Who is Alyssia Del Mar?

To Desmond . . . she is "the last movie star"—and the last chance to save his studio from ruin.

To Maxim . . . she is temptation in the flesh—and salvation for a price.

To Barry . . . she is the perfect wife—until her success outshines his own.

To Hap . . . she is the inspiration he needs to become the world's greatest director—unless their torrid affair explodes in scandal . . .

DREAMS ARE NOT ENOUGH

"All the necessary ingredients are in place: glamor, fame, wealth, travel, romantic complications and danger."

—Los Angeles Times

"Mar-velous!"

—Cosmopolitan

"Jacqueline Briskin keeps the plot simmering."

—New York Daily News

"There's more intrigue and suspense in this tale than in most Hollywood novels, and you'll love the surprising conclusion."

—Wichita Eagle-Beacon

Don't miss these other Berkley bestsellers by Jacqueline Briskin

TOO MUCH TOO SOON
EVERYTHING AND MORE
CALIFORNIA GENERATION

Books by Jacqueline Briskin

AFTERLOVE
CALIFORNIA GENERATION
DREAMS ARE NOT ENOUGH
EVERYTHING AND MORE
THE ONYX
PALOVERDE
RICH FRIENDS
TOO MUCH TOO SOON

DREAMS ARE NOT ENOUGH

JACQUELINE BRISKIN

B

BERKLEY BOOKS, NEW YORK

This is for

Ralph and Donna

Liz and Mort

Richard and Jeri

And, most especially, for

Bert

This Berkley book contains the complete text of the original hardcover edition. It has been completely reset in a typeface designed for easy reading and was printed from new film.

DREAMS ARE NOT ENOUGH

A Berkley Book / published by arrangement with the author

PRINTING HISTORY
G. P. Putnam's edition / February 1987
Berkley edition / October 1987

ISBN: 0-425-10179-7

A BERKLEY BOOK® TM 757,375
Berkley Books are published by The Berkley Publishing Group, 200 Madison Avenue, New York, NY 10016.
The name "BERKLEY" and the "B" logo are trademarks belonging to Berkley Publishing Corporation.

PRINTED IN THE UNITED STATES OF AMERICA

10 9 8 7 6 5 4 3 2 1

CONTENTS

BEVERLY HILLS, 1986

It had rained before dawn on that particular Wednesday in December of 1986, but by nine o'clock sunshine spread like warm butter through the green, landscaped folds of the overpriced Beverly Hills canyon.

A woman stood at a bedroom window, gazing at the sunlit morning. Even unadorned with her black mane of hair pulled austerely back, a peignoir hiding her apparently felicitous curves, she was lovely. For a moment she closed her eyes and her thoughtful expression altered to one of haunted dread. Then she shrugged as if reminding herself of a task, and moved briskly to a long, narrow dressing room. Behind a professional strew of cosmetics, the front section of the *Los Angeles Times* was folded and propped to show a photograph of her. With her artfully tousled head thrown back and her lipsticked mouth open in a breathless smile, her image on black and white newsprint appeared far tougher, that of an aggressively sensual woman. The caption read: ALYSSIA DEL MAR, THE RETURN OF THE RECLUSIVE STAR.

Alyssia del Mar hadn't made a film in six years. For long months at a time she vanished completely. Her reappearances were noted by television newscasts and the press—the *Star* and the *Inquirer* routinely sold out when they printed a rumor that she had been secluded in an exotic Katmandu palace, a Moorish castle, or a viceregal *estância* in the Brazilian jungle with some billionaire, say Adnan Kashoggi, or a notable like Prince Rainier. Legends have never thriven on the rocky soil of truth and Alyssia del Mar had transcended her own myth. What is more intriguing than a star—an international star of the first magnitude—who quits at the height of her beauty and fame? The public, who had suffered with her through illness, tragedy and lurid scandal, snatched at clues to the enigma.

Alyssia switched on a surgical array of lights, leaning forward to study her reflection. Her nose and chin were rather too delicate, but in the manner that exacts homage from the camera. Her upper lip was fractionally narrow for the lower, a flaw that made her appear provocatively vulnerable. It was the large, dark blue eyes, though, that one noticed—the eyes dominated her face and had mysterious depths.

During her lengthy, patient application of makeup, she kept tilting her head, listening for a sound that by her expression she anticipated with fear.

At precisely ten thirty, three cars turned in at the steep driveway on Laurel Way, following one another up the snaking curves of the long driveway to park near the sprawling bungalow whose pink stucco was in need of a painting crew.

Barry Cordiner didn't move, but sat fiddling with the keys of his dusty BMW. Beth Gold's lined but still pretty face was anxious as she peered into the mirror on the sun visor of her Cadillac Seville to straighten the impeccably tied bow of her slate-gray silk blouse. PD Zaffarano's expression proved a wary reluctance to get out of the Rolls with the personalized license plates AGENT 1.

Simultaneously, as if summoned by an inaudible bell, they left their cars. Calling out greetings in loud, overcordial voices, they merged in an awkward troika. Before they could reach the front door, a plump, middle-aged black woman in a maid's uniform emerged from the pink fencing that hid the service entrance. "Miss del Mar says will you please come this way to the backyard," she said. They followed her along the side path, Beth cautiously avoiding the huge, serrated leaves of overgrown birds-of-paradise.

The level area of the garden was taken up by a large patio and heart-shaped swimming pool—this coy pool had achieved a notoriety of its own in Andy Warhol's much reproduced portrait of Alyssia del Mar with her breasts rising bountifully from its blue water.

The early rain had washed away every trace of smog and the threesome could therefore decently ignore one another in the pretense of admiring the panorama that stretched from the faraway, snow-topped San Bernardino Mountains across the endless sprawl of city to the Pacific, where for once Catalina Island was visible, a lavender hump on the horizon.

Beth broke the silence. "Did either of you know she was back?" Even though her hands were tensely clasped, her voice retained its soft-pitched, melodious quality.

"It wasn't in the trades," PD said.

"I knew," Barry said. As the others turned expectantly, he rested a Dunhill tobacco pouch on his plump stomach, taking his time to fill his meerschaum, a writer's ploy to enhance suspense. "It was on the front page of this morning's *Times.*"

PD and Beth sighed with disappointment. After more inhibited silence, they heard a car snaking up the driveway. In due time, Maxim Cordiner emerged onto the patio.

Seeing them, he shrugged his wide, bony shoulders and formed a caustic smile. "Well, if it isn't the Widow Gold; Paolo Dominick Zaffarano, superagent; and that well-known American author, Barry Cordiner. The four of us."

Beth, thinking of when the four had been five, murmured, "Do *you* have any idea what she wants?"

Maxim lowered his thin, elongated self into a chaise. "The place gives off a distinct aroma of hard times. Possibly we're here to have the bite put on us."

"The run-down condition isn't significant," Barry said. "She's been renting it out. Besides, she never cared about maintaining a house."

"Well, I can hardly argue with *you* about that, Barry-boy. After all, you were married to the lady."

Their styles were completely at odds. Maxim wore an unpressed work shirt and Levi's so old that they were white at the knees, Barry a double-breasted navy blazer with unfashionably narrow lapels and brass buttons left open to accommodate his paunch, PD a black suit superbly tailored to his well-exercised body, while Beth's sedate gray outfit was adorned with pearls so large that most people believed them costume jewelry, but in actuality were from the waters off Ceylon and insured for a sheik's ransom.

In spite of their dissimilarities, a certain line of jaw proclaimed them kin.

Beth and Barry were twins, the only two on anything remotely resembling speaking terms, and their infrequent conversations inevitably centered on the care of their bellicose octogenarian father. Neither had seen Maxim or PD, their first cousins, in nearly two years.

Yet once, when there were five of them, they had been so inseparable that the Cordiner clan had nicknamed them Our Own Gang.

Beth persisted, "Waiting'd be easier if we knew why we're here."

"I don't know about you, Beth." Maxim fished a crumpled letter from his jeans pocket. "For myself, I'm on hand because a couple of hours ago a messenger brought this to my place." He read the ink-printed words, "'Imperative you be at 10895 Laurel Way at ten thirty, Alyssia.'"

"I got one like that." Beth's delightful voice rose shrilly. "Except I was told to bring Jonathon. But he'd already left for school." She said the last sentence tremulously, as if begging their exoneration for her son's absence.

"I had to put off a meeting with Spielberg." PD glared at the sliding glass windows, which were coated with a substance that repelled sunlight and turned the glass into greenish mirrors. "What's keeping her?"

Maxim formed his mordant smile. "When did the lady ever put in an appearance on time—or keep a commitment?"

Beth and Barry jerked, twin brother and sister acknowledging in this single unguarded motion that whatever had caused their umbilical cords to be untangled, they still shared memories of one secret time, sweet for both, when Alyssia had followed through on her promise.

"Given a choice, we'd all be schmucks to show," PD said. "Let's face it—she wrecked our lives and—"

"PD!" Beth interrupted, her face contorted with horror.

"Yes, PD," Maxim said, "let's merely count the minor wounds the lady inflicted. Breaking it up between you and Beth. Dropping Barry into the bottom of the bottle—it sounds like a fabulous miniseries."

PD nodded glumly. "Maxim, I can get you a major deal if you want to produce it."

In the sixties and seventies, Maxim Cordiner had been a startlingly innovative producer. Critics applauded him, the box office rejoiced in him, and his movies had brought him nearly as much fame as his glamorous marriages and affairs, yet, in 1981, after tragedy had engulfed his brother, he had abandoned filmmaking.

Barry got to his feet. "While we await Alyssia's purpose, anybody for liquid refreshment?"

Beth lowered her dark glasses, querying him with a somber glance.

"Not to worry, Beth," Barry said. "If there's one lesson the doyenne of this manor taught, it's that alcohol is a poisonous substance for me." The bar in the den had a Dutch door onto the pool deck and he opened it. "Still the same for everybody?"

It was. And the bottles on the otherwise empty shelves showed a care for these preferences. A chablis spritzer for Beth, Polish vodka for Maxim, Campari and soda for PD. Barry opened himself a Perrier.

Drinking, the men began to relax, and soon were talking shop. Barry's upcoming espionage novel, which would be published in hardcover the following April, was being auctioned off to the paperback houses. PD was closing a deal for Robert Redford and Sissy Spacek. Maxim had recently worked with his longtime friends, Jane Fonda and Tom Hayden, on a human rights committee.

Beth remained silent. The others feared disclosures from their past. She, however, was the only one with anything current to surrender. *Jonathon,* she thought with a shiver. *Why does she want him here?*

Barry poured fresheners. At a metallic screech, they all froze. The window of the master bedroom was being slid open.

Alyssia emerged. She wore her favorite color, red. In her tightly belted crimson cotton dress that displayed dazzling white cleavage, her face made up, her gleaming lips parted in a tremulous smile, she was a different woman—no, not a mortal woman. As she came toward them, back arched, hips swaying, she was the ultimate screen love goddess. Even at close range in the clear sunlight, she appeared to be in her mid-twenties, yet they knew that she had begun working at Magnum in 1960, twenty-six years earlier.

"I appreciate you coming here on such short notice," she said. Her voice was small and slightly husky.

"The question is, why?" Maxim retorted.

She gave him a little smile, then looked inquiringly at Beth. "Where's Jonathon?" she asked.

Beth paled until the freckles that covered her cheeks were clearly visible. "In school," she said pleadingly to her former sister-in-law. "When your note came, he'd already left for school."

PD, glancing around at his cousins, realized for the first time that Alyssia had gathered together the perfect group for him to package with her. Barry with a hot property, Beth with the financing, and Maxim the producer. He asked with atypical bluntness, "Have you got comeback in mind, Alyssia?"

"Isn't it possible I might like to be with family again?"

"Such a thought has occurred to me, yes," Maxim said. "After all, you have, shall we say, an overview of a certain episode that we Cordiners feel is best left in the shadows."

"Is that what you think?" Alyssia asked. "That I've invited you here to blackmail you?"

Maxim's mordant expression was gone. "Tell us what you want," he snapped. "Then we can get the hell away."

Without a word, Alyssia turned. Though something about her posture and walk suggested dismay, even sadness, the little group heard the click of her stiletto heels as ominous. She slid the window shut after herself.

Maxim narrowed his eyes at the uncommunicative, green-hued glass. "She comes out, she says nothing, she leaves. What the hell is that all about? Barry-boy, you and the lady shared many years of matrimonial bliss. Let's hear your theory on why she's called this chummy pow-wow."

Barry walked to the pool, frowning reflectively at a dead eucalyptus leaf afloat in the chlorinated water. *Why are we here?* He couldn't pursue the thought. His reasoning power had fled. Coming face to face with his ex-wife, disturbing enough after so many years, had fluttered the pages of his authorized history of their disastrous marriage, the version that laid blame for all their woes at her slender feet. Now, after being in her presence less than two minutes, it didn't seem so obvious, did it, that she had eternally done him the dirty?

BARRY

1959

1

On October 8, 1959—a blazing hot Saturday—three weeks into his senior year of pre-law at UCLA, Barry Cordiner took by far the most daring act of his twenty years. He eloped to Las Vegas with a girl called Alicia Lopez whom he had met exactly seventeen days earlier.

Barry couldn't remember his mother ever actually informing him in her rather nasal voice that, not being rich like his cousins, he had to earn top grades, be prompt and avoid the troublemakers at school. Neither could Beth. The twins therefore agreed that their obligations must have been genetically programmed: the ultimate requirements were that Beth graduate from college, then marry a Jewish professional man who had either already made it or would soon make it, while Barry must propel himself into a lucrative law practice before picking an equally suitable mate. Neither of them rebelled. How could they? Clara Cordiner bought her own clothes on sale at cheap stores like the Broadway while taking her children into Beverly Hills to outfit them at Saks or Magnin's; she prepared them nutritiously balanced meals. She taught them manners, for she had been gently reared.

Clara Friedman Cordiner's father had owned a large shoe store, and she, an only child, was cosseted. Right before her twenty-second birthday, she had been window-shopping along Hollywood Boulevard when Tim Cordiner, hurrying along, possibly a bit loaded on bathtub gin, bumped into her, knocking her down. He apologized by taking her for tea on the veranda of the nearby Hollywood Hotel. He was very tall, and his laughter rang loud and hearty. Being in the movie business, he knew Gloria Swanson, Tom Mix, Irving Thalberg, Louis B. Mayer, Art Garrison, Douglas Fairbanks and Mary Pickford. Clara had never met such a dashing man. Of course her orthodox parents would never let her date a *goy,* so she invented excuses to get out. Less than a week later she lost her virginity on Tim's Murphy bed. The following month, she missed her period. Tim, who was equally nuts about her, said, "We'll go tell your folks about us." In her large, immaculate home, Clara wept and vowed to rear her future offspring as good Jews, with Tim concurring—his virulently antisemitic Hungarian peasant forebears must have been twisting in their graves. After disowning their daughter forever, the Friedmans also wept, then sat *shiva,* the traditional seven days of mourning, counting her among the dead. Clara's missed period turned out to be a false alarm, and she took eleven years to conceive the twins. Early in her marriage she discovered that her husband, a studio grip, spent his days shifting heavy props: his knowledge of the Hollywood famous was garnered from his older brother, Desmond Cordiner, a bigshot at Magnum. Tim drank; he cheated on her. Yet when the chips were down—and in the Tim Cordiner household they often were—the couple clung together.

Barry understood that it was his obligation, as the only son, to make it up to his mother for his father's shortcomings.

During the long, hot drive through the Mojave Desert to Las Vegas he had been unable to entirely block the vision of his frail mother's impending horror; yet, standing at the gaudily painted altar with Alicia at his side, seeing the tears on her luminous, flushed cheeks, his heart seemed to swell, and he accepted there had been no stepping back from the madness that had overtaken him the first time he'd seen her sipping a Coke at Ship's Coffee Shop in Westwood.

Love at first sight had been accompanied by the classic symptoms: sleeplessness, loss of appetite, inability to think of anything but Alicia, a constant semi-erection. They had made out vigorously in his 1950 De Soto coupé, but hadn't gone all the way. Barry held Alicia in reverence, and also feared failure—his one experience with an aging pro on Main Street had been an unhappy one.

Barry was exceptionally thin: standing at the altar in his rumpled gray suit, he gave the impression of a malnourished adolescent who had grown too quickly. As he shifted on his storklike legs, he could feel the sweat running down from his armpits despite the extrastrength Mitchum's he had applied the previous night before setting out for his date with Alicia—it wasn't until they were embracing that he had seriously entertained the idea of elopement. The hairs on his neck prickled with awareness that his cousins and sister were staring at them, and he had a momentary surge of regret that he'd invited them. Alicia brought out a hitherto dormant protectiveness in him. During the six broiling hours in his un-airconditioned car, she had worried about looking a mess at her wedding—and from the guests' vantage point, she did. The rear of her scarlet crepe dress was puckered into ugly creases, causing its miniskirt to ride yet higher in back of her slim, shapely thighs.

Glancing sideways at his bride, Barry found himself unable to look away. He considered Alicia gorgeous, but he wasn't positive whether others did. From the heads swiveling in her wake he knew that most people found her riveting. True, her skirts were unfortunately short and her tops a shade tight so that the buttons pulled between her full, peach-shaped breasts, but this didn't fully account for the zephyrs of attention that trailed her: women turned as often as men.

Ignoring the justice of the peace, who was rumbling on about the duties of matrimony, Barry gazed at Alicia's profile, attempting to convince himself that he wasn't moonstruck, that she was indeed gorgeous. As usual, he was incapable of analyzing her face. Her skin assuredly was unique. Other women possessed faultless complexions, but he'd seen no other skin with this velvety incandescence. Light was not an external quality for Alicia, but appeared to emanate from within, as if an electric current flowed with the blood that now was pulsing rapidly in the subtly blue vein at her throat.

He realized she was clutching the wilted bridal bouquet (he had just purchased it in the wedding chapel's tiny vestibule) so tightly that the baby's breath trembled. Edging closer, he let his arm rest in moist reassurance against hers.

At noon, the temperature in Las Vegas was well above a hundred, and the chapel lacked air conditioning. The justice of the peace's bulging, magenta cheeks appeared to be melting into the creases of his double chin.

Hap, Maxim, Beth and PD were equally miserable.

The cousins had all been born in 1938 or 1939, the so-called Golden Age of Hollywood. Hap and Maxim were sons of Desmond Cordiner, the family emperor. Long before their births Desmond had been a major wheel in the Industry, second in command to Art Garrison, founder of Magnum Pictures, and after Garrison's death he had taken over as head of the studio. PD's father was Frank Zaffarano, the director whose sentimental, flag-waving films had made a bundle for Magnum. Barry and Beth's father, Tim Cordiner, never rose higher than a grip. The cousins, therefore, belonged to the top, upper middle and bottom of an industry with a well-defined hierarchy. This had not prevented the friendship forged between them in early childhood from binding them yet closer during adolescence and adulthood.

PD's button-down shirt collar had wilted into shapelessness and large globules of sweat showed on his face. The fresh handkerchief he took out to mop his classically handsome features was impeccably ironed: his mother, Lily Zaffarano, née Lily Cordiner, had a live-in maid and cook as well as a laundress who came in on Tuesdays to iron the voluminously skirted little dresses and petticoats of her daughters, Annette and Deirdre, but she personally attended to her husband and son's linens. Frank Zaffarano, who had left the hilltop town of Enna in Sicily at sixteen, kept the old Italian belief that a woman's purpose in life is to serve the men of the household.

Hap and Maxim appeared less uncomfortable, though the blue of Hap's sport shirt had a growing splotch between his broad shoulders.

The brothers were both six foot three, but here the similarities ended.

Hap, the older by thirteen months, was large-boned. He had thoughtful gray eyes, a wide forehead and a nose that once had been broken during football practice, leaving him with a rugged look.

Maxim spotted a sheet of old newspaper on the floor and he retrieved it. As he fanned himself, his narrow, well-shaped lips curled down in an acid smile. He had inherited a smaller, handsome version of his father's thin scimitar of a nose; his attenuated height was elegant. Women fell all over him—among the Cordiners, he had the reputation of being a cocksman.

Beth alone seemed cool, until you noticed the moistness where her silky brown page boy curled toward her throat.

Her delicate, unflushed face was lightly tanned as were the round arms bared by the sleeveless, powder-blue chemise that she wore with a strand of small cultured pearls. With her slightly too-thick legs tucked under the pew, she was the ultimate California coed.

She showed none of the inner anguish that she felt as her twin was severed from her and joined in wedlock to this cheap-looking girl, a girl whom Beth had not known existed until five thirty this morning when Barry had tapped on her window, whispering that she should dress and come to Las Vegas for his wedding. "Beth, no noise," he had warned through the window screen. "I don't want Mom and Dad in on this."

Beth had a far more deeply ingrained sense of responsibility than her twin. As she sat on the hard wooden bench she was thinking up ways to ease the blow for their mother, who suffered from a coronary condition.

The justice of the peace was inquiring in an orotund tone, "Do you, Barry, take Alee-sha to be your lawfully wedded wife to cherish and protect?"

"I d-do," Barry stammered.

"And do you, Alee-sha, take Barry here to be your lawfully married husband and promise to honor and obey him?"

Alicia murmured assent.

The justice said that by the power vested in him by the state of Nevada they were man and wife.

Alicia turned. Her lashes fluttered as Barry bent for the traditional kiss.

The justice of the peace clomped over to lean on the front pew, assailing PD, who was closest to the aisle, with odors of rancid sweat and raw onion. "Can I bother you and the little lady here to be witnesses for the happy couple?"

"Come on, Bethie," PD said.

Now a faint flush did show on Beth's smooth throat. Nobody, not even Barry, who was closest to her in this world, was aware that she was mad for PD. Her greatest childhood treat had been to stay overnight at Aunt Lily and Uncle Frank's house, occupying the small room adjacent to PD's. Her adoration had turned distinctly physical during her eleventh year, when she had simultaneously attained her menarche and learned about the Italian renaissance. In her secret thoughts she called PD by his baptismal name, Paolo Dominick, visualizing him as a Medici duke clad in velvet and satin. Beth knew her love was hopeless—she was irrevocably Jewish, PD a devout Catholic, and besides they were blood relations, first cousins. Being sensible as well as pretty, she dated many boys, thus becoming the most popular senior in USC's Alpha Epsilon Phi house.

She and PD waited while the justice of the peace with painful slowness readied the license for them to sign. Afterward PD linked his moist-jacketed arm companionably in hers and they went outside.

The others were waiting in a clump to take advantage of the sliver of noontime shade cast by the parody of a church steeple that topped the wedding chapel.

"Where'll we go for the wedding breakfast?" Hap asked. He was Our Own Gang's unofficial leader, originally because he was the largest, later because they respected his unerring instinct for fairness.

"This is a no-frills elopement," Barry replied stiffly.

"My treat," Hap said.

"Ours," Maxim added.

Hap and Maxim took it as a given that, as the ones with trust-fund incomes, they would foot the bill for group extravagances. PD was able to accept the largesse because his father was well known as a director, Beth because as a female she was accustomed to checks being picked up. Only Barry felt a poor relation with his manhood threatened each time he was treated.

"Not that I don't appreciate it—" he started.

"Come on, Barry," Hap said. "Alicia deserves some little celebration."

"It's not necessary," Barry said awkwardly. "We'll—"

"Jesus Christ, will you guys quit arguing in this oven?" PD interrupted, "I'll sign Dad's name at the Fabulador. He has privileges there."

The Fabulador, with its top-rank entertainers, opulently appointed rooms and five gourmet restaurants, was considered the best hotel on the strip. Dapper Uncle Frank must have dropped considerably more in the Fabulador's colossal casino than the family suspected. PD led the way to the Champs-Elysées, the most expensive of the eateries, and when he explained whose son he was, the beaming captain escorted them to a large booth. Flipping open stiff white napkins for Alicia and Beth, he suggested that they start with the blue points.

While the others tipped on horseradish, tabasco, red sauce, Alicia gripped the damask of her napkin. Noticing, Hap picked up the tiny pitchfork to pry the fleshy mollusk free, eating it without any doctoring. She watched, and followed suit. Swallowing the first oyster with a gulp, she hastily covered her mouth with her napkin. She played with the rest, twisting her fork.

At first the cousins were a little stiff, as if Barry's marriage had somehow elevated them all to another generation and they weren't yet certain of the ground rules. Even Maxim's sarcastic humor was blunted. But the champagne—a vintage Mumm's—did its work, and by the time the eggs benedict arrived, the five cousins were back to their usual bickering jests and digs.

"So tell me, Barry-boy," Maxim asked, "how do you intend breaking the news to your parents?"

"Quite simply. I'll point out that they eloped, too," Barry said.

"Alas, that's not the type of logic Cordiner parents accept," Maxim retorted.

Beth turned to her new sister-in-law. "And what about you, Alicia?" she inquired with the attentive smile she employed at rush teas. "How will your family feel?"

Alicia looked down at the table. "They're in El Paso." She spoke too rapidly.

At this nonsequitur there was a silence.

Then PD asked, "You're a Catholic?"

After a fractional hesitation, Alicia nodded. "Uhhuh."

"That makes two of us, then, and we both know there'll be repercussions. You've married out of the Church."

Her soft, full mouth quivered, her eyes looked a yet darker blue.

"Hey, they'll get over it," Hap said.

PD asked, "Barry, where'll you guys live?"

Currently, Barry lived in his parents' tract house, which had three tiny bedrooms, one bathroom and thin walls. "We haven't decided," he said, unable to repress his shudder.

Alicia touched his hand. "I'm pretty sure my boss'll let

us have the cute cottage in back that I told you about," she said comfortingly.

"Cottage?" Maxim asked. "Do you tend sheep or bake bread or what?"

"Housework," Alicia replied.

Barry's flush was so deep that his freckles disappeared. He dropped his napkin on the table. "We better get a move on, Alicia," he said abruptly.

"Good idea." Maxim grinned. "I hear tell there's a great shortage of motel rooms in this town."

"Really?" Alicia asked.

"He's kidding us," Barry said, embarrassment forgotten in a surge of masculine superiority. "PD, thanks."

"For what?" PD replied expansively. "The Fabulador's paying."

The newlyweds moved around the linen-draped tables, Barry putting his arm around Alicia's narrow waist as they reached the lobby.

Maxim said, "There goes Barry Cordiner with the hell shot out of his legal career."

His brother Hap retorted, "I didn't hear anything about dropping out of college."

"What was so wrong with skipping the ceremony and taking the fabulous little knockout directly to a motel?" PD wanted to know.

Maxim shook his head. "Jesus, a Mexican live-in!"

"He's cuh-razy about her," Beth said, her despair hidden by a jocular tone.

"If this doesn't kill your mother, nothing will," Maxim said. "Face it, Beth, on humane grounds, for Aunt Clara's sake, your twin should've foregone the legalities."

"One thing Mother isn't," Beth said hotly. "A bigot."

"Ahh, but she wants her half-Hebe chickadees to fly high," Maxim said.

Maxim, PD and Hap joked about PD's Catholicism and Desmond Cordiner's rise from nothing to Episcopalian, never catching on to Beth and Barry's invariable hasty changing of the subject when it came to their Judaism.

Beth looked down at the remains of her eggs benedict. "If it weren't for all the goop," she said, "I'd have guessed Alicia to be way younger than eighteen."

"You got that impression because she's a mite low on the brainpower," Maxim said.

"It's her wedding day. And she was too terrified of us to say anything," Hap said, leveling his gray eyes on his younger brother.

"We all know you rise to defend the underdog," Maxim retorted. "In this case, there's no need. i mean, with an ass and boobs like that, who needs an IQ?"

"Maxim, please," Beth murmured. "She's my sister-in-law."

PD gave Beth that warm smile, flashing white teeth. "That lust you hear from Maxim, Bethie, is pure envy."

Hap raised his glass. "To our new cousin," he said. "To Alicia. And Barry."

2

One eye cocked for a suitable motel, Barry cruised slowly along the gaudy strip.

"I've never been inside a place like that before," Alicia said.

Though scornful of the huge neon outline of a woman on the hotel's façade, Barry had also been awed by the Fabulador's grand scale. "It's crass," he said.

"Your family sure gave us a classy send-off."

"They have style," he said, nodding.

"Style," she repeated slowly, as if to imprint the word on her memory.

For a moment Barry relived that excruciating humiliation he had suffered when Alyssia had announced her occupation. Then, as she shifted across the frayed upholstery, her side snuggling against him, his anxieties and doubts fled. When he was alone with her and the world didn't impinge, another Barry Cordiner emerged from the skinny, insecure original: a man of the world, suave, assured.

His bride, he knew, came from a large, close-knit family in El Paso. Though she had mentioned them only sketchily—Mr. Lopez drove a big rig, Mrs. Lopez fixed sensational *albóndigas* soup—Barry's mind had developed a keenly precise snapshot of Alicia's dark and plumply pretty mother with one arm around the lean waist of the tall Lopez, their numerous offspring lined up in front of them. At eighteen, Alicia, the eldest, had no chance of college unless she earned the money herself, so she had left home to find work in Los Angeles.

Alicia's poverty made it unimportant that he was starting out married life with a five and two ones in his wallet. As a matter of fact, at this moment his lack of cash exhilarated him.

Through the dusty windshield he spotted a long, narrow motel dwarfed by a clump of tall, dusty Washingtonia palms. The trapezoidal shaped sign was emblazoned: $3, $3, $3, $3. The lowest-price accommodations that they had spotted. Slowing, he asked, "How does that place look?"

"Perfect . . ." She trembled as she spoke.

He drew her closer to him, wildly excited by what he would soon do to her, yet remorseful. He knew for certain that she, a good Catholic girl, was a virgin. Parking, he kissed her, a kiss that turned ardent.

Reluctantly he pulled away. "I better make the arrangements." Wiping the lipstick from his mouth with the back of his hand, he put on his jacket despite the heat—he needed to hide his hard-on.

The small office was empty. Pressing the bell on the counter, he looked out the full-length window. Alicia was putting on lipstick. He smiled. What a female female she was, smearing on that junk when the minute they were together he would kiss it away.

There were no sounds coming from behind the closed door with the brass sign: MANAGER'S OFFICE.

"Hey," he shouted, pressing on the buzzer again.

Again no response. Going behind the counter, he rapped on the door. "Anybody home?"

No answer. He lifted a key from its hook, assuaging his law-abiding soul by scribbling: *Nobody around, so I took the key to #7. Pay you later.*

Parking in front of number 7, he reached for the brown paper bag containing two new toothbrushes and a small tube of Pepsodent, their total baggage. (The Trojans he'd purchased at the same Thrifty were discreetly stashed in his jacket pocket.) He carried Alicia across the warped wood threshold.

The heat trapped inside smelled thick, as if the place had been unoccupied a long time. Kicking the door shut, he turned on the air conditioner before setting down his bride. He kissed her thoroughly, his tongue thrusting deep into her open mouth, both hands cupping the firm, gorgeous butt to bring her closer to him. With a small shoving gesture against his chest, she pulled away.

"Barry . . ." she murmured. "First can we shower?"

Disappointed, yet recognizing that after the desert drive in an un-airconditioned car, she was right, he touched his lips to her forehead. "I should've thought of it."

As the water began running in the tiny bathroom he felt the champagne combine with the previous night's lack of sleep. Sprawling on the dust-odored chenille bedspread, he lit a Tareyton and examined the barren, ugly cubicle. He imagined a future anniversary when they would clink their crystal wine goblets and chuckle at the crazy kids they'd been. By then he would be the main partner in a prestigious law firm (Cordiner, Etc., Etc., and Etc.) with a white streak in his hair and a couple of exceptionally fine novels under his belt. Alicia would be even more stunning in a long black sheath, the simple, elegant kind that his aunts wore to display their diamonds.

The shower was turned off. He stubbed out his cigarette expectantly.

Ten minutes passed with excruciating slowness before the door opened and she emerged, makeup complete, black hair atumble over her shoulders, a skimpy towel hiding the torso of that astonishing body.

"Your turn," she said.

Resisting the urge to yank off her towel, he stepped under the shower, rubbing the sliver of soap under his armpits, not taking time to dry himself. In deference to his bride's innocence, he wrapped the other threadbare towel around his waist.

The spread was folded onto a chair. She lay with the sheet pulled up to her throat.

Sitting on the edge of the double bed, he said, "Hi."

She managed a small, nervous smile.

Kissing her, he slowly drew down the sheet. Necking, he

had become acquainted in a tactile fashion with her body. Seeing it took his breath away—no figure of speech, he felt as if the air had been suddenly forced from his lungs.

That astonishingly luminous flesh seemed to collect all available light in the dim motel room. She was all slender, supple curves, the young breasts full and firm with nipples the pale pink of tea roses, the waist deeply indented, and the black leaf of hair startlingly explicit between the white hips. Gazing at her, his mind filled with names and images of love goddesses: Astarte, Venus, Aphrodite. . . .

He found himself kneeling at the foot of the bed, kissing each of the crimson nails of her small, soap-scented, high-arched feet.

Stretching out next to her, he pulled her nakedness to his own. He was incapable of holding back to put on the rubber. Moving on top of her, he forgot every technique he'd studied in sex manuals.

Penetrating her, he moved back and forth three or four times, sweat pouring from him as he ejaculated.

He held her, gasping. In a few minutes he'd calmed enough to reach for another cigarette. "Everything okay?" he asked tenderly.

"Fine . . ."

"I didn't hurt you?"

"Now I'm truly yours."

Her murmur held the emotional intensity of their exchange of vows.

Smiling, he closed his eyes.

For a full five minutes after his breathing lengthened into the steady rhythm of sleep, she lay very still, then slowly disengaged herself from his loosened grasp. Getting out of bed, she brushed a kiss on his forehead. He stirred. She poised, scarcely seeming to breathe until he rolled over to clutch a pillow with a long, contented, snorelike sound. Reaching for her large, shiny new imitation patent purse, she tiptoed into the bathroom, locking the door.

She unzipped the largest of the interior pockets, taking out a half-finished tube of contraceptive foam. She squatted to use it, her expression intent.

She was rinsing herself free of the medicinal odor when the hammering blows started.

"Open up, damn you!" shrieked a female voice from outside. "This is the manager!"

Alicia wrapped the towel around her nudity, running into the other room, where Barry was hastily skivvying into his shorts. His face was pale and guilt-ridden.

"What's going on?" she whispered.

"In the office nobody answered, so I took the key," he mumbled. "How am I going to explain?"

"Don't worry." Alicia yanked the covers into a semblance of order, lying down and pulling the sheet over herself. "I'll help you."

The shouts and hammering grew more overwrought.

Barry unlocked and unchained the door. The manager, whose platinum hair was wound around pink curlers, stood there, the sags of her face set as if in one of those primitive masks of rage.

"You punk bastard!" she shrilled. "Don't you know there's laws against breaking and entering? I got friends in the sheriff's department! You'll get six months!"

"Nobody answered the buzzer. I left a note for you." Grabbing his trousers, he drew out his wallet. "Here, let me give you the money."

"You damn rich suck-ups, you think you can wave a buck and get away with everything!"

"Please?" The tremulously unhappy girl's voice belonged to a stranger.

Barry turned to ascertain that only Alicia was in the unit.

The manager stared at her. "Jesus, and you got a kid with you. For that you can do life, buster."

"She's my wife," Barry said.

"Yeah, sure."

"We *are* married," Alicia said, holding up her left hand with its shiny new sterling ring. Then she raised up the sheet around her, whispering, "My parents wouldn't think we're married either. We went to that wedding place up the road. A justice of the peace did the ceremony. No . . . priest. . . ." She buried her face in her hands.

"Hey, no need to carry on like that." The manager's voice had softened.

"It's . . . a . . . a mortal sin. . . ."

"Dearie, it's okay, okay."

Alicia's head remained bent. Unconsolable little sobs drifted from the black veil of tousled hair.

The manager touched Barry's naked arm. "Pay me later," she hissed. "Go make it up to the kid."

When the door closed, he stared at Alicia. Her body shuddered as if with sobs.

"Hon, don't, please don't. I know how you feel. Remember, I told you my mom's parents disowned her because Dad wasn't Jewish. Listen, if you want, I'll become a Catholic. Religion's a big deal to Beth, but it means nothing to me."

Alicia looked up. She was convulsed with laughter. "The old bag," she managed to gasp out.

For a moment he was devastated that she had fooled him so completely. After three UCLA creative writing classes he considered himself possessed of a seasoned author's acute powers of perception.

Then he was realizing that Alicia, naked and unprepared, had gotten the witch manager off his back. *He* never could have pulled it off. He was fairly certain that few girls could have done so superb an acting job.

"You deserve an Oscar," he said. "Can I count on you to always come to my aid like that?"

"Of course," she said happily. "Aren't you my husband?"

Her remark aroused him. He *was* her husband. Pulling back the sheet, he lowered himself onto that lush body. "Barry Cordiner and Alicia Lopez Cordiner," he whispered.

3

Her name wasn't Alicia, her father hadn't been a Lopez, she didn't come from Texas and she wasn't eighteen but barely fifteen.

Her earliest memory was of endless rows of strong-smelling celery. "Now don't you go straying off," her mother had said with a slap. The pickers and packers had no time to smile even when she did her little dance. As the great yellow sun rose to the middle of the sky she felt like melting into tears, but she was nearly four, too old to be a crybaby. A distant clump of eucalyptus promised shade. Forgetting her mother's warning, she went toward the trees. A line of ants carrying fragments of green distracted her, and she knelt to watch. She was too absorbed to hear the footsteps. A heaviness on her head was her first inkling of the man.

"Ain't you the prettiest little tad of a thing with this black hair and them big blue eyes."

She had never seen him before. He had no teeth in front and his smile frightened her.

"I have to get back to my momma," she said as politely as possible.

He laughed in a funny, rusty way, squatting near her. "I buy my friends things. How'd you like a nice big cold Coca-Cola?"

She hardly ever got so much as a sip of Coke, and she was remembering how hot and thirsty she was. "Where is it?"

"First you gotta show we're friends." He stroked her leg. His breath smelled like doody, and his fingers felt slimy, terrible, as they crawled up her thigh.

"I'm not your friend!" she said in the tone her mother deplored as her Miss Snotty voice.

"Ain't long before you will be," he said. Now he was fingering his grubby pants. "Then you'll get your Coke."

She tried to move, but he gripped her leg tighter, and pulled out his pee-pee. The men often relieved themselves in the field, but they always turned away decently. This thing was an ugly red, fat and stiff as a baseball bat.

"First, you gotta stroke this." He grabbed her hands, pulling them to that ugly thing.

She used the only weapon she had, her even white milk teeth. Leaning forward, she bit him hard.

He gave a high squeal, releasing her. She ran as hard as she could in the direction of the truck and her momma.

Her mother, May Sue Hollister, wasn't sure where to put the blame for her younger daughter, Alice, but she'd had the hots for a looie in the tank corps, one gorgeous hunk of man with big baby blues. Whoever, you only had to look at Alice to see he hadn't been some Mex like Juanita's old man. "God, that older gal of mine looks pure pachuco, don't she?"

May Sue was one of the migratory farm workers who shifted up and down California in rattletrap trucks or ancient, trembly yellow buses that had been declared unsafe for schoolchildren. She worked the fields, stoop labor, twelve or fourteen hours a day of it. Many ranches had a row of plumbingless shacks for the seasonal labor, but others lacked even these minimal facilities, and then May Sue, with her girls, would cover the bare earth with corrugated cardboard and hang a makeshift tarp. She shopped at shabby, badly lit grocery stores, paying exorbitant prices for stale, fat-laden hamburger and white bread whose soft crust occasionally was green with mold. On payday she splurged on dago red or beer or candy bars or milk. Clothes came from cavernous Goodwill shops. (Decades later Alice would see a rerun of *Harvest of Shame* through a blur of tears: she knew only too well the way of life Edward R. Murrow had been exposing.)

Despite the grueling life that was reflected in her sagging body, May Sue retained a yen for pleasure. Traces of her girlhood prettiness remained and men were still drawn to what she called a little party-party. She had no energy left for her daughters. Alice's remembrance of her mother was not visual: Momma meant the mingled smells of beer and sweat and cheap perfume, the sting of a slap.

It was her half sister, Juanita, eight years older, who supplied the hugs, the warmth, the soft lullabying. "Nita, Jua-nita," she would croon, pressing her cheek against Alice's soft, black hair. "L-i-ingering falls the Southern moo-oon."

Other than the thick, lustrous black hair, the half sisters had no feature in common. Alice could have posed for a Gerber's ad with her enormous blue eyes, glowing pink and white skin, cute button of a nose, her wide smile that soon displayed perfect milk teeth. Juanita's face was too wide, her complexion large-pored and sallow, her teeth crooked. Her one good feature, beautiful dark eyes, were set in a perpetual squint because of uncorrected near-sightedness and astigmatism.

When Alice was five and Juanita thirteen, May Sue

found herself in need of yet another abortion. The old woman with the pink wart on her nose required a ten-dollar bill in advance and Juanita's assistance. Both of May Sue's daughters witnessed the gush of crimson that bore away the mouselike creature, their half sibling, saw the blood spread and spread, dripping between the planks of the old table as May Sue's cries grew feebler.

After May Sue's death, Juanita earned their living. The other pickers helped her as much as possible, telling her where the crops were coming in, whom to see about being hired. During the height of the strawberry season the younger children picked too, and Alice labored under the summer sun. At these times, foremen often refused to pay a child who didn't pick steadily. Alice would grow dizzy and the endless, plastic-shielded fields would shimmer and waver in the blazing sun, but she never quit.

Local authorities paid lip service to California's educational laws, not supplying teachers for the children of migratory workers but insisting they enroll in school. Neither Hollister girl attended any one school for more than three successive weeks. Juanita, with her feeble eyesight, never did learn to make out more than a few simple words, and May Sue's demise ended her education. Alice, though, was a quick study. She learned to read more fluently than most of her classmates, to spell with reasonable accuracy, to add and subtract so rapidly that she astounded her teachers. Otherwise her education showed startling gaps—she did not know George Washington had been the first president, she never learned cursive writing, she believed Spain to be located south of Mexico.

School personnel understandably disliked having these transients foisted on them.

The fourth grade marched along the pergola to the classroom marked LIBRARY. The pretty blonde librarian demonstrated how to make out their cards, how to sign the slips glued to the inside of every bookcover. Alice, excited by the incalculable wealth of books, couldn't wait for her turn. "I'm checking this out," she said, extending *The Secret Garden.*

"Alice, you haven't written an address on your card."

"It's Harrow Ranch."

"Are your parents picking Mr. Harrow's lettuce?"

Alice nodded. She always lied about her orphaned state: telling the truth, Juanita warned with an anxious squint, would get her hauled off to what the pickers commonly referred to as facilities.

"Then you'll need a signature from Mr. Harrow." The librarian, no longer pretty, yanked away the book as if Alice might infect it with cooties.

"Thanks a whole big bunch." Alice threw back her shoulders and stamped away.

Though teachers, cops, foremen and people like this librarian terrified her, she'd die rather than let them know it. Most of the other workers kowtowed to the authorities. Much as she loved Juanita, she despised that head-bent humility of hers.

The men stared at her a lot, so she stuck close to Juanita. (The pickers were a decent lot, and though they glanced at the luscious Alice, they would never consider molesting a child.) Juanita took her fostering seriously.

"Listen," she said when Alice was around seven, "if any man tries to do things to you, touch you, don't let him."

"*That* kind of thing? Don't worry. Yech. It's repulsive."

"If anybody tries, hit him hard here." Juanita pointed between her ample hips—at nearly sixteen she was short and sturdily built. "Then run as fast as you can."

When Alice was ten Juanita took up with a very short man called Henry Lopez.

From the start Alice loathed Henry passionately. He was forever cuffing her for having a big mouth, and a few times a month he beat up on Juanita, which in Alice's eyes was far worse—Alice's loyalties would always be greater than her self-interest. Henry, however, possessed one admirable feature. When he and Juanita were going to party-party—he called it have a bang—he would drive Alice in his rattly pickup to the nearest picture show and give her ten cents. She saw approximately three double features a week.

Adoring movies, she learned to do sharply honed imitations of Kirk Douglas, Ingrid Bergman, Rain Fairburn, Burt Lancaster. Sometimes during intermission a boy would buy her a Coke or a Uno Bar, and she felt an obligation to repay these munificent gifts by permitting a hot hand to cup the shirt over her blossoming breasts. But no more, *nada más*. In the spring before Alice was fifteen, Juanita's method of contraception failed. Henry Lopez, miracle of miracles, came through. They were married in Santa Paula. It was from the officiating priest that Juanita learned about a vacancy for a couple at the nearby Taylor Ranch.

For their full-time services, the Taylors gave the Lopezes $200 a month plus a furnished frame cottage with a working refrigerator, a real stove and, treasure of treasures, a black and white television with a wavery ten-inch screen. The Hollister sisters had stepped up numerous rungs in the social scheme. They were now permanent people, they belonged. Juanita, now called a housekeeper, held her head high as she hurried up the dirt road to the big, two-story white ranch house—Mrs. Taylor was unaware of the pregnancy.

Juanita would have done the work at the frame cottage, too, but Alice insisted on cooking, cleaning, doing a share of the Taylors' enormous pile of ironing as well as fixing a home lunch for Henry.

It was now that his attitude toward her changed drastically. He began following her as she moved between the stove and the refrigerator, stroking her arms, casually touching her breasts. She learned evasive tactics; he grew more impossible. To Alice, her brother-in-law's mauling demeaned Juanita and therefore was infinitely more painful than his casual blows had been.

She dreaded the lunch hour.

"Feel what you do to me," he said, grabbing her wrist.

"Cut it out, Henry!"

But Henry's large, dirty hand was extremely strong. Inexorably he drew her small hand downward, forcing her fingers around the hardness beneath his jeans. "Bet you'd like some of that."

With a violent effort she yanked away. "Your beans are on the stove!" she shouted, slamming out the front door.

"Here, baby, isn't this something?"

"Just button your fly, Henry. I'm warning you."

"You want me to tell Juanita you been making eyes at me?"

"She wouldn't believe it."

He gripped her shoulders, pressing her until she was kneeling. "Suck me off, you little cunt."

Her early memory surfaced. "I'll bite you, Henry."

"She'll throw you out on that pretty can of yours. Baby, come on, a little blow job. Who'll it hurt? You'll still be cherry." He pushed himself at her mouth.

For the second time in her life, she bit a penis. Not as hard as she could have, but sharply enough for him to sag back, whimpering, "Jesus!"

One July morning the thermometer sheltered by the nearby barn read 113. Alice sprawled on the big bed in the front room, wearing white shorts and halter that were hand-me-downs from the youngest Taylor daughter, reading the same girl's discarded *Seventeen*. Absorbed, she didn't notice Henry watching her from the doorway until the sound of his breathing grew audible.

The instant she looked up, he was a blur. Before the screen door closed, he was on top of her, mashing her with his wet, odorous, squat, strongly muscled body.

"Mr. Taylor says it's too damn hot to work," he panted. "The perfect day to have us a wonderful bang."

She struggled to escape, panting and gasping, but his hard-muscled thighs and one of his arms held her down.

"You're going to love it." His free hand fumbled with her shorts.

"No!" she cried.

He reached under the waistband, popping the button, which spun onto the floor as his fingers wriggled downward on her flat, silken skinned stomach.

She attempted to squirm away. "Get off me!"

"Been like a father to you," he muttered. "You owe me this."

He gave her halter a yank, tearing the strap in the back. Thrusting his face between her bared breasts, he dragged down her shorts and tore at the riveted buttons of his jeans. His engorged penis sprung out at her.

While she twisted violently, his fingers plunged inside her. Ragged nails cut the soft flesh. Parting her vulva, he thrust forward his erection. Alice thought frantically of gouging his eyes, then Juanita's long-ago advice presented itself. Her knee went up.

He grunted loudly, rolling off her, curling in a half circle as he clutched at himself.

"*Puta,*" he whimpered, continuing to clutch his groin.

His pain cut through Alice's panic. Retreating to the curtain that separated the rooms, her top dangling between her breasts, her shorts around her thighs, she asked, "Can I help? Get you some aspirin?"

Henry hunched on the edge of the bed, his dark, narrow-jawed face assuming the same righteous cast as when he beat up on Juanita. "You been begging for it ever since I known you," he muttered. "Only one thing worse than a *puta* and that's a prick tease."

As he lurched heavily down the uneven steps of the narrow porch, Alice began to shake uncontrollably.

She knew where he was going. To tell Juanita that she had made a pass at him. The thought that Juanita, who was everything to her, would believe this, increased her shakes. Sobbing, she changed her clothes.

At five Juanita came down the road, her flapping sandals raising puffs of dust around her bare brown ankles. She held one hand to the small of her back. Alice, going to meet her, concluded that the Taylors must be blind not to realize that their housekeeper was pregnant.

Juanita said nothing as they moved through the hot afternoon to the cottage.

Alice, filled with dread, chattered aimlessly about how she had started the lamb burrito mix and had put the refried beans in the oven. Then she heard herself ask casually, "Seen Henry?"

"I seen him." Juanita pushed open the screen door. Spicy aromas vibrated in the day's accumulated heat. "He came by the house. Said you was giving him the eye, and rubbing up against him."

Alice blinked rapidly, not denying the allegation. She wasn't about to hurt Juanita by telling her that her husband was a liar and an attempted rapist.

Giving a small shrug, she said, "I've been thinking of going to LA, getting a job, maybe an education." Then held her breath, praying that Juanita would nix the plan.

Instead, Juanita said, "Sounds like a good idea."

Alice's hands were shaking as she changed to her good outfit, a tight-topped red sun dress with a matching stole, and packed her possessions. Everything fitted in one large brown grocery sack.

Juanita, who was at the stove, fished a wad of bills from her apron pocket. "Here," she said.

"Nita, I can't take that, you've been saving it for the baby doctor."

The sweat on Juanita's face highlighted the dark splotches under the eyes as she made a sad smile. "A girl that looks like you needs a little cash to stay good in LA."

Here was her admission that she knew Henry had lied.

After a long moment Alice reached for the money, hugging her sister. She could feel the hard knot of the unborn infant. "Nita, it's going to be awful without you."

"Alice, look, I got something you oughta use." Reaching to the top shelf she came up with a partially used tube of vaginal foam. "Squeeze it into you."

Alice was too miserable to explain what actually had transpired. And besides, what if Henry had pushed it in far enough to start a baby? She retreated to the bathroom.

In Los Angeles, Alice tried for waitress jobs.. After three days and fourteen turndowns on the justifiable grounds that she had no identification to prove her age was indeed eighteen, she started riding the RTD busses to answer the ads listed under *Help Wanted, Domestic.*

Matrons examined her at their front doors, not allowing her across their threshold. "Oh, thank you for coming out, but the position's already filled."

The toll calls and fares to fancy suburbs, her slit of a hotel room, the chili dogs and Orange Juliuses that were her meals, rapidly depleted Juanita's money.

On the morning that Alice set out to answer the lowest-paying job in the column, she hadn't eaten in a day. The fumes and heat in the bus giddied and nauseated her. An old black woman wearing a shiny reddish wig plopped down next to her. Opening a paper sack, she said, "Have a donut."

"I just ate a huge breakfast, but thanks."

"I done did that big breakfast routine myself. But you looks like you'll pass out. Go ahead."

Faced with simple kindness, Alice broke down. Devouring a chocolate donut, she confided her problem.

"You ain't going to get no kind of housework, girl. You

too pretty. And they sees you's very young. Now, they ain't so fussy about Mexicans and us colored." The kind, bloodshot eyes examined her. "Mmm, you is very light. But with all that pretty black hair, you could pass as Mex. Can you speak it?"

"Sure." Who couldn't, in her line of work? "But what about my blue eyes?"

The face wrinkled into a smile. "You ain't got a thing to worry about. Talk that to them, and they'll never look you in the eye."

That morning Mrs. Young, mistress of the small, Mediterranean-style house in Brentwood, hired Alicia Lopez. Because of her lack of *inglés*, Alicia was underpaid and overworked.

Alicia had been with the Youngs two months on September 23, her fifteenth birthday. Since it fell on a weekend when the Youngs were out of town, she treated herself to a burger, fries and a Coke at Ship's in Westwood. Everyone else in the big coffee shop was laughing with their companions or deep into a conversation. Alicia, wearing her new red mini and five-inch red heels, felt even more miserably lonely than she did on the job. Quite apart from this devastating loneliness, Alicia missed Juanita in a manner so deep it was a constant, arthritic ache in her bones. Most nights she cried herself to sleep.

When the tall, skinny, redheaded man sitting next to her smiled, she smiled back. He had a class look, and she decided, correctly it soon turned out, that he was a college man from nearby UCLA. She pursed her lips around the straw.

"You don't look like you're enjoying that hamburger," he said.

She glanced down at the almost untouched bun. "I guess I don't have much appetite today," she said, discarding the Spanish intonations she put on with the Youngs. "But the food here's terrific."

"For hamburgers," he said authoritatively, "Tommy's is the tops."

"Tommy's?"

"You've never been there?"

"I've only been in LA two months," she admitted softly.

"Where are you from?"

After a long moment, she said, "El Paso." She had been reading about Texas in the *National Geographic*, which the following month would be in Dr. Young's waiting room.

"I'm Barry Cordiner," he said.

Another slight pause, and then she said, "Alicia Lopez."

Intuitively she accepted that disclosing the truth of her childhood would prompt him to pick up his check and leave her to her icy loneliness. Besides, hadn't she left Alice Hollister and the sickening smells of over-ripe crops far behind? Besides, she already liked this college man with the freckles and curly red hair.

He took her to see *Room at the Top* at the Bruin. He arranged to dine with her on chili-burgers at Tommy's the following night, which she had off since the Youngs were away. When he kissed her goodnight, she felt all warm and happy. Was this love?

On her wedding night she lay awake, the lusty whir of the air conditioner drowning out the gentle, regular breathing of her sleeping spouse. She knew she should feel guilty and rotten about deceiving him—but what choice had there been? He had led her from that awful, lonely pit, and she could not risk being thrust back there.

I'll make it up to him, she thought lovingly as she touched his bony ankle with her toe. She had already considered him immensely rich and knowledgeable, an "almost" lawyer who wrote wonderful stories, a creature so far superior to her that it was impossible to ever bridge the gap. And today she had learned that his family owned Magnum Pictures! Magnum, where they made so many of those double bills she'd seen in fleabag theaters.

Thinking of his sister and cousins, she sighed. Only that large blond one, Hap he was called, had looked at her with any degree of warmth. The others had been snooty and superior. *Hap*, she thought. *What a funny name.*

Then she reached her arms around Barry's thin body. His even breathing continued.

You'll never be sorry you married me, she thought fiercely. *I promise that you'll never be sorry.*

Alicia Cordiner was making a sacred vow. She was giving her husband her loyalty, which was boundless.

4

As Barry turned onto his mist-shrouded block, a jet roared overhead. This tract of modest bungalows, identical except for their gingerbread and clapboard trim, lay directly on the flight path into Los Angeles Airport.

He pulled into his driveway, parking behind his father's eleven-year-old Onyx sedan. Alicia slipped her comb in her purse. When they had entered the Los Angeles sprawl, she had turned on the interior lights and ever since had been combing and recombing her hair, wiping away pale lipstick to reapply it, attempting to finger-press the creases from the red fabric of that horrendous dress. Her jitters had heightened Barry's own uptightness about the coming encounter. Gripping the steering wheel, he wished that he'd been flush enough to take her shopping in Vegas, buy her a sweater and skirt and thus tame her exuberant beauty. By free association, he saw an image of Beth, so cool and conventional, the classic coed. *Bethie,* he thought. *Thank God she'll have already broken the news.*

Alicia intuitively caught the drift of his thoughts. "Barry, will your sister be home?"

"Sundays she usually is. She lives at the AEPhi house."

"Is she at UCLA, too?"

"No, USC." He didn't elaborate that his Uncle Desmond was paying his twin's tuition at the private campus as well as her sorority dues. Drawing a deep breath, he touched Alicia's arm. "Let's go in," he said.

Since there was no vestibule, they stepped directly into the living room. Beyond the pair of wing chairs and couch—all covered with the same worn maroon early American pattern—was the dining ell. Tim and Clara Cordiner sat opposite each other.

Clara's hair, dyed an uncertain shade between red and brown, had been brushed back rather than carefully ratted into a bouffant, and she wore a navy housedress. Tim had on his old blue tee shirt with the bleach fade.

As his parents looked up questioningly, Barry's stomach plummeted. *They don't know.*

"Where's Beth?" he asked stupidly.

"She stayed over at Uncle Frank and Aunt Lily's," Clara replied in that unfortunately pitched, nasal voice. "Dear, if you're not coming home, I do wish you'd call. I was awake nearly all night listening for you. Saturday morning I found Beth's note saying she was off to Las Vegas with you and the others."

Tim's eyes were going up and down Alicia's curves. "Aren't you going to introduce us to your friend?"

Barry grasped Alicia's fingers. "Sh-she's quite a bit more than a f-friend," he stammered. "Mom, Dad—this is Alicia, my wife. We were married yesterday in Las Vegas."

He might just as well have jabbed them with one of those electric cattle prods being used by Mississippi sheriffs against civil rights workers. Tim's leer was replaced by slack-jawed surprise. Clara's loud gasp faded into a drawn-out moan and her veined hand went to her chest. Since her coronary she had been preoccupied with the flurries and splutters of her unreliable heart.

Alicia broke the silence. "I'm very happy to meet you, Mr. Cordiner, Mrs. Cordiner," she said softly.

Tim pushed to his feet. This being Sunday, he hadn't shaved; his gray-blond hair had receded to the back of his pate, his belly bulged out in his faded tee shirt. Yet his height and the breadth of shoulders made him an impressive physical specimen, and now, in his anger, he was downright intimidating. "The hell you say," he growled.

"Married?" Clara whispered, the tendons of her thin neck straining. "You've never mentioned her. How long have you known her?"

"A month," Barry exaggerated.

"Alicia? What's her other name?" Clara addressed Barry, as if Alicia were a mute.

Alicia said, "Cordiner. But it *was* Lopez." Her voice held a note of defiant humor, but the hand that Barry held was shaking.

Clara went gray. Tim moved around the table to pat her thin shoulders with awkward tenderness.

Barry asked, "Aren't you going to say anything?"

"It seems to me you've said it all, buster!"

"Please, Tim. . . ." Clara murmured warningly. She knew that the Cordiner temper was at its most unregulatable in her husband. When the twins were nine, he had gotten into a fight with another grip, knocking him cold. The man had died on the way to the Magnum infirmary. It had taken all of Desmond Cordiner's considerable influence downtown to get his brother off without a prison term.

"Please what?" Tim bawled. "He barges in with some wetback chippy and tells us he's married to her. What the hell does he expect us to say?"

Barry had inherited a small share of the family temper, and at this moment, brown eyes glaring, thin shoulders hunched, the normally invisible resemblance between him and his father showed. "Something along the lines of good wishes and congratulations."

"For that, buster, you have to get married properly!"

"Like you and Mom did?"

A rumble came from Tim's chest as he took a step toward his son.

Clara's hand pressed tighter against her flat bosom. "Please don't the two of you start again."

"What do you mean, again?" Tim demanded. "When has this snotnose ever brought home a pachuco tramp that he's married to?"

"Come on, Alicia," Barry said tightly. "We're getting out of here."

The Cordiners' rejection filled Alicia with desolation, yet she said placatingly, "Barry, we took your folks by surprise."

"You!" Tim turned on her. "If you're expecting a free ride here, just forget it. We aren't the millionaire Cordiners, we're just plain, ordinary people." He lowered his head like a bull at Barry. "And as for you, if you're so damn grown-up, you don't need any more bucks from me."

"I work at the Student Union," Barry said.

"That money goes on books and gas. You pay your own room and board and we'll see how long you keep on with that fancy education of yours."

"Tim, he's got to finish!" Clara cried.

"Clara, you keep out of this. You've spoiled him long

enough. It's time Mr. Bigshot Married Man here learned what life's all about."

Barry's nails dug into Alicia's hand. "At least I know it's not about picking up women in bars and passing out in their beds!"

"You little turd!" Tim shouted at the top of his lungs. "Get the fuck out of my house, and take your Tijuana hooker with you!"

"Tim," Clara whimpered. "Tim, please. . . ."

Barry didn't hear the rest. Grabbing Alicia's upper arm, he propelled her down the short, unlit corridor and into his bedroom, where he yanked down the cordovan leather suitcase that had been a birthday gift from his Aunt Lily and Uncle Frank and began throwing in clothes. Alicia sat on the desk chair, her shaking hands clasped in her lap. The scene had destroyed what little there was of her self-esteem, yet she couldn't repress a ripple of sympathy for Tim. Not Clara—she'd never liked or respected whiners. But there had been something infinitely pathetic about the infuriated bull of a man in his old tee shirt. She wanted to urge Barry to go in and make up with his dad, but in Alice Hollister's world it was infra dig as well as downright dangerous to come between two furious men. She began folding the clothes that Barry had tossed into the suitcase.

The pencil jar jumped on the desk as the front door slammed.

"There goes Dad," Barry said, his brown eyes glittering with tears.

"Barry, we'll fix it up with them."

"After the way he insulted me—and you?"

"The shock—"

"We are not crawling." His boyishly angular face set, he began pulling books from the shelves. "*Never.*"

The door opened. Clara stood in the narrow hallway, her longish face like a white egg suspended in the dimness.

Studiously avoiding glancing at Alicia, she said to her son, "Dear, you mustn't take Dad seriously when he gets upset. We don't want you to leave."

"This time Dad's right," Barry said stiffly. "I have my marital responsibilities."

"Your, uhh, wife, could stay here, too. You've got the trundle bed."

"I refuse to sponge off of you."

"But how else will you finish school? Barry, you *must* finish school."

"I'll get that law degree, don't you worry."

"I can't bear any more of these family ruptures. . . ." Clara's jaw trembled. "It's ruined my health, you and Beth not knowing your grandparents. You will visit, won't you?"

"That's up to Dad. He'll have to apologize to my wife."

Clara blinked uncertainly.

"Barry, it's okay," Alicia said.

"I categorically refuse to enter a house where my wife's been insulted," Barry said sternly.

"You know Dad, dear," Clara sighed. "He means well, but he's never apologized to anyone in his life."

"Then it's about time he did."

"You used to be such a good boy," Clara said, and tottered away. She had not once permitted her gaze to rest on Alicia.

Barry shut the door. "So they'll let us have the cottage, the people you work for?" he muttered.

"Sure," she said, covering her uncertainty with a smile.

The Youngs were so shocked when they learned that their maid was married, and to a "white college student" (yes, Mrs. Young actually said it), that neither of them noticed that she had lost her accent. When Alicia asked if she could continue on the job and have the cottage for her and Barry, both Youngs put on grave faces, and Mrs. Young sank onto the slick plastic that covered the brocade upholstery, her somewhat protuberant eyes fixed on her husband.

He said obligingly, "Alicia, while Mrs. Young and I discuss this, will you and your husband step outside."

Alicia and Barry waited on the front step.

After a long ten minutes, they were invited back inside. Dr. Young did the talking, extolling the construction and plumbing of the room in back. "In a neighborhood like this we could get top rent for it," he said, neglecting to mention that the local zoning was R-1, restricted to single-family dwellings. "But Mrs. Young and I are very, very fond of Alicia, and so are Ronnie and Lonnie. And you seem like a sensible sort of young man, not wild or noisy. So we'll let you have it—on a trial basis, of course."

"You won't regret it," Barry said diffidently.

"Naturally we'll deduct a little from Alicia's salary. Does fifty dollars strike you as fair, Alicia?"

Alicia knew that at one twenty-five she was already being underpaid. Fifty dollars less? But what choice was there?

She nodded. "Fine."

"After you've done the dinner dishes, you're absolutely free to go out there," Dr. Young said. "Unless Mrs. Young and I have a date. Then, of course, you'll baby-sit in the house with the boys. Your husband—"

Barry coughed, repeating his name. "It's Barry Cordiner, sir."

"Yes, Corder. You understand of course that this arrangement doesn't include food."

Mrs. Young said, "I won't tolerate Alicia feeding you from my kitchen."

Alicia leaned toward Barry, anticipating some of the hot temper he had displayed with his parents. But he nodded docilely. "Of course."

In parting, Mrs. Young said, "Alicia, we expect you here at six thirty, sharp."

They checked into an ancient motel on Pico. A radio blared the music of Argentina on one side, on the other a drunken marital argument rose and fell. When Barry climbed on top of his wife's luscious body his erection turned to marshmallow.

The evening had reached its final defeat.

5

Neither of them slept much. The next morning they arrived at the Youngs' well before six thirty.

Leaving Alicia whipping Birds Eye frozen orange juice to a froth in the Osterizer, Barry went into the small backyard. Alicia's word, cottage, had roused in him visions of a vine-draped setting for *Werther* or somesuch rustic romance, so it took him a full minute to accept that she had meant the room stuck behind the garage.

Yanking open the unlocked, warped door, he was blasted by the pungent aroma of fertilizer. Dr. Young, a gardening enthusiast, stored his weedkillers, trowels, clippers and other equipment on the rough redwood shelves, using the floor space for huge plastic sacks of Bandini steer manure. Moving gingerly around the bags, Barry opened a plywood door, gagging involuntarily at a toilet whose interior was a stygian brown.

He had to straighten the garage before he could begin shifting tools and those endless, heavy, odiferous sacks. At ten thirty, when Mrs. Young drove off in her two-tone Dodge, Alicia came out.

"What a fabulous job you've done!" she exclaimed.

She dumped an entire bottle of bleach in the toilet, leaving it there while they scrubbed walls, windows and the warped floorboards. Mrs. Young had granted them certain furniture stored in the garage loft. After making the box springs and mattress, Alicia surveyed their quarters. "When I hang a sheet in that corner to rig up a closet and put your books on the shelves, it'll be perfect." Her face glowed with a light film of sweat and happiness.

Barry didn't know what to say. His requirements, to his own mind, were modest; he hadn't been reared in architectural splendors like his cousins, but God knows one needn't have grandiose expectations to want better than a scuzzy lavatory and the ineradicable stink of manure.

That night she returned after nine, bringing with her the scent of hand lotion. He was at the table studying for the following day's poli-sci quiz. Bending over him, she circled his throat with her arms, drawing his head back against those voluptuous breasts. He got up for a welcome-home hug, not intending anything sexy—he still had to learn several more points of the Volstead Act—but she pressed her palms to his buttocks, crushing against him as she made small whimpering sounds. Her passion astonished him. Previously she had responded with shy pleasure, never taking the initiative.

"Make love to me, Barry," she pleaded hoarsely. "Make love to me."

He responded with an instant hard-on. "Let me get a rubber."

She was pulling him down onto the mattress, guiding his hand beneath her short uniform and under her panties to the hot, slick wetness.

Summoning every ounce of willpower, he pulled away from her embrace. "Be right back."

The sight of the toilet bowl, now a paler but equally evocative brown, demolished his erection.

He returned to find their one lamp dimmed by a scarf and his wife stretched naked on the bed. The nipples pointing up at him were the palest pink while the vulva exposed by her spread thighs was deep rose. Again he thought of goddesses, but this time of the ancient ones before civilization began, the deities served by fertility rites.

His hardness reasserting itself, he fell on top of her, grasping the full curves of her breasts so tightly that she cried out.

"Is this what you like?" he demanded hoarsely.

"Yes," she whimpered.

"What do you want me to do?"

"Make love to me."

"No, say the word."

"Fuck. . . ."

"Beg me."

"Fuck me, please fuck me."

His own hoarse breathing filling the universe, he entered her, pumping deeper and deeper into her rosy mysteries, coming so intensely that it ached far up in his balls.

When his gasping ceased, he kissed her ear. "Hey, when you're hot, you're hot." Wishing he were uninhibited enough to tell her of those favorable comparisons with goddesses, he fell asleep almost instantly.

Alicia pulled the blanket over his shoulders, then began to cry. But why was she crying? Hadn't she accomplished what she had set out to do? Hadn't her husband just made love to her?

Alicia, too, had brooded about the previous night, deciding the failure was hers. *I'm just not sexy,* she had thought miserably. *Maybe he can't make it because he senses I'm not leveling with him.*

But honesty was out of the question.

When she'd first spoken to Barry Cordiner at Ship's

Coffee Shop, an infallibly sure intuition had informed her that he might be educated and say things she'd hitherto only read in books, but he was utterly naive about one word: poverty. He had no comprehension how deep and shameful a thing poverty could be. He believed that being poor meant having a father named Lopez who was occasionally laid off from his trucking job, scratching together the mortgage payments and maybe eating beans at the end of the month. He didn't know about sleeping on the damp earth, going hungry until you were giddy, peeing in the fields. The reality would assuredly send him packing.

She knuckled her eyes dry, tiptoeing into the bathroom to use Juanita's vaginal foam. It probably would have been safer if she could have squeezed it in before *and* after as she had in Las Vegas, but this time he'd had on a Trojan, so she guessed it was okay. She wished Juanita were here to discuss the problem with. *She doesn't even know I'm married.* Then Alicia thought, *I wonder if she knows anything about Barry.* Alicia had written glowingly about him, but Juanita, humiliated by her functional illiteracy, might not have asked Henry or anyone to read the letters to her. Alicia, barely fifteen, longing for the half sister who had been a mother to her, began to cry again.

The following morning, when everyone had left the house, Alicia walked the mile and a half to San Vincente Boulevard to the nearest pay phone. She called the Taylor Ranch.

Mrs. Taylor answered. Juanita and Henry, she said in a clenched tone, were no longer there. Mr. Taylor had been forced to fire Henry. The Lopezes had left no forwarding address.

Of course they hadn't left an address. Pickers don't have addresses. There was no way of telling Juanita anything. No way of finding her. Ever.

Dropping the phone so it dangled by its cord, leaving the little pile of coins on the shelf, Alicia blindly left the booth.

Three weeks later Barry and Beth sat drinking coffee on the broad, crowded flight of steps in front of Ackerman Hall. Barry, who had not spoken to anyone in the family since the disastrous night he'd left his parents' house, was surprised and delighted when Beth showed up just as he was getting off work at the Student Union. Since it was lunch hour, all available tables inside and out were taken, and students were eating on the red brick steps. Over the roar of laughing conversation and the clashing of crockery, he boasted about the fabulous cottage and about the three articles he was writing for the *Daily Bruin* on John Hersey's *The Child Buyer.* He needed to prove to Beth—and the entire Cordiner clan—how excellently he was managing.

"Barry, listen," Beth said. "Things haven't been going well since you left. Mom's been in for an EKG. And Dad's gotten into a running battle with the head grip."

"Now tell me what I'm meant to do about it? Come crawling back to beg their pardon for marrying a terrific, fine girl I happen to be crazy about?"

"How are her parents taking it?"

Barry's defensive truculence faded momentarily. When Alicia had told him she'd phoned her family, her huge blue eyes had been wet. She didn't say anything about the call, but he was positive the Lopezes were coldly unforgiving about her marrying outside the Church.

"You see?" Beth said. "Everybody's upset. Uncle Desmond, Aunt Rosalynd, Uncle Frank, Aunt Lily—"

"Stop laying a guilt trip on me!"

"I don't mean to."

"Why else're you here?"

Playing with her narrow gold bangle, she said, "PD asked me to talk to you."

"PD? How's *he* in on the act?"

"He's invited us all down to Newport." Frank and Lily Zaffarano owned a bayfront house there. "This Sunday."

"Us?" Barry asked. "Define the word 'us.'"

"You, me, PD, Alicia, Hap, Maxim."

"Give PD our regrets," Barry said. "Beth, you might as well be aware of this for future reference. Until Dad apologizes to Alicia, I'm not exposing her to the family."

"PD wants us to get together, that's all. Us. Not Dad and Mom—or any of the aunts and uncles."

"You're sure?"

"Positive."

"Well, let me see how Alicia feels about it." Barry used a stern tone. But as far as he was concerned, a Sunday away from the dreadful room was one notch below paradise.

6

Newport curves along a narrow spit of land across from Balboa: the paired resort towns cuddle around a large, boat-filled bay. During the summer Angelenos flock down, clogging traffic for miles. In mid-November the roads weren't jammed, but nevertheless Barry concentrated on his driving. This morning they'd had their first spat. Barry had suggested Alicia wear shorts, but since she owned only the Taylor girl's hand-me-down white ones, ancient and mended, a too graphic reminder of the Henry Lopez incident, she'd put on her red sundress with the stole. Barry had not commented, he had simply remained silent. Since then he had responded to her attempts at conversation monosyllabically. She was anxious enough about an entire day with his sister and those rich cousins, and his silence made her stomach twitch.

In Newport, Barry turned left, crossing a short, humpbacked bridge. "Lido Isle," he announced. "The most exclusive of the exclusive."

"It's nice," she said, grateful that he had spoken, yet unsure why these houses jammed so close together were considered special.

Barry parked, leading the way to a two-story, white-shingled Cape Cod. As they walked along the side path, Alicia realized how deceptive the frontages were. The Zaffarano house went back at least a hundred feet. In the bright noon sunlight, the acres of fresh white paint gleamed, blurring in front of her eyes. She reached for Barry's hand. His fingers dangled, limply unresponsive.

They turned a corner, emerging onto a planked deck. A brisk breeze shimmered whitecaps across the azure bay. The big Chris-Craft with the royal blue canvas cover that matched the house's royal blue shutters bobbled and banged its bumpers against the swaying dock. The deck was protected by high glass walls, and in the still warmth,

PD, Hap and Maxim were stretched out sunbathing. Beth, fiddling with a camera, wore a sleeveless yellow blouse and matching shorts.

Barry called, "Hi, guys."

The others looked up.

Alicia, acutely conscious of the tightness of her sundress top, and of the black patent shoes with the killing pointed toes and stiletto heels, formed a smile.

PD pushed to his feet. His compact, well-muscled, dark-tanned body agleam with Coppertone, he strode toward them. "Welcome," he said, smiling. "So you finally made it."

Maxim raised up on one long, thin arm, giving Barry and Alicia his acid smile. "Hell, PD, you know these horny honeymooners, they probably pulled over for a quickie."

Beth held up her finger, smiling. "Hold it." Bending her smooth head, she aimed her camera at PD, who was standing between Barry and Alicia.

After the click, Hap moved into the group. Alicia, who even in her heels was nearly a head shorter, couldn't help noting that the curly blond hairs covering his chest became brown as they cut in a narrow line down to his navel, turning almost black where the line disappeared beneath his faded madras trunks.

Hap punched at Barry's shoulder in greeting before he kissed Alicia's cheek. The light touch of his lips caused a surprising tingle of pleasure and her sense of being on enemy territory dwindled.

"Beth's made guacamole," PD said. "Her one big specialty."

"Yeah," Maxim added, "and the bitch refused to serve it up until her twinnie-twin-twin arrived. So hurry and suit up before we starve."

Barry glanced down, his lips pulling into a line that wasn't quite a smile, an expression that Alicia had come to dread: it meant she had somehow embarrassed him.

She said quickly, "I forgot to bring a suit." Actually she didn't own one, and hadn't been able to sneak off for an hour to buy one at any of the intimidatingly smart little boutiques lining San Vincente Boulevard.

"No sweat," PD said. "Mom keeps a slew in the dressing room for all sizes and shapes."

On the other side of the house were twin doors with bright brass silhouettes designating the sex of the users. Alicia found herself in a kind of sitting room approximately twice as large as their cottage and furnished with wicker and bright plaids. A row of swimsuits hung from wooden pegs. Three cotton-ruffled numbers for little girls. Two outsizes with skirts to cover dimpled, matronly thighs. She tried on the remaining four. The red and the pink bikini were both far too loose. The black one-piece knit was too tight on top. The white Lastex, also one-piece, fitted to perfection. It dipped to a deep V between her breasts, while cutouts revealed the curves where her waist met her hips. Turning this way and that on her bare feet to view her image in the mirror, she had to admit that the suit was a knockout on her. Then she frowned uncertainly. Would Barry get that embarrassed little smile when she emerged?

A rap sounded on the door. "It's me, Hap. I was getting worried. You decent?"

"I'm not quite sure."

He came in, staring at her. "Hey," he whispered. "Hey."

"It's okay on me?" She could feel herself coloring. The intensity of his gaze embarrassed her, yet at the same time she felt a delightful melting in the pit of her stomach.

"Spectacular." His voice was husky, and he seemed incapable of looking away from her.

"Yes, but am I . . . you know . . . cheap?"

"You're incredible is all. Liz Taylor, only younger and more gorgeous. Take it from me, Dad'd sign you right away."

"Sometimes Barry—" She stopped abruptly, before she could say anything that would imply disloyalty. "I really don't know anything about style."

Hap's head tilted, and his gray eyes were no longer crinkled into a smile. He had very dark lashes for somebody with such light hair. Alone in the room with him, she was acutely conscious of how his suit bared him, the odor of salt and tanning lotion on him, and how large and muscular he was. Barry's narrow height did not make her feel diminutive like this, or fragile and weak.

"You're nervous, aren't you?" he asked quietly.

"Me? Why should I be shook? Because I've never been

in a house like this? Or because PD's father is a famous director? Or because your father owns Magnum—"

"He works for Magnum," Hap interrupted. "He's vice president in charge of production. It's a job like anyone else's."

"Yes. Except he runs a big studio."

Hap sat in one of the chairs, apparently unconcerned about the effects of suntan oil on the plaid fabric. "He didn't always."

"No, he was a boy. A rich boy."

"Is *that* what Barry told you?"

"We don't talk much about families." The way Barry kept silent about his made it clear that questions on the subject were off limits: the sum total of her knowledge about her husband's background was that his Jewish grandparents had disowned his mother for marrying Tim Cordiner.

Hap's thoughtful gaze seemed to go with his size, and maybe for that reason the way his gray eyes remained on her, rather than draining her limited supply of self-confidence infused her with more of the commodity. She sat on a wicker ottoman. "But I'm interested in knowing."

"My grandparents left Hungary when Dad was a few months old," Hap said. "The name, incidentally, wasn't Cordiner, but some unpronounceable mouthful that the immigration official wrote down as Cordiner. They were starving—the local baron had sold the two fields where they grew rye out from under them. Grandpa became a contract laborer at a Pennsylvania steel mill—"

"Contract laborer?"

"In those days the mills paid the passage for cheap foreign labor. In return grandfather agreed to work seven years for a pittance. The only hitch was that the mill owned the town. Rents and prices were exorbitant and Grandpa never did work his way out of debt. There was no money for luxuries like medicine or doctors. Grandma had nine children. Only Dad, Aunt Lily and Uncle Tim survived."

"I'm sorry," she said.

"It gets worse." The gray eyes were somber. "Grandpa was drowned—or boiled maybe—in tons of molten metal. This was a couple of weeks before Aunt Lily was born. It goes without saying there were no widows' pensions or free rent. They moved to Pittsburgh. Dad—he was ten at the time—ran errands at a cheap whorehouse. His tips supported the family. And, by the time he was sixteen, he'd saved enough for fares to Los Angeles. Here, he lugged heavy props at Magnum, which Art Garrison had just started. Within a year he was producing two-reelers and had gone into hock for a big house for the family in the Wilshire District. He has a reputation for being cutthroat in business, Dad, but he's a terrific family man. Anyway, you can see the Cordiners aren't exactly quality folk."

Alicia nodded. The reassurance of Hap's person, rather than his story, had calmed her. The horrors of another generation were historical events, and the Cordiners *were* quality now, rich and important.

"Thank you, Hap," she said.

"For what? Telling you about your new family?"

He reached out as if to touch her bare shoulder reassuringly. She knew from the heat in her cheeks that she was flushing. His hand dropped to his side, and his voice was again huskily deep as he said, "Don't worry about the suit, it's great on you."

"It's not like there was any choice," Alicia said. "This is the only one that halfway fit me."

It was just after one. The others were inside changing to go out for lunch.

"Halfway is the crucial word," Barry said tightly.

"Oh, Barry, don't ruin the day."

"Thank God Beth's finding you a shift to wear over it. Otherwise they'd never let you in the Crab Cooker," he said. Then, realizing that his embarrassment over the explicit lushness of his wife's body had led him into gratuitous unkindness, he added in a conciliatory tone, "What were you and Hap doing down there anyway?"

"Talking."

"About what?"

She realized that Barry wasn't questioning her out of jealousy but curiosity. She also understood that although her husband resented his role of poor relation, his pride was intricately tethered to being part of the shining Cordiner galaxy. He would not care for Hap's dimming the family glow. "Oh, just stuff," she said lightly. "Nothing special."

Alicia had been anticipating a formal, stiff restaurant like the one in Las Vegas, but eating at the Crab Cooker was as casual as a picnic. The chowder came in Styrofoam bowls, and seafood main courses were served on paper plates. Amid the smells of barbecuing fish, the rush of tanned young waitresses, the laughter of casually clad people, Alicia, wearing the flowered shift Beth had found in a guest closet, traded quips with Our Own Gang. Afterward, the six of them crowded back into PD's open Chrysler convertible, the salty breeze blowing away their loud rendition of "Itsy Bitsy Teenie Weenie Polka Dot Bikini" as they drove back to the house.

A large black Rolls-Royce was parked imperially to block the Zaffaranos' three-car garage.

"Jesus, that's Dad's car," Hap said.

"What's Uncle Desmond doing here?" Barry asked. He was blinking rapidly, as if a bug had caught in his eye.

"Who knows?" PD said. "Maybe he got his weekends mixed up."

"Dad?" Maxim said. "PD, you weasel, try again. Why is he here?"

"Okay," PD said agreeably. "He asked me to get Barry and Alicia down so he could settle this crap between Barry and his folks."

"You're a shit, PD," Barry said, his voice clenched yet frightened. "And my marriage and my parents' reactions to it are nobody's concern but my own."

"Evidently, *paisan,* Uncle Desmond doesn't agree," PD replied equably.

7

The casual ease with which Desmond Cordiner lounged against the dock rail would convince a stranger that he was the proprietor of the big Chris-Craft and Cape Cod beach house. In his slip-on loafers with discreet gold buckles, well-tailored gray slacks and open, gray-striped sport shirt with a paisley ascot tucked in, he was infinitely distinguished. The two wings of silver in his thick, recently barbered black hair appeared placed there by aristocratic heredity. His tall, well-toned body—at sixty thickened a bit around the beltline—gave no hint of childhood deprivation. Neither did his face offer a clue to his peasant origins. The grooved forehead was high, the nose long and narrow, and in relaxation, the mouth showed a quirk of superiority.

In the seven years since Art Garrison, the near-dwarf founder of Magnum Pictures, had died and Desmond Cordiner had taken over as studio chief, the Magnum publicity department had been planting items linking the current boss with world-class celebrities. Desmond Cordiner had been on the cover of *Life* in a golf cart with President Eisenhower, and visited Hyannisport to spend a weekend with Senator Kennedy, who was currently campaigning to get the Democratic nomination for the presidency. A much televised strip of film showed him relaxing aboard HMS *Britannia* with Her Majesty and Prince Philip. A recent issue of *Forbes* devoted to an in-depth article on Magnum Pictures pointed out that Desmond Cordiner was no vulgarian like his dead boss, Art Garrison; no crude Harry Cohn; no malaprop-making Louis B. Mayer; no *arriviste* Skouras or Zanuck: here was one movie mogul capable of holding his own with the patrician New York bankers who financed films.

As his sons, his nephews and niece came into sight, he showed his slightly oversized white teeth in a fond smile, moving up the steps, greeting them indulgently.

Barry mumbled, "Uncle Desmond, this is my wife, Alicia."

Desmond Cordiner took off his sunglasses; his dark eyes fixed on her.

She had never seen eyes quite like this. As he stared at her they seemed to turn to black glass, depthless and flat. The worldly gentleman faded and there were only the coldly assessing eyes probing into her flesh, her skull, her guts, her ovaries.

"So you're the hot little number who's caused all the fuss."

Alicia hid her trepidation in the usual way, with bravado. "Guilty," she said blithely.

"Well, you do have something. Even in a town of pretty girls, I have to admit you have something. Maybe the eyes, maybe the skin. . . ." He shrugged as if reminding himself he wasn't in his office considering some young actress's physical attributes. "You and Barry come on inside."

Barry made an uncertain sound in his throat.

"Dad," Hap said, "we were all at the wedding. It's legal and binding."

Desmond Cordiner replied genially, "When the law's in question, Hap, I get advice from the head of legal." He opened a glass door, glancing from Barry to Alicia.

Barry went inside, and a second later Alicia followed. *He has a reputation for being cutthroat in business, Dad, but he's a terrific family man,* Hap had said. Now if only she knew whether she were business or family.

The living room of the Zaffarano beach house had a wall of windows overlooking the bay, which made it appear yet more expensive, not that it needed such embellishment. Centuries-old Provencal tables and chests mingled with deep chairs and couches upholstered in various patterns of blue and white toile de jouy. Desmond Cordiner went to the paneled bar, poured himself a large shot of J&B and carried the drink to an ell at the far end of the room where they could not be seen from the deck, indicating with his free hand that Barry and Alicia should sit on the *bergère* chairs facing him.

"Barry," he said jovially. "The good news about this is it proves that you're not a faggot." Desmond Cordiner stubbornly manifested his hatred of homosexuals in a business where a large number worked with great and indispensable talent. Of necessity he hired gay people, but whenever problems arose on a film, he laid the blame on them. His loathing was psychotic—and implacable.

Barry smiled uncertainly. "Were you worried, Uncle Desmond?"

"Hardly." Desmond Cordiner spoke in a way that indicated such proclivities were impossible among *his* relations. "On the other hand, the bad news is you're a horse's ass."

Barry's left eyelid began twitching.

Alicia shifted in the deep upholstery, moving closer to her husband. "You don't have any right to talk to Barry like that, Mr. Cordiner," she said.

The drink splashed violently in Desmond Cordiner's hand. He was the tribal chieftain, and nobody in the family had ever dared tell him what he could or could not say. His face was terrifying. It was as though the tanned skin were stretched into a mask—obviously the mannered charm could be put on and off like a piece of clothing. "Since when do I need a fucking right to talk to my nephew?"

"You weren't talking to him, you were insulting him." Alicia's heart was banging so hard that she was positive the erratic movements were visible through the borrowed shift. "And whether you like it or not, we're married."

Desmond Cordiner turned to Barry. "Barry, I'm about to show you how easy it is to become a single man again."

"Uncle Desmond . . . I don't w-want—" Barry stammered.

But the sunglasses were fixed on Alicia. "How much have you got in mind?"

"Much?"

"Money."

"We have enough," she said.

"Of course you do. That's why you're scrubbing other people's shit out of toilets."

Alicia's surge of fury blanked out fear. "For the time being, Mr. Cordiner, I work. Later on Barry'll support me."

"Bullshit."

"He'll have his law practice."

"If you've a brain in your head you'll see that he'll never make it through college, much less law school, if he's married to you."

"I will, Uncle Desmond," Barry muttered.

"You don't have the staying power, you never did. Beth got the stamina and sense of responsibility. All you want to do is waste your time at the typewriter and pretend you're Ernest Hemingway." His shielded gaze returned to Alicia. "I want your claws out of my nephew—so tell me the tab."

"Uncle Desmond—"

"Shut up, Barry. This is between me and Mrs. Bigmouth Cordiner here. One thousand bucks?"

"You're only embarrassing yourself, Mr. Cordiner."

"I'll do a damn sight more than embarrass myself to get one of my family out of hot water. Fifteen hundred?"

"I don't want your money." The fury that gave her courage had blanched her face.

"Two thousand."

Alicia got to her feet.

Desmond Cordiner's frightening tension remained, but for a moment his head tilted as if her continued refusal not only surprised him but also challenged him. "Twenty-five hundred." He shifted his weight so he could reach into the back pocket of his slacks to draw out a large wad of bills that were divided by five paperclips. Heavy paper thumped and metal clicked as he tossed the money on the coffee table.

Alicia stared. Angled across the corners of the visible bills was the number 100. She had never before seen a hundred-dollar bill. It was incomprehensible to her that anyone, even a man who owned—no, ran—Magnum Pictures, could carry all this money, much less toss it at a stranger.

"Not a nickel more." Now Desmond Cordiner was smiling benignly. "Cash on the line."

"Barry," she said quietly, hiding her sudden, panicky dizziness, "I'd like to go home. Right away."

The blood drained from Barry's head. Desmond Cordiner was the man before whom all Magnum trembled, and none of the hierarchy of executives, none of the major stars or the thousands of employees—including his father and uncle—dared walk out before he signaled the interview was over. Yet Barry found himself mutely leading the way to the front door.

The instant Alicia got into the old De Soto, she crumpled and began to weep.

Barry drove jerkily down the block and was toiling up the humpbacked bridge before he realized that he'd left the handbrake on. "Jesus, Alicia, how can I drive with you caterwauling?"

She wept harder. ". . . I've stolen . . . your aunt's swimsuit and shift."

She drenched his spare handkerchief and then used the

dirty one. Barry, by now even more distraught about her hysteria than his uncle's rage, patted her knee. "Stop worrying. As soon as we spot a pay phone, I'll call the house. Beth'll bring up your things and take back Aunt Lily's."

Even though he made the promised call to his sister, Alicia wept all the way to Disneyland. As they passed the enormous parking lots her tears finally ceased.

Wiping her swollen eyes, she stared up at the fake Matterhorn. "Barry?" she said.

"What, hon?"

"I never saw a hundred-dollar bill before."

"Mmm," replied Barry, who hadn't either.

The next morning, Monday, the door chimes sounded before nine. Mrs. Young bitterly resented being wakened so early. Alicia, anticipating Beth's arrival with the clothing swap, reached for the big paper bag containing the swimsuit and shift, both of which she had carefully laundered, darting through the hall before a second repetition of the loudly unmusical sound.

At the front door stood an elderly black chauffeur. "Does Mrs. Cordiner live here?" Politely he removed his peaked cap. "Mrs. Barry Cordiner?"

She nodded. The Rolls-Royce at the curb told her whose chauffeur he was, and therefore she felt no surprise to see Desmond Cordiner emerging from the gleaming limousine. Yet instinctively she took a step backward.

"We didn't get a chance to finish our conversation," Desmond Cordiner said as he gave her short, tight nylon uniform the once-over. "That Pucci thing you wore yesterday didn't do you credit. Your body's top grade."

Did he think to flatter her out of marriage? Or was he making a pass? Did men this powerful and rich make passes? "Mr. Cordiner," she said, "I'm not allowed to have company."

"Alicia?" Mrs. Young, frowning irritably and tying her chenille bathrobe, came into the hall. Then her eyes bulged at the apparition in a handsome black silk suit that had cost more than the entire contents of Dr. Young's closet.

"Mrs. Young," Alicia said, "this is my husband's uncle."

Desmond Cordiner formed his urbane smile. "I hope it wasn't my man who woke you, Mrs. Young."

"No," she said, glancing out the open door. The elderly chauffeur was rubbing a chamois on the Rolls-Royce's windshield. "No, of course not. Alicia, dear, why don't you take Mr.—"

"Cordiner," he said with another smile. "Desmond Cordiner."

Mrs. Young recognized the well-publicized name. She said respectfully, "Alicia dear, take your guest in the living room."

Desmond Cordiner made himself comfortable on the plastic-covered couch. "My approach yesterday was crass," he said affably. "But you'd be surprised at how often the actual sight of green does the trick."

"Barry and I want to stay married."

"So you made abundantly clear," he said, pausing. "I could have been far, far worse, you know."

"Mr. Cordiner, there was no point in your coming here."

"How do you know what I have in mind?"

"To separate me and Barry."

"Many, many years ago I learned not to waste energy on losing battles," he said. "I've decided you'll support your husband in a more dignified manner."

"He works at the UCLA Student Store, and that should be dignified enough for two."

Desmond Cordiner's manicured hand waved away her protest. "I admire loyalty, Alicia, but have you ever considered the marriage from his point of view?"

"All the time."

"Then you must realize that Barry would rather be doing a jail term than living in a maid's room."

"We have our own place out back."

He eyed her again. "You really are a knockout," he said. "A bit exotic, although I wouldn't for a minute believe there's anything Latino about you."

"My name is Lopez!" she protested.

"Let's try Hollister," he said with a wry smile. "So you see, I could have been far less pleasant yesterday. Or does Barry know you're a fifteen-year-old bastard who worked in the fields when you were six—or was it five?"

She gripped the paper bag closer, as if it were a shield from the naked truth.

"Don't look so surprised," he said. "A private investigator easily uncovers that kind of thing."

"So what?" she blurted out. "At least I never ran errands for cheap whores."

His eyes turned that icy black as he peered at her. "Barry told you *that*? How the hell does Barry know? Even Tim never knew."

That Hap had entrusted her with so closely held a secret shocked her. "Nobody told me," she evaded. "I made a stab in the dark."

Desmond Cordiner continued to stare at her. She looked away first.

"I'll kill you if you tell anyone," he said quietly.

The threat did not sound like hyperbole—Desmond Cordiner would know where to hire a hit man.

"We'll both keep quiet," she said.

She expected him to attack her for this audacity, but instead he leaned forward as if they were two merchants discussing business. "How would you like to be an extra?" he asked.

"Extra?" She frowned, momentarily incapable of grasping his meaning.

"You know what an extra is," he said impatiently. "The money's pretty fair, and I'll make sure you get enough work at Magnum so you and Barry can manage. I hire hundreds of extras a day. You might as well be one of them."

An extra. . . . She bit her full lower lip. Being an extra meant she would be up there on the screen. "Barry won't let me do it," she said finally.

"I've known Barry since he was two hours old—I know how his mind works. It's killing him to live in that bug-eyed woman's house, married to the housemaid."

"He's very upset about the way his parents treated me and the things you said yesterday. He'll never let me take a thing from the family."

"Believe me, you won't have the slightest connection with the family." Desmond Cordiner's tone was cold and flat. "I'm not offering a relationship, I'm offering work."

"Barry's very proud, he hates favors. There's no way he'll allow me to accept your help."

"Try him," Desmond Cordiner said, rising to his feet and walking to the front door.

8

As the day passed, Alicia's head pounded and she became increasingly tense. She was realizing that for the first time in her life she was being offered what Juanita had called the real breaks. What could be more of a break than a chance to be in movies? Her headache spread to the back of her neck as she attempted to think up ways of presenting Desmond Cordiner's offer in its most alluring light to her proudly defiant husband. This was Dr. Young's night to work late and it was after ten before she locked the back door behind her. She was wild with impatience to talk to Barry.

He lay on the mattress, a long pad of yellow lined paper propped on his thighs as he scribbled—he was writing three essays on some book for the college newspaper.

Not looking up, he said, "Talk to you later, hon. The narrative flow's coming."

Her planned cajolements vanished. Sitting next to him on the bed, she blurted out, "Your uncle was here."

Barry's ballpoint dropped, clattering onto the floorboards. "Uncle Desmond?"

"Yes."

"When?"

Her voice rushing and childishly pitched, she reported the visit, omitting the exchange of secrets. "It wasn't anything like yesterday. He was quite nice, actually. Barry, uhh, I've been sort of thinking. Do you think it's really dumb? I mean, *could* I be an extra?"

"There's no creativity or skill involved," he said in a dismissive tone. "Extras aren't expected to be actors."

"Then you aren't against the idea?"

"It's up to you."

The hundreds of arguments she had fretted into existence spun away. "You wouldn't mind?"

"I just told you," he snapped. "It's strictly your decision."

She could tell by the way he didn't look at her but bent down to retrieve his pen that he hoped her decision would be affirmative.

The following morning Alicia called Magnum Pictures. Desmond Cordiner's executive secretary said her boss was tied up in a conference, but she'd been alerted to take a message.

Alicia said, "Will you please tell him that his, uhh, nephew's wife wants to accept the offer he made yesterday."

On Monday, one week to a day after Desmond Cordiner's visit, the Barry Cordiners moved into a furnished bachelor apartment in a run-down section of West Hollywood. Barry counted out the first and last month's rent from Alicia's savings, then the couple drove to the nearby Van Vliet's supermarket. When the checker returned their change, Alicia fingered the two worn dollar bills and the coins. This was all they had. The precariousness of their finances didn't appear to faze Barry, normally a worry wart about money. He helped her stow the groceries in the old-fashioned, built-in refrigerator, he laughed when she discovered the oven of the ancient, high-legged stove didn't work, he peered into every shelf of the kitchenette and bathroom.

After they ate their hamburgers, he suggested they open up the couch.

He hadn't made love to her since the night before Newport. (Alicia took the avoidance personally; however, the infrequency of their conjugal relations had no connection to her appeal. Barry's sex drive, never high, had been perilously drained by their ugly, odiferous room.)

Finishing, he followed his pattern of falling instantly asleep. Alicia got up to use the foam, which she now left out on the sink ledge—Barry was delighted about what he called double insurance. Her bruised breasts seemed oddly huge; her pelvis felt engorged. Her body appeared to be awaiting something further. With a sigh, she decided that she wasn't any good at being a wife.

Three days crept by. Desmond Cordiner hadn't contacted her since his visit to the Youngs', and now she nursed dark doubts. Had she misinterpreted his offer? Had he really intended to help her become an extra? Or was it possible that the secretary had neglected to tell him of her call? Maybe he'd mislaid her note with their new address? Or changed his mind? Her worst and most persistent fear was that he'd concocted a monstrous game to punish her for not accepting his bribe. Desmond Cordiner was too complicated and too powerful for her to figure. All she knew for certain was that unless something happened soon, it would be back to seeking employment in the *Help Wanted, Domestic* ads, which would mean the demise of her marriage—she had not realized the full force of Barry's aversion to living in the cottage until they had moved here.

On the fourth morning after Barry left for UCLA she was too jittery to even turn the bed back into a couch. Sitting on the rumpled blanket, she drank another cup of stale coffee. She jumped, nearly gagging on the hot brew, as a rap sounded on the screen door.

A tall Oriental boy wearing cut-off jeans called out that he was a Magnum messenger. She signed for a large manila envelope with the Magnum leopard's head logo in the left-hand corner.

Opening it with fumbling fingers, she found a Screen Extras Guild membership card made out to Alicia Lopez, and a creased, extremely authentic looking Texas birth certificate for Alicia Elena Lopez, dated July 2, 1941. Clipped to the IDs was a handwritten memo. *You are not permitted to use the name Cordiner.* It was not signed, but she knew the spiky, near illegible sentence had been scrawled by Desmond Cordiner. Later the note would both infuriate and desolate her, but now, giddy with relief, she crumpled it into the plastic garbage can under the sink.

There was also a typed letter explaining that Alicia Lopez had been registered for preferential treatment at Magnum. She should call Central Casting immediately.

There was a job for her. At the bottom, in lieu of a signature, were the words: *Dictated but not read by Desmond Cordiner.*

They could not afford a telephone and Alicia trotted the long block to Santa Monica Boulevard, using the Standard station's pay phone.

The number given in the letter rang fifteen times before an unpleasant voice snapped, "Central Casting."

"Do you have a job listed for Alicia Lopez?"

"Nothing," snarled the voice.

"But there's supposed to be. Maybe at Magnum Pictures."

A long pause. "Here it is, Lopes." The name was pronounced as a single syllable. "Why didn't you say Lopes? You're in *Paris Lovers*. Report to Magnum at eight tomorrow, Stage Fourteen."

"What shall I wear?"

"Street clothes." The phone went dead.

At seven thirty Barry was edging along the slow left lane of traffic on Gower. Alicia, who had never seen a studio, peered through the morning haze at a high, block-long stucco wall painted a nondescript shade of mustard yellow. Barry braked at the open gates through which cars were streaming. High overhead on the wrought-iron arch was worked a leopard's head and an intaglio of Gothic lettering: MAGNUM PICTURES.

"See you here at five thirty," he said, leaning over to peck her on the cheek.

"Wish me luck?"

"Hon, I've told you again and again not to agonize. You'll simply be a body in the background."

The cars behind them were honking persistently and Alicia jumped out. She watched the De Soto disappear around the corner of Sunset. Drawing a breath, she started toward the iron arch. Then she noticed a turnstile beside a window. Neatly painted above the window were the words: EXTRAS REPORT HERE.

A full-cheeked old man sat behind the grille. "What's your name, sweetheard?" He hit a *d*, not a *t* on the end.

"I'm Alicia Lopez, working on *Paris Lovers*."

"Lopez?" He consulted his clipboard. "Yup, here you are." He smiled and handed her a voucher.

She read the slip of paper. "Where's Stage Fourteen?"

He waved at a pretty, pouty-mouthed driver who was vaguely recognizable, then turned back to Alicia. "First day, huhh? Those big buildings are called sound stages. Walk straight ahead past two of them, turn to your left and go two more. The third on your right is Stage Fourteen. And, sweetheard, break a leg—that means good luck."

She gave him a blazing smile of gratitude and went through the turnstile onto the lot. Hurrying past the huge buildings, she went up a half dozen cement steps. Pushing open a heavy metal door, she gasped.

She appeared to be in some high, endless subterranean cavern. In the distance to her left was one brilliant splash of light. As she went toward it she saw a canvas backdrop of a city skyline. In front were fake grass, fake bushes to hide the ugly wood crates in which real trees grew, and a small carousel. Around this gaudily lit pseudo park were maybe a hundred people, mostly casually clad men and a handful of women. A foursome of propmen carried park benches, two electricians walked along overhead scaffolding, but nobody else appeared to have a job. Alicia peered at men drinking coffee, men reading the trades, men laughing and chatting, trying to figure whom to report to. She spotted a gray-haired, motherly-looking woman knitting.

Approaching her, Alicia said politely, "Excuse me, but where do the extras go?"

"Shit! Now I've dropped a stitch." She glared up at Alicia. "*You're* an extra?"

"Yes."

"Then where's your makeup?"

Alicia, who had spent nearly an hour at dawn in front of the bathroom mirror putting on what she presumed would be enough makeup for any camera, realized that the face thrust belligerently forward was coated with orange pancake, while long false lashes quivered above the glinting little eyes.

"Think you're a star, huhh? Think you'll be given your own makeup woman? Well, let me tell you—the rest of us are ready to earn our money when we get here." The woman viciously dug her long steel needle into red yarn.

Alicia backed away. She spotted a little girl sitting on a stool. Entirely covered by a voluminous pink cape, the child held her face tilted upward, eyes closed, as a red-headed makeup woman patted an enormous powder brush on the small nose.

As the child trotted away, Alicia went over. Swallowing hard, she asked, "Uhh, could I please borrow some of your stuff?"

"New, ehh?" said the makeup woman amiably. "C'mon, sit down, I'll give you a lesson."

A few minutes later, as Alicia's mouth was being painted, a masculine voice shouted, "Okay, you guys, get over here!"

"That's the assistant director calling for a runthrough of you extras," said the kindly makeup woman.

As Alicia got to her feet, she sucked in her breath.

Standing by a complicated-looking boom mounted with a camera was Hap. In his clean white shirt with the sleeves rolled up he looked improbably strong and handsome.

"Hap," she called softly.

He turned. "Alicia! What are *you* doing here?"

"I'm an extra. You're a surprise yourself."

"Meet the second assistant cameraman," he said.

Now she remembered Barry telling her that both Maxim and Hap worked at Magnum, while PD had a job in the contracts department at Paramount—the point of his story had been that he and Beth were the only two of the cousins with more than a year of college. She also recollected that in Newport Maxim had made a remark about Hap's goal of becoming a director.

"Hap," called the man behind the camera. "We need more film."

"Right away," Hap called. He said to Alicia, "You better get on the set, but what about lunch?"

"Wonderful," she said and ran.

Twenty or so extras were gathered around the assistant director, a thin, nervous man wearing a gray suit. She was assigned to move along the park path left to right. Her knees locked and she fell. They went through it again. This time the assistant director advised her to slow it down, she wasn't running the hundred-meter dash.

Then Hap was in front of the camera, closing a clapper chalked with words that he called aloud. "Scene twenty-six. Take one."

The camera bugged her hideously. Her ankles wobbled

above her good patent shoes. This time when she stumbled, the entire crew was in on it.

"My first day on the job," she said with a nervous snicker, "and I'm about to be blacklisted from the entire motion picture industry."

"Why?" Hap asked. "I looked through the lens at you and you photograph sensationally—of course, the secret of making it as an extra is to stay away from the cameras. If you show up in the rushes—that's the day's exposed film, which get looked at every night—you won't be called for other scenes."

She filed away the information. "There's so much to learn," she sighed. "But you saw me fall all over myself."

Thoughtfully Hap pulled the saran wrapping off the two chef's salads he had just set down. Alicia had been expecting a glamorous studio dining room, but they were in a cafeteria with linoleum floors and undecorated walls. The chipped Formica tables were jammed. Some people were made up like her, and a few had on Western costumes, but there were also painters in smudged coveralls, elderly women who looked like they were secretaries but were script girls, and grips and electricians.

Hap asked, "What do you think about when we're shooting?"

"Getting to the other side of the set—what else?"

"Maybe this is a girl enjoying the sunshine and thinking about her boyfriend?"

"Mmm," she said, nodding. "You'll be a really good director."

He smiled. "Now tell me how you got the job."

"Your father."

Hap tore off the end of his French roll, buttering it. "But when he left Newport, I smelled the brimstone."

"He stopped burning."

Hap smiled again.

That afternoon, when she passed in front of the camera, she sauntered slowly, imagining herself a girl dreaming of her lover.

It was not quite four thirty when the director called out, "Print it!"

It was too late to start another setup, so cast and crew were dismissed.

The hot kliegs around and above the set were doused, people gathered up their possessions, farewells and footsteps echoed in the murkiness. Alicia, having an hour to kill before Barry picked her up, sat on a folding chair in the shadows.

"Ever see that black-haired extra before?" a nearby masculine voice inquired.

"The one who tripped? Nope. And I'd sure as hell remember. She oozes it, doesn't she?"

"That she does. The sweetest little ass—and those big jugs. How'd you like to—"

Her face was hot as the voices faded, yet she couldn't help smiling.

"Alicia?"

She jumped, then said, "Hi, Hap."

"What're you doing here?"

"Barry's not coming for me until five thirty."

"I'll drop you off. Just give him a buzz."

"Uhh, we don't have a phone."

"Then come on, we'll have coffee."

"Hap, the makeup woman, Madge, she told me there's a place up on Sunset where they sell professional makeup—"

"Gower Cosmetics," he said. "Be glad to drive you over there."

They were back at the gate before Barry drove up. As Hap opened the car door for her, he said, "Hey, Barry, since Alicia and I'll be on the same film for five or six days, I might as well give her a ride home and save you the trip. Your place is right on my way."

"Good deal," Barry said. Having turned in the three pieces on *The Child Buyer*, to the *Daily Bruin*, he had started what he called a novella that might stretch into a novel, filching time from sleep and his studies to write.

As the De Soto inched along in the rush-hour traffic, Alicia sat back wearily. All day she had been mentally etching details to describe to Barry—the other extras, the kind makeup woman, the director—however, now she found herself staring at the oncoming headlights in silence and thinking of Hap.

9

Alicia worked on *Paris Lovers* six more days. Driving home each evening, she deluged Hap with questions about the movie business. She seldom asked questions, having learned in numerous schools that to admit lapses in her education was tantamount to an admission of inferiority, but the adept way Hap handled his small MG, the darkness, their proximity, made it easy to confess ignorance. He told her about the unions, the pay scale, the equipment, what it was like to go on location, the front office. He would park at the shabby apartment court, walking her past the orange-scented pittosporum bushes, coming in to chat with his cousin.

When the *Paris Lovers* shooting schedule finished with extras, Alicia felt a letdown, almost a depression. She called Central Casting every morning, each day getting a negative response. But she had received her paycheck: even after the deductions there was enough left for the Barry Cordiners to put in a telephone and go to the movies to see *Sons and Lovers* and dine on spaghetti Bolognese, the cheapest item on the menu at swanky Perino's.

At the beginning of December she worked on Magnum's big-budget espionage story, *Killing*. The spy, played by John Gielgud, wandered in and out of nightclubs where extras danced. Alicia had never danced in her life, but she had watched Gene Kelly and Cyd Charisse, she had seen Chubby Checker do his twist. She threw herself around to the beat, or easily followed her partner.

Her assurance was an act. She was still frightened down to the pointed toes of her high-heeled shoes, but she had assigned herself the role of Movie Person, slipping into the part as she entered the Magnum lot. Movie Person was somewhat along the lines of, say, Marilyn Monroe, walking with a bit of a strut, smiling with her head tilted back, wetting her lips to keep them shiny, a desirable, slightly brash young actress in whose vocabulary the words *doubt* and *insecurity* had never existed.

Though Hap wasn't on *Killing* he drove her home. The third night, he parked and sat gripping the steering wheel.

"I have to work late for a while," he said. His voice was flattened, and she knew he was lying.

She felt a peculiar tightness, and couldn't catch her breath.

"I'm sorry," he added.

"Hey, it's okay," the actress in her responded brightly. "And Hap, thanks for the terrific taxi service."

Every year the Cordiner family celebrated Christmas en masse at the Desmond Cordiners' massive, Tudor-style house above Sunset Boulevard in Beverly Hills. Leo's Florist swagged holly on every wall and decorated the twenty-foot spruce in the hall with twinkling lights and Rosalynd Cordiner's collection of antique ornaments. Glitteringly wrapped gifts extended for yards around the tree. Caterers prepared three obscenely large turkeys with every conceivable trimming for the mob of relatives, in-laws, in-laws of in-laws.

As December advanced, Barry felt increasingly cut off from his family. With pangs of homesickness he thought of his parents, Beth, his uncles and aunts, Our Own Gang and the younger cousins all gathered together, the men talking shop, the women displaying their new jewelry, the children energetically bouncing around with new toys. Until now he had been able to consider his exile if not with pleasure, at least with equanimity based on pride: like the Duke of Windsor, he had given up everything for the woman he loved. Holiday time, though, memory attacks. He sunk himself into his novella and—though he didn't intend to—behaved with sullen remoteness toward Alicia.

On December twentieth he received a letter typed on Magnum stationery. *Dear Barry, Aunt Rosalynd and I are expecting you for Christmas.* It was signed, *Uncle Desmond.*

Barry made a ceremony of tearing the thick paper into the wastebasket.

"Why not go?" Alicia asked.

"It doesn't bother you, being excluded?"

"Maybe he meant me, too," she said, her voice trailing away as she remembered: *You are not permitted to use the name Cordiner.* "Anyway, why can't you show up for an hour or so? It's Christmas."

"Jesus, what a masochist! Do you enjoy insults and slaps in the face? Can't you understand? I'm doing this for you!"

She had her period, and this brought her emotions considerably closer to the surface. Her eyes grew wet and she wanted to bawl. Instead, she decorated the apartment. Barry had given her driving lessons in the De Soto, and she went to Van Vliet's for a poinsettia plant. She taped the few cards she had received from new friends at the studio around the arch to the kitchenette. She had no way of knowing how pitifully her attempts compared with the decor at the Desmond Cordiner home.

On Christmas morning Barry and Alicia exchanged presents. She had bought him a navy and white checked sport jacket, a good one that she would be paying off until July. He gave her an envelope with a ten-dollar bill. Since the oven didn't work, she couldn't even roast a turkey drumstick. She fixed *arroz con pollo,* angry at the traces of self-pity she discerned within herself. After all, had Alice Hollister celebrated sumptuous Christmases?

They finished the chicken around one. Barry pushed his plate away. "Hon, I need to get out for a bit, okay?"

"Now? Before dessert?"

"I hate myself for being such a killjoy. But Christmas is bad for me. The Jewish side always squares off against the *goy.* It's a bloody fight." His laughter was forced. "I'll be back before it gets dark." Grabbing his old windbreaker—not his new jacket—he darted out.

He's going to the party, Alicia decided. She turned on the small-screen television that came with the apartment. Unable to concentrate on the laughter that brayed from every station, she turned off the set, changing to old clothes. She did the dishes, then embarked on a cleaning spree.

She was using a toothbrush with scouring powder in the shower when she heard the screen door open. Positive her husband had returned earlier than intended, she called out joyously, "Hi, I'm in here!"

"Where?" Hap's voice called back.

She jumped to her feet, glimpsing her reflection in the door mirror. She'd yanked her hair back with a rubber band and her hand-me-down pink blouse had an old stain down the front.

Hap stood in the middle of the room, his arms clasped around two large, beribboned boxes. The intensity of his stare made her yet more embarrassed by her disheveled appearance. "Ho, ho, ho, and a merry Christmas to you." She managed a lively, actressy smile.

"I brought by your presents," he said. "Where's Barry?"

"Isn't he at your folks'?"

"No." He cocked his head at her. "Alicia, you look—"

"A slob," she supplied.

"No. Without makeup you're even more beautiful, and the hairdo shows it off." Reddening, he extended a metallic green and crimson box with a gold Saks label. "For you."

She sat on the couch, her fingers stiff as she fumbled to untie the green satin ribbon. As she lifted the lid, for the first time she inhaled the luxurious perfume of expensive new clothing. She drew out a royal blue cardigan, touching the soft wool with reverent fingertips—the ultra rich wore sweaters like this. Without thinking, she folded the garment back in its creases.

"Hey, what's wrong? Aren't girls wearing cashmeres anymore? Alicia, I thought it matched your eyes, but it's fine with me if you return it for something you like better."

He had not only spent a fortune, he had gone to considerable effort. "I'm crazy about it." She undid the gold buttons, slipping her bare arms into feather-soft sleeves.

"Fits you perfectly," he said.

"We didn't get anything for you."

"Big deal. How was your Christmas?"

"Great. Really nice."

"You're lucky you weren't at our place. Dad was in a foul mood. Uncle Tim arrived at the house already stoked to the gills and then proceeded to have a half dozen more.

Aunt Clara barely spoke. Uncle Frank lost a small fortune at the poker table and Aunt Lily got uptight. One of the little kids threw up."

"Actually it wasn't much fun here, either," Alicia admitted. "I'm pretty sure Barry wanted to go to your place, but your father sent a letter that sounded like he wasn't inviting me?" Her voice rose in a query.

Hap busied himself folding tissue paper back into the box.

"What do you think?" she pressed.

"About Dad inviting you?" He sighed, then said, "Alicia, Dad's extremely complex, and I never can get a bead on him. But he *is* big on family, and if Uncle Tim and Aunt Clara didn't want you—"

"I understand," she said bleakly.

Hap sat on the couch next to her. She could smell his after-shave and a faint hint of clean soap. "Today must've been tougher on you than on any of us," he said. "You're absolutely cut off from your family and everything you know. The *piñatas,* the enormous stars—a friend of mine once described Christmas in El Paso."

Alicia lowered her eyes. "I've never been there," she whispered.

"Where?"

"Texas."

His head tilted and his gray eyes questioned her.

"I've never been out of California," she mumbled. "I lied about my name, my family, everything."

"But why?"

"You don't know, you just don't know." As she spoke, it became imperative that he did know. If he despised her thereafter, so be it.

Hugging the sweater around her, she went to the window and in a low voice began unraveling the story of Alice Hollister. She told of her unknown fathering, of the tramp in the celery field, May Sue's sudden red death gush on the old plank table. She described Juanita's nurturing and her dark, beautiful, but weak eyes. She told of the endless hot work in the fields where no toilets were provided so that little girls wet their pants and women workers felt as if their bladders would surely burst. She told about her sporadic schooling and often sleeping with only cardboard protecting her from the bare earth. She mentioned the dingy movie houses that had filled her with dreams. She described Henry's aggressive forays and why she had come to Los Angeles, and how Juanita had been lost to her. She even told him her true age. Incapable of looking at him as she talked, she faced the overgrown court, watching dusk fall.

When she was finally silent Hap said nothing—he hadn't spoken during her entire narrative. In another apartment somebody kept playing "Adeste Fideles" over and over. *O come, all ye faithful, joyful and triumphant* . . . Finally she turned to look at Hap. It was too dark to make out his expression.

"I'm ashamed," she sighed. "So ashamed."

"Why?"

"Why? You heard. We lived like animals."

"It's everybody else in this country who ought to be ashamed." He blew his nose. "What does Barry say?"

"I've done a terrible thing . . . I . . . He thinks I'm Alicia Lopez from El Paso."

The confession that she had told him what she feared telling her husband hung between them in the dimness.

O come ye, O come ye to Be-eth-le-hem.

Hap came over to the window. His eyes glittered with moisture and she realized he'd been crying.

"The reason I stopped driving you home," he said in a low voice, "is I was getting in too deep. Way too deep."

The recorded carolers exalted during the long minute that Hap and Alicia gazed at each other. Then the blinking Christmas lights strung in the pittosporum came on. Hap shook his head as if arousing himself.

Neither of them spoke as he opened the door and went out.

10

The luminous green hands of their alarm clock showed twelve forty-three when Alicia heard uneven footsteps and the fumbling of the key. As the door opened then closed, the heavy smell of beer reached her, an odor disturbingly reminiscent of Henry Lopez. In the darkness a chair toppled.

She switched on the lamp.

In the sudden light, Barry blinked. "Sorry, hon," he muttered. "'Pologize for deserting you on Christmas." He stood with his hands dangling at his sides, his head bent penitently like an overgrown, guilty first grader.

"It's okay, Barry. Uhh, Hap dropped by with our presents."

"Just as rotten as Dad."

"It's not the crime of the century to have a few."

"Rotten, rotten. . . ." He fell on the bed, clutching her. "Need you so much, hon." He fell asleep, still wearing his windbreaker and loafers, his beery breath gusting about her.

She stroked his crinkly, reddish hair. Why should he feel guilty? *She* was the one who'd been indulging in adulterous reveries. She slipped off his loafers and spent the remainder of the night planning kind ways to explain to Hap that his original impulses to avoid her had been wise.

As January moved forward Alicia worked steadily in Magnum's television department. Hap did not call Barry—or her. Once she saw him walking on the studio street, his breeze-tossed fair hair visible above the other heads. A few days later she spotted him driving out the gate with LouLou Rodier, the gorgeous French dancer. Both times she waved. He didn't wave back although she was positive he'd seen her. With a profound sense of desolation she decided that he had needed no further warnings to stay away from her: Alice Hollister's life story had repelled him.

Days of Repose went on location in Guatemala without a word of goodbye to the Barry Cordiners from the second assistant cameraman.

"Okay that I've asked Beth, Maxim and PD over for dinner Sunday?" Barry's freckles were glossed with a light sweat, his eyes were shining. "I've promised you'd make your burritos."

His excitement was a welcome change from the previous week, when he had been sunk in a misery that he refused to share. Alicia hugged him and said, "Sure."

Beth arrived first, handing Alicia her hostess gift, a pound box of See's chocolates. She was followed almost immediately by Maxim and PD, who drove together. Alicia, acutely conscious of the absent cousin, returned to the stove. Barry, who had chilled a bottle of California champagne in the refrigerator, opened it with a loud pop. Pouring the bubbly liquid into their mismatched glasses, he raised his own small tumbler.

"This is a celebration," he announced. "You're looking at a man who's just sold a story to *Southwest Review.*"

The stove top sizzled as a few drops of Alicia's wine spilled. The others were all shouting at once. Beth cried, "I'm so proud, Barry!" "Hey-hey-hey Barry-boy!" Maxim laughed. And PD asked, "How much did you get?"

"The pay's in copies, not cash," Barry replied rapidly.

"Who said writing's like prostitution?" Maxim asked. "At first you do it because you love it, then you do it for a few friends—that's *Southwest Review*—and in the end you do it for money."

Laughter.

Alicia stirred the mixture of lamb, refried beans, chilis and tomato. A sentiment that resembled betrayal curled painfully in her throat. *Why didn't he tell me first?*

They were at the table when the phone rang. At the loud, seldom-heard jangle, Barry and Alicia exchanged questioning glances over half-eaten burritos.

It was Alicia who went to the phone. "Hello?"

"Is this the Cordiner place?" inquired a vaguely familiar masculine voice.

"Yes."

"Give me Barry, will you?"

She looked at Barry. "For you," she said.

He got up. "Dad?" he whispered. He listened silently, blinking, his face going white. "Where is she?" Pause. "We'll be there right away."

Hanging up, he stared at Beth. "It's Mom," he said. "She's at Cedars. It's her heart."

Beth, her lips trembling, was already opening her purse for her keys.

"No," PD said, gripping her arm. "Let's not risk an accident here. I'll drive."

"We're in my car, cousin," Maxim pointed out.

They were at the doorway. Alicia ran to turn off the stove, reaching for her blue cashmere.

"Hon," Barry said. "It'll be best if you stayed home."

Beth added in a politely placating tone, "They won't let anyone see her except the immediate family anyway."

The door closed on the four of them.

Odors of champagne and Mexican food surrounding her, Alicia didn't move for a full minute. Abruptly she yanked off the soft wool sweater and began clearing the table.

Maxim and PD dropped the twins off at the bottom of the long flight of steps that fronted Cedars of Lebanon Hospital. It was after visiting hours. Alone in the elevator, Barry gripped Beth's hand and was still holding it when they emerged.

Footsteps sounded heavily in the empty corridor. Their father came toward them, a tall, thickset man whose burly shoulders were slumped beneath a shabby car coat.

Barry couldn't speak.

It was Beth who whispered, "How's Mom?"

He peered at them with bloodshot, frightened eyes; the once handsome, fleshy face seemed collapsed. "Not too good, but she's resting."

Beth, who had been fearing to find her mother dead, murmured. "Thank you, God. *Sh'ma Ysroel. . . .*" Unlike Barry, Beth knew the prayers and could read and speak Hebrew—not only to please her mother but also because her mixed heritage disturbed her and she needed the structure of the sternly traditional religion.

Tim reached out hesitantly to Barry and they hugged with masculine awkwardness.

"It's good to see you, Dad," Barry said, choking back his desire to weep.

"Uncle Desmond's arranged for Doctor Prinzmetal to come to see her tonight." Myron Prinzmetal attended to the overstressed hearts of the Industry's upper echelon. "And I got her a private room and private nurses around the clock." Tim voiced these extravagances with pathetic pride.

"Can we see her?" Barry asked.

They had been walking up the corridor. Tim tapped on room number 513.

A capped gray head popped out. "No visiting right now, Mr. Cordiner. Our girl needs her rest."

"My son and daughter wanted to look in on her."

"Oh, you must be Barry," the nurse said. "She's been asking for you."

Barry slipped into the dimly lit room. Clara Cordiner's thin face looked as white as if the skull beneath were showing.

"Mom?"

Her eyes opened slowly. "Barry. . . ?"

"Hi."

"My heart. . . ."

"Don't try to talk, Mom," he said, smoothing her hair. "Doctor Prinzmetal's on the way. He'll patch you up."

"Missed you. . . ."

"And I've missed you, Mommy." How long since he had called her that?

"Your school. . . ?" she whispered.

"Practically have a Phi Bete key in my pocket." The still hospital air seemed to vibrate with his lie. He hadn't even told Alicia the bad news when his self-addressed postcards had arrived with ten units of Ds and four of Incompletes. "Mom, I sold a story. A famous literary magazine's going to print my work."

Clara's white lips curved in a weak semblance of a smile, then her eyes closed.

The nurse tapped Barry's sleeve. As he left the room, thick tears spurted. Embarrassed, he ran up the corridor to the men's room, where he gasped out his filial remorse. When he emerged, he saw his Uncle Frank standing with his arm around his brother-in-law. Frank Zaffarano was five four, and Tim Cordiner nearly a foot taller, but the director, virile in his alpaca sport jacket, appeared the dominant figure.

Seeing Barry, Frank raised his clenched fist. "You're lucky we're in a hospital, Barry. If we weren't, I'd give you a good beating." In his thirty years in California, Frank had lost much of the Sicilian accent of his youth, but the final syllables of his words became more lyrically inflected when he was in the midst of emotion-drenched family brouhahas like this. "What sort of son are you, staying away from your mother?"

"Uncle Frank," Beth murmured, "Barry came the minute Dad called."

Frank shook his head, from which thick gray hair grew in profusion, as if bewildered by the ways of irresponsible sons. "And where has he been all these months?"

"Barry, how's Mom?" Beth asked.

"She spoke to me," Barry said, trying to sound confident.

Frank tapped his stocky chest. "Seeing her son is the best cure for a mother's heart."

Myron Prinzmetal pronounced his patient's condition to be serious. Tim Cordiner and his two children sat up all night in uncomfortable hospital waiting room chairs. When the doctor arrived at seven he reported that Clara's condition had stabilized. The twins and their father returned to the tract house in Westchester.

The breakfast was like thousands of others, except that Beth, not Clara, scrambled the eggs. Barry and Tim ate, then lingered over black coffee at the kitchen table, splitting the *Times,* Tim reading the sports section while Barry turned to Robert Kirsch's book review. Despite his guilty anxieties about his mother, Barry felt more at peace than at any time since he'd left this house with Alicia.

11

"Do you think it's a good idea for me to buy a used car?" Alicia repeated.

"What did you say, hon?" Barry's pen stopped racing, but he continued to scan his yellow notepad.

"I've been thinking," she said. "We have enough for a down payment on a car. You won't need to drive me to work."

"If a car's what you want, fine with me."

"Can you go with me to look this weekend?"

Barry had begun to write again.

This was one of their rare evenings together: he had gone to the afternoon visiting hours at the hospital.

During the five weeks that Clara Cordiner had been at Cedars of Lebanon, Barry had spent at least two hours every day with her. On the night of her heart attack, horrified by her absolute weakness, he was convinced that if he'd been around she never would have been stricken. And he was positive that she would recover only if he dedicated himself to becoming a far better son than he'd ever been.

Clara no longer needed private nurses; she was wearing her gift bedjackets and reading her gift books, yet that slave-driving guilt brought Barry back each day. He never suggested that Alicia accompany him—after all, hadn't their marriage quite literally broken his mother's heart? Usually he had a bite afterward with Beth and their father and whoever in the family happened to be around.

"Barry?" Alicia said.

Frowning, he looked up. "What?"

"Is Saturday or Sunday better for you?"

"This'll be your car. Pick whatever you want."

"I don't know the first thing about motors and stuff like that, or financing."

"I can't spare the time," Barry said, then softened. "But PD has a good grasp of financing. Let me see if he'll go with you."

Saturday afternoon Barry went to see his mother. Alone in the apartment, Alicia peered critically in the bathroom mirror. Barry's pointed exclusion of her at the hospital had increased her insecurity about being with his family. Would PD think her new white slacks too tight? And what about the sweater? It had come from Saks, Hap had made the selection, so it had style . . . yet wasn't the royal blue garish on her, and the fit too snug over her breasts?

A firm tap sounded on the door.

"Coming, PD," she called.

But it was Hap who stood outside.

The blood drained from her head, and she experienced

the same weakness in her legs as when she had passed out picking strawberries in Oxnard.

The Central American sun had deepened Hap's tan, and streaks of his hair were bleached to tow. Dressed in a white Oxford shirt and khaki slacks, he looked top drawer—and far too handsome. And he'd been avoiding her.

Self-consciously wetting her lips, she bestowed a dazzling stage smile. "Welcome home from Guatemala," she said. "When did you get back?"

"Two weeks ago."

"I was expecting PD."

"He asked me to fill in. That okay with you?"

She made another smile.

"Otherwise PD can probably do it tomorrow," Hap said, adding, "He's a much better bargainer than I am."

"You took me by surprise, that's all," she said, reaching for her purse.

Traversing the rows of freshly waxed cars at Baumgarten's Used Chevrolets, she decided that Hap's easy friendliness and calm advice was proof positive that he, as opposed to her, had recovered from being in too deep.

She liked a two-tone '56, but the down payment was out of her range.

They drove two blocks east to Alton's Foreign Cars.

A roly-poly salesman in a navy suit and navy shirt bounced over to them. "Well, sir, and what can I do for you and your gorgeous little wife?"

"This is my cousin. She's buying the car," Hap said, explaining Alicia's needs and price limit. They were led to a maroon Volkswagen bug with fifty-three thousand miles on the odometer. They drove around the block and Hap decided the engine seemed in good shape. In a small, airless office, he cosigned the sheaf of forms. The rotund salesman told Alicia that when her loan application was approved, the VW would be hers, "—and the bank's, hahaha."

"How long will it take?" Hap asked.

"You know how banks are. Slo-o-ow." The salesman laughed again. "The little lady won't have her VW until Wednesday at the earliest."

As they left the lot, Alicia said, "I really appreciate you cosigning, Hap."

"You're not going to run away, are you?" he asked. "Besides, Dad's got you on the preferential treatment list, so you're good for the payments."

"Anyway, thank you."

And then he smiled.

He hadn't smiled since he'd picked her up. Hap didn't go in for forced joviality like PD, or polite laughs like Beth, or a nervous baring of teeth like Barry; he was never wittily caustic like his brother Maxim, but on the other hand, he never went for hours like this without cracking a grin.

His smile had a reassuring warmth. "You're wearing the sweater," he said.

"I do all the time. I love it."

He opened the door of his MG for her. A Buick was waiting for the parking space, but he didn't start the motor.

"When PD asked me to fill in," he said slowly, "I almost refused."

"Why didn't you—" She coughed to clear the rustiness in her throat. "Why didn't you turn him down?"

"I wanted to see you."

"But it's been months. I thought. . . ."

"What?"

"It's nothing."

"No, tell me."

In the hazy March sunlight she stared at him, knowing the attraction of the magnet for the pin, and heard herself come out with the unadorned truth. "I figured you'd been avoiding me."

"I was."

"Ohhh. . . ."

"I explained, Alicia."

"Yes, but by then you'd heard my life story. A major turnoff for anyone."

"You sure don't understand me very well," Hap said. The driver of the waiting Buick honked rapidly. Hap ignored the blasts, taking her hand, twining his large fingers between hers. She began to tremble. He raised her hand, pressing their clasped knuckles against his cheek. "You don't understand me at all."

On Monday Alicia was in a street scene on the Magnum back lot. In the early afternoon Hap dropped by to suggest he drive her home. Her face was hot when she phoned the apartment. "Great!" Barry said enthusiastically. "This way I can head right on over to Cedars."

But Hap did not take her home. He drove along Hollywood Boulevard turning left on a side street, pulling up at Don the Beachcomber's. The restaurant, decorated as a Polynesian jungle with rocky nooks and a warehouseful of plants, was extremely dark, and the candlelit hurricane lamp on their table cast a glow on Hap's face, intensifying his tan. She requested a Coke. Hap ordered a rum drink that came in a coconut shell.

"Want a sip?" he asked.

She sucked at the red cellophane straw. "Mmm, delicious."

"That's why I chose it—I figured you'd like it." He paused. "Alicia, isn't it lonely for you with Barry gone so much?"

"He's swamped," she said, defending her husband. "There's his studying, his work in the Student Union and his writing—I guess you heard he sold a short story to a big literary magazine? And to top it off there's his mother's illness."

"I wasn't knocking him, Alicia. Yeah, I suppose I was. So he never takes you to the hospital?"

"I'd hardly help Mrs. Cordiner's recovery."

"Did he tell you that?"

"Sort of," Alicia sighed. "He says it'd upset her and that might be dangerous."

"You wouldn't have to be in her room. Everybody else drops by and afterwards has dinner with him and Beth and Uncle Tim."

The Cordiner gatherings were news to her. She said nothing.

"Why let Barry shut you out?" The knobs of Hap's jaw showed.

He's mad at me, she thought, and immediately understood that his anger was directed not at her—or even at

Barry and his parents—but at the injustice of the situation.

"He's not really shutting me out," she said, and changed the subject. "I've been getting a lot of work. Hap, when I went to those cruddy theaters, I used to tell myself one day I'd be up there on the screen, but in my heart I knew it was a ridiculous daydream. And now look at me—I feel like Alice through the looking glass. The dream's come true."

"Dreams are not enough," Hap said, refusing to be diverted. "If Barry took you there every night, Uncle Tim and the others would accept it. You'd become part of the family."

"Mexican maid mingles with Hollywood high society?"

Hap's jawbones showed again. "Uncle Tim's a grip."

"And what about Mr. Zaffarano? And you know who your father is."

"Uncle Frank freely admits to arriving in California with less than five dollars. And I explained about Dad."

"Hap," she said, "let it go."

"Don't you see? Barry's always had a massive inferiority complex. Because *he's* insecure, he's making it impossible for you to ever fit in with the family."

Although she had known since the post-elopement scene at Barry's parents' house that she never would be accepted by the Cordiners, hearing Hap say it demolished her. She bent over her Coke.

After a moment or two he said gently, "I'm sorry, Alicia. I didn't mean to make you feel worse. But by now you must have figured that what hurts you hurts me too."

She looked up. The flame of the hurricane lamp flickered in his gray eyes. He was gazing at her with such transparent supplication that words were unnecessary. He reached out to cover her wrist. Once again his touch made her tremble. He didn't move his hand and as they stared at one another inexplicable tears formed in her eyes.

"There's motels on Cahuenga." His voice was stretched out of shape.

"Yes," she whispered. "Yes. . . ."

12

On Thursday, March 16, the same day that Alicia picked up her VW from the dealer, a Schaefer ambulance took Clara Cordiner home. On the small crabgrass front lawn Tim and the twins were waiting to greet her.

Clara smiled weakly up from the gantry. "This is what makes it all worthwhile," she murmured. "Having my family around me."

Five nights a week Barry drove the traffic-clogged miles to the Westchester tract house. He, Tim and Beth—when she was not on a date or at an AEPhi chapter meeting—shared the salt-free, fat-free, taste-free dinners prepared by the elderly, officious practical nurse, eating at awkward metal TV tables in the sickroom. He seldom returned to the apartment before eleven. Routinely he found the lights on, the Late Show movie rattling away, and Alicia asleep tightly curled into a fetal position. He had no reason, therefore, to speculate on how she passed the numerous evenings that he was absent.

"Hap. . . ."

"What?"

"Hap . . . that's not your real name."

"Harvard," he supplied.

"Harvard? Like the college?"

"It's mother's maiden name. When I was a baby they nicknamed me Hap and it stuck."

"A good thing. You're not a Harvard, it's way too pompous." She kissed the fair, crisp hairs of his chest.

They had already made love once, and a provocative, musky odor surrounded the thrown-back sheets. He had been caressing her slippery epithelial flesh, she had been running her fingers on his hard, deliciously silken penis. The Cahuenga Inn, their regular meeting place since their precipitous departure from Don the Beachcomber's a little over six weeks earlier, did a brisk hourly business. They would arrive discreetly in their own cars, Alicia waiting a full two minutes to follow Hap to whichever door she had seen him unlock.

She had stored up nuggets of information about him. Some were intimidating: his mother came from a wealthy and philanthropically inclined old family, he knew celebrities by their first names—he called Lauren Bacall Betty and Rain Fairburn Marylin, Henry Fonda Hank and Edward G. Robinson Uncle Eddie. On the other hand, it delighted her to discover that, unlike his brother Maxim who bed-hopped in the best Hollywood tradition, Hap had slept with only three other women. (His reticence was partially due to a nice, sensitive shyness and partially because he felt that entering a sexual entanglement meant you were serious.)

"You're a man of mystery," she said. "All I know about you is that you're upright—"

"Very," he chuckled, clasping her hand tighter around his penis.

"—and strong and good."

"The exact opposite of the correct adjectives to describe a guy in bed with his cousin's wife." The amusement was gone.

"Don't let it bug you so much, Hap."

"How not?"

"*I'm* his wife, *I'm* the one who's cheating."

"And what about me? Not only his cousin but his so-called friend."

"It's different for the woman."

"That's the double standard, love, and I don't believe in it."

"The rest of the world does."

"You can't argue me out of feeling like a shit." He drew a sigh whose depth she felt and heard beneath her ear.

She raised her head, peering at him. "Sorry we started?"

"Jesus, no. How can you even think that's what I meant? I was trying to explain having a go at other people's wives isn't my usual style."

"That's not how it sounded." Because of her sudden

fear that he might want to break off, she spoke too forcefully.

"*I* won't be the one to end it."

Her pupils were enormous as she said, "You're free."

His arms tightened around her. "No, love, I'm not free."

He strained her body closer. Caressing the curve of her back and buttocks, he kissed her eyes, then her mouth. She returned his kisses with equal fervor, stroking the muscles of his arms, his shoulders. Away from Hap, the memory of his tactile qualities—the strong body hairs, the large bones, the musculature that was well developed without being grotesquely delineated—could make her grow wet and ready. And when she was with Barry, though she despised herself for it, she couldn't help making comparisons—her husband was smaller and narrower *everywhere.*

She and Hap were both shaking violently as he entered her, and her gasp filled his open mouth. Their caresses grew more languorous and then ceased entirely as he moved within her or she undulated around him. She thought only of the exquisite sensations of the moment. All at once she gave an involuntary, wavery cry. Every cell in her body was suspended, absolutely still, poised waiting. She was no longer conscious of the room, nor of Hap, nor her own body, just of the anticipatory stillness. Then the frenzied spasms began, and she thrashed without control, clinging to Hap's waist as she gasped out, "Darling, ahh . . . ahhh . . . ahhhhhh Hap . . . darling. . . ."

It hadn't happened the first time. Hap had been too quick, she too nervous; but since then she always reached climax—climaxes. The first took a long time: after the initial powerfully relentless waves of pleasure that turned her body inside out, every part of her skin wet, tingling, alive, she would drift, then feel herself rising higher and higher, hovering until she fell in gentler yet equally blissful release, drifting again and again in that orgasmic sea. She considered her perennially fresh joys a physical manifestation of the tender yet violent emotions that bound her to Hap.

As she dressed, she thought, *The worst thing we do to Barry is my going back to him afterward.*

* * *

"Barry," she said, pausing. "Have you ever thought about, uhh, moving in with your folks?"

Slumped over his typewriter, he heard her voice but the question didn't register. Looking up, he grunted, "Huhh?"

"Wouldn't it be easier if you slept at your parents'?"

"That's a wondrous strange question. This is where I live, remember?"

"You're not here all that much and—"

"Are you giving me an ultimatum?" he interrupted, his freckles showing darkly.

"It makes more sense, that's all."

"Am I receiving an ultimatum?" Barry raised his voice because she'd gone into the bathroom to undress. How long, he asked himself, had she been changing in there? It went back to when she'd bought two sets of baby-doll pajamas—before that she'd slept in the raw. A couple of months ago, give or take a week, he decided.

She returned, the short froth of white nylon ruffles not quite hiding the curves of her body. "Barry, look, this is the first night you've been home all week."

As Alicia bent to open up the bed she reminded Barry of a Degas bronze ballerina at the County Museum, pliant and feminine yet also magnificently, casually strong. Then the light bulb flickered and she seemed to dwindle and fade, moving farther from him. In this instant he recognized the full extent of his dependence on her earthy strength, her ability to cope, and yes, even her inferiority.

"You can't hold Mom's illness against me," he said hoarsely.

"I'm not accusing you, Barry." She tucked in the corners of the sheet. "I'm just saying we already both go our separate ways."

"Have you been seeing somebody at the studio?"

"This is about us—you and me," she said.

"Yes, absolutely!"

Concentrating on the other corner of the sheet, she said, "Can't we talk sensibly?"

"Why don't you talk sensibly with *him*?"

If Barry had not been so distracted by his fear and jealousy, he would have noted her increased pallor.

"Talk about what to who?" she parried.

"The guy you're going your separate way with!" Grabbing up his old windbreaker—he'd never worn that loud checked sport jacket that she'd given him at Christmas—he rushed out.

He drove to the nearest bar, a dim, narrow place with an outsize television screen tuned to a pro basketball game. At every Laker basket, the clientele roared approval and thumped on the counter. Barry, uninterested in sports, hunched in a booth, ordering Schlitz after Schlitz, attempting to drown the memory of Alicia's huge, concerned blue eyes as she suggested that he move out.

Two hours later, reeking of beer, he managed to steer the De Soto home. In the darkness he stumbled, sprawling on the rug. The light went on and Alicia bent over him. He pressed his cheek against her bare foot, beginning to sob. "Hon, don't leave me."

She stroked his heaving shoulders. "Barry, get up."

"Sorry I've been spending so much time with Mom."

"Here, let me help you."

He did not take her hands. Instead he pressed his lips to her polished, lotion-scented toes. Even drunk, he understood the ridiculousness of his abject pose, but he could not prevent himself from begging. "Promise you won't go?"

"Come to bed, Barry."

"We're married . . . on an eternal basis. . . ." His sobs were loud, hoarse, agonized.

Finally she sighed, "It's was just an idea, Barry, that's all."

In bed, he kissed her breasts, sucking noisily on her nipples, an overgrown, bristle-faced baby nursing as his limp penis pressed against her thigh.

The incident saddened her and reminded her of her vows, which she had certainly never taken lightly. Yet each time she entered a room at the Cahuenga Inn the idea of divorce filled her mind.

13

On a damp, smoggy afternoon in early May, groups of costumed extras waited on the folding chairs strewn at the south end of Magnum's Western street. Alicia, swathed from neck to ankles in calico, sat a bit apart, engrossed in *The Idiot.* A passionate reader, ignorant of which author was designated as a genius, she approached every novel on Barry's eclectic shelf—Melville, Agatha Christie, Thomas Wolfe, Balzac, Flaubert, O'Hara, Hersey, the Russians—with a near carnal abandon: teach me, compel me, carry me away. She was oblivious to the extras as well as the crew.

"Alicia Lopez?"

Blinking and startled, Alicia left nineteenth century, mystical Russia to look up at a young messenger who was extending an unstamped envelope. Inside she found a small memo sheet: *Report to Mr. Cordiner's office at six thirty.*

Shivering, she stared at the note until the assistant director bawled through his megaphone, "Extras! We're ready for you!"

At the end of shooting, she returned her costume, which would be cleaned for the following day, hastily creamed off her makeup, then jogged the quarter mile to Magnum's red brick and stucco Executive Building, an exalted place where she had never set foot. In the decades before television had put the stamp of decline on the industry, the Executive Building had been overcrowded. Now, the curving staircase to the unoccupied second and third floor was blocked by a long table.

Desmond Cordiner's outer office, however, retained its aura of prosperity. Behind the curves of two elegant old mahogany hunt tables sat a pair of equally decorative secretaries, neither of whom appeared cognizant that the workday had ended. The young, voluptuous blonde continued her rapid typing while the trim, fortyish brunette looked up, questioning Alicia with a demi-smile.

"Mr. Cordiner sent for me. I'm Alicia Lopez."

"Oh, yes," said the brunette, her smile fading. "Will you take a seat."

There was no clock in the office, Alicia didn't own a watch, so there was no way to properly gauge the passage of time. The blonde typed, the brunette put through a minimum of five calls to her boss, while beyond the undrawn maroon plush draperies the dark blue dusk turned black.

A peculiar thought occurred to Alicia: *I won't be kept waiting when I'm a somebody.*

Not *if,* but *when.*

Although she thought of herself as being a mere worm amid the lordly Cordiners, undeniably her association with them had elevated her ambition level. As a child she had fantasized about being any one of the beautifully dressed girls on the screen, but now she understood that the clothes of extras and bit players belonged to the costume department, while their stately homes were shells. What she yearned after was respect. If she were a star and respected, she would not be waiting in this outer office, perspiring lightly, a sharp knot of anxiety in her empty stomach.

Finally a buzzer sounded on the desk. "You can go in now," said the brunette secretary.

When Desmond Cordiner had taken over as head of Magnum, he had not altered Art Garrison's office. Garrison, a near dwarf, had placed his desk up four steps, forcing all visitors to walk the near fifty feet like supplicants to his altar. Here, Desmond Cordiner hunched over papers without acknowledging her entry. Alicia, gazing up at her husband's uncle—her employer—was struck by awe and fear. Throwing her head back, she traversed the distance in her Movie Person strut, worrying her quivery legs might give out.

As she reached the dais, Desmond Cordiner looked up. "Listen, you little cunt—" In this flat, conversational tone, the obscenity, one she loathed above all others, rang more venomously than if he had ranted. "—I've had it up to here with you."

"Now what have I done?" she said, inwardly astonished at the contrast between the strength of her voice and the weakness of her body.

"None of that big blue-eyed innocence. You know the fuck why you're here."

"Give me a clue."

"I will not have you screwing up Hap's life."

Her breath expelled loudly. A blinding light expanded painfully within her brain. Believing those clandestine meetings at Cahuenga Inn to be totally secret, she had never once considered Hap as the reason behind her summons. "How did you find out?" she asked in an oddly pitched tone.

He ignored the question. "Stay away from him or else he'll hear about the shithole you crawled out of."

"He knows," she said, digging her nails into her palms. "And it doesn't matter to him."

"The kid's always been too decent for his own good," Desmond Cordiner said in that same restrained tone. Then suddenly his rage broke its dam, inundating her. He slammed his fist on the massive desk, rattling papers. "I want you away, cunt!" he bellowed.

"You mean out of the country? Or the world?" Her mouth was dry, yet somehow she managed a note of defiant humor.

"You get out of Los Angeles! If you don't I'll phone the cops and tell 'em you're peddling ass *and* horse."

"Ass and horse. Cute."

Desmond Cordiner's eyes narrowed. Braced for further assaults, possibly physical, she tensed her muscles. But he took off his black-rimmed glasses, wearily rubbing the bridge of his scimitar nose. "It's been a bitch of a day," he said, descending the steps to mortal level. "Let's start over."

In an industry of wily, often dishonest negotiators, Desmond Cordiner was famed: a real pro, his peers and underlings called him admiringly. Fury, obscenity, blackmail, threats, offers of advancement or prestige, sympathetic gentleness, appeals to human decency—he could switch from one to another deftly and with unparalleled success. "Here, sit down," he said.

Her legs were about to give way, so she didn't argue but sank into the deep, comfortable leather chair.

He sat opposite, leaning toward her. "Alicia, a few months ago you refused to give up Barry. Now you think you're in love with Hap. You're very young. Isn't it possible that this is another infatuation?"

"It's totally different," she said. "And Hap's twenty-one."

"A veritable Methuselah," Desmond Cordiner said with a tired smile. "What about your marriage?"

She shrugged.

"I talked to Hap this morning, asked him what the hell was going on."

"What did he say?"

"That it was none of my damn business." He paused. "By now you've certainly realized that Hap's thoroughly decent—he must've inherited the virtues from his mother's side—*she* comes from good blood. So I cannot believe he enjoys sneaking into motel rooms with his cousin's wife."

Alicia tried to control her expression, but she had not yet learned acting technique: her bleakness showed.

Desmond Cordiner went on. "Granted Barry's been goofing off in the worst way."

"His mother—"

"I respect that loyalty of yours, Alicia. But Clara's been out of the woods for a while now. Barry should be home nights with you. What's with that boy? Leaving a wife who's not only gorgeous and sexy, but has brains and spunk. And not keeping up his grades—"

"Last semester he got all As."

"Ds and Incompletes. I checked." He shrugged sadly. "The dean says he's killed his chances at a good law school."

"But it's only one semester!"

"The grades are on record. Now listen to me, Alicia. We both know Barry's always fiddled with writing. I'm suggesting we give him a chance at it. Clara'll threaten another coronary, I grant you that. Damned if I know why she's so hot to have a lawyer for a son. Probably has something to do with her being Jewish. What a family! Catholics, Jews, Episcopalians, a Christian Scientist—even a crazy Rosicrucian."

And one itinerant farm worker. "You're positive he won't get into law school?"

"Maybe one of those shyster mills." Desmond Cordiner laced his fingers. "Alicia, I have a good friend in France, Philippe Saint-Simon. Perhaps you've heard of him."

Who hadn't? Saint-Simon wrote, directed and produced. He had put his stamp on French film as Fellini had done in Italy, as Bergman was doing in Sweden. Even the most vituperative critics mellowed when reviewing a Saint-Simon movie, often using the word *genius*.

"If you could become one of his troupe, you'd have a go at an important career."

Career. . . . The word had a rich patina, like fine old silver. Despite her innocent pride at being an extra, she knew it was merely a job. Career?

"You and Barry could learn your respective professions."

Profession, another evocative word.

"It's become a damn rat race here, but it's different in France."

France. In France she'd be separated from Hap by thousands of miles. Not to see him, feel him, taste him, smell him?

Desmond Cordiner was watching her. "Have you ever considered how much this is damaging Hap?"

"I'm not hurting him," she said through numbed lips.

"Not you, Alicia, the situation. Before this, he's never behaved in any way that wasn't absolutely aboveboard. I pride myself on being a judge of character. You're too good a woman to turn him into something less than he is."

"But what if—"

"If you leave Barry? Hap would feel even more rotten. It would gnaw his guts constantly."

"I'm not hurting him," she repeated.

"Think about it, at least." He got to his feet. "Saint-Simon is a good friend."

Drained and hopeless as though she'd been tried for murder by a hanging judge, she closed her eyes, thus missing Desmond Cordiner's satisfied little smile.

14

When Alicia left the Executive Building, she saw by the round clock above a sound stage door that it was nearly eight. Since Barry was to be with his parents, she had arranged to meet Hap at the Cahuenga Inn. He always waited in his car until she arrived. How else could she see him emerge from the office with the key? How else could she follow him to the right room? She accepted now that these were the clumsy maneuvers of a man unskilled at adultery—or any other form of chicanery.

As she trudged shivering toward the parking lot, the chill wind that gusted along the dark, empty studio street seemed a fit companion. Once Henry Lopez had beaten up on her with a plank of wood, and that was how her interview with Desmond Cordiner made her feel. Bruised, weak, dazed. She—low-life Alice Hollister—had corrupted Hap, a knight nonpareil. In her demoralized state, she rushed into an anguished decision.

I won't show up tonight.

I won't talk to Hap. I'll end it now. Quickly. Quickly. Quickly.

Halting, she leaned against a cement-block wall, overcome by sobs. She remained hunched and gasping, the cold wind tearing at her clothes, then a passing car's headlights bathed her in yellow light and she straightened, heading for her VW and home.

When she opened her front door, the phone was ringing. Positive it was Hap, she stood over the instrument with her hands tightly balled into fists until the insistent sounds ended. When, a few minutes later, the ringing began again she pressed her hands over her ears.

The following night Barry stayed home. His realization that he needed Alicia had combined with its frightening corollary: she might walk out on him. He was trying to cut down on the number of dinners he ate with his parents.

Alicia was doing the dishes when the phone rang. Barry answered.

The conversation lasted no more than thirty seconds, and he replaced the instrument with a baffled frown. "That was Hap," he said. "After lo these many moons, he calls. And for what? To ask when Mom's birthday is."

The next night, Saturday, it was raining, and Clara begged her son not to risk driving the slippery roads. So again it was Barry who answered Hap's call. And again they spoke briefly. "What's come over Hap?" Barry said mystified. "He's the reliable, steady type, never discombobulated. And you know what he wanted? To find out what to get for Mom's birthday—and I told him yesterday it's not until August. Sometimes I can't figure the guy out."

Sunday was brilliantly clear and Barry elected to spend the day with his parents. The phone rang on numerous occasions but Alicia did not answer. And neither did she on Monday, when Barry stayed late at the UCLA Research Library.

Tuesday she worked at Columbia on a ballroom sequence: having invested in a black sequined minidress and a fake mink coat, she was eligible to earn the higher wage scale available to dress extras.

She arrived home to find the familiar note propped against the lamp. *Am at the folks. Be back around 10.*

She felt light-headed, as if she might pass out. Since her summons to Desmond Cordiner's office five days earlier, she had drunk gallons of black coffee and bottle after bottle of Pepsi, but downed no more than a few forkfuls of solid food. Telling herself she must eat, she peeled a small russet potato, slicing it into cold salted water, lighting the stove. She hung up her formal, sliding out of the cheap nylons that bit uncomfortably at the thigh. In the bathroom she slathered Albalene cream on her face, neck and shoulders, tissuing off the greasy layer of brownish cosmetic. As she soaped herself, the front door buzzer sounded, but with the faucets on she didn't hear.

"Alicia?" Hap said.

She jerked up. She hadn't locked the door, and Hap

was standing in the middle of the room. Snatching the towel, she draped it around her waist—what idiocy to hide herself from Hap, who had kissed every part of her nakedness. "Be with you in a sec," she said, pushing the bathroom door shut.

She held on to the washbowl, feeling as if her raw flesh were contained only by the thinnest membrane of skin. She resolved to muster all of her strength. *It's breakup time,* she thought as she rinsed her face. *Do it quickly. Quickly. Quickly.*

She emerged from the bathroom with Barry's terrycloth robe pulled high around her throat and the sash knotted tightly.

"Why've you been hiding?" Hap asked. There were bluish smudges under his eyes.

"Hiding?"

"You know what I mean."

"We had a fling and it's over. That's all." Desmond Cordiner would be proud of her calmly unemotional tone.

"You call what went on between us a fling?"

"For me it was."

He took a step, grasping her shoulders. "Like hell. I was there, Alicia. You weren't faking it." He paused. "What's happened?"

"Nothing," she said numbly.

"Don't you think I'm entitled to the truth?"

"Let's just say I came to my senses. One person has to first."

"You damn well weren't over it the other night."

Probably because Hap was a large man and apparently self-assured, many people considered him impervious to mental anguish. Alicia knew him better. From his voice and expression she understood how profoundly she had hurt him—and was hurting him now.

"Hap," she sighed, "sooner or later we have to stop. Sooner's easier."

"Why is breaking up inevitable?"

"We both know the reason. I'm married."

"Barry doesn't remember it often."

She went to turn off the potatoes. With her back turned, she said, "Once I suggested to him that we split. He rushed out and got loaded, then came home and cried." She winced, trying to black out the memory of Barry groveling on the rug, of the slobbery, teary kisses that wet her feet.

"He'll recover," Hap said expressionlessly.

"Maybe. But *you* won't. He's your cousin, one of your closest friends. You even felt guilty talking to him on the phone. None of the conversations lasted a full minute."

He was gazing at her, his lips parted and soft. When she opened the door at the Cahuenga Inn he would look at her like this, as if his eyes were indelibly photographing her. She drew a shaky breath, her body traitor to her resolve. She was ready and Hap must know it—he could see the flush of warmth rising from the collar of Barry's robe, the moisture in her eyes.

He stared at her another few seconds, then lifted her off her feet, carrying her in two strides to the couch, pushing aside the lower half of her terrycloth robe while unzipping his fly. They were both shaking violently. She flung one slim leg up on the sofa back while dropping the other on the floor, opening herself utterly to him.

This was the truth, the only truth. She belonged to Hap.

It was artless, swift. Afterward, still tingling, she smiled at him. "Is that your caveman act?"

"I didn't hear any complaints." He stroked back the mass of moist black hair. "Were those potatoes for your dinner?"

"It *was* my dinner."

"I'm taking you to a restaurant. No arguments. And if somebody sees us, good!"

At the Pacific Diner, they devoured the rolls, laughing at each other's jokes, falling silent when the waiter brought their steaming slabs of beef and football-shaped baked potatoes. She ate hungrily, but the heroic platter proved too much for her. Hap reached over for the filet she had pushed aside.

"How do you know I'm not going to finish that?" she asked.

"Simple. *I* am."

Laughing, she threw the end of a sourdough roll at him. He fielded it. "Nice catch," she said.

"Hey, who do you think you're patronizing? Sitting in this booth is a three-year letterman in baseball, a man whose Little League team went to the All Star game."

"It's not in the Guinness *Book of Records* yet," she said. But his words had struck a slender dart into her unfettered euphoria. *What's Little League? There's so much in his life that I don't understand.*

"Hap, what time is it?"

He glanced down at his gold watch. "Nine thirty."

"Barry'll be home around ten," she sighed.

"When we get back," he said, his voice also emptied of buoyancy, "I'll tell him."

"You?"

"Who else?"

"Hap, I explained how shook he was when—"

"I can't keep lying."

"Neither can I. What I mean is, let *me* tell him."

"No way. If you think I'm about to let you do the dirty work—"

"He's married to me," she interrupted. "I care for him—not love, like us, but I *care.*"

"So do I. We'll tell him together, then."

She clenched her napkin in her lap, aware of her disloyalty as she explained rapidly, "Barry's got this real bug about being a lesser Cordiner. He feels he's not quite up to snuff in the family." Her final betrayal sickened her, and she mumbled, "When it comes to your branch, he feels a total nothing."

"Why not? We walk on water."

Hap's bitterness was so uncharacteristic that she looked up at him. For the first time she saw a resemblance between him and Maxim, his sarcastic, mercurial brother.

She touched Hap's large, tensed hand. "It'll be a low enough blow if *I* tell him. But at least he won't need to be ashamed."

Nearing the apartment, she could see the cracks of light coming from behind the closed Venetian blinds. *Barry's home,* she thought, and a shiver passed through her. Physically braced for the miserably unhappy scene ahead, she opened the door. She was greeted by the thunder of hoofbeats. Ten to eleven Tuesday was the slot for high-rated *Apache 45*, a Western made by Magnum Television, a series that Barry derisively scorned.

Desmond Cordiner sat watching on the daybed/couch so recently used for love.

"You ought to lock your door," he said benignly. "If you locked your door, Hap and I couldn't barge in."

Instinctively, she lied to protect Hap. "Hap? I went out to Dolores Drive-in for pecan pie. Alone. By myself."

Desmond Cordiner drew a folded paper from his breast pocket. "Hap arrived at six forty-three and left with you at seven twenty-seven. The two of you drove in his MG to the Pacific Diner. You ate steaks, but no pie—or any other dessert."

"You're a spiritual comfort," she sighed. "Putting detectives on your own son."

"The man was keeping an eye on *you.*" Desmond Cordiner rose to turn off the television. In his black silk suit and gleaming white shirt, he made the one-room apartment seem yet shabbier. "Alicia, are you old enough to remember who Collis Brady was?"

Startled by his conversational shift, she said, "Collis Brady? Wasn't he the drummer who lost his hand in an automobile accident years and years ago? The one who killed himself right after?"

"He killed himself, yes. But losing the hand was no accident. Brady was hanging round Elaine Pope. In fact, he was having a red-hot affair with Elaine Pope." In the forties and early fifties Elaine Pope had been a star of the first magnitude, her roles were similar to the sweetly feminine parts played by Olivia de Havilland and Greer Garson. "If you'll remember, Elaine was married to Jack Rexford, so she certainly wasn't getting any at home. Rexford was one of the boys." Desmond Cordiner's unalleviated loathing of homosexuality showed in his unpleasant smirk. "*He* was Magnum's virile he-man lover. When Louella put a blind item in her column about Elaine and Collis, Art was beside himself. He laid down the law to Elaine. The affair got more recklessly open. So then Art warned Brady to quit. Brady pointed out that he was a musician with no ties to Magnum so he could do as he damn chose, and he just might choose to tell the world Rexford loved to get plugged in the ass. Thereby destroying two of Magnum's biggest box-office stars. It wasn't many days after this conversation that Brady met with his accident. Not much of a future for a one-handed drummer. He killed himself. There were no more problems with Elaine."

Alicia managed a smile. "Mr. Cordiner, I do believe you're threatening me."

"There've been more than a few such maneuvers in the Industry. It's not unheard of in other businesses either, when people step out of line."

She swallowed sharply, remembering the dark blood around the crushed corpse of a union organizer run over by a truck. "If something happens to me, Hap would guess."

"Who said anything about *you*?"

"But Barry's your nephew, Hap's your son . . ." Her voice dropped a horrified decibel. "You wouldn't."

Desmond Cordiner scratched the side of his aquiline nose in cryptic silence.

The door opened.

"Hi, hon, I'm—" Barry's greeting halted abruptly. "Uncle Desmond."

"You're home late, Barry," Desmond Cordiner said.

"I dropped in on Mom, but if I'd known you were here I'd've left sooner."

Smiling at them, Desmond Cordiner said, "I've been waiting for you before I told Alicia my big news."

"News?" Barry asked.

"Philippe Saint-Simon's a friend. I'd heard that he was looking for a young American girl to play in his new film, so I shot him off a clip of Alicia—Alicia, there's a close-up of you crying in *Marked.* Saint-Simon called tonight to say you had precisely the quality he wanted, an exotic innocence, whatever that means."

Had Saint-Simon called? Would Desmond Cordiner ring him later? Alicia twisted her wedding band.

"It's not a big part, of course, one line, but Saint-Simon keeps a troupe, so it's a beginning."

"I thought he loathes Hollywood," Barry said.

"He's shooting in Normandy—he's begun already."

"Normandy?" Barry asked.

"Normandy, France."

"Then Alicia will have to go over there—to France?"

"Naturally."

Barry was blinking. "Uncle Desmond, you've been wonderful to us, and Alicia and I appreciate it," he said in a stilted tone. "And naturally I'd never stand in her way.

But I have the rest of my senior year at UCLA, and then there's law school."

"Barry, Barry. Of everyone I know, you're the least cut out to chase ambulances. You're too sensitive and creative. Clara showed me those articles you did about Hersey's *Child Buyer* for the college newspaper. Topnotch stuff. Tell me, have you ever given serious thought to writing as a career?"

Involuntarily Barry glanced toward the locked drawer containing the scrawled yellow sheets and neatly typed Eaton's Corrasable Bond. "Well, uhh, vaguely."

"This would be the perfect opportunity to give it a whirl."

"The thing is, Mom really counts on me becoming an attorney. She and Dad sacrificed a lot for my education."

"I grant you Clara'll be disappointed—until you publish your first book to rave reviews."

Barry glanced at the drawer again. His novella would outshine the work of Hemingway, Fitzgerald.

"Uncle Desmond, after all this effort on your part, it would be churlish of me to drag my feet. I can certainly go with Alicia for a few months."

"Attaboy. As I said, Saint-Simon's already shooting. He wants Alicia the day after tomorrow."

"I can't," she whispered.

"Why not?" asked Desmond Cordiner.

Barry answered for his wife. "She's nervous," he said. "But, hon, remember the shambles you were before you started as an extra? And now you know it's mere idiot work. There's no reason to be afraid. Saint-Simon's a genius—he could get a performance out of a circus chimp."

Desmond Cordiner gave her his most avuncular smile. "Barry's right, dear. No need for the jitters. My office'll arrange for the tickets—yes, yes, Saint-Simon's promised to pay the fares for both you kids."

Barry gripped his wife's icy hand. "France, hon. Just think, we're going to France. . . ."

Alicia understood that the choice was no longer hers. She had been severed from Hap. And now, at the moment of amputation, she was too numb to feel anything except an awful internal draining, as if her lifesblood were oozing away.

BEVERLY HILLS, 1986

Barry turned away from the heart-shaped pool, walking slowly across the sunlit patio to where the other three sat nursing their drinks.

Pushing back his sparse red hair, he said, "I can't tell you why Alyssia's asked us here. In fact I've been mulling it over and I don't understand much at all about her. I'm reasonably certain she didn't want to go to France."

Maxim laughed. "Oh, Jesus Christ, that is rich! She didn't want to work with Saint-Simon? Barry, buster, during your marriage didn't you notice her motivations at all? Your ex is the world's top-ranked ambitious bitch."

"Yes, Barry, you're being dumb," Beth said. The sisterly warmth of her smile restored her youthful prettiness. Glancing toward the mirrored windows, she lowered her voice. "Whose career was forging ahead when the two of you were in France?"

"Beth and Maxim are right," PD said. "Speaking as an agent, let me tell you that an extra has one chance in a million of making it to stardom. And who fixed the odds in her favor? You, Barry. You with your Cordiner name. Without that, there's no way she could've maneuvered a job with Saint-Simon."

"She didn't maneuver anything," Barry said sharply. "He was looking for an American girl to play a bit in *Bibi* and Uncle Desmond sent him a clip of Alicia."

Maxim's thin legs, still bent on the chaise, jerked as if a doctor were testing the knee reflexes. "Dad? Why? Oh, God—Hap? That was his way of prying her loose from Hap? Strange, until now I've never made the connection."

"Why would you? I didn't either—of course I didn't know about the two of them in those days." Barry spoke without reproach or jealousy. He added, "All those years

I was learning my craft, she supported me without a murmur."

"We're all sweating bullets trying to figure out why she's brought us here," Maxim said. "So don't you come down with a terminal case of writer's nobility."

Barry rubbed the flesh under his chin. "I'm only pointing out there's something to be said on her side."

Maxim's face exaggerated disbelief. "You want us to start a foundation to aid Mexican domestics who become superstars? Barry, she not only as good as murdered my brother, but can't you see she used us? And used. And *used.*"

"She became a disaster area for you, Maxim, I grant that," Barry said doggedly. "But you'll have to admit she gave you—and poor Hap—your initial chance to do a film."

Maxim's eyes narrowed as he squinted at the ridiculous pool, and he appeared ready to hurl the lightning bolts of his sarcasm at his stout, balding cousin. Then he shook his head, a slight gesture as if clearing his thoughts.

Impossible as it seemed in retrospect, hadn't he once viewed Alicia—no, by then she was Alyssia—as a symbol of hope professionally? Hadn't he seen her magnificent body as a feasible way out of his personal hells? But that, of course, was before the tragedy inextricably linked with the production of *Wandering On* had wiped such dreams and hopes from his mind.

MAXIM

1966

15

On a cold night in late February of 1966, Maxim Cordiner inched forward, part of the long line going into the Bruin Theater in Westwood. Edging into the lobby, he stared at the glassed-in poster:

Saint-Simon presents
BRAVURA
Claude Tissot—Jacqueline d'Abrantès
Also starring Alyssia del Mar

He could have borrowed a print of *Bravura* from Magnum's excellent library, but he had grown up with the knowledge that the paying audience is the final arbiter of a film's success. He had seen every movie made by Saint-Simon, whom he rated up there with Bergman, and thus had watched Alicia's growth from that first silent bit in *Bibi*. Then, her face had been childishly full and her eyebrows plucked into thin, naked curves, yet even amid the sophisticated French actors she had shown a tenuous talent of her own, somehow managing in her brief close-ups to convey musky yet innocent sex. Three films later he raised his opinion of her. She came across as carnal, true, but with a nice comedic flair. Her roles had grown larger. Two years ago, after she did the Fellini film and Saint-Simon gave her also-starring status, the American press had started taking notice.

Maxim took a seat in the rear of the theater, cupping his chin in his hand as the lights dimmed. There were no opening credits. Instead, the camera races up the Champs-Elysées as if attached to Claude Tissot's Harley Davidson, panning jerkily to a group of hip young Americans, focusing on the back of a shapely girl with long black hair. As she turns, the surroundings veer wildly and there is a skidding crash. The camera cuts to the American brunette—Alyssia—and the audience let out a mass chuckle of lascivious amusement. Her dress has popped a button, and her high, firm breasts are almost exposed, jiggling in an interesting way as she rushes to the aid of the sprawling Tissot. From her concerned expression it is apparent that she's oblivious to what has caused the accident. The woman in front of Maxim said to her companion, "Oh, don't you just adore her!"

Unconsciously Maxim leaned forward. Here was the missing ingredient for *Wandering On.*

Wandering On, the loosely structured, New Wave film that he was planning to produce, seldom strayed from his thoughts.

The film would make his father see him favorably.

Though Maxim hid his emotions from others with his laser sarcasm, his self-honesty was brutal. He admitted to himself that from earliest memory his goal in life had been to get his father to love him. Rationally Maxim knew that his IQ was over 160 and his appearance rakishly handsome, yet under Desmond Cordiner's dark and piercing gaze, he invariably felt too tall, too skinny, a buffoon, unlovable, shallow of intellect; he felt taken apart like some cheap toy, with his negative attributes exposed. Through the years his father had managed to convey to Maxim that Hap, a scant thirteen months his senior, possessed the qualities woefully lacking in him. Yet for some inexplicable reason Maxim had never resented this bias. Indeed, the wall that he had erected around himself was weakest on the side that abutted his brother. He loved Hap.

Maxim jerked to attention. Alyssia was on screen again. He noted that everyone appeared to be paying attention—the popcorn buckets had stopped rattling. She possessed the indefinable magnetism that nobody can put a name to and without which no star is born.

He stayed for the next showing. While the chattering crowd found seats, his mind ferreted after means to convince Alyssia to leave Saint-Simon and defer salary to work on a low-budget film with a novice producer and director. A difficult task at best, made yet more complicated by the obstacle that whenever family members went to France Barry saw them alone while Alicia—now Alyssia—kept aloof.

This has to be played delicately, Maxim thought as the lights dimmed. *I'll have to go over.*

"Barry, Maxim here."

"Maxim. It's been eons!"

"Should I put a senile quaver in my voice?"

"Where are you?"

"Home in Los Angeles. But ask the question next week and the answer'll be Paris."

"Tell me your flight number. I'll motor up and act as your cicerone in the City of Light."

"What's wrong my dropping by your country place?"

"Well. . . ."

"We have a rotten connection. I can be there next Thursday."

"The twenty-seventh?"

"Yeah, the twenty-seventh. Will Alyssia be around?"

"No, she's rehearsing a new film. Magnificent timing. You and I can catch up on auld lang syne."

"She come down weekends?"

"Uhhh. . . ."

"This damn connection. Will Alyssia be with you that weekend?"

"Uhh . . . yes."

"I'll be there Saturday, that's the twenty-ninth, around five. Let's hear the directions from Tours."

On that rainy Saturday afternoon in March of 1966 darkness fell long before five. Alyssia had removed both vanity lamps' old-fashioned fringed shades to bare the feeble light bulbs. Leaning toward the round mirror, she held the corner of her left eye, painting a fine blue line just beneath the taut lower lid. The portable electric heater battled ineffectually against the chill.

The conditions definitely weren't optimum to show the place off to Maxim.

Summer endowed a certain ingratiating charm to this eighty-year-old gray stone country house. The small, bramble-draped park was verdant if unkempt, the white roses that wandered over the pediment arch of the front door bloomed lush and fragrant. Now, with the wind-driven rain dancing the skeletal shrubs and trees, the place had a *walpurgisnacht* desolation. Interior walls were moist to the touch and drafts prowled the halls.

Two years previously Barry had found this house with twin turrets shaped like witches' hats. Though the sparse furnishings were battered, numerous windows broken and the front door hanging off its hinges, the Renaissance Revival architecture had sparked fantasies within him. He told Alyssia the derelict château, as he inaccurately termed the property, would be an excellent investment. She closed out her savings account at the Crédit Lyonnais for the required payment, then borrowed enough from Saint-Simon to make the most vital repairs. Barry, his sleeves rolled up to show skinny, freckled arms, his brown eyes snapping, his French rotten but decisive, directed the trio of unskilled boys recruited from the nearby hamlet of Belleville-sur-Loire. When there was no cash left to pay his laborers, he lapsed back into morose moodiness. He seldom drove up to Paris, immuring himself within these stone walls.

Alyssia had gone into hock primarily to bring him out of his depression.

The novella started at UCLA had been rejected by twenty-seven publishers in the United States and England. His subsequent opus, all 1407 pages of it, was halfway through the same unhappy round. Barry, always secretive about his writing, now maintained top security. However, his outbursts of temper, slumped shoulders and the silence of his typewriter told Alyssia that failure had blocked his third endeavor.

Her career, on the other hand, while scarcely classifiable as a blazing rocket, had ascended gratifyingly.

After *Bibi,* Saint-Simon had said, "Alicia Lopez? Ees thees a name?"

So once again she acquired a new identity. Alyssia del Mar, actress.

Saint-Simon recommended an octogenarian marquise to teach her the tongue of Racine and Balzac, and an almost as superannuated acting coach. She took singing lessons, she entered a ballet class, and though she would never be a diva or a prima ballerina, she acquired flexibility of voice and body. She learned how to swim, ski, ride a horse, as enhancements to her craft.

Alyssia del Mar was addicted to an old narcotic—work. Work was the sole anodyne for the loss of love; work kept at bay her sick shame at the manner with which she had left Hap.

That night of her conversation with Desmond Cordiner, her alarm had been more for Hap and Barry than herself. Unable to come up with a logical explanation for her abrupt departure that did not incriminate his father, she was afraid to contact Hap. The adolescent panic remained with her for over a year. By the time she recognized that Desmond Cordiner would never harm his son or nephew, it was too late for letters and phone calls. Hap was engaged.

She had learned about the betrothal one May evening in 1961. After a strenuous rehearsal session she returned wearily to the little apartment that she and Barry leased in the 14th Arrondissement of Paris. He was out. On his desk lay Beth's weekly letter. Though these long, typed letters were addressed to both of them, the references were generally meaningful only to him, so Alyssia seldom did more than scan. This time the opening paragraph jumped at her.

> The big family news is that Hap's engaged! To a truly gorgeous redhead called Sara Cowles. She's a Kappa at USC, and her father is a senior vice president at Hughes Aircraft. The perfect match. Naturally Uncle Desmond and Aunt Rosalynd are walking on air. There was a big party at the Cowleses, and Sara is terrific. Not that I had a chance to talk to her alone. She and Hap stayed glued together. . . .

Alyssia set down the letter. She was crying too hard to read.

That summer, though she was rarely ill, she had a bad bout of flu, then a series of summer colds. She found herself weeping at inappropriate times.

Seven months later, when Beth wrote that the engagement had been broken off, Alyssia loathed herself for her lightness of spirit.

By then, encouraged by Barry, she had signed a five-year contract with Saint-Simon.

The contract was nearly up and she had become, if not a star, at least a known quantity. In December, *Elle* had done a fashion layout with her, and this month *Time* had run her picture in the People section—*Alyssia del Mar, the exotic American with a Spanish name, is France's favorite sex kitten.*

Alyssia yearned to expand her range.

As she licked her mascara brush, there was a tap at the door.

"It's me, ma'am," said a woman's servile voice. The door creaked open to admit a short-legged, heavy-hipped, Latino-looking woman. She wore a neat uniform and her gray-streaked black hair was cut in bangs that reached her glasses.

It was Juanita.

Pushing the door shut, Juanita peered through her bottle-bottom lenses at her half sister. "I figured you'd be dressed."

"You know me, traditionally tardy."

"What're you wearing tonight?"

"I thought the blue velvet."

"It's gorgeous on you, but you'll catch your death."

"*Avec* long johns, *naturellement.*"

Juanita laughed. Her laughter was soft, surprisingly melodious. "You crack me up with that dry little voice."

Alyssia put her arm around the pudgy shoulders, squeezing. "Ahh, Nita, how did I ever manage without you?"

It had taken an interfering friend to reunite the sisters.

The past August, Alyssia had found in her sheaf of fan mail a letter postmarked USA. Since most of her American correspondence consisted of either obscenely worded propositions or subliterate warnings that even though Jesus loves us all, He does not tolerate immorality, she had slit the envelope gingerly.

Dear Alyssia del Mar,

Yours truly is a friend of Mrs. Juanita Lopez. She being not so grate in the letter-writing dept, asked my help. She seen you in *Incroyable,* and wants you to know you was fablous. She says you and her are related, but left me in the dark how close. So here comes the part Im not meant to write. Things is very bad for her since her kid died last year. Right after the funeral, her husband beat her up so bad she needed the ambulance, then he took off, the bum. Since then she's been trying to pay the Drs. and hospital. If you could spare some cash, it'd be a blessing. You could mail it to me, her frend, Lucy Cobin, Box 198, Fresno, Ca.

Alyssia air-mailed a substantial money order and a one-way Air France ticket. At Orly the Hollister girls embraced. Alyssia, radiantly exquisite in a cream Dior suit (she had bought it from Saint-Simon at quarter cost after wearing it in *Sabine*) and Juanita in her J. C. Penney green stretch pants with a baggy, mismatched green nylon sweater, Alyssia used every atom of her acting technique to disguise her horror at the changes in her sister. One of Juanita's front teeth was gone, a raised magenta scar bisected the wrinkles in her forehead, and two deep lines lay between the fine dark eyes, for she needed to squint fiercely to see. It was impossible to believe that Juanita was not in her fifties but only thirtyish.

On the drive to the 14th Arrondissement apartment, they caught up with each other's lives. Juanita laughed about Alice's christening herself Alicia Lopez to get domestic work, and sighed deeply when she heard that Alicia had been in love with an unnamed guy but had stayed with her husband. When Alyssia learned the specifics of the death of her little nephew, Petey—from spinal meningitis and medical ineptitude—she wept.

Over supper, Alyssia said firmly, "Of course you'll live with us."

"Where *is* your hubby?"

"He doesn't come into Paris much—it interrupts his writing."

"The last thing you need is a pachuco sister."

"Nita, don't talk like that. Please? You can't leave me, not now. I've been so lonely."

"Who said I was taking off? I never had anything but

you and Petey. But you don't need a long-lost slob sister, and you sure could use a maid."

"Be my servant?" Duck terrine from the nearby *charcuterie* dropped from Alyssia's fork. "That's the craziest thing I ever heard! You *raised* me!"

"And now you're a movie star."

"I'm a bit player."

"You never did know what you got, Alice," Juanita said.

"Okay, a feature player. And *you're* my sister."

"In private we'll be the same as ever. In public I'm working for you."

"No!"

"Does your hubby know what sort of life you had? Before that Alicia Lopez business?"

"No. . . ."

"If you introduce me as your sister, he'll sure as heck find out."

Alyssia sighed but refused to surrender. "And don't you think he'll be suspicious we both have the same last name, Lopez?"

"There must be a million Lopezes—five million." Juanita spread brie on a hunk of baguette, using her finger as a knife. She said thoughtfully, "We'll kill two birds with one stone. I'll tell him I heard your real name was Lopez, which made me write you a fan letter and ask for help in finding a job." She licked the cheese from her finger. "Alice, quit arguing. It's the only way I'll stay. This place is a mess, and I'm proud of being good at housework and cooking."

"Are you positive that Mexican food's okay for this rich cousin?" Juanita was asking.

Just then Barry opened the door.

His hair was receding from his forehead in an uneven W, and that adolescent boniness was gone forever—his thick Irish tweed jacket hid a slight paunch.

"Hon, you're nowhere near dressed, and you promised you'd be ready before five," he said, taking a long drink from his nearly full glass.

Barry had been nipping *vin ordinaire* since before lunch. His nerves were tangled into a cats cradle. His sharp-tongued, rich cousin would see the château at its worst *and* be thrown in with Alyssia. The infrequent times that Barry had played tour guide to visiting Cordiners, he omitted his wife from his elaborate plans. Despite his inverted, unexpressed pride in her status, and despite what he considered their stable marriage, he had never outgrown that early sense of shame about her.

Alyssia, who had been nursing her own anxieties *(How'll it be, seeing Hap's brother?)*, found her husband's nervous state unbearable. "What's the rush? Maxim isn't here yet."

Juanita edged out.

"At least we don't have to worry about the dinner," Barry said. "That woman's a gem." He had accepted Juanita's story without a question. "Listen! Isn't that a car?" He yanked aside the faded red plush drapes. Headlights glared through the rain. "I'll go down and let him in—hey, there's two of them."

Alyssia's throat tightened. She ran to Barry's side. A man was darting up the rain-obscured steps ahead of Maxim. Or was it a woman wearing slacks and a trench coat? What difference did it make? The figure was far too short and slight to be Hap.

"I'll tell Juanita to set another place," Barry said. "And, hon, let's not take the remainder of the twentieth century, okay?" He barged from the room.

Alyssia back-combed her hair fashionably. Pulling on thermal underwear, she slipped into the hostess robe with the deep décolletage that she had bought after *Couscous avec Crème,* clasping on her gold and sapphire necklace—the gold was plate, the stones fake, but the piece was an antique, and she liked its soft, worn look. Her instincts told her she looked smashing. She tilted her head. But . . . wasn't she overdressed for the country?

She changed to a red flowered evening skirt with a fluffy angora sweater, then to a black pantsuit, then she returned to the blue velvet with the *faux* sapphires.

Maxim and his companion had been in the house nearly an hour before she descended the unlit stone staircase, guiding a hand along the cold balustrade in order to avoid the broken step.

16

Barry and his guests were in the drawing room, their chairs drawn close to the blazing logs in the baronially carved fireplace. As Alyssia entered, they rose.

"Hey hey." Maxim gave her his mordant grin. "Finally. The inimitable Alyssia del Mar, star of half the world's wet dreams."

"Piker. Why not all of them?" She raised her eyebrow with actressy drollness.

"Saint-Simon doesn't get major distribution, that's why," Maxim retorted, opening his campaign immediately.

"Diller, this is my wife, Alyssia," Barry said. "Hon, this is Diller Roberts."

Diller Roberts, standing as he was between the two tall cousins, appeared yet shorter than his actual five eight. With his slender build, his shock of Indian-black hair, his vulnerably angular face, he bore a slight resemblance to Montgomery Clift. There was a sympathetic quality about Diller, and Alyssia liked him immediately.

"Alyssia, I can't tell you how much it means, meeting you," he said. "When Maxim said he was coming here, I tagged along. I hope you don't mind."

From the way he managed his voice and his nonregional American diction, she knew that he had trained as an actor—and was using this training to hide a nervousness similar to her own.

"I'm glad you did," she said. "Buried down here, we hardly ever have company." She tilted her head. "Diller, don't I know your work?"

"That depends on how many forgettable, low-budget films you see. Oh, and I worked on this year's Brando turkey."

The flames leaped as Juanita opened the arched door a crack to nod at Alyssia.

"Dinner is served," Alyssia announced.

The dining room had not yet been renovated, so they retired to the pine table in a snug corner of the cavernous kitchen. The *albóndigas* soup, the meltingly rich tamales and spicy enchiladas, the refried beans, were devoured with numerous compliments directed toward Juanita, who hovered near the ancient black behemoth of a coal stove.

The cousins dominated the conversation, lapsing back into their old relationship, Barry deferential yet touchy, Maxim barbed.

After the richly caramelized flan and the coffee, the host pushed swaying to his feet. "A banquet to which Maxim's Hennessey's will mark a fitting end."

Back in the *salon,* he opened the gift brandy while Maxim, with Diller's assistance, maneuvered another thick elm log onto the fire. Alyssia settled into the worn, puce-colored upholstery of the Récamier couch.

"Alyssia," Maxim said, "do I have a deal for you."

"Deal?" she asked, bewildered.

"It's like this. My grandmother Harvard, so ripe in her years that she was known as Grandma Veggie, died two years ago. Her will, finally passed through probate, leaves her two grandchildren a sum of three hundred and sixty thousand bucks. We've decided to blow it on making a movie, Hap and I."

The harsh wind coming from the Atlantic drummed rain at the bay window.

"Hap?" she asked.

"Maxim's brother," Barry reminded.

"How could you forget him?" Maxim said. "He's too large to forget." He sat back in the wing chair. The jumping orange flames lit his lean face. "Just one minor problem. We don't have a leading lady."

"I'm under contract to Saint-Simon."

"I had Magnum's legal department check," Maxim said. "Your contract's only got a few months to run."

"A Magnum movie?" she said, aware she sounded inane.

"You *are* being dense. Hap's and my movie. A Harvard Productions film. The distributor'll probably be Magnum—it so happens I'm acquainted with somebody there."

Diller gave an actor's chuckle.

"We anticipate a major, major release," Maxim went

on. "You should relate to that. Also, the female star will do more than bare her boobs—not that I'm knocking yours, understand. It's just you're ready to move on to more meaningful roles."

She cleared her throat. "Does Hap know you're asking me?"

"He's scouting locations."

"He doesn't know then."

"I'm the producer. The producer's task, as you know, is to hire the talent and enable it to function."

"Maxim, Saint-Simon's planning a better role for me." As far as she knew, a total lie.

Maxim sipped his brandy. "Is that a no I'm hearing?"

"Yes, a no."

"A definite no, or a maybe no?"

"A *definite* no."

Maxim tilted his head, holding out his free hand, a gesture that meant, *Lady, fine by me if you want to give up the chance of a lifetime.*

Wind howled, redoubling the force of the rain.

"Listen to that," Diller said.

"It's like a genuine Magnum storm," Maxim said, megaphoning his hands as if on the set, calling, "Okay you guys, get your rain machines ready!" He lowered his pitch to normal. "I'm not avid about that drive back to Tours."

"You're spending the night here," Barry said, nodding tipsily. "You're staying here."

Alyssia wanted nothing more than to be rid of Maxim's acid smile. "Yes," she said. "I insist—I hope you and Diller don't mind sharing a bed."

"Dill?" Maxim asked.

"All I can say," Diller retorted, "is it beats getting killed on that bastard of a road."

"Did you know about Maxim's plans?" Alyssia asked as she stepped into the heavy flannel nightgown. "The movie, I mean?"

Barry was already in the high-legged *lit matrimonial.* "Before you came down he waxed eloquent about the production—I'd forgotten the flights his wit can take."

"Wit?"

"Oh, he kept up a running commentary about being forced to star Hap's girl."

Hap's girl? In the years since Beth had reported that Hap's engagement to Sara Cowles was broken, there had been no mention of any serious entanglement—but certainly Hap must have been involved. Alyssia turned away. "Then she's an actress?"

Barry yawned. "That's the point. She's not. Her name is Whitney Charles. Of the Charles-Boston bank. She's tried her hand at commercials. She's made three of them, all for companies controlled by Charles-Boston."

"Think they'll go with her, then?"

"How can they? You know how abysmally uncertain the movie business has become. Magnum stockholders would rise up en masse if Uncle Desmond were to commit the gross nepotism of distributing a film his sons made with a star whose sole expertise is vanity commercials. That's why he wants you. You might not be Bardot, but people *have* heard your name."

"Think I was wrong, turning him down?"

"Hon, don't we have a mutual nonintervention pact? You manage your career, I manage mine."

She turned out the light and climbed into the big, soft bed, pulling the goosedown quilt high to her ears. Barry rested a hand on her shoulder. A comradely gesture, not a suggestive invitation. They hadn't had sex in four months. Prior to that the interim had been more like five. This infrequency was never mentioned, it being a source of private shame to both of them. Though she had been approached by Saint-Simon, who buzzed like a stout, whiskered bee amid the distaff side of his ensemble, and by Claude Tissot and some ten others, she put them off with deftly humorous tact that roused no animosity. Among her friends, who were also her co-workers, she was considered to be that American perversity, a faithful wife. She accepted that her archaic fidelity was more closely tied to Hap than to Barry.

Barry exuded a vinous yawn and rolled away from her. *My poor sweetie,* she thought, rubbing his leg affectionately with her big toe. *His rich relations still intimidate him—that's why he got loaded.*

She invented excuses for Barry's drinking. Despite their lackluster sex life and the empty spaces he left in their marriage, her loyalty to him had deepened, and because of this she never considered herself as one of the main reasons he hit the bottle. Despising himself for his failures, he bitterly resented her for her successes.

Within two minutes his loud, jagged snores competed with the assaulting storm. She lay on her back with her eyes wide open.

To star in a film, to play something more than a sex kitten, would be a challenge—and tremendous for her career.

But of course taking the part was unequivocally impossible.

She couldn't face Hap.

She knew that to him her hasty departure without a word of explanation must inevitably have appeared cruelly meretricious and self-serving. Kept in the dark about her motives, he could only conclude that she had chosen a chance to work with Saint-Simon over a life with him.

Suddenly she saw herself opening the door of a drab, beige motel room, saw Hap waiting for her, his gray eyes warm and intent. With a whimpering moan, she rolled onto her stomach, pressing against the mattress, tightening her vaginal muscles as she rubbed back and forth, a humiliating, unsatisfyingly inconclusive compromise for love.

She was sickeningly jealous of Whitney Charles of the Charles-Boston Bank.

Sunday morning the wind had lulled, but a light rain still fell. While Alyssia dressed by the little electric heater, hastily skivvying into lined woolen bell-bottoms and two layers of sweaters, Barry crouched in the bed with the feather comforter pulled up around him.

She asked sympathetically, "Want me to bring you up a raw egg with Worcestershire sauce?" His favorite hangover cure.

"Thanks, but I've got to put in an appearance."

He lurched from the bed, drawing his plaid robe around himself. "Once more into the fray," he said.

She planted an encouraging kiss on his prickly cheek—his breath smelled sour—and they linked arms as they went down the staircase. Reaching the bottom step, they saw that the library door stood ajar. Maxim was bent over the desk, reading.

Barry paled. With a wordless growl he careened across

the dilapidated stone floor of the hallway. He yanked Maxim from his desk.

"You don't go prying into my things," he panted.

"What the fuck—" Maxim started.

Barry shoved at his cousin, who fell backward onto the nineteenth-century arched wooden trunk where various drafts of manuscripts were stored. Maxim, recovering his balance, charged back at Barry, aiming a series of rabbit punches at the stained plaid of his robe. Barry, crying out, slapped at Maxim's hands. A humorously amateurish scuffle.

The noise brought Diller from the kitchen. "Jesus," he said. "What the hell's up?"

"Barry never lets anyone see his writing," Alyssia explained. "Not even me."

Alyssia and Diller stood, their breath showing in the cold air, their hands dangling, duelists' seconds aware that they should stop the clumsy battle but not knowing how.

Maxim caught Barry a hard blow to the chest, Barry staggered, then rushed forward, flailing at Maxim's tensed face.

Blood spurted from Maxim's nose. Barry dropped his hands. "God, Maxim, I didn't mean that."

Maxim struck his final assault at his now undefended opponent, raising his knee upward. Clutching at himself, grunting, Barry bent double.

Alyssia rushed to her husband's side, leading him to the desk chair.

Diller offered Maxim his handkerchief.

"Thanks," Maxim panted, stanching the blood. "What the fuck was that all about, Barry old chap?"

"Ever think of asking before you look?" Barry's question ended in an embarrassed quaver.

"In my ignorance I assumed writing is meant to be read," Maxim said.

"Not until the final draft."

"It's pretty good."

Barry straightened.

Maxim added slowly, "In fact, pretty damn good."

"Well, if nothing else, the battle's cured my hangover," Barry said cheerfully. "Had coffee?"

"I'll have another cup," Maxim said. "Barrymore, I never meant to castrate you."

He meant it, Alyssia thought, following the men into the warmth of the kitchen.

That morning Barry and Maxim stayed very close, the two exchanging family nostalgia as if to reassure each other that fisticuffs were nothing compared to their tribal past. On Barry's invitation, Maxim—with Diller—agreed to spend another night.

Diller volunteered to go into Tours with Alyssia to buy food. Though rain turned the rolling countryside desolate, and the narrow road was slick and difficult, the shopping trip seemed exceptionally short. Diller was excellent company. He had a ruefully gentle way about him, a likable pliability that she associated with certain homosexuals. But *that,* she decided, was highly unlikely. If Diller were, would Maxim, a highly publicized lady's man, be touring Europe with him?

17

Alyssia, with Juanita next to her in the car, returned to Paris early the following morning for a rehearsal of *Le Feu.* The session, one long, uninterrupted Gallic argument, lasted until after six that night.

As Alyssia let herself wearily into the flat, a masculine voice said, "Hi."

Maxim lounged in the easy chair, elegantly mod in his Harris tweed jacket and faded jeans.

"What are you doing here?" she asked sharply.

"I read my horoscope. It says this evening is for repaying hospitality. We're having dinner, you and I."

"Maxim, I'm too tired to move. Besides, Juanita's already fixing something for me." She glanced around for corroboration. But the open doors revealed the emptiness of the bedroom with its pair of narrow, monastic twins as well as the tiny slits of kitchen and bathroom.

"When I explained we were going out, she decided to take in *Sound of Music.*"

Alyssia's temples throbbed painfully. "What makes you so sure you can control everyone?"

His narrow, handsome face drained of its usual tension and the newspaper on his lap rustled onto the rug. "Alyssia, you have no idea how humorous that remark is."

Pressing two fingers to her aching head, she told herself that in the six workaholic, often homesick years that she'd spent building her career in France, Maxim's invitation was the first overture made by any Cordiner other than Barry.

"All right," she assented. "Give me a few minutes to change."

"No sweat. Our reservation at Lapérouse isn't until eight thirty."

As she moved to the bedroom, he reached out, patting her derriere. The light caress roused nothing in her, not even mild anger.

Lapérouse spreads through an ancient, charming house. Initially they were seated in the large downstairs *salon,* but Maxim spoke briefly to the captain and they were led up the highly polished old staircase to a secluded ell overlooking the dark Seine with its brightly lit boats.

After their orders were taken, Alyssia said, "If this evening's about the film, the answer is still no."

She anticipated a wittily cutting retort, but instead he turned in the banquette to look at her with somber earnestness. "Let me level with you, Alyssia. I need you badly. Both of you."

"Both?" she asked in surprise. "Barry, too?"

"We don't have a script, only a story line. The novel he's working on covers roughly the same ground."

"It does? He never discusses his work with me," she admitted. "What's it about?"

"A loose, episodic journey. His title's the same as the original, *The Odyssey,* ours is *Wandering On.* His locations are the lushest hostelries in Provence, we move up and down the Oregon and California coastline in a psychedelic bus. Our characters are anti-Vietnam, pro pot, pro sex."

"Experimental stuff?"

"Very powerful stuff. New for American film, yes, but the time's right. Alyssia, I meant it when I said you've grown beyond those dumb, leg-spreading American chicks. You deserve a real role. You *are* the sixties, the new woman, intelligent, loose, no hangups about sex."

Nary a one, unless absolute fidelity to a near-celibate marriage would be considered a hangup.

A chic, elderly couple was seated at the nearest table. The man glanced at Alyssia, did a double take, then murmured to his Chanel-clad wife, who after a discreet half minute turned to look. Generally Alyssia took innocent pleasure in recognition. In her current mood, the sliding glances vexed her.

Darting a frown at the offenders, she said in a low voice, "Maxim, I'm sorry. But I have my own reasons for refusing."

"What about Barry? Have you ever stopped to consider the kind of life *he* has? Never earning a cent, living off you?"

"That," she retorted, "is *our* business."

"Oh, absolutely. Barry explained that never your twain careers shall meet. But I say bull to that. You owe him, Alyssia, you owe him. Minus you, he'd be a lawyer, pulling down large fees, at peace with Aunt Clara and Uncle Tim—"

"You *do* realize you're being obnoxious?" Alyssia snapped. After a few beats she said quietly, "Barry wouldn't do it anyway. You know how often he's called movie writers whores."

"That's what all the virgins say. It comes from fear—fear of not being asked, fear of being rotten at the job. Believe this, Alyssia. He'd leap through flaming hoops to script *Wandering On*."

"Then why not let him at least do a treatment?"

The first course had arrived. Maxim watched the ceremonial serving of their *turbotin braise aux échalotes*.

When they were alone again, Alyssia said, "He's a completely dedicated writer."

Maxim took a bite. "This is topnotch."

"Give him a chance."

Maxim continued savoring the food as if she hadn't spoken. "Taste it. There's an herb I can't quite identify."

"Is this your way of saying the film's a package deal? If I'm not in it, you won't use Barry? Is that what you're telling me?"

"I'm telling you to eat your *turbotin* before it's stony cold."

As usual on Friday, Saint-Simon broke the rehearsal at one. Alyssia and Juanita loaded the Citroën, halting in Belleville-sur-Loire for fresh baked baguettes.

As they entered the house, they shared a glance of astonishment. Behind the library door, typewriter keys clattered furiously.

"There's something I haven't heard for a while," Juanita said.

The typing continued, its crescendo unabated until the dinner hour. When Barry emerged his eyes were bloodshot, his face slack with fatigue, but he grabbed the wine bottle from the kitchen shelf, capering over to Alyssia, enfolding her in an exuberant bear hug.

"Hon, you are about to have the plum role of your career!"

She pulled away, gaping at him. Juanita, stirring the spinach bisque, watched impassively.

"You don't know?" Barry asked.

Alyssia shook her head.

"Didn't Maxim tell you? I was positive he said he'd already cleared it with you. . . . Or did I say I'd do it? The way I've been an adjunct to the typewriter, I can't remember my own name." Another hug. "I know you're nervous about tackling Hollywood and a proper starring role, but believe me, you're ready."

"Saint-Simon—"

"You'll have time to finish *Le Feu.* And he's not a pettifogger, he won't hold you to the few extra months of your contract. I've never interfered before, hon, but you can't turn this down."

Alyssia sighed. "Barry, you truly want to do the script?"

"This film's exactly the boost you need in your career," he said loudly. "So much so that I've agreed to do the outline gratis."

"I'm doing this for *you*!" Barry shouted.
"Soup's ready," Juanita called from the stove.

"You turd," Alyssia said. "You unspeakable turd."
"One day," Maxim retorted, "you'll be on your knees thanking me."

It was the following afternoon. He had arrived alone at the château around eleven in the morning, closeting himself with Barry. The heavy library door muffled their outbursts of anger.

"You got him to do it without pay!"
"Writing on spec is routine for a novice."
"And if I refuse to take the part, you'll reject his outline?"
"I'd have to."
"He could turn in a treatment that's the best since *Gone With the Wind,* and you'd still reject it?"
"What choice would I have?"
"Don't you care that you'll destroy him?"
"Alyssia, you're in the business, I shouldn't need to spell this out for you. Without you we won't get any studio to release *Wandering On,* so there won't be any film. Barry's destruction isn't up to me. It's up to *you.*"

The rest of the week Maxim stayed at the château to help Barry pare down his overblown treatment. The cousins argued day, night and over meals. At Le Nègre, the two-star restaurant in Tours, the cousins disagreed about a scene so virulently that they were asked to leave. By Friday they had an outline, and late that afternoon, Maxim departed. Barry celebrated with a vintage Beaujolais. The following morning Alyssia gave her husband a raw egg with Worcestershire sauce, and he retired to the library to begin work on the actual script.

When Alyssia's scenes in *Le Feu* were completed, Saint-Simon formally released her from the remainder of her contract. His bushy whiskers prickling her cheeks, he wished her goodbye and "*Bonne chance en Ollywooood.*"

Barry yearned to return home in first-class triumph. But since both his and Alyssia's salaries for *Wandering On* had been deferred, and since she was still in hock to Saint-Simon for the house repairs, he sat crammed shoulder to thigh with his wife and her maid on a Paris/Los Angeles charter flight.

When he dozed, Alyssia and Juanita went to stand by the bulkhead near the toilets.

Juanita turned to her sister. "Now we're going home, why don't you explain all this to me."

"Explain what?"

"I know you're only making this movie on Barry's account. What I can't figure is why you're so antsy. I've never seen you like this before. Is it to do with Barry's uncle, Maxim's dad? You told me he wanted you out of the country."

Alyssia gazed down at the clouds. "That was a long time ago—six years. By now he doesn't care where I live."

"So if you aren't afraid of him, what've you got against California?"

Alyssia rested her cheek against the small oval window. "Remember I told you I was in love and we broke up?" she said slowly. "It was Maxim's brother, Hap."

"The one who's directing?"

"Yes. Hap's nothing like Maxim. He doesn't have that clever mouth, he's totally decent. I told him all about our lives, how I grew up, and it didn't faze him. He's got gray eyes and blond hair and he's big. You trust him right away. Mr. Cordiner arranged for Saint-Simon to hire me to separate us. There was no way I could tell Hap about what his father had done, so he must've thought I picked a chance at a career over a life with him. He's going with a very rich girl now."

"And after all these years, you're still carrying a torch?"

Alyssia's assenting sigh fogged the window. "I know it's not logical, but yes. Oh Nita, how am I going to bear being with him every day, knowing he despises me? How am I going to bear seeing him with this girl?"

18

Hap had selected Mendocino and Fort Bragg in northern California for the *Wandering On* location. The neighboring small towns, situated on the ruggedly scenic coastline amid stands of redwoods, each represented a major constituency in the two divergent factions ripping at the seams of American society. The straight quality of Fort Bragg, a lumbering community, showed in the bars and gun shops, in the short-haired males, in the flags fluttering at gas stations and stores. Mendocino, the quaint remnants of a Portuguese fishing village, drew hip young vacationers as well as weavers and potters whose galleries were decorated with peace symbols. College dropouts peacefully tended small patches of cannabis hidden in the nearby forest.

To this optimum site Harvard Productions transported a skeleton crew of less than thirty people including the half-dozen actors. All were successful and sought after. Yet because *Wandering On* made a strong pro–Civil Rights, anti-Vietnam statement, each had agreed to accept union scale. Despite this political solidarity the immutable caste system of the Industry prevailed. Nowhere was it more obvious than in the housing that Maxim had arranged: the assistant director, the assistant cameraman, the script girl, the electricians—all the lesser folk, among them Juanita—took over a spartan motel outside of Fort Bragg. The prettily shingled cottages scattered around Three Rock Inn sheltered the producer, the director and his lady, the cinematographer, the stars and the scenarist.

"I damn well smell it's going badly," Barry said, his pugnacity bolstered by Johnny Walker.

Maxim replied, "And of course your nose is attuned to these things, being a long-term film-sniffing veteran."

"I've been close enough to the business to know any production with a script that's being constantly rewritten during shooting is in serious trouble."

"Barry-boy, we aren't grinding out dead studio sausage. *Wandering On* lives and breathes. Therefore your immortal prose must inevitably be altered. Which, if you recall, is why you're here."

Their argument was taking place in a small, crammed trailer. The double bed built into the rear remained, as did the red breakfast booth where Barry crouched behind his typewriter, but all other fittings had been removed to make space for a small copying machine and a large, pink hairdresser's chair now occupied by Alyssia. For her role of Cassie, she wore a long madras dress glinting with bits of mirror, leather sandals, a half-dozen turquoise and silver necklaces. Ken Papton, his face intent, dexterously tousled her hair while she watched her husband and Maxim.

She had always considered Maxim the most arrogantly spoiled of the cousins—the family wastrel. But during the two weeks of pre-production rehearsals in Los Angeles and the ten days on location her opinion had altered radically. Maxim rivaled Saint-Simon in organizational ability. He cajoled, coerced, expedited, outdoing the frugal Frenchman in thrift. When July rain had fallen, days that other crews (on full pay) would have been playing cards, knitting, or listening to KMFB on the radio, Maxim had kept them working. He was a genius at location logistics.

Since filming had begun he had lost five pounds, and now, leaning with one hand on Barry's table, he resembled a wire-thin, Giacometti statue.

With ostentatious movements, Barry inserted a new sheet of paper into his typewriter. "I'll have new lines for you by noon," he said, glaring at Alyssia—it was for her role that Maxim had requested the additional dialogue.

The hairdresser said, "Spray coming."

Alyssia curved her hands on around her cheeks and forehead as hard-scented lacquer hissed through the trailer.

Maxim coughed. "The next best thing to Mace," he said, opening the door. "Come on, Alyssia." He trailed a caress down her flank as she edged past him.

Maxim was forever giving her long, knowing smiles or touching her. Yet she could not quite believe he meant serious business. For such a famed philanderer, his smiles lacked intimate heat and there was something noncommittal about his touch, as if his fingers were tracing a road map rather than her flesh.

Though this was the latter part of July, the cloud cover sagged like a cold and sodden army blanket. Today they were shooting in an area the locals called the Pygmy Forest—here, for some lack in the soil, the pines grew no taller than man-high.

As Alyssia hurried to where the crew worked around a bus gaudily decorated with slogans and signs, Maxim easily matched her pace. Draping an arm on her shoulder, he let his fingers dangle possessively near her breast. She broke away, jogging to a clump of scrubby trees where Hap, wearing a sleeveless quilted vest, stood talking intently to a tall, extraordinarily striking blonde.

Whitney Charles of the Charles-Boston Bank played Louise, a minor, also-featuring role. Other than her part there was nothing minor about Whitney. A great deal of money had gone into producing the nearly six foot, athletic yet curved body, and at least a million strokes of a brush held by nannies and governesses had polished the blonde hair which fell straight and gleaming around her shoulders. The shearling coat thrown over her costume was no ordinary sheepskin, but had been designed for her by Revillon.

As Alyssia neared them, Hap turned, smiling. The smile could be the standard for courteous respect. His mouth curved amiably, his gray eyes showed nothing but polite pleasure.

"Brought you our starwoman," Maxim said. With an adieu pat to Alyssia's hip, he continued to the generator, talking to the electrician.

"Hi, Alyssia," Whitney said. Her color-slashed cheeks, glamorous in repose, drew in so deeply when she smiled that the lower part of her face appeared hollow.

After Alyssia returned the smiles and greetings with forced animation, she moved to the white tape that was her marker.

The morning thus far had proceeded with the predictability that had given *Wandering On* its surreal quality. Everybody was behaving so true to form as to be distorted self-parodies. Since landing at LAX, Barry had drunk steadily, blaming her for the stream of script changes. She knew that every alteration forced on him caused him to feel he'd failed not only as a novelist but also as a scriptwriter; however, the knowledge didn't help her transcend the often public humiliation he heaped on her. Maxim, on the other hand, stalked her like a predator. She kept up the pretense that his interest was a running gag between them, but the cast and crew, aware of Maxim Cordiner's randy reputation, watched for further developments with interest bordering on the salacious.

Then there was Hap.

At the first rehearsal—after six long years—his greeting

had been, "Alyssia, I can't tell you how I admire your work. I'm a novice at directing, so I'd appreciate any feedback you can give me." He had spoken with the deference granted to long reigning stars, and no other intonation. "Uhh, it's good to see you again, Hap," she had murmured. When the actors had started their initial reading of lines she had drawn on all her craft, but even so her voice had quavered embarrassingly. After a few minutes she had pleaded a sudden onset of the twenty-four-hour flu and left.

The assistant cameraman held up the slate board (SCENE 45/TAKE 1), clapping the two pieces together loudly.

"Quiet everybody," the assistant director called. "This is a take."

Hap looked encouragingly at Whitney, who blew him a kiss before she began her designated stroll past the psychedelic bus.

Alyssia stepped forward on cue. She thought: *To me it was the love affair of the century, to him nothing more than a few highly forgettable boffs. What was Desmond Cordiner so worried about?*

19

"Why not forget going up to dinner tonight, Mrs. Cordiner," Juanita said, folding a silk nightgown on one side of the turned-down patchwork quilt. "I'll go up and get you a tray."

"Juanita's right, hon," Barry called from the bathroom. Recovered from this morning's petulance, he was in a mood that could only be described as chipper. "You look worn-out. Why not just get into bed."

"I'm perfectly fine," Alyssia lied. Fatigue dragged at her muscles and her nerve ends felt rubbed raw.

She was in almost every scene, and this had caused a

full-blown case of star's overload, the most terrifyingly lonely of all show-biz fears. What if she couldn't summon up a credible performance? What if she couldn't carry off Cassie's transformation from outcast, oddball town girl to a free spirit? What if because of her, *Wandering On* flopped? In addition to the doubts that haunted her, she was shooting exteriors in rough weather conditions. The sensible course, as suggested by Barry and Juanita, would be to go to bed with a light supper. Instead, and this seemed the ultimate in masochism, every night she accompanied Barry to the table reserved for Maxim, Diller, Whitney and Hap in the inn's dining room. Like a helpless moth fluttering to the light, she was unable to stay away from Hap.

Alyssia sat poking at her roast beef while pretending to listen to Maxim. Lounging in the captain's chair next to hers, he was entertaining her with stories about the film Marilyn Monroe had made at Magnum. Hap's head was inclined toward Diller as they discussed the rushes, which came in from a San Francisco lab on the daily commercial flight. At the far end of the table, Whitney was inquiring, "Barry, don't you agree that John Barth's the greatest living American writer?" Being an English major at a finishing school in Virginia had nudged her toward Barry, the company's man of letters.

"—her skirt whirled out and the crew got a mass hard-on." Maxim stopped abruptly. "Alyssia, you aren't listening."

"Marilyn wasn't wearing underpants."

"You missed the key sentence. Nobody knew it, but she *was*."

"No tests tonight, Maxim," she said wearily. "Please?"

"You do look run-in." He pressed his warm, bony calf against hers.

She shifted as far from him as the large chair permitted. "Working in the cold's always rough on me."

He glanced at the sleekly modern brass clock hands affixed to the rough rocks above the fireplace. "Nearly quarter past ten. Time for me to escort this worn-out star to her cottage."

"No!" she snapped. "Barry'll take me." She glanced down the table. "Barry?"

Her spouse continued to wax erudite on *The Sot-Weed Factor*.

"Barry?" she repeated more loudly.

He finally turned away from Whitney. "Yes, hon?"

"I don't think I can last through dessert."

"Go on ahead then, hon." He poured Napa Valley Bordeaux into Whitney's glass and his own. "I'll be down in a little while."

"So much for Barry-boy," Maxim said *sotto voce*, adding normally, "Can't have shadows under those big blue eyes tomorrow, can we? Come on, Alyssia. Beddie bye."

Diller gave her and Maxim a sliding glance. From allusions and gratuitous smirks around the set, she had learned for certain that he was homosexual, and—though neither a glance on his part nor a word of gossip verified this—she intuited that his affections were directed toward Maxim. Maxim's flagrant pursuit of her must therefore be as painful to him as she found witnessing Hap and Whitney enter their shared cottage.

She continued to protest. "You ordered chocolate soufflé, Maxim. Stay and eat it."

"We can't have you tripping."

It was then that Hap turned to her. "I'll see you down, Alyssia," he said.

She had been taking a final sip of wine. The glass shook and red drops spilled on the white cloth. Although Hap epitomized professional solicitousness, he had never before extended personal chivalry. To be alone with him in the pine-fragrant darkness? After those dreams about him, dreams from whose eroticism she awoke with her thighs clenched? What if her control failed her, what if she threw her arms around him, kissing him—what if she found herself caressing him in the old, explicit ways?

"I appreciate all the concern, guys," she said resolutely, and stood. "But I'm a big girl."

Maxim, too, was standing. "Alyssia, forget the women's lib business," he said. "Come along."

Clasping her cape tightly around herself, she walked apart from Maxim as they crossed Highway One and circled the three enormous gray boulders that gave the inn its name. A fog had rolled off in the Pacific and the occasional lamp suspended from the tall sequoias cast hazy, aureoled pools of light on the winding path ahead of them.

Maxim broke the silence. "What gives, Alyssia?"

"I was thinking about tomorrow's lines."

"Stop being obtuse. I meant about us."

"Oh, Maxim, come on."

They were passing the fork that led to Whitney and Hap's cottage. Maxim halted under the light to extend both hands. "Look," he said. "Not a finger missing. No symptoms of leprosy."

"Let's forget this pointless conversation."

"I'm asking about you and me, chick."

"There's nothing," she said.

"Nothing? Isn't nothing exactly what you're getting from Barry?"

"He's all upset." She was too weary and too caught up in fending off Maxim's advances to realize that this defense of her spouse answered the question. "He doesn't understand that scripts are written to be changed."

"Let's omit his problems as a writer as well as his obvious difficulties with the bottle. What's pertinent is, can he get it up?"

Alyssia started toward the next lantern.

"So he can't," Maxim said. "Then why not you and me?"

"Oh, get lost!"

Gripping her arm, he halted her again. His eyes glinted in the darkness for a long moment as he stared down, then he bent to kiss her. His lingual foray toward the back of her throat, a slithering, curling exploration, nauseated her.

Wrenching her neck backward and to the side, she managed to escape. "No!"

"Nature didn't intend a body like yours for celibacy," he muttered.

Exerting her muscles, she pushed both hands at his bony chest. Surprisingly, he released her. Adrenaline flooding her, she dashed downhill toward her cottage.

At the gingerbread fretwork porch, she fumbled with the large iron key. Maxim, catching up, took it to unlock the door.

"See you tomorrow morning," she said.

"It's not goodnight time yet."

He shoved her into the tiny vestibule, grasping her arm, dragging her into the bedroom.

She shouted, "Goddamn you, Maxim, get away from me or I'll kill you!" She slapped, kicked, but her cries and blows had no more effect on him than if she were a paper cutout.

"You need it, need it badly," he muttered. "And I'm really hung up on you."

Pushing her on the bed, he pinned her shoulders to the quilt. By the dim, brown cone of light from the bedside lamp that Juanita always left on, Alyssia saw that Maxim's thin lips were twisted.

His expression was one of yearning grief.

Maxim sad? Impossible.

Then his mouth came down on hers for another brutal kiss. She wrenched away. "Get out of here," she panted. By now terror ruled her. Though his hands immobilized her shoulders, she flipped and twisted in the same way as a landed fish attempts to escape the boat deck, a struggle over which her brain had little control. She tried to knee him, but he anticipated her, capturing her raised thigh between his thin, strong thighs.

"Maxim, get out!" she panted. "Do you hear me? Get the hell out of my room!"

He jerked her onto her stomach.

One hand manacling both her wrists behind the small of her back, he managed to drag down her slacks and French silk underpants. Thrashing, she thought of Henry Lopez—had she been quicker and stronger then, or was Henry a more clumsy rapist than Maxim? He was on top of her, his hands roughly spreading her buttocks.

She had never been sodomized. An indomitable part of her refused to let Maxim know the full extent of pain he was inflicting on her, so she buried her face in the smooth cotton folds of the quilt, smothering her agonized groans.

His hands clasped her waist and his body hammered against hers more furiously. Then, with a drawn-out groan, he fell away from her. Almost immediately the mattress shifted and he got up. As he left the cottage, the lock didn't catch. The door blew open and shut and for an immeasurable length of time she lay with the cold, damp air slapping in gusts at her naked buttocks.

Slowly she clambered from the bed, inching to the vestibule. It wasn't until she had locked the door that she realized the warmth trickling down her thighs was not only semen but also blood. She turned on the shower. Resting her shoulders against the tiles, she sagged downward until she was squatting in near-boiling water. The rape had banished Alyssia del Mar. She was Alice Hollister again, and as her skin turned crimson she expended the feeble remnants of her strength on hating the Cordiners, one and all.

The following morning, when she emerged, made up and coiffed, from the trailer, Maxim was waiting to drape an arm around her waist and give her a proprietorial smile. Seemingly by osmosis, everyone on the film—except Barry—knew that Maxim Cordiner had scored again.

During shooting, Alyssia's entire body ached and certain motions tore unbearably. Thank God Hap broke early for lunch. Alyssia ignored the buffet, heading back to the trailer.

Diller caught up with her. "Alyssia, can we go someplace to talk alone?" he asked quietly. He took off the brightly embroidered denim jacket that was part of his costume, draping it over her shoulders. "I promise not to keep you long."

Dreading the reproaches or whatever else might ensue, she said, "Dill, I'm zonked."

"*Please?*" His voice shook.

"Let me get some tea first."

She took a few sips from the Styrofoam cup as Diller led her deeper into the scrubby little trees.

"Alyssia, we're friends, aren't we?"

"Of course we are. Dill, you don't need to spell anything out. I understand. And it's never mattered to me what a person's preferences are."

"Sure I'm gay." Diller shrugged. "I came to terms with it years ago. This thing with you and Maxim—"

"Put your mind at rest," she interrupted bitterly. "It's totally one-sided—part of his obsession with the female half of the human race."

"Maxim's obsession is hiding from his father." Diller held aside a branch for her, then said, "It's no secret how Desmond Cordiner feels about homosexuals."

She stumbled as Diller's meaning penetrated. "I can't

believe what you're telling me," she said in a shocked whisper. "Maxim? But he's been married. He's had a million girls."

"We've been lovers for three years."

The Styrofoam had cracked and lukewarm tea dripped onto the long skirt of her granny dress, but she didn't notice. "So then I'm a beard. But . . . if he just wants to stay in the closet, why not keep on with the public passes? Everybody thinks he's superstud anyway. Why did he have to jump my bones?"

Diller's eyes were moist. "Alyssia, he's convinced that you're his key to a straight life."

"Me? He can't believe that, Diller. He knows my feelings are totally negative. Me? The idea's so far out it's crazy. . . ." Her protestations faded as she recalled the cone of lamplight and Maxim's peculiar expression of yearning grief.

"He wasn't like this with his wife or the others—they really were beards. He never stops talking about you."

"To you? He has a true gift for cruelty."

"Cruelty's one of his tunes, yes. But, Alyssia, he's so much more than that. He's witty, totally honest with himself. He can be kind. He's brilliant."

"Why are you telling me this?"

"So you won't hate him."

Turning back toward the set, she said quietly, "You're a truly good person, Dill."

"No I'm not. I'm jealous as hell. But, Alyssia—don't hate him."

20

Maxim gloomily tapped the end of his ballpoint on the shooting schedule. "We're going six days over."

"And that's if things run like clockwork," Hap said.

Both brothers grimaced. It would be unrealistic not to anticipate any time-consuming screwups.

Hap warmed his hands on his steaming mug of roasted grain "coffee"—the Pagoda of Health in Mendocino served no stimulants, but since their conversation demanded privacy they had foregone caffeine at the crudely hearty six o'clock breakfast set out by the catering truck. "Face it, Maxim," he said. "It was inevitable that we couldn't keep to the schedule. This is my first directing job."

"And my first production. Barry's first screenplay, Whitney's first movie. We ought to change the title to *Virgins*." Maxim jotted down figures. "This puts us around a hundred thou over budget."

"That much?"

"Probably twenty-five more. It's ulcer time, Harvard."

Sipping ersatz coffee, Hap said, "Where can we find financing? We can't go to Dad."

They exchanged glances. Each was recalling a poolside conversation at their parents' Palm Springs house. After they had unveiled their plan for *Wandering On,* Desmond Cordiner said, "Why not flush that inheritance of yours down the crapper and save yourself a lot of work and heartache? There's no chance whatsoever of bringing in anything commercial for that kind of peanuts."

Hap asked, "D'you know anybody with investment capital?"

"To lend virgins? You're a comedian."

"What about PD?"

"PD? Now you've got me laughing so hard I'm rolling on the floor. *Paisan* can't even pay his office rent."

PD had left the MCA agency earlier this spring to venture forth on his own. He represented a few lackluster clients, and though he kept up a good front, the family was aware that every month he borrowed from either Frank or Lily Zaffarano.

Hap said, "He knows how deals are put together."

Maxim's index finger tapped against the counter for nearly a minute, then he asked, "Got any change?"

They both emptied their pockets.

Maxim went to the pay phone, dialing 213, the Los Angeles area code. "Yes, you dumb wop, sure I know the time. But this weekend we need a conference. . . . Yes, I know you have dates, you have nuts, don't you? . . . Yes, sure. . . . Listen, PD, Hap and I're in so deep we're wearing rubber boots. *We need you.* Great, great. . . . Yes, naturally the room and fare are on us."

They were shooting every day, including weekends, but when the Saturday flight landed Maxim was on hand.

To his surprise Beth preceded PD down the metal ladder.

"Hey, Beth." He bent to kiss his trim, dainty cousin. "You've shocked the socks off me. I wasn't expecting the big lady executive."

Upon her graduation (summa cum laude) from USC in June 1960, Beth had been hired by Magnum as an assistant reader. Highly literate yet acutely practical in selecting material for the screen, conscientious to the point of compulsiveness, she had risen without a whisper of nepotism (or as Maxim inquired, was it niecetism?) to become head of Magnum's story department. As she had been the perfect coed, so now, in her ice-blue sleeveless linen shift, she epitomized the young California career woman.

She said a shade breathily, "When PD mentioned he was flying up, it seemed a fun opportunity to see Barry."

"These twins and their twisted umbilicuses," PD joked.

Maxim had reserved a single room for PD in the main building of the Three Rock Inn. Leaving Beth at the desk competently arranging her accommodations, the two men went upstairs.

PD, a connoisseur of luxury in all its permutations, glanced disdainfully around the cubbyhole. "Talk about going all-out."

"I got you a private bathroom, didn't I?" Maxim retorted.

PD was already starting the shower. Embarrassed by his overactive sweat glands, he nursed the family myths about his fetish for cleanliness.

Maxim sat on the narrow bed until PD emerged, a towel wrapped around his short, muscular body, a gold cross dangling amid the moist black hairs of his chest.

"Now what's all of this about?" PD asked. "Why drag me up here to the boonies?"

"Should I waltz you around first or give it to you straight? We're over budget."

PD gave an agent's shrewd nod. "When you talked this project to me, I figured you'd never bring it in at three sixty. Even on a shoestring, I decided, you'd need five hundred. Was I close?"

"Not too far off. We need another hundred and twenty-five thousand."

PD skivvied into black bikini shorts. "If Magnum's releasing, why not get it from them?"

"There's no way we'll go to Dad."

PD, who had inherited old-country ideas about *famiglia* sticking together and helping one another, looked baffled. "Why not?"

"For a great many reasons, none of which is germane to this conversation."

"At this point, talking strictly from a business angle, you have what amounts to a half-finished student film."

"One minor detail. We're working with professionals like Diller Roberts and Alyssia del Mar."

"Diller's never had proper career guidance. And Alyssia's never carried a film. Still, she's not exactly chopped liver." He tugged ruminatively at his cross.

"You've got that cagy look, PD."

"I know people in Vegas. They're friends and fellow countrymen of Dad's. . . ."

Casino people, Maxim thought. In Hollywood circles, Frank Zaffarano was better known for his gambling than for his directing. Frank would bet on anything, people said, then would cite an example. Once, on location, he had bet Clark Gable a hundred dollars which raindrop would crawl fastest down a windowpane. He had bet Henry Fonda when the Fonda children would cut a tooth. He had standing poker games; he patronized several bookies. His preference, though, was for the high-stakes tables of Nevada.

Maxim asked, "What makes you think your chums would put up cash?"

PD pulled on a sport shirt magnificently pressed by Lily Cordiner Zaffarano's manicured hand. (Though Lily paid two full-time servants she continued to iron her menfolk's linen.) "Since I've been on my own, they've expressed interest to me about financing films. Magnum, MGM,

Fox, Warners, Columbia—all of the majors—steer clear of Nevada money. One day it'll be different, but as of now—"

"In case you've forgotten," Maxim interrupted, "my brother rivals Superman in incorruptibility."

"I'm pretty sure a bank would handle the transaction. You needn't tell Hap."

"How much of the package will they take?"

"Fifteen percent. That's the going interest rate for production loans. They want their show-biz investments to be strictly legitimate."

Maxim stared out the window. It was a high blue summer day, and from here he could see an inlet where brilliant azure breakers curled and crashed spuming against massive boulders. "What about you?" he asked.

"If I can help out, why not?"

"No finder's fee?"

"We're family," PD said reproachfully. "I'll just bring you together and let you work out the deal." He was pulling on ironed black socks. "Now tell me about Alyssia. Is she good?"

"A terrific piece of ass on the screen—and off."

PD grinned. "Maxim, you shit. Poor old Barry."

"We're family. I'm giving transfusions to a troubled marriage."

PD laughed and shook his head. "Is she turning in the same caliber performance she does with Saint-Simon?" He asked this a fraction too loudly. Though PD Zaffarano paid lip service to the art-house boys—Fellini, Bergman, Buñuel, Saint-Simon et al.—he disliked and avoided foreign films. He had never seen Alyssia onscreen.

"Better. Hap's really fabulous with her. When she's in the frame, you can't look anywhere else. No denying those fantastic boobs help, but it's more than that. Come on, I'll show you. There's a fleapit in Mendo."

After dropping Beth off at the trailer to surprise Barry, they proceeded to the Royale, where Maxim slipped the manager and projectionist each a joint to run yesterday's rushes before the kiddies charged in for the Saturday cartoon matinee.

The clips showed different versions of three scenes. In the long love scene, the camera was in so tight that the fine hairs on the nape of Alyssia's neck showed.

PD held his breath. All his life he'd been exposed to movie sirens, but Alyssia had something unique. It wasn't her luminous flesh, those large, sultry blue eyes, her mouth with that sensual lower lip or her startling body—after all, many actresses came well equipped. It was the mysteriously conveyed message that her sexuality was too heavy for her to carry alone, and she needed a man—PD Zaffarano in this case—to help her with the burden. He'd never had the least inclination toward his cousin's wife, yet watching her on the screen he got a hard-on.

The receptionist yelled, "That's it, Maxim!"

PD came to his senses. "Wow," he said reverently. "And she can act, too."

That night, with PD and Beth at the big table by the fireplace, Our Own Gang was once again complete. Wisecracks and laughter bubbled. Only once did the conversation touch a serious note.

PD said, "You heard about *Far Country*?" *Far Country,* Magnum's big summer release, had become this month's media joke, a catchphrase for failure. "Word is that Uncle Desmond's job's on the line."

"Dad?" Hap and Maxim questioned in shocked unison. Whatever filial resentment they nourished, neither had known Desmond Cordiner as anything other than invincible and invulnerable.

Beth set down her fork. "I hear all the Magnum gossip. Rio Garrison isn't blaming Uncle Desmond for the last few flops." Rio was Art Garrison's widow, and the company's major stockholder. "Still, in a way you're right, PD. She expects one huge moneymaker this year. Everyone's saying to trust Uncle Desmond, he'll pull a rabbit out of the hat like he always does."

Alyssia, forcing herself to appear brightly in control, joined the laughter. Not only was she drained from work, but she was self-conscious at being with the sister-in-law who embodied everything that intimidated her. A college graduate, a sorority girl, coolly collected, discreetly dressed, virginal.

Beth and PD lay curled across the four-poster bed in her big room on the second floor. He was naked except for his cross; she wore only her delicate gold Star of David.

"Mmm," she said, her lightly freckled arms nurturing him.

"Mmm," he replied. "Good?"

"Couldn't you tell, darling?"

PD returned unobserved to his own small quarters. At dawn, after showering and dressing, he hot-wired the Harvard Productions pickup to go into Mendocino for early Mass.

Later that Sunday he was knocking at Alyssia's trailer. "Our flight's in a few minutes," he said. "So I thought I'd drop in to say goodbye and to tell you again that you're turning in a smash performance."

"*Wandering On* is a terrific film."

"You'll have to learn to blow your own horn. Modesty's no virtue in Hollywood."

"We aren't staying. We're going back to France."

"That's a major mistake careerwise, Alyssia," PD said soberly. "Hollywood's where it's at."

The door opened without a knock. Maxim came in. Touching a kiss to Alyssia's hair, he grinned over her head at his cousin.

"In case you haven't guessed, Alyssia," Maxim said, "old *paisan* is here to hustle you."

"Up yours, Maxim," PD said without rancor. He picked up his Vuitton bag. "If you ever need business advice, Alyssia, pick up the phone. As family, I'll give you the straight dope. And there's no strings."

21

PD called the following day, Monday, to tell Maxim that the loan of $125,000 was set with his Las Vegas connections. In passing on the good news to Hap, Maxim neglected to mention who the lenders were, explaining instead that their financially astute cousin knew of some tax loopholes that made the deal highly attractive to investors.

That night, Barry, Whitney and Maxim dined alone at the Three Rock Inn. The others were shooting a night scene—Duke and Cassie's last tender moments before the redneck sheriffs' climactic destruction of them and the bus. Diller's on-camera forgetfulness had increased to embarrassing proportions, but mercifully the scene had no dialogue, so he couldn't go up in his lines.

After the first take Hap said, "That's a wrap."

To transport cast and crew, Maxim had hired local people to chauffeur their own cars. Alyssia, so weary that her spine felt crumpled, drove the few miles in a Buick sedan. Her cottage was unlocked. Barry, cautious by nature, always secured it. *He must've gotten really loaded at dinner,* she thought. Pushing the door open, she heard her own sharp gasp.

Maxim sprawled with one long, lean leg propped on the back of the sofa. Closing his paperback copy of *Demian,* he said, "You finished early."

"Where's Barry?" she asked, keeping the fear from her voice.

"With skullface—Whitney. He didn't expect you home so soon. It seems I owe old Barrymore an apology. Apparently he *can* get it up."

Alyssia let Maxim's information slide away to be dealt with later. She was remembering her rectum being torn, the degrading fear that she might soil herself.

"Don't take the action to heart," Maxim said. "All sins of the flesh committed on location are automatically absolved."

"Maxim, I've been working fifteen straight hours and I'd like to get to bed."

"Is that an invitation?"

"What do I have to do to convince you that I'm not interested?" She remained standing just inside the doorway.

"What do *I* have to do to convince *you* that what I feel for you is not the common, garden variety of hots." Bleakness showed around his eyes.

She hated him, feared him—and felt sorry for him. What was the matter with her? Why couldn't she dam up this inanely misplaced pity?

"Maxim," she said, sighing, "I don't mean to be cruel, but the answer is no. Absolutely no. And I do need my sleep. It's another long day tomorrow."

He pushed to his feet, coming toward her.

She bolted from the cottage.

Leaping the front steps in one stride, she sprinted up the thickly shadowed path. Her knees pumped, her breath burst forth loudly. Her mind was cleared of extraneous thoughts and fixed on one goal. The Three Rock Inn. Maxim wouldn't try anything in the lobby under the eyes of hotel guests sipping their after-dinner drinks. Those lights glimmering through tree branches represented safety.

Abruptly she pitched forward.

Stars, she thought dazedly. *No. These aren't exactly stars, more fireworks.*

Then full consciousness returned.

Maxim! She peered back. The path was empty, but she jumped up. She felt no pain. Her left leg simply refused to support her weight. Once again she fell, this time like a slowly released marionette.

"Hey, Alyssia." The man who spoke was a few feet ahead of her.

The pain had begun, blossoming in her ankle, radiating upward, bringing involuntary tears to her eyes, and she didn't recognize Hap's voice.

Then he squatted next to her.

"What's wrong?" He sounded faraway.

"I must've tripped over a root," she whispered. "My ankle's sprained."

"Which one?"

"The left."

As his warm hands touched her skin, she let out a whimper.

"It's broken," he said gently. "You need a doctor."

She avoided the medical profession. The rare occasions when May Sue or Juanita had handed a doctor a small but painfully earned sum, the treatment had been given disdainfully—and was often harmful. "An Ace bandage'll do," she said, struggling to sit up.

"The bone's broken, Alyssia. There's a twenty-four-hour clinic in Mendocino. I'll get Barry."

"He's not in the cottage, he's—" She stopped. "He's at the bar. In no condition to drive."

From the way Hap ducked his head she could tell he knew about his girl and her husband. "I'll run you into town," he said. "Can you walk?"

"I think so."

Using his bicep as a crutch, she hopped once, biting back her groan.

When he swung her into his arms, she didn't protest. His solid warmth eased the world of pain.

The frosted glass door of the Mendocino Medical Building was opened by a very young man with red hair and freckles so vivid that he could have been cast as Huck Finn.

"I'm Doctor Shawkey," he said. "Miss del Mar! Is that you? You look like you're in trouble."

"It's her ankle," Hap replied. "But the first thing she needs is a painkiller."

After Dr. Shawkey threw away the disposable hypodermic, he said, "Now while you relax a bit, I'll go wake the nurse to take X-rays. She's sleeping in back. No raised eyebrows, please. She's my mom."

The shot of Demerol took over quickly, and the pain seemed remote by the time Nurse Shawkey, a plump little woman with a crest of hair retouched in the same carroty red as her son's, came down the corridor. Helping Alyssia onto the X-ray table, she reported in a confidential tone that she had been dying to meet her—an actual movie star.

A few minutes later Dr. Shawkey announced, "A bad fracture."

After he had finished wrapping the wet, plaster-coated bandages to form a cast high above Alyssia's knee, he adjusted aluminum crutches to her height. "Stay off your feet entirely for a week, Miss del Mar. And take it very easy for the next month."

"Stay off my feet! How can I do that? We're shooting!"

"I give medical advice, not cinematic," he said with a boyish grin.

As Hap lifted her into the high pickup—it was the same one PD had hot-wired the previous morning—she said with Demerol-induced euphoria, "No problem to work this out. A few changes in the script to explain my cast, that's all."

Hap was standing by the open door, his eyes on a level with hers. "Now's not the time to talk about it. You need to sleep."

"You know that scene where Cassie falls? She could break her ankle. Hey, that's terrific. If she's pinned down, the ending'd have way more zing. She couldn't even consider making a run for it—she'd be utterly helpless for the rape."

The keys dangled from Hap's hand. "To explain a broken ankle, you'd have to shoot extra scenes. That means you'd be standing."

"What other choice is there?"

"We could," he said, "scrap the whole project."

The drug had closed off whole sectors of her brain—Maxim's hot and heavy pursuit, Barry's infidelity, her broken ankle. She felt only the pleasure of being with Hap, of talking without that wall of politeness between them. "We'll do close-ups," she said.

He rounded the pickup to the driver's seat. "Close-ups won't be possible all the time. You'll need to stand, and the doctor said to stay off your feet."

"Hap, all of us have put too much into *Wandering On*. We can't scrap it."

"You're in no shape to decide anything tonight. Take a couple of days and then see how you feel." He started the engine.

He drove swiftly but smoothly, winding out of the dark, silent town and along Highway One. Beyond the shadowy trees, occasional black slabs of ocean showed.

Hap broke the night silence. "Why did you run?" From the low timbre of his voice, she understood that he was not inquiring how she had come to fracture her ankle.

Far away, her heart skipped a beat, yet she said without hesitation, "Your father arranged a job with Saint-Simon."

"I figured Dad had a hand in it. But what about saying goodbye to me?"

"I didn't know how to explain."

"Oh? Or was that part of the deal? If you contacted me he wouldn't help you?"

Was Demerol related to sodium pentothal? She didn't

even consider lying. "He told me how Collis Brady lost his hand because of Elaine Pope."

The pickup swerved slightly. "Collis Brady? His suicide's a famous Hollywood warning. But . . . I had no idea Dad set up the accident."

"He didn't. Art Garrison did. Hap, I was dumb enough then to believe you or Barry might be hurt."

"Dad's a master at getting people to do what he wants." Hap negotiated a hairpin turn, then said ruminatively, "The funny thing is, when I was a kid I thought of him as right up there with God. My dad could make miracles, too. On my tenth birthday I got out of bed and saw a circus tent pitched on the lawn. The whole school showed up for the party. Gene Kelly was one of the clowns, Mr. Lancaster did a trapeze act, there were elephants, hot dogs, peanuts, the works."

"It sounds like a dream," she said.

"As Maxim and I grew up, Dad changed. No, that's not true. He didn't change, the way he treated us changed. To remain leader of the pack you need to subdue all male rivals, even your own sons. He still loves us, but he puts us down constantly."

"Maxim said almost the same thing."

Hap stared ahead as the narrow highway twisted to reveal Three Rock Inn. Did he believe her Maxim's adoring lover? Hap was highly intuitive, but if he hadn't guessed about her and his father, how could he imagine the labyrinth of her relationship to Maxim?

Pulling into a parking slot, he said, "You won't be able to walk down to the cottages with those crutches."

"I was thinking I'd move to the main building."

She waited in the lobby, her cast propped on an ottoman, as he made the arrangements with the bearded young night clerk.

Returning with a key, he said, "I'll go down and get your things."

"No!" she said sharply. "I mean, I'll be fine for tonight."

She swung on the crutches down the corridor, Hap pacing himself to her lurching slowness.

At her room, he said awkwardly, "Alyssia, I can't tell you how rotten I feel. All these years I assumed Dad held out the bait and you took it."

"Exactly the conclusion you were meant to reach."

"Sure, but I wasn't a hero-worshiping ten-year-old."

"Hindsight's always twenty-twenty, Hap."

He smiled, unlocking the door for her. "Can you manage alone?"

"Didn't I just do the hall marathon?"

"You're sure?"

"Positive. I'll see you tomorrow at the location."

"That's a decision you're meant to sleep on."

"It's only a broken ankle, nothing fatal," she said. "I'll be ready for shooting at eight."

"Thank you."

"Hey, don't *I* have something at stake here, too?"

"Thank you," he repeated.

She watched him go down the corridor. After all these years with actors who had studied how to walk, he seemed possessed of fine, unconscious strength. Reaching the lobby, he turned. Seeing her still there, he raised a hand.

She blew him a kiss. A gesture she immediately regretted. As far as Hap was concerned, what had been between them lay dead in the unrecapturable past.

22

Alyssia put in a bad night. The Demerol wore off, and Dr. Shawkey's Empirin Codeine barely dulled the pain. She brooded incessantly about the gross coyness of that blown kiss. When she finally dozed off, her body tried to curl into its accustomed ball and she awoke. By five thirty she was in the bathroom, attempting to get into a position to wash a streak of dirt from her ankle.

The bedroom door opened. "It's me," Juanita called softly.

"In the bathroom," Alyssia replied. "How did you know I was up here?"

"Hap came to the motel with a spare key a few minutes

ago." Taking off her coat, Juanita surveyed her sister. "You sure smashed yourself up but good."

"My ankle's broken, that's all. The cast up to here makes it look worse than it is."

"I'll sponge that for you. Come lie down." Juanita supported her to the bed.

"Thanks, Nita. Did Hap drive you?"

"Who else? He's heading on up to the Golden Pagoda to get you a bite."

"That's not necessary."

"He seemed to think it was." Juanita returned with a towel and wrung out washcloth. "What happened?"

"I tripped over a big root."

"So Hap said." Behind the thick lenses, Juanita's fine, dark eyes glowed with compassion. "This is me, Alice. You've never been a klutz. Who was you running from? That Maxim? Or did Barry have a hand in it?"

"Oh, Nita. He's having a fling with Whitney."

The broad face showed no surprise.

"So you knew?" Alyssia said.

"All anybody in the movie bunch does is gossip. If you listen to 'em, there's an affair a minute." Juanita paused. "And what about you and Hap?"

"Nita, you can see for yourself. It's ancient history for him."

"I'd of said that yesterday, but he's sure running around over this broken foot."

"He's very caring. Besides, he knows shooting'll be difficult for me. He wants to make it a bit easier."

Juanita gave her another look. "Well, whatever, he's a nice man. I guess you'd call him the white sheep of the Cordiner family."

They were shooting on a cliff a few miles south of the inn. A brisk wind swept in from the Pacific, and as Alyssia and Juanita drove up, two electricians struggled to hold onto the ballooning banner spray-painted in red: IT'S ONLY A SAYING, ALYSSIA. YOU AREN'T REALLY MEANT TO BREAK A LEG. BUT GOOD LUCK ANYWAY. The crew crowded around, kidding and following the big-bellied gaffer who insisted on carrying her to the trailer.

On the Formica counter stood a professional arrangement of red roses and white stocks. Juanita handed Alyssia the tiny envelope. The card inside had a single word: *Sorry*. The distinctive backhand was Maxim's. How had he managed to rouse up a florist in this tiny town—and before seven? *His father all over again,* Alyssia thought, shivering.

She reshot a short scene that came late in the story. When she hitched herself into the trailer Barry was rattling away at the typewriter. Jumping up, he embraced her.

"Jesus, this is awful, hon." His voice shook with sincerity. Then his tone shifted upward. "If I'd only known, I'd've driven you to the doctor. But last night I tied one on—Beth and PD leaving cut me to ribbons. Maxim had to put me to bed on his couch."

The lie was accompanied by a rapid fluttering of his eyelashes against her cheek. For the umpteenth time she experienced the emotions that tied her to him. Loyalty, protectiveness, a form of comradeship, ancient gratitude. And pity. Pulling away, she patted his shoulder. "He did? Well, you better go easy on the *vino* for a while." Unlike her husband, she had been tutored to lie convincingly.

The next few days they attempted to adhere to the schedule as well as reshoot scenes to accommodate Cassie's broken ankle, and Alyssia understood the wisdom of the medical advice to stay off her feet. When she stood, the cast dug into her thigh. The weather had done a complete turnabout, the temperature rising to the high eighties by noon. In the heat, her bruised flesh swelled against the plaster. Recalling the Demerol-induced sense of well-being, she would find herself glancing at the assistant cameraman—he had a local dealer. But always she had shied away from drugs.

Can I talk to you alone tonight?

Diller had slipped the folded note in her palm and she had waited until she got back to the trailer before unfolding it. She stared at the dark slash underlining *alone*. Later, on the set just before a tight two-shot, she murmured, "Make it around eight. I'll be alone." (She no longer joined the group in the restaurant, but ate in her room.)

* * *

Diller ducked inside, pressing the lock.

"What's going on, Dill?" Alyssia asked. "Is this a Hitchcock thriller?"

He didn't smile. "Maxim thinks I'm in the head now. He's a bloodhound when you and I're together. He blames me."

"For what? *He* knows why I ran and tripped."

Diller pulled a chair to the bed, sitting tensely. "He's positive if I hadn't mentioned his switch-hitting, you'd have fallen into his arms."

"But Diller, I never said a word about our conversation."

"He's got a sixth sense about things like that." Diller's deep-set eyes were haunted. "He's leaving me, Alyssia. Leaving me. He's threatened before, but this time it's for real. We've had our battles, but never like last night. It went on for hours and hours—he even said that I indoctrinated him, that before me he was straight."

"Was he?"

"We met at a New York party. Nobody was a flaming queen, but nobody was straight, either."

"People say a lot of things they don't mean when they fight, Dill."

"All he thinks about is you."

She shuddered. "Once the movie's finished, he'll never see me again."

"Maxim won't give up. With you, he says, he'll be completely heterosexual. I told you, he's in love with you."

"Whatever he feels, it's not love."

Diller's eyes filled. "How am I going to live without him?"

"It won't be easy—believe me, I know. But people survive."

"Not me, Alyssia, not me. I don't know what I'm doing anymore. I'm really crazy."

The sheriffs' rape of Cassie takes place in the slain Duke's bus. Playing a scene of this emotional intensity in such cramped surroundings with the stifling heat of the weather plus the lights, the strong odors of numerous sweating bodies, required Alyssia's utmost concentration. At two, when they finally broke for lunch, she began to tremble and pains darted from her left ankle to engulf her entire body. She could scarcely propel herself to the trailer. Barry and Whitney, as usual, lunched at the shaded barbecue tables near the buffet. (Though Whitney wasn't in any further scenes and therefore off the payroll, she still slept in Hap's cottage, causing Alyssia to ask herself a hundred questions, all of them hurtful.)

Juanita, standing at the trailer door, held a glass of water with a codeine capsule.

Alyssia downed it gratefully. "Thanks, Nita. It was a grim morning. I better take two."

"That's all there is. I figured this one would last out the day. But I can get a ride into Mendocino now. Here's your lunch."

The last thing Alyssia wanted was food. As soon as Juanita left, she set the untouched, crowded plate on the Formica table in back of Barry's typewriter and stretched on the rear bed. The sheer nylon curtains sucked back as the door opened.

It was Maxim.

She jerked to a sitting position. *Don't be ridiculous,* she told herself. *Maxim's been a doll the last few days. And besides, he's not about to pounce on me in a trailer with an unlocked door.*

"I'm not saying the original scene wasn't good," he said. "But today's had dimensions beyond dimensions."

"Thank you."

"The thing is," he said, "guilt and misery are destroying me."

She breathed shallowly and said nothing.

"I am offering apologies."

"You sent flowers for that."

"Yes, and you had your girl toss them." He paused. "Tell me I'm forgiven or I'll bleed all over the trailer floor." His narrow mouth was pulled into that amused smirk, but his hands were clenching and unclenching. Once again that freak compassion trickled through her.

"I've forgotten," she lied. "Why don't you forget it, too?"

"What I'm trying to do here is get a fresh start on our relationship."

"Our relationship is that I'm married to your cousin. Period."

"If it's kneeling you want, kneeling you get." He dropped in front of her, flinging his arms around her waist.

She pushed at him. "Don't be ridiculous, Maxim!"

"Ridiculous? I'm so hung up on you I can't see." He pressed kisses on her lap.

She pushed at him. "Maxim, I do not want you near me! Ever! So cut it out!"

Neither of them heard the door open.

"Maxim!"

Hap's gray eyes were narrowed, his fists clenched. In two swift steps he crossed the trailer to yank his brother to his feet. Maxim, startled, stepped backward, banging into the table and overturning her lunch plate, scattering coleslaw and tuna salad. Immediately he regained control of himself, and his lips curled into a knowing smirk.

Looking pointedly from Hap to Alyssia, then back at Hap, he said, "So that's how it is."

"Get out," Hap said.

"How long has it been going on?"

"Listen, if you don't get the hell out I'll—"

"You'll what? Hit me? Not you, brother, never you." Maxim gave a mirthless chuckle. "The attachment's long-term, isn't it? You always were a card-carrying bleeding heart, so why wouldn't you fall for the first sexy pachuco domestic who came along? Now that I think about it, when the Barry Cordiners hastily departed for *la belle France,* you went around for months like Chicken Little after the sky fell in."

"Listen, you—"

"No, *you* listen. My amorous inclination for the lady must have blinded me to the reason behind your heavy politeness to each other."

Hap took a step to stand within a few inches of Maxim. "I'm telling you to get your ass out of this trailer. And stay away from Alyssia. Is that clear enough?"

"Clear as glass, big brother, clear as glass," Maxim said. "Enjoy your fun and games now, kiddies. Repercussions will come in the future."

The trailer shook as the door slammed behind him. His jaunty whistle receded, fading in the direction of the remote buzz of lunchtime voices.

"Okay?" Hap asked.

Drawing a breath, she murmured, "Embarrassed."

"He's been coming on to you all the time, hasn't he?"

"Uhh . . . sort of." So Hap, like everyone else in the straight world, was ignorant of his brother's true preference. How could Maxim keep such a secret? *By being desperate enough,* she thought.

"He'll be talking about us," she said softly.

"Do you mind?" He was watching her carefully.

She shook her head. "No."

"Then neither do I," he said.

23

She woke to the certainty that someone was in her room. She heard nothing, and—peering into the darkness—saw nothing. Not a movement, not a misplaced shadow, yet the sense of not being alone pervaded her. Her mouth tasted of copper, and a vast stone seemed to weigh down her chest. *Don't move,* she told herself. *Breathe regularly, pretend to be asleep.*

Yet that foolhardy nut within her was whispering aloud, "I know you're there. Who is it?"

Then the sound began. It wasn't quite human, more like the rubbing of skeletal tree branches, yet she recognized it as laughter. "He's on his way to Mendo," said a sepulchral version of Maxim's voice.

"Who. . . ?"

"My father." The eerie laughter sounded again. "Repercussions will come."

Alyssia woke drenched in sweat. Since the shattering of her ankle she had been bedeviled by anxiety dreams and nightmares. None, however, came close to enveloping her in this sense of impending doom. She pressed the switch of the bedside lamp. Normalcy showed in the crumpled Hershey wrapper, the pink pages with tomorrow's script changes.

I'm safe, she told herself. *I'm fine.*

But she did not turn off the light.

This was the last day of shooting. By ten o'clock Fort Bragg's temperature had risen well above ninety, but the heat had not discouraged an astonishing crowd for so small a town. Women clad in shifts and men in short-sleeved shirts were packed behind the ropes that blocked off this portion of the street, which was patrolled by three sweating, off-duty cops hired for the day by Harvard Productions.

The drugstore's sign was covered by another sign with gold-painted Gothic letters: WINSLOW'S DRUGS. Alyssia sat on the curb, the cast hidden by a maxiskirt, her tie-dyed tee shirt revealing the lack of a bra.

Hap, who had been examining her through his viewfinder, conferred briefly with Maxim. At the same moment, both brothers raised a hand to squint up at the sky: the blaze of sun was cut off by a slow-moving, puffy white cloud. Hap glanced at Alyssia, signaling her that he was nearly ready. Maxim formed a circle with his thumb and forefinger, smiling at her. *Here we are,* she thought, *the three of us, not a hint of yesterday's emotional pyrotechnics, simply a director, producer and actress cooperating.*

Again Hap glanced up at the sky, then nodded to the assistant director.

The assistant director shouted, "Start your action!"

The extras—local recruits—began walking from left to right, right to left, a dusty old Chevy and a new Onyx sedan drove along the block. The sun came out at the moment the colorful bus pulled up in front of Alyssia, a dazzling effect Hap and Maxim had been timing.

Diller kept stumbling over his lines.

When finally he got an approximation of the dialogue, Hap called it a take. Somebody handed Alyssia her crutches. Maneuvering to a standing position, she glanced across the street.

Between an obese, shirtless man and Nurse Shawkey stood Desmond Cordiner.

Alyssia gazed at him, feeling no surprise. May Sue had sometimes boasted about dreaming things before they occurred—the gift of second sight, she'd called it. *My mother's daughter,* Alyssia thought.

Six years had not altered her old antagonist. His hair remained the same dark pewter, and from this distance no new wrinkles or sags showed in the tanned face. He smiled at her, then lifted the rope. The hired cops, awed by his tailoring and supreme confidence, did not move to halt him. He strode over to her.

"Alyssia," he said. "That was some performance."

"Thank you."

"I talked to PD yesterday. He was extremely positive when he discussed you—in fact he sounded very much like an agent pitching a client to me."

"You've got PD wrong, Mr. Cordiner. He knows as soon as *Wandering On* is launched, we're going back to France."

"Oh? And what about Barry's new career as a screen-writer?"

With a bright smile, she said, "He's dying to finish his novel."

Maxim and Hap had come to greet their father.

"Why didn't you phone you were coming, Dad?" Hap asked.

"I only got it into my head yesterday," Desmond Cordiner said.

Desmond Cordiner was a man on the brink of the bottomless chasm.

Magnum, his fiefdom, like all studios, had eroded disastrously. The across-the-board industry decline had started in 1950, when the courts handed down an antitrust ruling that studios must divorce themselves from their theaters. This meant Magnum no longer had an automatic outlet for its product. Revenues declined. But the true harbingers of disaster were the television antennas burgeoning from more and more rooftops. People didn't go to the movies, they stayed home to watch Jackie Gleason, Dinah, Ed Sullivan; to see Mary Martin fly through the air and Lucy get the best of Desi.

The audience who ventured forth to a theater wanted more than the sanitized fare available gratis. Accordingly Magnum, like every other studio in Hollywood, made widescreen epics loaded with stars, crowds, violence and sex—productions that cost a fortune.

Recently Desmond Cordiner had done the unforgivable. He had given the go sign to three of these extravaganzas that had flopped in a row. To round off his problems, the company's major shareholder, Rio Garrison, the luscious widow of the studio's founder, had taken a lover who was a shrewdly successful businessman. Upon scrutinizing the company books, he pointed out to Rio that although her enormous dividend checks continued to arrive quarterly, the cash came not from profits but capital. To pay for the bombs, Magnum had quietly divested itself of the company's East Coast headquarters on Madison Avenue as well as the ranch in the Valley.

Desmond Cordiner knew that Rio was about to give him the old heave-ho. Though outwardly unchanged, inwardly he had reached a near demented state. His mind circled obsessively around a single thought: *I must come up with a major blockbuster.*

He, who had always rescued his family, needed to determine whether PD was right, whether his two sons could somehow save him. Was *Wandering On* the sleeper that would recoup Magnum's losses? It was the end of shooting, but impatience tore at him. He flew to Northern California in a studio-rented Lear.

He promptly caught the tensions between Hap and Maxim. In Los Angeles he had heard rumors connecting Maxim with Barry's wife, that little extra he had given a start, a girl so far below the social ladder that she had pretended to be a wetback in order to reach the bottom rung. Obviously Hap was at her again, too. He ignored the sexual computations. A man about to be shoved into nothingness cannot concern himself too deeply with where his grown sons choose to put their cocks.

"I'd like to see the rough cut," Desmond Cordiner said over the remains of his apple pie à la mode. He, Hap and Maxim were in the rear booth of Fort Bragg's top eatery, Lucy's Cafe, two blocks south of the location.

"You'll have it sometime in September," Hap replied.

"A month to see the *rough* cut?" his father asked.

"Dad," Maxim said smiling, "you ought to know by now that your number-one son is a perfectionist. Left to Hap, nobody'd see an inch of film until the final print."

"We've got the project penciled in for an October release."

"October?" Hap exclaimed. "But this is August! We planned six months for the scoring and editing."

"Hap, if Magnum's going to release your film—what's the title? I never can remember." In every negotiation, no matter how close to home, Desmond Cordiner kept his opponents in full possession of their uncertainties.

Hap's gray eyes didn't blink. *"Wandering On."*

"If we decide to give *Wanders* a major release, I'll have to okay four million on advertising and promotion. If it bombs, I'll be on the firing line with the stockholders for backing my own sons' cheapie with big bucks."

Hap was already having a problem staying on an even keel with his father—he kept thinking about that long-ago coercion of Alyssia. He inhaled deeply, then exhaled. "Dad," he said, "there's no point trying to frighten us—"

"Frighten you? I'm merely pointing out a fact that you both already know. October's a more advantageous month to release than January or February."

On the way out, the trio passed Alyssia and Diller, who were in the front booth. Maxim reached them first.

"Our star people, lunching *à deux,"* he said. As his father caught up, he added, "It's rare to find Diller with a lady." A quirk of his left eyebrow made the innuendo abundantly clear.

Desmond Cordiner's benign smile didn't falter, but appeared to solidify.

"Knock it off, Maxim!" Hap snapped.

"I'm only trying to point out to Dad, who's hot to trot with *Wandering On,* that there's not much chance of Magnum's publicity department drumming up a romance between our two leads."

"A shame," Desmond Cordiner said, looking coldly down at Diller.

Diller flushed, then peered around the cafe in bemusement, as if uncertain of where he was.

That afternoon Diller and Alyssia did another shot on the sidewalk. Diller kept blinking dazedly at the camera and despite the cue cards could not get his lines.

Alyssia murmured comfortingly, "Dill, you know Maxim didn't mean anything. He's just a born gadfly."

"What's wrong with the sound people?" Diller asked. "Why don't they turn off that damn radio? Jesus, how I hate waltzes!"

"Dill, there is no radio," she said.

After fourteen takes under Desmond Cordiner's piercing gaze, Hap called, "That's all. We'll use Alyssia's reaction shot."

Diller wandered as if aimlessly to one of the production cars, a maroon Dodge, and talked to the driver. Alyssia, the perspiration on her nose being powdered, wanted to go over and say something upbeat and soothing, but they were waiting for her.

She watched Diller drive off alone in the Dodge.

It was after seven and growing dark when they completed the final day's shooting. As Alyssia returned to Three Rock Inn, her leg throbbed mercilessly: to divert herself she watched the passing scenery.

At the curve where the road almost touches the cliff she saw tire tracks, black double lines that swerved for yards across the asphalt, growing invisible on the granite.

"Do you remember those skid marks this morning, Victor?" she asked her young, short-haired driver.

"Beats me, Miss del Mar. But this is one dangerous curve. Last year a car went off the cliff."

Alyssia felt a prickling of apprehension on her skin. "Maybe there's been another accident. Mind if we go back?"

The driver slowed, turning.

In less than a minute they were parked. "I'll go take a gander, Miss del Mar," the driver said. "Be right back."

As he peered over the cliff edge, he jerked backward, holding his hand over his mouth.

Alyssia hopped out of the car, scarcely aware of the pain or the hampering cast, moving more rapidly on the crutches than she ever had before. The roar of the breakers grew louder, thundering through her as she reached the edge of the cliff.

A hundred feet below, a wave was spuming around a maroon fender. The foamy swirl hid the interior of the Dodge. Then the wave ebbed. Alyssia felt a physical shock in the pit of her stomach, a jarring pain.

In the front seat floated a dark-haired, masculine body.

24

She couldn't move. The sun, a flaming coin, was dropping below the horizon, and in this last red light she gazed hypnotized as the waves broke and receded to show Diller's body drifting in its steel and glass coffin.

"We better get some help, Miss del Mar," the driver muttered shakily.

Staring down at the precipitous tumble of rocks, she said, "You go."

Barging back to the highway, the youngster jumped into his car, digging away.

Her eyes fixed on evidence of mortality, her ears filled with the sound of the Pacific, she didn't realize that Maxim was standing next to her.

"Your driver passed me yelling out something." Maxim peered down. His face was contorted into the odd, half-humorous rictus one sees on a corpse. "So good old Diller finally did it."

"God. . . ."

"No shock to me, Alyssia. The guy never quit about not being able to stand any more of life." Maxim gave a discordant laugh. "Snuffing himself was a preordained act."

Barry had once pointed out to her that whenever Maxim was distraught, his protective sarcasm grew more frenetic, an astute character analysis that she forgot in her outrage.

"Preordained?" she cried. "You forced him to it!"

"Diller Roberts was a faggot with suicide programmed into his genes."

"He was kind, talented, good. He loved you. God knows why, but he loved you."

"So the pansy *was* spilling all to you."

"How could you have blamed him because I didn't want

you? And that crack in the cafe—God, wasn't he down enough? How could you broadcast it, you, of all people?"

"You dumb, castrating bitch—Diller Roberts was an aberration in my life! Ask any one of a hundred women. You want references, I'll give you references." Maxim's voice rose and the words rushed out frenziedly. "Better yet, I'll give you proof!"

He turned, clutching at her, kissing her, thrusting his tongue deep into her mouth. Through her blouse she could feel the iciness of his hand as he squeezed her breast hurtfully. A crutch fell, skittering across the granite. He drew away, staring at her.

His eyes glittered, and that death-mask smile again twisted his lips. Then he locked her body against his, lifting her from her feet, carrying her a few steps to the point. From here the cliff fell in a sheer drop.

There was no ground beneath her. Nothing to keep her from falling except the inescapable, bony strength of Maxim's arms. A hundred feet below, a breaker crashed, spuming over the maroon car and the rocks with their sharp barnacles.

Her breath rasped loudly through her arid throat; Maxim's breath rushed at her. Her eyes widened as she stared into the glint of his eyes. The remaining crutch dropped, falling into the murderous surf, and she accepted that she might follow. Perspiration covered her face and body. She felt her bladder go loose.

Then Maxim lurched backward, setting her down.

She crouched, pressing a hand to the rough, still warm stone. Her blood pulsed so strongly through her carotid artery that her neck vibrated. She was so dizzy that she worried she might faint. But it was more than vertigo that made her touch the rock. She needed reassurance that the earth's substance was beneath her.

Maxim, staring down at the crashing sea, began to laugh.

Obviously he had gone around some hairpin bend in his sanity. It was impossible to calculate his next move—would he hurl her down to the barnacle-covered rocks below? The anesthesia of terror numbed the agony of putting weight on her left leg as she escaped through the gathering darkness toward Highway One.

Oncoming headlights shone on Maxim's Porsche (he

was the only member of the production crew to drive his car nearly the length of California to Mendocino), and a Ford Fairlane sedan glided to a halt. Before it had fully stopped, the rear door opened. Hap jumped out, followed by his father. Obviously her driver had spread the word to them as well as to Maxim.

Alyssia waved violently. Hap, reaching her, put an arm around her shoulders. "Okay?" he asked.

She leaned into his side. "It's horrible. . . ."

"Diller?"

"God . . . yes, Diller."

Desmond Cordiner and Mrs. Kelley, owner of the Fairlane, had caught up.

"You mean the darling actor?" Mrs. Kelley cried. "Is he dead?"

"His car went over the cliff," Alyssia whispered.

"They never did bank that curve right." Mrs. Kelley's voice rose shrilly. "And in the late afternoon the sun blinds you. There's been a slew of accidents. Just last summer another car went over." She stared at the cliff.

Maxim was clearly silhouetted, his shoulders rising and falling. Obviously he remained trapped in that crazy laughter.

He can't be exposed to strangers, Alyssia thought. "I wouldn't go to the edge if I were you," she said to Mrs. Kelley. "The rocks are very slippery." She held out her hands. "I lost my crutches."

Desmond Cordiner was staring at the cliff. "Isn't that Maxim?"

"Yes, and he's really upset, Uncle Desmond," Alyssia said, using the appellation for the first time.

Desmond Cordiner peered at her, nodding. He had spent a lifetime keeping the press and other interested parties from the scandals inevitable with a group of highly exposed, highly nervous people. "Son," he said to Hap, "you and Alyssia go ahead with this kind lady. I'll drive Maxim's car."

A half hour later, Alyssia, Hap, Barry and Whitney sat in the Three Rock Inn's shabby, comfortable office, where the two police officers had asked them to wait until somebody they respectfully called the Lieutenant arrived to take their statements. Barry, prompted by the solemnity of death, maintained a marital proximity to Alyssia, sitting with her on the sagging tweed couch. The manager had dug up a pair of old wooden crutches in the storeroom for her, and she gripped them tightly. Her eyes appeared a darker, more intense blue.

Whitney said, "What can be holding up Maxim?"

"He's having a drink is my guess," Hap replied quickly.

"It was pretty grim," Alyssia added.

Headlights shone through the window as cars turned off the highway. After a couple of minutes the door opened. A short man with thinning, slicked back gray hair and a brown plaid sport jacket strode in briskly, followed by a youthful, narrow-jawed man in a khaki uniform.

"I'll be investigating this case," said the gray-haired man, going directly to the manager's desk, sitting in the swivel chair as if it were his own. "The name's Lieutenant Mikeleen."

As they introduced themselves, the younger man began scribbling rapidly.

Mikeleen said, "Low tide is early tomorrow morning. We'll haul up the Dodge then. No point risking any more lives tonight. Miss del Mar, did you see the deceased in Harve Escabada's car?"

"It was Diller Roberts."

"Are you absolutely certain it was him?"

"I'm positive."

"Young Victor Johnson says it was too dark to make an identification." Mikeleen's voice had a badgering note.

"I saw a black-haired man wearing a Levi jacket embroidered exactly the same as Diller's costume."

A soft rap sounded on the door. "Desmond and Maxim Cordiner are out here, Lieutenant Mikeleen," called a deferential bass voice.

"About time. Send 'em in."

Maxim's expression lacked all evidence of his recent craziness. For a moment Alyssia pondered the use of a sedative, then decided sedation wasn't necessary: his father's presence worked on him like a drug.

"It's my fault we're late, sir," Maxim said. "Dad stayed with me while I was on the phone to Ohio. Being the producer of *Wandering On* means I'm in charge. It seemed wrong to let Diller's mother hear the news on television—"

"All right, all right," Mikeleen cut him off brusquely. "We're in the middle of the interrogation."

There were no vacant chairs in the crowded little office. Maxim leaned against a metal filing cabinet while Barry and Hap both rose to give Desmond Cordiner their places.

Desmond Cordiner, however, showed no inclination to take a passive position. Aware that a film's chances are radically damaged by the star's suicide, he was determined to prevent any such cause being written on the death certificate. Placing both hands on the scarred desk, he stared down at Mikeleen. "Now maybe you people will do something about banking that curve."

"Highway repairs aren't the subject of this investigation," Mikeleen retorted.

"Last year on this same stretch you had another fatal accident."

"A case of drunk driving," Mikeleen said coldly.

"The curve's not banked." Desmond Cordiner leaned farther forward. "Magnum dislikes bad publicity. If we didn't, Mendocino County would find itself in a suit for major damages. So let's settle this unfortunate accident as quickly as possible."

"We haven't ascertained it *was* an accident."

"I fail to see any other conclusion."

"Cars can be steered over cliffs."

"Diller Roberts was alone, so there couldn't have been any foul play."

"He might have steered it himself."

"Surely you can't be suggesting that he killed himself?"

"It's the top possibility."

"An actor who's struggled for years and is finally on the brink of well-deserved stardom? Lieutenant, this was a young man with everything to live for." Desmond Cordiner paused reflectively. "I knew him well. He was a magnetic and dedicated personality. Magnum's lost a valuable asset. I better confer with our legal department before I make any decisions against filing that suit."

Mikeleen fingered back his thinning gray hair. "All we're here for now, Mr. Cordiner," he said with a small cough, "is to ask a few questions about what actually occurred."

"Then let me talk straight. You'd be one hell of a lot better advised to ask your questions about your highway than to cook up wild reasons for the death of a brilliant young actor."

By the time Mikeleen and the others drove away, the restaurant was closed and the chef had gone home, so the manager's full-cheeked wife offered to cut roast beef sandwiches and brew fresh coffee.

Alyssia wasn't hungry. She bowed out.

Hap said, "I'll walk you to your room."

As they went slowly down the long corridor, he asked, "Dad browbeat them into accidental death, but do you think Diller did kill himself?"

"Maybe," she sighed. "He's been terribly on edge."

"And it got worse this last week. Any idea what was wrong?"

"It could have been a hundred things," she hedged.

"That dumb dig of Maxim's at lunch! I wanted to kill him. Diller was a good guy, so what difference did *that* make. To anyone except Dad, I mean." Hap shook his head. "Jesus, what a way to choose to die, water filling your lungs—it takes five minutes."

They had reached her room. Visualizing Diller's last five minutes, his frantic, animal-instinct struggles growing feeble, she shook her head. "I saw him getting the car. I should've gone over. . . . Stopped him. . . ."

Hap put both his arms around her, holding her. She was shamed by the comfort she got from the cotton shirt that smelled of him, his warmth, the beat of his heart, then horrified that a faint fringe of desire stirred within her.

"I love you."

The words were a low rumble, and she wasn't positive if he had spoken or if she had heard a nonexistent voice.

Pulling away, she said clearly, "I never stopped loving you."

He gazed down at her, the overhead light gleaming in his questioning eyes. Had he actually spoken? If he hadn't, then her remark must be an embarrassing nonsequitur to him. The exterior door at the end of the corridor opened and a heavy-hipped woman in purple slacks tramped inside, peering at them, showing recognition. She halted a few doors away, dawdling with her key as if she hoped to hear their conversation.

"You must be hungry, Alyssia," Hap said in a friendly, offhand tone. "Want me to have them bring you milk?"

"Please—oh, and a candy bar."

"A Hershey with almonds," he said.

"You remembered," she said.

"I haven't," he said, "forgotten anything."

Alyssia, more tired than she could remember, her leg aching ferociously, sipped the milk but found it impossible to eat more than one square of chocolate. Fully clothed, she stretched on the bed, attempting to consider the significance of her brief conversation with Hap. But instead she kept seeing Diller's corpse bobbling, drifting.

She blinked in surprise at the yellow sun flooding between the undrawn drapes. Last night it hadn't seemed feasible that she'd sleep, but she had.

A rap on the door had wakened her, and another sounded now. Positive that Juanita had arrived, she called, "Just a sec." Unhooking the chain, she turned the lock.

Maxim stood there.

Instinctively she pushed the door to close it.

He gripped the wood, wedging in his shoe. "I need to talk to you. Please?"

"If you don't go away, I'll scream." In what Saint-Simon film had she said that line?

"I'm not wearing my Jack the Rapist suit, I swear I'm in no mood to attempt any assault or the least battery. But I haven't slept. Been doing what you might call some heavy thinking. You're the only person who'll understand."

"Me? As far as I'm concerned, you're a complete mystery. I don't understand one thing about you."

"Alyssia, if I don't get some of this garbage out, I'll explode. *I am begging.*"

His eyes were mapped with red veins, and the shadows beneath were nearly black. *Diller asked me not to hate him.* Warily she released the door.

He crossed the room, sagging into the chintz love seat. "What happened on the cliff?" he asked. "The scene we played isn't exactly clear in my mind."

"You really can't remember?"

"I yelled a lot of ugly things about Diller, and you yelled back. Then suddenly you were on the ground. Did I hit you or what?"

"You held me over the cliff."

"I what?" His bloodshot eyes were incredulous.

"You lifted me off my feet and dangled me over the edge of the cliff."

"Jesus."

"It seemed like a year, but was probably less than a minute. One of my crutches dropped into the sea."

"I knew I went bananas, but I didn't realize it was that bad."

"It still doesn't ring a bell?"

He shook his head. "I felt something inside me snap—it actually sounded like a bursting balloon—when I saw him floating and rocking like some sort of aquatic animal in that damn car."

"It was horrible." She shivered.

"He meant too much to me," Maxim said. "And that frightened the hell out of me. I'd had guys before him, lots of them. During the act I was both titillated and terrified by how my honored sire would react if he could see me. When I met Diller, he became the only person I wanted . . . and I wanted him excessively. I don't mean just sex, although God knows I was insatiable. I wanted to be around him every second. So there I was, trapped in a form of involuntary servitude and scared shitless by it. I couldn't stop hurting him. But you've got to believe this, Alyssia. Even though he kept telling me he couldn't bear any more of what I was slinging at him, I never, repeat never, thought that he'd drive any cars over any cliffs."

"Neither did I."

"Does this sound like a laying off of guilt? When I said I was terrified of what I was, maybe I wouldn't have been if it weren't for Dad."

"Maxim, so you're afraid of your father. Who isn't?"

"Dad's why I needed marriage plus the signed affadavit of every starlet in the greater Hollywood area that Maxim Cordiner is the stud of studs."

"What could be more natural than trying to cover up?"

"Nothing I've done in my life has ever been perfectly natural, Alyssia. Unless you count falling in love with Diller. I went to France to sign you for *Wandering On,* and when I saw you in that drafty barn, all dolled up in your blue velvet and fake sapphires, I thought to myself, *This chick's something else. Maybe playing around with her will cure me of Diller.* But then I began to see something of him in you. It was the eyes. His eyes and your eyes have mysterious depths. I did care about you. Not like Diller, you understand—I never could love a woman that way. But a genuine emotion flickered. And you rejected me."

She sighed. "The flicker wasn't there for me."

"Yes, your interest is in the noblest Cordiner of them all." He paused. "Anyway, on my part, rejection or no, I began to view you as the sexual savior of my reprehensible life. I kept building up what I felt for you. And crushing down what I felt for Diller. God, the things I did to him. And said to him. I told him he swished, I told him he ought to come to the set in drag. I told him—ahh, fuck, what didn't I tell the poor dead bastard?"

He bent his head into his hands.

She moved to the love seat, sitting close to him. "It's over."

"Over?" Maxim said, his voice muffled. "At this very instant they're on the rocks dredging up the car, taking him out of it."

"Oh, Maxim." She put an arm around his shuddering back. "Maxim, Maxim."

". . . How am I going to live?"

Diller had asked this same question in this same room. Her answer then had been that people survive. She didn't offer this cold and disputable comfort now. She let Maxim cling to her, and when he buried his wet face between her breasts, she kissed his russet hair.

"How am I going to live?" he gasped out.

BEVERLY HILLS, 1986

A breeze stirred across the patio, rippling the heart-shaped pool. Maxim gazed broodingly at the wavelets. "Without Alyssia," he said finally, "*Wandering On* would have been long strips of celluloid running through a machine."

"Exactly." Barry nodded. "But I've never quite understood how you convinced her to do it."

"If you'll recall, Barry-boy," Maxim replied, "in those days your career had not reached its current splendor, and you were panting to earn your first buck. I spelled out to her that you and she were a package deal. If she didn't play Cassie, no script for you."

"I should've guessed it was something like that," Barry said. "She's always had a fine generosity of spirit."

"Are the two of you crazy or what?" Beth's voice rose from its natural, pleasantly modulated level. "She came back for one reason. Hollywood is where it's at. You didn't convince *her,* Maxim, she used *you.* And she used Barry and she used Uncle Desmond and she used poor Hap. She used all of us."

"It's bad enough she's a driving bitch," PD added, "but educated word is that she had a hand in Diller Roberts's death."

Maxim took off his dark glasses, staring at PD for a long moment. "She didn't," he said harshly.

PD turned away, gulping at his Campari. Though estranged from his cousins, he had joined with Barry and Beth in vehement condemnation of *Diller Roberts and Montgomery Clift: The Inside Story of Two Actors,* the 1981 smirky dual biography that had devoted a full chapter to a supposed affair between Maxim and Diller. In defense of Maxim's heterosexuality, they cited their cousin's four marriages and numerous well-publicized affairs. At publication, though, Maxim had issued no denials, filed no libel suits, remaining incommunicado on his island off the Gulf Coast of Mexico.

"If Alyssia's so marvelous, why did we all come rushing over today?" Beth's aging, pretty face was pink. "You both know the answer as well as I do. We're terrified of what she can do to us."

Barry glanced nervously at the inscrutable windows with their sun-protective coating, saying in a low voice, "Maxim and I weren't canonizing my ex-spouse, merely pointing out she's hardly a reincarnation of Jezebel."

"Bull," PD said. "That's exactly what she is."

"Why so rough on the lady, PD?" Maxim inquired. "Time was when you would have gone up the length of California on your knees like a *penitente* to represent her."

"She was my client, yes. And I always say the agent knows a client best."

"Why not? You guys imbibe ten percent of their blood," Barry said, then forced a laugh.

"In this particular case, let me tell you, my client was the one who fucked me over." Mopping a linen handkerchief over his forehead, PD moved to sit in the shade.

Alyssia had been difficult, yes, but inwardly he had to admit that she quite literally had saved his life.

PD

1966

25

Because of Diller's death, Maxim and Hap had to stay in Mendocino, taking charge of what the local undertaker called "the sad remains," but the rest of the *Wandering On* ensemble departed on a chartered DC3.

An August hot spell engulfed Los Angeles. PD, who picked up Alyssia, Barry and Juanita at LAX, kept the air conditioning in his Cad roaring all the way to their furnished rental in West Hollywood.

It was three blocks from their original bachelor apartment and nearly as shabby. Barry had written to Beth from France requesting that she rent them a house in a nice neighborhood. But Los Angeles rents had shot up, and though she searched long and conscientiously, this was the best she could find.

Barry and Juanita sweated copiously as they hauled in the luggage. PD helped Alyssia to the couch, responding with alacrity to her murmured request for water.

She downed two more codeines: she had taken two on the plane. The typed instructions on the brown phial read *one every four hours,* but the pain was unbearable. She told herself it was the heat.

"First thing tomorrow," PD said, "you have an orthoped look at that leg."

"Doctor Shawkey said the cast should be on for a month," she responded weakly.

"Shawkey's fine for the boonies, Alyssia, but now you're back in civilization." He took a Tiffany silver card case from his pocket, writing a number on one of his cards. "This is my guy—Uncle Desmond uses him, and so do Liz, Marlon and Natalie."

"Thanks, PD." She dropped the card on the coffee table.

"You're not in shape for socializing right now, but let's do lunch before you go back to France."

"France is on the shelf."

"Good girl! My professional advice is to hold off until October. I heard today that the premiere's set for the fifteenth."

"That's less than two months." She shifted on the couch, wincing at the shooting pains. "Why is Magnum pushing so hard for the release?"

"Here's the situation. Uncle Desmond is enthusiastic. And Uncle Desmond is in urgent need of a hit."

Barry puffed through the front door, setting down the biggest suitcase. "What've you got in here? The Rosetta Stone? I'm acquiring a goddamn hernia."

"Don't you remember? You asked Juanita to save the drafts of the script."

"Oh," he said without contrition. "PD, a drink's your reward for picking us up."

"Nothing, thanks." PD glanced at his watch. "I'm due at the l'Orangerie to meet with a friend—he's producing the new Redford." It was in actuality a friend of Frank Zaffarano's.

As PD's Cadillac backed out, Barry went into the kitchen to pour himself a drink. The phone rang. He picked up the extension. "Hello," he said. Then his voice grew inaudible.

Alyssia knew Whitney was on the other end.

When he returned to the living room, he said, "That was Beth. She's on her way home, and'll drive me to see the folks." He didn't look at Alyssia. "I said I'd walk down the block so she won't have to make the detour."

"Barry, why're we playing games?" Alyssia asked quietly. "We both know you're meeting Whitney."

He flushed. "Is that your hypothesis?"

"I'm not accusing you, Barry. Just saying there's no point in all this covering up we've been doing."

"We? Am I correct in assuming you're referring to your little fling with Maxim?"

"Maxim's got nothing to do with this."

"But Whitney does?"

"Can't we make this a reasonable conversation?"

"All right," he said loudly. "I'm admitting there's somebody who cares about *me*, somebody whose top priority isn't a multinational career. Whitney has total belief in my writing. She thinks *Wandering On* is a fine piece of work."

"Barry, I made so few suggestions for changes."

"Yes, but we both know how Maxim arrived at his complaints."

"Will you stop dragging in Maxim," she sighed wearily. "It was a great script, Barry. From now on things'll be good for you."

"But not so hot for you. Maxim changes women like he changes shirts."

"Maxim's my friend, nothing more." She spoke with a hint of exasperation.

"Yes—your fidelity's intact."

She drew a breath, then said, "Before we went to France I had an affair with Hap."

Barry swallowed his Scotch and soda the wrong way. He burst into a coughing fit, hacking uncontrollably for nearly a minute. By then the spasms had affected his vocal cords so that he spoke in a high-pitched squeak. "Hap? Him too? I don't believe this. Hap? He's the cleanest guy I know."

"We were going to tell you. But your uncle found out . . . he didn't want Hap and me—"

"That I can believe. I vividly remember that day in Newport when he tried to pry *me* away."

"He fixed me up with Saint-Simon. I was a kid, I was terrified . . . there's no excuse. I bolted."

"And began spreading your legs for Frenchmen."

"Oh, Barry, will you stop it? The only time I've cheated on you is years ago with Hap. I loved him then and I still love him. Look, we made a mistake when we were very young, and now's the time to put it right. A divorce isn't the end of the world."

"Divorce? Who's talking about a divorce?"

"We are, Barry."

"No! The answer is no!"

Barry's face was crimson. Alyssia could not know it, but Hap had always been the person in this world that her husband most admired, most envied. In his incoherent shock (Alyssia and *Hap?*) Barry's reason fled utterly while his lifelong jealousy spoke.

"If you're both expecting me to meekly fold my tent and steal away, you can just forget that goddamn idea!"

"But you and Whitney—"

"*No divorce!*" he screamed, slamming the front door.

Juanita, accustomed to their marital eruptions, asked no questions, walking to the nearby McDonald's, bringing home supper. Alyssia, who normally relished fast food, grew nauseated at the aroma of the hamburger and fries. Though the evening was warm, she shivered and put on extra covers. *I must be coming down with the bug,* she thought.

That night she slept heavily and woke feeling nauseated again. The constant darting pain in the leg had spread to her torso. When Juanita brought in a breakfast tray, she shook her head. "I have some kind of flu."

She was dozing off again when the door opened. Barry stepped inside.

"Hi," he said in a quiet voice.

"Hi."

"Ankle still bothering you?"

"A bit."

"The pain should have stopped by now. You really ought to have it looked at."

"You know me and doctors. I'll go when it's time to take off the cast."

He sat on the end of the bed. The mattress shifted and the pain in her leg intensified. She bit her lip and rested her head back on the pillow.

"I'm sorry about last night," he said penitently. "That scene I put on was petty and vindictive."

"Barry, one thing you should know. When I married you, I truly thought I loved you. It might not have worked out well for us. But always I've cared, cared very much. And I still care."

"So do I. Listen, I'm going to move out."

"Where?"

"Whitney's place."

"Then we're separating?"

"I guess. For the time being, though, hon, let's not make any permanent decisions."

"But if you and Whitney are living together, why not?"

"It's better this way," he muttered. He was mad for Whitney, who aroused his never-strong libido. Yet at the same time his deep-rooted and jealous inferiorities toward Hap prevented him from relinquishing Alyssia. "No need to rush out of marriage the way we rushed in."

Alyssia closed her eyes, engulfed by a sickening rush of pain.

"I'll be in touch," he said, kissing her forehead. "Hon, you're burning up."

"I've got the flu," she whispered faintly.

Juanita helped him stow his suitcases and typewriter in the trunk of the low-slung, yellow Corvette that he'd borrowed from Whitney.

Alyssia slept, mumbling and tossing.

By four thirty, when Juanita tried to waken her, she was delirious. Terrified, Juanita searched for Barry's number, but he hadn't left one.

PD's business card lay on the coffee table.

In a high, rushed voice, she told PD that Mrs. Cordiner was sick, really badly sick.

Galvanized by the terror in the maid's voice, PD left Matty Gorlick, a big CBS honcho, to rush over to that dump Barry and Alyssia were renting. One glance at the beautiful, ravaged face, one whiff of that strange, meaty odor, and he carried Alyssia screaming to his car.

While Juanita wept over her, he broke the speed limits consistently on the few miles' drive to Mount Sinai, the nearest big hospital. Acting with instinctive good Samaritanism, he didn't realize until he watched Alyssia being wheeled swiftly away that he might just have given himself the wedge that he desperately needed with her—if she made it. As he walked to his car, he thought, *Poor kid,* and said a prayer for her.

26

She was on fire.

Her left leg was the igniting flame that sent fire blazing through her body. The inferno raged the hottest within her skull, and once she actually saw a horde of tiny, crimson-clad demons bending and swaying as they stoked the conflagration, miniature devils that were frighteningly real. Another time, a huge grower with slablike features stood over her, forcing her to pick an endless row of lettuce under a white-hot sun even though sweat poured from her and strange whistling hoots sounded against her eardrums.

The figures in white who came and went were equally hallucinatory torturers. She knew they were doctors and nurses because May Sue had told her. Her frizzy blonde hair a halo around her raddled face, May Sue had perched on the bed. "What are you doing in a hospital, Alice? Don't you know hospitals are the place they take people to die? Listen to your momma and get away while the getting's good."

She tried to escape. A faraway voice warned her not to move. After that she was pinned down.

Afloat in fever and pain, Alyssia drifted with the hours and days—or was it weeks and months?

"Mrs. Cordiner. Mrs. Cordiner. Alyssia."

She opened her eyes, peering up at the fuzzy outline of a man in a white coat.

"Ahh, that's better. You're awake. Do you know where you are?"

"Hospital. . . ?"

"Yes. You've been in Mount Sinai for nearly three days. You have an infection in your leg."

"Want to . . . go home. . . ."

"Alyssia, you must try to concentrate. This is very important. You have the fever because the infection is extremely serious."

"Take off . . . cast."

The doctor sat near her, talking intently and clearly. "Unfortunately the infection appears to be spreading. We've been discussing amputation."

"We"? Who were "we" to cut off her leg? Obviously "we" were ranged with the hostile, ominously all-powerful authorities. May Sue was right, she should have escaped.

She tried to shout *no*! The word came out a feeble whisper.

"You have to realize how gravely ill you are. We want to save your life."

"Never. . . ."

"Alyssia, we'd cut below the knee. It wouldn't interfere with your acting. You could even learn to dance."

"No. . . ."

"Your husband agrees with us."

"He's . . . not my husband."

The doctor turned to a hazy figure at the window. "Barry, I'm afraid there's no point in this. You'll have to sign the consent for surgery. She's delirious again."

"She might not be." A nervous cough. "We'd, uhh, we'd just agreed to separate."

"You're her nearest relative."

"Hap. . . ." she repeated.

"There, you see. She's really out of it."

"Hap's my cousin. She wants to see him." Another nervous cough. "He directed her in the movie. She has, uhh, a lot of respect for him."

"Oh? Is he around?"

"You met him in the corridor."

"The big guy with the blond hair who hasn't left since the day before yesterday? It's worth a try. Maybe he can convince her."

The masculine voices moved away. Alyssia knew that she must not sink back down into timelessness. If she so much as catnapped she would be mutilated. With stubborn difficulty she fought to hold her eyes open, staring at a dark, wavery blob that was the television screen.

"Alyssia," Hap said.

She tried to focus, but saw only the oval above her. Then a strong hand clasped hers, and cool lips rested on her forehead. *I must smell awful.*

"Hap. . . ?"

"I'm here, love."

"Everything's blurry. . . ."

"It's probably all the antibiotics and drugs they're dripping into you."

"No . . . amputation."

"Love, they're worried the infection in your leg might spread and kill you."

"Don't let them . . . please?"

"But if you die—"

"I won't." Her voice was louder.

"Stop being brave, Alyssia, I couldn't bear it if you die."

"Don't let them. . . . Hap, promise?"

His grip on her hand tightened.

"Hap?"

His sigh cooled her cheek. "I'll tell Barry to have them wait on the decision as long as possible." He released her hand.

"Stay. . . ."

The large hand enfolded hers again. The fever seemed to lift a bit, and she saw a funny vision of Hap in a fireman's red hat battling the blaze with her. Then she tried to remember coming here. Nothing was clear except a memory of consuming pain when PD lifted her into his car.

27

When PD had left MCA to open his own office on the Sunset Strip, only six of the clients in his charge went with him. These half dozen were old buddies of Frank Zaffarano's, but they did not leave the prestigious agency out of friendship. Self-interest was their motive. All were on the sharp downward curve of a major career, with only PD between them and the Motion Picture Retirement Home in Woodland Hills.

At his parents' parties, at his Uncle Desmond's Sunday barbecues, at screenings, on private Bel Air tennis courts and the fairways of Los Angeles Country Club, PD never ceased flashing his white smile and spreading his considerable charm on anyone who might possibly give his clients a part.

Nevertheless, every month the PD Zaffarano Agency went deeper in the hole. It was impossible to remain solvent on ten percent of the earnings of his half dozen, difficult-to-place geriatric clients. He needed young blood. Not the pretty, talentless nobodies of both sexes who waited tables while hoping for the one in a zillion chance of making it in the Industry, but a star who would bring in big bucks and also put a stamp of authenticity on the agency. Nobody of stature would talk business. PD kept trying—he was a born hustler.

Last January his innate drive had become near pathological.

From early puberty he'd been drawn to his opposite, the calm-voiced, conventionally pretty cousin who looked at him adoringly. In a not altogether unpleasant attempt to break the attachment, he entered the sexual arena early, screwing his way through a brigade of flamboyantly attractive females. Nothing helped. Finally, on the morning after New Year's Eve, he had succumbed to an affair with Beth.

They were on his living room couch, Beth sitting, PD stretched out with his head on her lap, she wearing his beige silk robe, he in his black robe. The aroma of broiled lamb chops surrounded them. Several nights a week she would drive from Magnum to his apartment, which was furnished with expensive, oyster-white hand-me-downs acquired when his parents redecorated their Beverly Hills house. First they would use the low white king-size bed, then Beth would broil a big porterhouse or chops, tossing a salad. After dinner they would sometimes return to the bedroom. Beth, who still lived in her parents' Westchester tract house, invariably left before eleven. These unpretentious evenings formed a serene oasis in PD's striving life. Beth had been a virgin when he took her to bed. And for him it was a first, too. Never before had he experienced the honest passion and wondrous ease of being with a woman he loved, a woman who loved him in return.

He longed to marry her. He had never discussed marriage. He wasn't making a living. But even if he were, the mammoth impediments of their blood relationship and their religions barred the way.

Beth was irrevocably bound to her Jewishness. And she was a completely devoted daughter. She often said with no hyperbole in her tone, "It'd kill Mother if I didn't raise my children to be Jewish."

PD, on his part, was also a believer. With Beth, his unbaptized cousin, he could never have a marriage performed on the altar of the Church of the Good Shepherd in Beverly Hills—or any other Catholic altar.

Beth stroked back PD's hair. He was telling her about his most recent visit to Mount Sinai.

"So Alyssia's that bad?" she asked.

"She's in terrible shape. I'm surprised Barry didn't tell you about it."

"He hardly ever mentions her to me."

"To save her, they're talking amputation."

"Amputation! God."

"Can you imagine a sex symbol with a wooden leg?" PD asked, sighing. His heartfelt prayers for Alyssia's recovery were entwined with his own problems. "There goes the perfect client."

Beth smoothed his hair again. She understood him completely.

"It's not that she's talented," he mused. "She is, but that and a dime'll get you a cup of coffee. With those small, delicate features and knockout eyes, she photographs well, but so do a lot of other girls in town. She's luminous. But it's something more than her looks. Beth, those *Wandering On* rushes floored me. Nobody can explain that certain something, but she's got it. She reaches out from the screen and grabs up in your gut—and other places."

"They certainly *are* high on her at Magnum." Beth paused. "I feel rotten, not knowing her better. But Mother and Dad were so upset about the marriage that Barry's been paranoid about getting us together."

Because PD loved Beth, he didn't say that in his opinion her twin had turned out to be a real loser, and neither did he mention that Barry wasn't racking up much time at the hospital.

"Poor kid, she was too gutsy for her own good, working with that broken ankle. The way they're talking, the doctors, it might be curtains."

Beth's eyes filled with horror. "But what about the amputation? Won't that save her?"

"They don't sound all that certain about anything." PD sighed deeply. "Bethie, she's younger than us. To cash in the chips at her age. . . ."

* * *

The next afternoon PD finished his last phone call forty-five minutes before he was due at Scandia to buy dinner for a casting director, so he decided to drop in at the hospital.

It was toward the end of visiting hours. Hurrying down the corridor, he was surprised to see Hap emerge from room 1001. If he were in there again, PD decided, it must mean she was up to company. "So she's feeling better?" he asked.

Hap shook his head. His gray eyes were bloodshot with weariness, and thick, fair stubble showed on his jaw. "Jesus, PD, she's burning up. They've got restrainers on her because of the IVs, but she's too weak to move."

"What about the leg?"

"She made such a fuss that I convinced them to hold off on the amputation. What if it's the wrong decision?" Hap slumped in the chrome and tweed chair kept by the door. His usual calm had deserted him and he was struggling for composure. "How could I have let her keep on working?"

Sitting next to his cousin, PD said, "Stop blaming yourself. She gave you the go-ahead. Any director would've done the same."

Hap said nothing.

PD changed the subject. "Hap, what gives? You and Maxim put up your own money and work your butts off. And now, at the most crucial time for any movie, Maxim's away incommunicado and you hand over the final cut to another editor."

"George is a good editor."

"George isn't good, George is dynamite. But ever since you and Maxim began the project you've been saying that this is a new kind of film for Hollywood, and only you guys know how to make it."

"The studio wants a rush job. Right now I can't put in the time." Hap gnawed on his thumb knuckle.

PD's mouth folded shrewdly, and his active brain made a connection that he would have reached far, far earlier had it not been for those sly sexual confessions of Maxim's in Mendocino. *It's not Alyssia and Maxim, it's Alyssia and Hap.*

After a few seconds PD said, "Hap, this is in the nature of a warning. I ran into Barry and Uncle Desmond in the lobby. I think Uncle Desmond was telling Barry he ought to be here more. So I imagine he'll come up to tell you to be here less."

"Screw him," Hap said savagely.

"Only trying to help," PD said.

"This is Dad's first visit. Barry was here exactly two minutes yesterday. Uncle Tim and Aunt Clara haven't even phoned for information."

"I lit candles for her."

"Jesus, I didn't mean *you.* If you hadn't brought her in—"

The private nurse, one PD hadn't seen before, looked out with a pinched, plaintive expression. "Where's Miss del Mar's husband?"

Hap had jumped to his feet so abruptly that his chair fell. "Is she awake?"

"For the moment."

"I'm the one she wants to see," Hap said, barging by the nurse.

With a questioning look, she closed the door behind them.

PD walked amid other departing visitors. At the long windows, he paused to gaze broodingly at the night, his absent gaze fixed on lights glinting on the Hollywood Hills. *Hap and Alyssia,* he thought, and tried to figure how this new configuration affected him. He could no more control his dexterously agile mind than his heart rate. *You prick,* he told himself, and moved briskly toward the bank of elevators.

As he waited, one of the doors slid open and his uncle and cousin emerged.

From Barry's hunched shoulders and his nervous little smirk it was obvious that Uncle Desmond had been lambasting him.

PD greeted them and, since it seemed top priority businesswise to be in on what transpired, he gave himself permission to be tardy for his appointment. He hurried back down the corridor, keeping pace with his uncle.

Reaching room 1001, Desmond Cordiner fixed his glittery, dark eyes on PD. "I thought Hap was here."

"He went inside."

Desmond Cordiner gave Barry a sharp nod and Barry scuttled into the darkened hospital room.

After a full minute Hap emerged alone. "Hello, Dad," he said calmly.

"How is she?"

"Sleeping."

"Then she doesn't need company, does she?"

Hap stared levelly at his father. "Dad, just butt out."

"It's Barry's place to be in there."

"Dad, no more fucking us up," Hap said in a low, rumbling voice.

"So she told you."

"She should've in the first place. And I'm repeating—just butt out."

PD feared his uncle would explode. But instead, Desmond Cordiner removed his glasses, rubbing the bridge of his narrow, impressive nose. "If that's the way you feel, Hap, fine. But remember, from now on in unless we handle it right, the press'll be shredding both you and her."

Hap's stubborn, weary eyes remained on his father for a second more, then he turned and went back into the room.

"Uncle Desmond," PD said. "Not to worry about a scandal. This isn't the forties."

"Stop conciliating, you little agent shit," Desmond Cordiner snapped. "I know the goddamn decade, and I know what they're like in Podunk." Then he stared at Alyssia's door, frowning thoughtfully.

The following afternoon at visiting hours the family began showing up at the hospital. Barry was accompanied by both parents. Lily Zaffarano arrived with her elder daughter, who was married. Rosalynd Cordiner brought a huge gilt box of Godiva chocolates. Desmond Cordiner and Frank Zaffarano came in the evening after work. Beth dropped by. Other family members showed up. It seemed immaterial to these visitors that they couldn't get in the sickroom. They chatted with one another in the hall, repairing in twos and threes to the ground floor coffee shop.

The Magnum publicity department, though a skeleton of what it had been in earlier decades, generated enormous coverage for the illness. Hollywood correspondents and television crews crowded the hallways, conferring with any available family member, nurse, doctor or hospital employee. A woman from UPI put on a green uniform and wheeled a bucket into room 1001. When she removed a small Nikon from amid her cleaning equipment, the private nurse on that shift, a two-hundred-pound black woman, shoved the newshen bodily out the door. After that one of Magnum's security force sat stationed outside.

It was variously reported that Alyssia del Mar, the American who had made it big in France by baring her bosom, was dying, was recovering, that her leg had been amputated, that her leg was fine, that she was in a coma, that she was already reading scripts for a new film. The telegram sent by President and Mrs. Johnson, the air-delivered orchids from Saint-Simon's Paris greenhouse, the more conventionally delivered flowers from the Burtons, who did not know the invalid, and Ingrid Bergman, who had met her once, were reported on in detail. Only Joyce Haber mentioned that Harvard Cordiner, director of the patient's latest film, had access to her room, and that item was in conjunction with a story lauding Alyssia's pluck at continuing to film *Wandering On* despite a critical injury.

For a week the world kept up with Alyssia del Mar. On the seventh day, a press conference was called at Mount Sinai, and Alyssia's team of doctors announced that she was off the critical list, calling her condition guardedly grave. But whatever happened, she would keep the leg.

"Good morning," Alyssia said when Hap arrived at seven—he had wangled dispensation from the floor nurse to sneak up whenever.

"You're looking—"

"Almost human," Alyssia supplied. Her weak voice held a hint of humor.

"No, great," he said, glancing at the large, kindly, black nurse.

Nodding sagely, the nurse said, "If it's okay with you, Miss del Mar, I'll get me my wake-up coffee."

When they were alone in the flower-filled room, Hap buried his face in the pillow next to Alyssia's black hair, which was stringy. The clear liquid continued dripping into her veins, the monitors behind the bed moved in their customary computerized jogs and Hap Cordiner wept with relief.

28

As the ambulance drove up to the house, neighbors and a half dozen journalists waited on the sidewalk. Barry, currently domiciled in the Beverly Hills Hotel bungalow maintained by the Whitney-Charles Bank, emerged from the doorway—Desmond Cordiner had ordered him to be on hand to greet his wife. He trailed the gantry from the ambulance to the front door, a progress recorded by Nikons and shoulder-held television cameras.

The drab living room was exuberant with roses: miniature pink Cecil Brunners in water glasses, crimson American Beauties regal on their three-foot stems, big fragrant yellow roses in baskets, buds of white roses in ceramic holders. Although Alyssia no longer had on the cast and could walk a few steps, the attendants carefully transferred her to the couch. Juanita covered her with a pink cashmere afghan—having lost twelve pounds, Alyssia was perpetually cold. Barry wrote a check for the ambulance charges. After the attendants left, Juanita returned to the kitchen and Hap emerged, kissing Alyssia's forehead and sitting on the couch next to her.

The threesome waited in awkward silence while the immediate neighbors were being interviewed outside. The press cars drove off and onlookers straggled back to their houses.

"I'm on my way," Barry said. "Farewell."

"There's the door," Hap said.

"What kind of tone is that?" Barry retorted. "I'm not entangled with *your* wife."

"Just get the hell out," Hap said, rising to his feet.

Barry stalked out of the house.

Alyssia asked, "Aren't we going to be civilized?"

"Exceedingly civilized," Hap told her. "If he makes any more trouble, I'll strangle him in the most civilized way."

"More trouble? What trouble has he made?"

"It's quite a list. The booze. Relying on you to support him. Humiliating you with Whitney in Mendocino. Leaving you alone here when you were practically dead. Avoiding the hospital until Dad laid into him."

"He does the best he can," she said, annoyed at her defensive anger on Barry's behalf—and almost as irritated at Hap for rousing the hackles of her wifely loyalty. "It's not like you to bad-mouth anybody, Hap. And you know Barry—he means well, but he's just sort of weak. Things'll be better for him when he marries Whitney."

"Marry Whitney? I got the impression she avoided that kind of thing."

A whisper of her old jealousy—*Whitney and Hap disappearing nightly into their cottage at the Three Rock Inn*—brushed Alyssia. "He says she's taking him East to meet her parents."

Hap's jaw tightened. His anger, Alyssia was discovering, generally arose from a conviction that some injustice had been perpetrated.

She changed the subject. "The flowers are gorgeous." She touched a pink petal. "Who sent these?"

"PD," Hap said.

PD had ordered a stream of cologne and flower arrangements from the Helping Hand Gift Shop on the hospital's ground floor.

"He's been terrific," Alyssia said. "And the rest?"

"Me and Juanita."

At that moment Juanita came in with a bowl of fruit. "Mostly Hap," she said.

During their hospital vigil, Hap had formed a friendship with the reluctant Juanita. She had succumbed to his warmth when he pointed out that there was no point calling him Mr. Cordiner. *I know you're Alyssia's sister.*

"Thank you, both of you," Alyssia murmured.

After supper Hap carried Alyssia to the bedroom.

"Put me down, Hap. I'm supposed to walk."

"This is a special occasion," he said, depositing her on the double bed.

"Special? Mmm?"

He reddened. "Your first night home."

She smiled, still looking up at him.

"Juanita's making up the couch for me," he said.

He was of course running true to form. As a gentleman, he was leaving it up to her to indicate a readiness for sex. Longing to feel his comforting strength and warmth all night, yearning to wake up next to him, she was on the verge of saying: *We could sleep together, just sleep*. But then she decided that cuddling, though Barry's game, would be cruel and inhuman punishment for Hap. And sex was indeed contraindicated, not only because of her general weakness, but also because of the leg, which still ached deep in the marrow.

Alyssia recuperated with astonishing swiftness. After a week she was walking slow laps with Hap around the backyard. (When she ventured into the nearby streets, gaping children trailed after her and adults peered through windows.) Every day Hap managed to come up with a small gift to make her laugh—a windup plush bird that played "La Paloma," a tee shirt with a huge red heart over the left breast, a Peter Max poster. She regained her appetite with a vengeance: Hap brought home Uno bars and Snickers, chili dogs, donuts and Twinkies—all the denied luxuries of her childhood. By the end of September she had regained five pounds, and her health.

Those hot fall nights there was a tension between them, a near awkwardness. It was caused by the currents of sexual electricity in the air.

Alyssia's entire body ached for Hap. All she had to do, she knew, was stroke his hand or look at him in a meaningful way, and he would be in her double bed. She was totally unable to act out the gesture. By the bright daylight, her reticence seemed idiotic—wasn't Hap proving by word and deed how crazy he was about her? But darkness inevitably reminded her that he was the studio chieftain's son, and that she worked in the fields.

Riding on the coattails of Alyssia's cliffhanger recovery, Magnum's publicity department racked up a miraculous campaign for *Wandering On*. *CBS Evening News* bumped a story on Fellini for an interview with the Cordiner brothers, while the *New York Times* invited Whitney Charles,

Hollywood newcomer, to model styles that went with the *Wandering On* hippie mood. *Newsweek* devoted a double-page spread to the making of the film. Alyssia wasn't well enough to beat the drums, but a soapy article detailing her brush with death appeared in *TV Guide*.

Theater owners who previously had dismissed the film as uncommercial altered their booking arrangements. *Wandering On* would open in over a thousand houses on the fifteenth of October.

Early in the afternoon of the premiere a top hair stylist, a thin makeup woman and a volatile perfectionist of a wardrobe mistress arrived at the small house. These Magnum employees were still fussing over Alyssia at seven thirty when Maxim, like Hap in black tie, arrived in a stretch limousine. Juanita, who had refused Hap and Alyssia's persistently offered premiere tickets, set out huge pink shrimps. Maxim, new lines etched into his face, ignored the platter, prowling around the living room. "Alyssia," he called. "Let's get the show on the road."

"Relax, Maxim." Hap dipped a shrimp in red sauce.

The wardrobe woman finished sewing up the back seam of Alyssia's white satin gown—the zipper ruined the line, she had earlier announced. The hairdresser swirled his ultimate brushstroke, as he followed Alyssia out the door.

The limo sped northward to the Beverly Hills Hotel, where Barry and Whitney waited under the green and white overhang. Magnum personnel had been working on Whitney, too: various shades of blusher accentuated her good cheekbones; her upper eyelids gleamed with striations of greens and mauves. Taking out her mirror, she turned from side to side, narcissistically examining her face. Barry poured a large Scotch from the limo's bar—he was already loaded. Maxim's long fingers tapped on the satin stripe of his trousers. Alyssia and Hap sat unnaturally straight. The tension in the limousine had a name: preview nerves.

Traffic came to a near halt on Hollywood Boulevard. At Grauman's Chinese, spotlights cut fingers into the darkness, fans jammed the temporary stands and an eagerly shoving crowd jostled in the courtyard that was embedded with the hand and footprints of Hollywood immortals.

Hap emerged from the car first.

"Nobody!" shouted a woman with angry disappointment.

As Hap handed out Alyssia and Whitney, though, a murmur went up from the crowd: they must be somebodies, these elegant creatures: the blonde in sequined black, the brunette in white satin. Alyssia's skirt was slit high on the left side to quiet *Confidential*'s poisonous hints regarding a prosthesis and, aware of the night chill, she slung her white fox boa (on loan from Magnum) around her throat. She put her silver heels down hard, managing her high-voltage walk despite the pain darting up her left side all the way to her collarbone.

"It's Alyssia de Var," a fat woman cried. "God bless you, Alyssia!"

A wrinkled crone in a micromini shouted, "I prayed for you, Alyssia!"

The Newmans were getting out of their chauffeured car. The crowd roared. The *Wandering On* group hurried inside to the lobby, where Army Archerd, one eye cocked for Paul and Joanne, interviewed them.

When the lights went down and the curlicued M inside a cartouche, Magnum's logo, appeared on the screen, Alyssia crumpled in her seat, closing her eyes. For a full five minutes she let the hard rock of the musical score fill her. Then Hap grasped her hand. She looked up, meeting Diller's hugely magnified, haunting gaze.

29

PD stood squarely in front of Alyssia, a highball raised in one hand, the other hand pressed against the paneling, thus tucking her away in a corner of the Desmond Cordiners' crowded living room.

"From here on in, Alyssia," PD said, "they'll kill to have you."

"One movie," she said wryly.

"One smash performance," he retorted. "You can be the biggest there is. Bigger than anyone here."

PD threw a meaningful glance at the guests assembled in the impressive room. When Rosalynd Cordiner's father had built the house for himself in 1919, no expense had been spared: the fifteen-foot ceilings were molded with Tudor tracery, each windowpane was beveled, the parquet floors inlaid by European master craftsmen, the antique furnishings imported by Lord Duveen, a formality that was largely dissipated by the oversized, comfortable modern couches. The background befitted the gathering. Alyssia had already been congratulated by Veronique and Gregory Peck; the Fondas, Henry, Shirlee, Jane and Peter; by James Mason; by Audrey Hepburn; as well as by several scores of less famed but equally illustrious movie people. The invitations had been issued verbally by Hap, Maxim and their parents at the premiere, but the party was far from impromptu. A string trio played in the entry hall's minstrel gallery, a brace of bartenders plied a brisk trade, the waiters passed steaming hors d'oeuvres.

A honey-colored hand extended a silver tray. PD dipped a miniature potato blini in sour cream and Beluga caviar. Alyssia shook her head. She had not eaten since breakfast, but the emotional turbulence of being in this house made digestion seem a long-forgotten skill. Although she had been aware that Hap and Maxim's mother came from old wealth, a queasy sense of intimidation had settled around her the moment the limousine curved around majestic trees to the battlemented entrance bay, where blue-jacketed parkers rushed about taking the cars.

Wiping his mouth, PD said, "I predict it'll be Magnum's biggest moneymaker ever. The studio's struck a vein of gold. Alyssia, it was your performance that took their heads off."

"Hap's a marvelous director."

"He had you blazing in every damn frame. Hey, there he is. Hap! *Hap*."

Hap, holding a long-stemmed Baccarat champagne flute, made his way through the crowd, halted at every step by congratulations. Women in magnificent jewelry tiptoed to kiss him, important-looking men slapped his back and shook his hand.

When he reached them, Alyssia saw that his face radiated excitement, and he couldn't control his smiles. He hugged her tightly to his side, then turned to PD. "Hey, cousin, this isn't the time to grab my date to talk business."

"Relax, cousin. I am only offering the star my sincerest compliments."

"I'll just bet, cousin."

"Cousin, no shit. And also telling her that your directorial skill brings out her best."

"Thanks, cousin."

"You're welcome, cousin," PD said, raising his highball glass as in a toast. "Naturally, I *would* like to talk to her before the small-timers, Swifty or Wasserman"—both were present—"get in their pitch."

"Tomorrow, cousin, tomorrow," Hap said. He hugged Alyssia again.

Her insecurities settled into manageable proportions.

"PD, tomorrow's Sunday," she said. "Drop by for brunch around eleven thirty."

PD nodded, making a mental note to tell Beth—across the room chatting with a pair of Magnum writers—to come to the apartment an hour later than usual.

Hap affectionately punched PD's bicep. "See you then," he said.

He guided Alyssia through the living room. In the entry hall, directly under the enormous crystal chandelier that his grandfather had imported from a ducal estate in Scotland, Maxim held court to an implausibly handsome young group. One hand draped casually over the breast of the tall, exquisite redhead, he was obviously telling a joke, his expression alive with comical, sardonic grimaces. Once, at the premiere, Alyssia had glanced at him. Maxim Cordiner's set profile might have been carved onto Mount Rushmore.

In the dining room, the buffet had opened and a half dozen firstcomers were being helped by solicitous waiters, while in the game room, onlookers surrounded a tense poker game.

"Christ," Hap said.

"What's wrong?"

"That's Uncle Frank." Alyssia followed Hap's gaze to a short, gray-mustached man whose black tie had been loosened and whose cards were clutched close to his barrel chest. "He promised Aunt Lily he'd quit. Again."

"Then he's a gambler?"

"A compulsive one."

Hap drew her into a long lanai massed with green plants. Here, in the relative quiet, older guests sat chatting. A couple in street clothes was perched on one couch like drab city sparrows thrust into an aviary of brilliantly plumaged tropical birds.

It took Alyssia several beats to recognize Tim and Clara Cordiner. Her in-laws appeared several decades older than on the one occasion she had seen them seven years earlier.

They were talking to a regal woman in a long, midnight-blue gown. Even if Hap hadn't pointed her out at Grauman's Chinese, Alyssia would have known that Rosalynd Harvard Cordiner was his mother.

He had inherited that broad forehead, the gray eyes set deep in their sockets, and the large bone structure—features considerably more felicitous in a man than a woman. Rosalynd Cordiner was nearly six feet tall, and although not fat, she had the pillar shape and impressive bosom of a Wagnerian soprano. Her sole adornment was a long strand of pearls, luminously pink, as large as walnuts. *They're too huge to be real,* Alyssia thought, but continuing her glance at Hap's mother, she reversed her opinion. These were neither fake nor cultured and must have cost a minimum of five times what May Sue could have earned if she'd lived to old age.

Hap's mother, perhaps feeling Alyssia's gaze, looked up and saw her. For a moment the gray eyes grew remote, as if Hap had brought home a pup that wasn't housebroken.

Then Clara Cordiner turned and saw Alyssia. The mournful lips tensed, and a thin hand clutched at the brown wool over her sunken chest.

Tim was staring at them, too, his face mottling with red.

Alyssia stepped backward, but Hap's stubborn clasp drew her toward the couch. Clara got jerkily to her feet, moving automaton-like to the sliding glass window, pretending to stare down at the brightly lit tennis court.

"Hello, Uncle Tim," Hap said in a controlled voice. "I must've missed you and Aunt Clara at the Chinese."

"We weren't there." Tim was standing, a large man with

a greenish-gray plaid jacket open to show a pendulant stomach. "It goes without saying that we're dying to see Barry's movie. But his home situation has been very hard on your aunt. Frankly, it disturbs the hell out of me, too. We're only here because we couldn't believe *she* would have the nerve to come." He glared at Alyssia.

That awful trembling of her hospital stint overcame her. Impelled to cover up her weakness, she said brightly, "But Mr. Cordiner, surely Barry's passed on the word. We're separated."

"From the beginning we knew as soon as you'd gotten all the juice you could from his connections, you'd drop him."

"Uncle Tim, you've had a few too many," Hap said in a clenched polite tone.

"You're acting like a dope, Hap, but I can buy that. At your age it's understandable, being a total ass."

"It appears to be a family condition regardless of age," Hap said in the same courteous tone.

Tim's face darkened to a more dangerous red. Rosalynd rested her large, well-proportioned hand on the sleeve of her brother-in-law's jacket. Her adeptness at sweeping unfortunate situations under the rug was as famous in Hollywood as her husband's unpredictable swings of business tactics.

"Tim, dear, they're serving the buffet. Why don't you take Clara in." While not in the least condescending, she somehow managed to give the impression of a duchess jollying along a grumpy retainer.

Tim glanced uncertainly at his rich sister-in-law.

Rosalynd gave him an encouraging smile. "I especially asked Milton to make that veal you're so fond of."

Tim joined Clara, and the couple stood whispering with their backs to Alyssia.

Rosalynd took a handkerchief from her gold minaudière, wiping a palette of lipstick shades from Hap's jaw and cheeks. "Dear, I can't tell you how proud I am of you and Maxim. I didn't understand everything tonight, but the film was unusual, and exceptionally fine."

"I'm glad you liked it, Mother." He held Alyssia tighter. "Mother, this is Alyssia. Alyssia, my mother, Rosalynd Cordiner."

"I'm very pleased to meet you, dear. You were most convincing."

"Thank you, Mrs. Cordiner," Alyssia said. "And I want you to know how much I appreciated your chocolates."

"Chocolates?" Rosalynd Cordiner looked bemused—and remote.

"When I was in the hospital, that huge box of Godiva. I'm a chocolate freak, and I wolfed them all." A white lie. She had been too ill then to even sip water.

"Oh yes." Rosalynd touched her pearls. "They wouldn't let me in, but then probably it wasn't the best time for you to meet Barry's family."

"Mother," Hap said, "Barry's left Alyssia."

"Yes, of course."

"And I've explained to you and Dad how I feel about Alyssia."

"Of course you did, dear." She patted his cheek again. "Alyssia, it was delightful meeting you. Now if you'll excuse me, I must tell our guests that the buffet's open."

She proceeded regally into the hall, where she paused to talk to Barry and Whitney. Barry's face was lax, and Alyssia knew from long experience that within the next ten minutes he would find someplace to sit, then promptly fall asleep—pass out would be a more accurate term.

Tim turned, looking at her. The venom in that glance!

She felt herself on the brink of passing out. "Hap, where's a bathroom?" she murmured.

"First door to the left of the front door."

Mercifully the powder room was free. Pressing the lock, she sank onto the velvet bench. The reflection in the vanity's triple-paneled mirrors showed a tawdrily made up brunette in a tight satin dress that exposed too much bosom. *Cruddy, cruddy,* she thought, bending her face in her hands to weep in great rasping sobs.

The bronze door handle was tried several times, but she didn't notice. She was attempting to do the therapeutic breathing exercises that she used to calm herself when anxious hyperventilation struck her on the set. Finally she regained control, but immediately visualized the remoteness in Hap's mother's gray eyes—crueler by far that chill than Tim and Clara's overt loathing—and her weeping began afresh.

Knocks barraged against the door. "Are you spending the night in there?" snarled a masculine voice.

Alyssia picked up a sharp-edged bottle from the vanity. She dug the pointed stopper into her palm. As the blood flowed, her hysteria faded. Wrapping a linen guest towel around the wound, she Kleenexed away muddy trails of eye makeup.

Her dress felt oddly loose. Turning, she saw in the mirrors that her crying jag had pulled apart the wardrobe mistress's temporary stitchery. White satin gaped, exposing her sumptuously curved body from the small of her back to her naked buttocks.

There's no way I can sew it up by myself.

More hammering. "Hey, have a heart!"

Alyssia edged out. A heavily wrinkled man darted in.

The buffet line now extended around the hall, and since the wraps were hung in a deep alcove directly across from the powder room, there was no way to retrieve her borrowed white fox. Forming a smile, keeping her back to the wall, she slipped toward the front door.

She sidled down the marble steps, positioning herself so that the parking attendants couldn't see her back. The limo drove up. She heard more stitches go as she maneuvered into the rear seat.

Back in the shabby little bungalow, the TV blared. Juanita, wearing her old chenille robe, a box of Cheez-Its on her lap, sat with her chair drawn up to the set. The couch was already made up for Hap.

"What a night!" Juanita cried. "You've been on every channel." Then she glanced around. "Where's Hap?"

"They're having a monstrous party at his parents'. And I met with an accident. . . ." Her intent to play it light withered. Turning to show the damage, she began to cry again.

Juanita gathered her in an embrace that smelled of Tabu cologne, cheese and comfortingly familiar perspiration. "Shh, baby, shh."

"I wanted to die, just like when . . . I was little and had to . . . pee in . . . in the fields. . . ."

"Oh, Alice, that's over."

"Never. . . ."

"You're famous, a real movie star."

"I'm a . . . nobody . . . and he . . . Nita, you should see that mansion."

The screen flickered with a black-haired actress smiling provocatively.

A feminine voice-over intoned, "Alyssia del Mar, who nearly lost her leg because she refused to quit, found that it was all worthwhile tonight. The plucky actress emerged from the premiere of *Wandering On* as Hollywood's newest star. Alyssia del Mar's first performance in an American film is the stuff Oscars are made of. . . ."

The dulcet televised voice was drowned out by Alice Hollister's desolate weeping.

She was in bed, still crying erratically, when a car pulled into the narrow drive. It was well after three, and by now her rib cage ached while her throat was raw and clogged. When her door opened, she blinked in surprise. Hap never came in her room after dark.

"Why did you leave without me?" he asked in a low, restrained voice.

Aware she should make a jokey excuse about her dress, she said instead, "I was tired."

"So you just came home?"

"It's not a criminal act."

"No, just a thoughtless one."

"I'm terribly sorry."

"Yes, you certainly sound it. I can understand that you were suddenly felled with weariness, but couldn't you have stayed awake long enough to find me? We could have left together."

"You and Maxim were the guests of honor."

"Odd," he said. "I always thought you were the bravest person I'd ever met. But put you up against a pair of losers like Uncle Tim and Aunt Clara and you run."

"Oh, leave me alone."

"I have been, dutifully."

"So that's the problem." Her raw throat tightened, but the actress in her got the words out easily. "Well, there's no commitment. You're free to find whatever you want, wherever," she said, her skin prickling with shame.

He stared a fraction longer, then quietly closed the door.

She could hear him in the bathroom, the whir of the

Water Pik, the flush of the toilet. She began weeping again, silencing the sobs against her pillow.

"Alyssia?" This time she didn't hear the door open, and he didn't turn on the light. "You asleep?"

"No. . . ."

"You're crying, aren't you?"

"So what."

He got on top of the covers. He was not touching her, but she could feel his warmth.

"I kept looking for you, asking," he said. "Finally PD said he'd seen you leave—the parkers told me you'd gone home. I stayed until the bitter end, pretending to have a blast. But I was positive you'd taken off."

"Taken off?"

"Like when you went to France. I still have nightmares."

"My dress ripped," she mumbled.

"What?"

"That's why I left. Where Minnie sewed me up, the seam split. I couldn't fix it."

"So that's why you couldn't come find me?" The mattress shook. "First you have me crying, then laughing."

"Were you crying, too?"

"I'm not as secure as you seem to think I am."

She was stroking his arm. Her fingers began to tremble. "Come under the blankets," she whispered.

"You're sure it's okay?" He was whispering, too.

"I've wanted to for weeks."

"Then. . . ?"

"I'm far more insecure than you seem to think I am."

He pulled back the covers. At first he put his arms around her, holding her gently, as if she were friable, but when she pressed against him, shaking as she caressed his shoulders, the deep indentation of his spine, the hardness of his butt, his arms tightened, strong and demanding.

"Oh, God," he whispered hoarsely. "More than six years . . . six long, lonely years."

30

They brunched on Juanita's tantalizingly spiced *huevos rancheros,* Hap and Alyssia on the couch, PD cross-legged in front of the coffee table, Sunday papers strewing the rug around them.

Alyssia was concluding her lighthearted explanation of her previous night's hasty exit because of a split seam.

"You were bare-assed?" PD asked, chortling loudly. "Alyssia del Mar, that boundlessly talented star, bare-assed?" He reached for a section of the *Times.*

Hap and Alyssia both groaned.

"Not *again,*" Hap said.

"You can never get enough of a good thing," PD retorted, his chest expanding under his navy French-knit shirt as he drew breath to read. "'It is a rare book or film that can capture the spirit of an entire generation, but *Wandering On* does exactly that. Its youthful director and producer, sons of Desmond Cordiner, the head of Magnum Pictures, are definitely the best and brightest of the new Hollywood. Working on a shoestring budget of $350,000, they have put the old Hollywood to shame. No film this corrosively honest, no film of this political persuasion, could have been made under the timidly stodgy aegis of the studio system. Yet, for all their antiestablishment frankness, the Cordiner brothers never forget that the first duty of any film is to entertain. Harvard Cordiner, making his directorial debut, gets the jumpy edginess, the manners and mores of today's youth so perfectly that one feels as if one is eavesdropping. By some sleight of magic he also manages to make credible the often hilarious yet ultimately tragic screenplay by another family member, Barry Cordiner. Diller Roberts, the talented actor who died recently in a tragic automobile accident, gives a brash yet haunting performance as Duke, the hippie wanderer.

But it is Alyssia del Mar who endows the film with its heart and humanity. Miss del Mar's boundless talents have hitherto been wasted playing dumb American broads in European films. The actress combines the breathtaking raven-tressed, sapphire-eyed beauty of a young Elizabeth Taylor with the delightfully comedic sexiness of Marilyn Monroe, but her sizzling charm is uniquely her own. Take note of October 15, 1966. On that date a star was born and her name is Alyssia del Mar.'" PD looked up. "In case you don't know it, Alyssia, you don't often see that kind of rave."

"Finish your eggs," she told him, blushing. "Nothing's more fickle than luck."

"You call that performance luck?" Hap asked. Pulling her closer, he nuzzled his unshaven cheek against her smooth one.

Alyssia's glow deepened and she kissed his nose.

In the hospital PD had seen how hung up the couple were on each other, but he had never seen them display such open affection. They seemed unable to stop touching.

Still holding Alyssia close, Hap grinned at PD. "Now she's softened up, PD. It's the right time for your pitch."

PD set down his empty plate. "I'm the wrong agent for you, Alyssia," he said somberly.

"What?" she exclaimed. "That's not how you were talking last night."

"I hadn't had time to think it through," PD replied. "Alyssia, you're hot, hot as they come. We're talking a major career. You're entering uncharted waters, so let me give you some input. The new trend is for the big boys to package talent—nowadays often the script, the director, the stars, all come from the same agency. No way I can compete with that." He paused. "Alyssia, if I were you—"

"Thank God you're not," Alyssia interrupted. "If you were, who'd have saved my life by racing me to the hospital?"

Juanita brought in the coffee tray, setting it in front of Alyssia. PD waited until she had gathered up the plates and returned to the kitchen before speaking again.

"Being grateful," he said, "is an entirely different thing from choosing representation."

"Aren't you a good agent?" She handed him his coffee.

"Thanks," he said as he took the cup. "I'm good, very—I do battle for my clients. But I'm still in the minors."

"A big agency'd make me uncomfortable," she said, pouring Hap's coffee. "Do I come to your office to sign papers or what?"

"I've never required a contract," he said. Why should he? His elderly, spritely clients would never depart his hard-driving representation. "A handshake does it."

"Then . . ." She extended her hand.

"This wouldn't be meaningful to me if you're doing it out of obligation."

"Will you quit playing hard to get." Alyssia wiggled her fingers. "Shake."

PD gripped her hand.

Alyssia smiled. "Finally I have an agent."

"And that means, lady, from here on in you come to me with your business problems. Never listen to the big bozo here."

"Now it's the bozo's turn, PD," Hap said. "Tell me how you're going to guide *my* career."

"With your contacts you don't need me."

"I've never been great on making deals. Besides, with Alyssia and me you have a minipackage. Star plus a one-shot director."

"It'd arouse a certain interest," PD said.

The cousins grinned and shook hands.

Spooning sugar into his coffee, PD made an inward prayer of gratitude to the blue-robed Virgin at Good Shepherd. His intense campaign had paid off, and he had nailed them both.

That same week Barry signed with Talent Management Corporation, and was handed over to a pompous young man in the literary department. Whitney also signed with TMC: she explained to Barry it was due to her family connections that Martin Naderman, TMC's founder, had taken her directly under his wing.

The under-thirty crowd waited in long lines for every performance of *Wandering On,* and within three weeks an impressive $33,700,000 had been pushed through the box-office grates of houses showing the film. The gross was unprecedented for a Magnum release.

Rio Garrison swept into the executive dining room for a celebratory lunch. Before taking her late husband's chair at the head of the oval table, she embraced Desmond Cordiner in full view of his minions, several of whom had been angling for his job.

"Desmond, you genius! Not even Art ever brought in a hit that cost so little." Her dark eyes moistened emotionally. "He must be looking down and applauding."

And her lover chimed in, "So the winning team's all in the family, ehh, Cordiner? What's the next project?"

"PD, be at the office at three this afternoon," Desmond Cordiner snapped over the phone.

PD exulted that he hadn't been forced to call his uncle. "Uncle Desmond, let me see if I can juggle my appointments—"

"I said three."

PD arrived a few minutes early, kibbitzing away the time with the younger of his uncle's two secretaries, a girl with spectacular legs whom PD had taken to lunch several times at the nearby Brown Derby on Vine Street.

At three promptly, the buzzer sounded.

His uncle remained behind the altarlike desk. Not inviting PD to sit, he snapped, "What's this crap I read in Joyce Haber about Alyssia working over at Fox?"

The moisture already trickling beneath his shirt, PD said, "She's doing that big-budget Western of theirs and—"

"Get her out of it."

"Out of it? Uncle Desmond, I've worked like a dog on the deal. I've got Fox up to one eighty plus two points of the gross, which I don't have to tell you is pretty damn good. Naturally I'd have come to you first, but you gave no indication that Magnum had interest in Alyssia and I hate to take advantage of the relationship—"

"Quit stinking up my office with pigfart," Desmond Cordiner snapped. "I'll give her two hundred and two points."

"Oh? Then you have a project with her in mind?"

"The Colman McCarthy best-seller I bought last year."

"*The One Mary*, mmm . . . a thriller. Weren't you talking to Julie Christie?"

"She's too British."

PD sat in one of the deep leather chairs. "Uncle Desmond, I'll lay it on the line. Fox also wants Hap. They have a project aimed at the youth market and they've offered him a hundred plus a point and a half."

"They did? He never told me."

"You know Hap—too much integrity for his own good. He thinks *you*'d think he was pressuring Magnum for that kind of deal."

"They won't be working together at Fox."

"Would they be here?"

"Of course. Him, Alyssia and Maxim."

"I don't handle Maxim so I can't answer for him. But . . . that two and two for Alyssia is firm?"

"You heard me."

"And what about Hap?"

"One ten and a point and a half."

"He'd be in on the other film from the beginning. Casting and—"

"One twenty-five, and that's my limit."

"Hap'd never sign unless he has approval of the final cut."

"*No final cut!*" his uncle thundered.

"Uncle Desmond, we have here a delicate situation—" He bit off his words.

Desmond Cordiner had rested both arms on the desk and was leaning his head into them. His shoulders heaved and odd muffled snorts escaped from him. Worried about the high incidence of coronaries among elderly, top-of-the-ladder executives, PD jumped up, leaning across the huge desk. "Uncle Desmond, are you okay? Let me pour you some water."

His uncle looked up. PD saw that he was racked with uncontrollable laughter. Desmond Cordiner was nightmarishly unpredictable, and PD now worried that this entire negotiation had been a wild hoax.

Finally Desmond Cordiner's guffaws calmed. "Hap gets the final cut," he said, wiping his eyes. "To be worked over by my own sister's kid, a snotnose."

"I'm twenty-eight."

"You've still got plenty to learn, frotz. You should've

played me along a bit more. I'd have upped Alyssia to two fifty and Hap to one fifty."

"I'll have to remember not to jump the gun," PD said.

He left the offices sedately. Once alone in the corridor, though, he permitted his highly polished black shoes to do a wild little tap dance. For the price of three Cobb salads at the Brown Derby, he had learned from the secretary with the great legs that Desmond Cordiner refused to go any higher than two hundred thousand for Julie Christie and one twenty-five for the top-ranked director, Bill Kenelworth. And he'd gotten that same amount *plus* a percentage of the gross.

Whistling, he drove to the writers' building, which housed the story department. Beth was in conference, so he waited for her amid the neatly ranged galleys, books and manuscript boxes. His exhilaration drained as he considered how wondrously simple it would be if money were the sole obstacle that prevented him from making those serene evenings of theirs permanent.

31

Maxim had holed up on Izumel, a remote little Mexican island unconnected to the world by telephone lines. Desmond Cordiner dispatched a three-page telegram that laid out generous terms for his son to act as producer on *The One Mary*. Maxim replied with a terse sentence: BUSY ON MY OWN PROJECT.

A promising young studio line producer was assigned to *The One Mary*, and principal shooting began on February 17, ending on April 3.

Before Hap started the editing, and Alyssia her next film, they vacationed for a week in a tile-roofed bungalow high above La Jolla's rocky beach. They never went into the pretty resort town. They made love between sheets that smelled of sea-must, they made love in front of the fireplace, they made love on the sunlit walled patio with the faraway roar of the Pacific in their ears.

Monday night as they drove the freeway back to Los Angeles, Alyssia drifted into a delicious, languorous silence.

Hap reached for her hand. "Want me to get you a lawyer?" he asked.

Her spine straightened. "Lawyer?"

"You'll need one for the divorce."

It was the first time either of them had brought up the subject of legalizing her separation from Barry. Turning, she gazed at the ghostly white surf. Partings of any kind, even a morning goodbye, were difficult for her. It was a profound form of loyalty stemming from multiple causes—her peripatetic childhood, her mother's death, her lack of family. And to sever any relationship, no matter how tenuous, was a near impossibility for her.

"First, I'll get together with Barry and discuss it with him," she temporized.

The following morning thick gray clouds sagged, a match for her mood. After Hap went off to a Magnum editing room, she steeled herself for nearly an hour before she could dial the Beverly Hills Hotel. A switchboard operator informed her that Mr. Cordiner was no longer a guest, but could be reached at Columbia Pictures, giving the number.

Mercifully, Barry didn't inquire why she was calling after all these months, but agreed to meet for lunch at Musso & Frank's, in Hollywood, which she suggested because it was geographically convenient for them both, and because she knew the choice would please Barry—the restaurant was renowned as a hangout for writers.

Being nervous, she was late, but Barry arrived even later. The booths were starting to empty out by the time he got there.

"Story conference ran over," he explained, lifting his hand for their waiter. "Whitney's sorry, but she couldn't make it."

Alyssia said nothing. With personal matters foremost in her mind, she hadn't considered Whitney might be present. The waiter was looking at her. She ordered a Coke.

"And I'll have a Dewar's on the rocks," Barry said. "Make that a double."

Unable to get bluntly to the point, she asked about his job at Columbia.

"A vapid romance. I'm the third writer," he said, downing his Scotch. "They're delighted with my structure."

By the time they got their steak sandwiches, though, he was sloshed enough to admit that all was not cozy at Columbia. He was saddled with a producer who knew every one of the million plots ever to go before a camera—and expected him, Barry, to come up with a fresh twist.

His assiduous invocations of Whitney plus his ejection from the Whitney-Charles bungalow at the Beverly Hills Hotel drew Alyssia to an inescapable conclusion. Not only was he having professional difficulties, he was also in a deep hole personally. Pitying him, she longed to clasp his hand in their old, comradely way.

She found herself unable to bring up her reason for inviting him to lunch.

Rain was falling in hard, silvery lines when they left the restaurant.

"We ought to do this more often," he said in the stiff tone he used when most sincere. "I've missed you."

And before she could reply, he darted across Hollywood Boulevard's gold-starred pavement, weaving a bit after his shoe splashed in the running gutter. She watched him rush across the street before the light changed, a tall, harried, prematurely balding man with a slight paunch.

When she got home, Hap was stretched on the couch, scraps of paper covering his broad chest.

"You're back early," she said.

"I wanted to make sense of these notes I jotted down in the editing room," he said. "Did you and Barry get things settled?"

She kicked off her black patent pumps: the soles were wet through.

"Alyssia?"

She sighed. "As soon as he sat down, I could smell the liquor. He never used to drink in the morning. And it was always wine. Today it was Scotch. He kept ordering doubles. I hope he made it back to the studio okay."

Hap hadn't shifted from his recumbent position. "What about the divorce?" he asked.

"He's so . . . I don't know. Pathetic. They're taking his guts out at Columbia. He kept dragging Whitney into every remark, as if he were rubbing a rabbit's foot. He's not at the hotel anymore, so things can't be too great between them."

"Am I right? Divorce was never mentioned?"

She sighed again. "At the moment he has enough problems."

Hap got up abruptly, scraps of paper scattering on the rug as he came over to her. In her stockinged feet, she felt like an insignificant dwarf.

"Barry's problems," he said in a low, contained voice, "are no longer your problems."

They had not fought since the night of the *Wandering On* premiere. Even during those frantic final days of shooting *The One Mary,* when all tempers were frayed, they had remained kind to each other.

"He's between a rock and a hard place!" she snapped. "And you're not even trying to understand!"

Hap squatted to retrieve his scraps of paper.

"Stop being the perfect gentleman—yell at me!" She bent, helping him to gather the notes. After a few moments, she asked quietly, "Would *you* kick him when he's down?"

Hap shook his head. "Nope. But that doesn't stop me from being jealous as hell of him."

The banal concept of masculine jealousy had never occurred to her before for one simple reason: she held Hap in too high esteem, herself in too low. How could anyone from his background, with his looks, his talent, be jealous of *her*?

"It won't be for long," she said. "Soon he'll find another girl, a more understanding producer."

Kneeling, he kissed her lightly. "You have any idea how much I want us to be married, to have children?"

"I do, because I feel exactly the same," she said, pressing her cheek against his.

At Hap's suggestion, she registered with a Beverly Hills real estate broker, and within a couple of weeks they leased an old Mediterranean house whose grounds sprawled across three acres in Laurel Canyon. Beyond the cracked, Olympic-sized swimming pool stood a three-room guesthouse for Juanita, and behind that, chaparral-covered hillside.

The exploitation press devoted much space to the family intertwinings of Alyssia del Mar and Hap Cordiner as well as their housekeeping arrangements, but the country's moral climate had altered drastically in this, the sixties, and the publicity had no negative effects on their careers.

In their rambling, isolated old house, they found something remarkably akin to paradise.

32

A little after eleven on the hazily sunlit morning of September 20, 1969, PD found himself once again taking in the view. Though he had already been in his new offices three weeks, he couldn't prevent himself from sneaking glances at the plate glass wall that gave him the whole goddamn smoggy Los Angeles basin. Everything about his new quarters—even the astronomical rent—pleased him. The thick beige carpet, the teak paneling, the spacious reception room presided over by Lana Denton, his stunning black secretary, the two smaller offices occupied by a bright and bearded agent of amorphous sexual preferences and by his original secretary, a plump blonde who now took competent if not inspired charge of the geriatric clients.

PD himself was constantly on the go. Alyssia's name, and Hap's, had enlisted several stars, two of whom had their own long-running series. The PD Zaffarano Agency was no longer a joke in the Industry. Though PD's extravagances prevented him from being completely solvent, his financial prospects were auspicious.

"Mr. Zaffarano." Lana's disembodied voice sprang

from the intercom. "Mr. Cordiner's here—Mr. Barry Cordiner."

"Ask him to take a seat, Lana," PD said. "I'm tied up right now."

It seemed to him that the gaze from Beth's black and white photograph in its oval sterling frame was reproaching him, but he brushed off his guilt about stalling his fiancée's twin. Barry was fifteen minutes late, and PD, positive his cousin wanted representation, knew it to be a tactical error to start off on the wrong foot with a floundering TV writer.

After that rewrite job at Columbia, Barry had been unable to find work on another feature. Television also had proved inhospitable. He sold sporadically to a couple of low-rated detective series.

Momentarily PD's attention remained fixed on Beth's portrait.

When they had announced their engagement, his parents had put up the anticipated squawks, which echoed his own initial reluctance. Constantly reiterating that they adored Bethie, that she was like one of their own girls, Lily and Frank Zaffarano never lost an opportunity to remind PD of what he knew far too well; that such a marriage was not only invalid in the eyes of the Church, but also incestuous.

Uncle Tim and Aunt Clara had not given their blessings either. Indeed, Aunt Clara had gone around looking sallow for months. Not because of the cousin angle, but because he could not bring himself to promise that the kids would be reared Jewish.

He looked away from his fiancée's picture, opening *Variety* to the page with the review of *Ace of Clubs,* Alyssia and Hap's latest effort. In the three years since *The One Mary,* Hap had made four movies, Alyssia starring in them all. (Under PD's aegis, she had also worked with other topflight directors: Lean, Nichols and Penn.) The review ended, "*Ace of Clubs* should be another solid hit for the team of del Mar and Cordiner."

After a half hour, he buzzed Lana, telling her to send Barry in.

Barry's paunch had expanded, and PD, who pumped iron at the Beverly Hills Health Club, sucked in his well-muscled gut with a sense of superiority. As he gave his cousin a warm hug, all his boyhood affection surfaced.

"Sorry about the delay," he said. "Well, how goes it with the writing?"

Barry blinked rapidly. "My work's precisely what I wanted to discuss with you."

"Any advice I can give, I'll be happy to. But, Barry, it's a rule of mine never to step on another agency's toes."

"TCM has quagmires and quicksands, eddies and currents," Barry said. "You know . . . the Whitney and Naderman situation."

PD didn't comment. In 1967 Martin Naderman, head of TCM, had left his wife to live with Whitney Charles in Malibu. Within six months, Whitney had lost interest in a film career—and Naderman. In the ensuing years Naderman had hooked up with a succession of long-legged, libidinous beauties. But Barry, poor SOB, was still vociferously blaming his being Whitney's previous lover for the neglect with which TCM routinely treated minor clients. "What about your contract there?"

"It expired the first of the month." Barry leaned forward. "I need to sink my teeth into another feature."

"Barry, that's not exactly a lead-pipe cinch. You're a TV writer."

"*Wandering On*—"

"That was *years* ago."

"The film was Magnum's biggest box-office smash, and my script earned the highest critical accolades."

"Barry, any writer would give his left testicle to have that particular credit. But you're my cousin, my *paisan,* my future brother-in-law, my friend, so I can't bullshit you. The only thing the producers want to know is what you've done lately." He spoke with difficult sincerity, then added, "Listen, I've got a terrific in at *Ironside*."

"*Ironside!* Exactly the genre of garbage I want to get away from!"

A flush showed on PD's tanned cheeks, but he said easily, "Their ratings are fabulous, and that's the name of the game."

The half hour in the waiting room had subdued Barry. "Okay, go ahead," he muttered. "But I *do* have several excellent concepts for a feature."

"Send outlines." PD glanced at his watch and rose: he had a one o'clock lunch with Lee Rich of Lorimar. "Come on, Barry, let's talk on the way down to the garage."

The uniformed attendant brought Barry's dusty Dodge, then PD's new Coupe de Ville. On the way to the Lorimar offices in the Valley, PD figured to whom he could present Barry's feature ideas. He was constitutionally incapable of missing a bet for a client.

It was well after three when PD arrived back at the office. Lana was saying into the phone, "—still out, Mrs. Zaffarano, but I'll tell him the minute— Oh. He just walked in. Mr. Zaffarano, your mother's on line three. She called a few minutes ago. It's urgent."

Visions of disaster dancing in his head, PD ran into his office. "Mom? What's wrong?"

She blurted something about his father, but she was weeping too hard for him to make out anything more. His mother was not a weeper. She had not even wept when he broke the news of his engagement.

"Mom, calm down," he said. "Are you home?"

"Yes . . ."

He went weak with relief: any dire illness or accident to near and dear, and she'd be at a hospital. "Hang in there, Mom. I'll be right over."

With a hasty command to Lana to cancel his afternoon appointments, he rushed back to the elevator and was in the underground parking before his car was put away.

33

Lily Cordiner Zaffarano, a handsome woman in her early fifties, normally presented an immaculate appearance. In a town full of girl-sized matrons, she was maturely plump, and her innate practicality informed her that she therefore must put forth more effort. A masseuse arrived with a folding table at the house every Monday, Lily had standings twice a week for facials and shampoos, and when it came to clothes, her one minor deviation from prudent chic was to always wear some variation of the purple tones. Frank Zaffarano rewarded these wifely efforts with uxorious fidelity, no minor thing in Hollywood.

As PD jerked to a halt in front of the big Colonial house on Beverly Drive, his mother rushed onto the pillared portico, her hair and clothing disheveled.

The apparition was so out of character that he goggled.

"Quick!" she shrilled. "Get inside!"

Slamming and locking the front door after them, Lily leaned against the wood, panting.

PD glanced around to ascertain that neither of the maids was present to witness his mother's descent into apparent madness. The sole movement came from sunlight flickering on the rock crystal chandelier. They were, thank God, alone.

"Mom—what's all the excitement?"

Breathing in those animal gasps, Lily stared mutely at him.

"Come on, Mom, let's go in the den."

She didn't move.

Suddenly it occurred to PD that maybe his father was dead. "Mom, is Dad . . . is he okay?"

"For now. . . ." Her mouth pulling frantically, Lily burst into tears.

Conquering his filial compunctions, PD slapped his palm hard across both her cheeks. Tears continued flowing down the smudged, reddening marks of his slap, but the hysterical gasping ceased.

"Mom," he said gently. "Hey . . . what gives?"

"This came while I was getting . . . dressed."

He realized her left hand was crumpling a piece of paper. Taking it from her grip, he straightened the slick, photocopied page.

It was a copy of an IOU written in his father's hand. *Frank Zaffarano promises to pay the sum of $425,000 to Robert Lang on or before September 14, 1969.* Over the photocopy, in different writing, was pencil-slashed: SIX DAYS OVERDUE.

"Robert Lang is Bart Lanzoni's son," she said.

PD nodded. Bartolomeo (Bart) Lanzoni and Francesco

(Frank) Zaffarano, *compaesani* from the same impoverished hilltop town in Sicily, had been closest friends. Frank had gone around red-eyed for weeks after Bartolomeo had died of multiple myeloma. Robert Lang (PD did not know at what point the name had been anglicized) had inherited his father's interests, the most public being the Fabulador Hotel in Las Vegas, where Barry and Alyssia had had their wedding breakfast almost exactly a decade ago.

Though PD had never met Robert Lang, he had been close enough to Bartolomeo Lanzoni to call him Uncle Bart, and the old guy had slipped him a folded five-dollar bill at every meeting. How could a round-faced old sweetie like him have a son who put the screws to people?

Then PD reminded himself that Uncle Bart was no saint either, but part of the New Jersey bunch who had migrated to Nevada after World War II.

"Let's go sit down," PD said, putting his arm around his mother's plump shoulders, leading her into the den. Lily sat on one of the leather game chairs and buttoned her lavender blouse.

"Have you talked to Dad?" PD asked.

"He's on location today, he won't be back until late." Lily was talking with her usual sensible coherency. "PD, there's no way we can pay it."

"How much *can* you pay?"

"Nothing."

"What do you mean, nothing? Mom, this is me. Your son, PD. I've hit you for a loan often enough to know you've got money stashed in every bank in Beverly Hills."

Lily shook her head. "There's nothing left in any of the accounts. Two weeks ago I drew out everything to give your father. He told me he needed it to pay Robert Lang off or else something dreadful would happen."

"Lang threatened to *kill* Dad?"

"Or me, or you, or Annette or Deirdre." Lily's voice sank. "Or even Jeffie." Jeffrey Fitzpatrick, Annette's five-month-old, the first, the only, the adored grandchild of the Cordiner clan.

"How much did you hand over to Dad?"

"Two hundred and twenty-three thousand and forty dollars. He lied to me and said it'd cover his marker, and then went to Vegas for the night. To pay Robert Lang, he said. But he must have tried to get the full amount and lost it all." She spoke without recrimination.

PD stared for a long, bitter moment at the copy of the IOU, thinking of the immense salaries his father had earned for many years, the bonuses, the stock options, the Newport Beach house which had been sold at a substantial profit.

"Why was it addressed to you?" he asked.

"That's the worst part. . . ." Her ample bosom rose and fell in a gasp, but she said with reasonable calm, "I was getting ready to go to a Mary's Guild tea and Dilly brought up my mail. The envelope only had my name."

"You mean no address, no postmark?"

"Mrs. Lily Zaffarano—nothing else."

"Where is it, the envelope?"

"I must've left it in the dressing room."

PD followed her up the curving staircase and through the big airy bedroom that she shared with his father. She handed him a thin white envelope across which MRS. LILY ZAFFARANO was penciled in huge letters.

"Somebody must have dropped it in your mail slot."

"That's what's so terrifying. Don't you see, PD? They're watching the house."

"Jesus," he whispered, wondering why this hadn't occurred to him immediately.

Moving to stand well back from a window, he looked out at the large, comfortable houses and manicured green gardens that were the choicest of Beverly Hills real estate. A peaceful, nostalgically familiar scene. There were no pedestrians, and the Jag and the Mercedes across the street were as empty as his Cadillac.

Yet, a half hour ago, immediately before or after the mail delivery, this envelope had been dropped in the mail slot by some hood who knew the neighborhood intimately.

Lily was twisting her wedding band and staring at him with frightened eyes.

"There's no choice, Mom," he said. "Dad'll have to find the four twenty-five."

"He can't," his mother whimpered. "PD, he can't."

"What about the house and cars?"

"We have three mortgages, no equity. We owe the bank more on the cars than we'd get for them secondhand."

"Mom, I'd give it to you in a moment, but I'm in hock, too. I owe for my new Cad, the office furniture." And for Beth's ring, but he didn't mention this. "What about friends?" he asked.

"PD, *everybody* knows about Dad. Who'd lend him that sort of money?"

"Uncle Desmond always comes through for the family."

"He won't anymore." She drew a long, wavering breath. "The last time your father had to borrow from Desmond, Desmond told both of us that we had to understand this was the last loan from him. And furthermore, if he heard of any trouble in Las Vegas again, he'd fire Dad instantly."

"A threat. He'd never carry it out."

"PD, you know the ins and outs better than I do. Before *Wandering On,* Desmond nearly lost the studio. He's still fighting for his life. You must have noticed he's letting a lot of family things go by the board. In the old days he would have stepped in between you and Beth." Though she said the words unemotionally, her lips quivered. "And you know how he feels about Hap living with that Mexican girl Barry's still married to. Do you think he'd let *that* go on if it weren't for her films bringing Magnum out of the box-office slump?" His mother glanced in the dressing table mirror, noticing a misplaced strand of hair. Smoothing it compulsively, she went on, "Mind you, I'm not blaming Desmond. He raised me in a fine home, gave me a college education, he's helped Dad from the beginning—he's been more like a father than a brother to me. I owe him everything."

"Mom, I understand. You don't want to beg anymore."

"Beg? I'd crawl to the studio if it'd help."

"Let me talk to him, then?"

Lily gave him a doubtful look.

"What can we lose?" he asked.

She patted his cheek. "You're a good boy."

He managed a grin. "Didn't you raise me that way, Mom?"

"And, PD, your father's a very talented man. The best husband a woman could want—generous, loving, warm. And he's been a good father. You mustn't think any the less of him because he has this weakness. It's as if he has a disease. He can't help himself."

"I'll go see Uncle Desmond and drop back afterward," PD said soothingly.

As he left the house, he was wondering what was so good and wonderful and loving and warm about a man who exposed his family, even his baby grandson, to murderous Nevada casino owners.

34

Not having an appointment, PD waited over an hour to see his uncle. The conversation in the inner sanctum went exactly as his mother predicted, yet PD was unprepared for the raging tirade of refusals.

Stunned and not a little frightened, he forced himself a step closer to the desk. "Uncle Desmond," he said earnestly, "I never would have asked, but Mom's petrified. Lang had one of his goons hand-deliver the IOU to the house."

"Robert Lang—another dago out of *Cosa Nostra* country. He's Mafia and so was his father." Desmond Cordiner leaned across his desk, thrusting his long, scimitar nose toward PD. "Don't you know they've been sniffing around this studio? Before I let them in the door, I'll see Frank Zaffarano in hell!"

"But, Uncle Desmond, this is for Mom, the girls, Jeffie."

"Your father should have thought of them when he had his fun. I've warned that has-been often enough. He's worked his last day at Magnum."

"No way!" The never-dormant agent within PD burst forth. "He's got over two years to go on his contract!"

The vibrant anger left the tanned, wrinkle-creased face.

Desmond Cordiner was expressionless as he said, "Magnum contracts have a morals clause."

Holy Mother of God—he doesn't care if Lang puts holes in all of us, thought PD. "Uncle Desmond," he said placatingly, "Dad's in the middle of a film."

"Tomorrow morning another director will take over," his uncle said, buzzing for his secretary.

Frank Zaffarano sat slumped in his chair at the head of the dining table. In this rare pose of dejection, his short neck appeared nonexistent, and the bristle of thick gray mustache almost completely hid his sensual, very pink lips. In front of him was spread a banquet. A large, compartmented dish held the antipasto—purplish red Gaeta olives gleaming with garlicked olive oil, pimentos, marinated mushrooms, proscuitto ham sliced thin enough to be transparent, redolent Tuscan finocchiona salami. Wedges of heavy textured bread nestled in a silver basket. The tomato and fresh basil sauce congealed atop the *penne.* Nothing had been touched.

Lily came in from the kitchen, a long mauve hostess skirt rustling around her, a covered dish in her hands. When Frank was late, she sent the maids home, personally serving the fine Italian food she lovingly prepared for him.

As she set down the dish, Frank lifted the cover, replacing it listlessly. "I have no appetite."

They both turned at the slam of the front door.

"Hi Mom, hi Dad," PD said.

"You're back," Lily said, giving her son an anxious smile. "I'll fix you some fresh pasta."

"Mom, I need to talk to Dad. Privately."

"Your mother knows everything," Frank said. "There are no secrets in this house."

"Frank, I have some calls to make about the retreat for young marrieds—I told you I'm in charge, didn't I?" Lily said.

As she touched a kiss on her husband's bushy gray hair, a sigh shuddered through his body and he clasped her hand silently.

Reaching the hall, she said, "There's fruit for dessert. The espresso's made."

PD held himself in check until an upstairs door opened and closed, then he snapped, "I could kill you!"

"I almost did the job myself."

"Have you made Mom the usual promises that you'll quit?"

"Your mother knows I don't have enough money to flush the toilet, much less bet."

"She should be canonized, staying with you."

"Desmond called right after I got home." Frank's voice momentarily regained a fraction of its loud verve. "He told me I should come in early tomorrow and clear out my office. I asked him what the hell he was talking about. He said you'd come to him with my difficulties. Then he fired me."

"You've pissed away several fortunes, and now it's *my* fault?"

"Who asked you to interfere in my private concerns?"

"Uncle Desmond's always helped before. And Mom was a wreck! Jesus, I barely recognized her. Believe me, if it hadn't been for her and the girls and little Jeffrey, I'd've forgotten the whole shitheap."

Frank slumped back into his chair. "My luck was good that night. To get the whole four and a quarter seemed a sure thing."

"Dad," PD said quietly, "is what Mom told me true? If you don't pay, will Lang get you—or somebody else in the family?"

Frank's skin turned gray. "He meant it."

"How do you know he's not bluffing?"

"Stories."

"What do you mean, stories?"

"Remember Bart's cousin, Carmine?"

PD shrugged. Who could keep all the *compaesani* straight?

"Carmine had borrowed from Bart for years. After Bart died, the boy—Lang he called himself by then—asks Carmine to pay up. Carmine refuses. A few weeks later, he disappears."

"Disappears? How?"

"Everybody says he's at the bottom of Lake Mead."

"Maybe he ran off with a hatcheck girl, old Carmine," PD said, taking an olive. "Coincidences happen."

"And accidents happen to whoever Lang thinks owes him. Never anything provable, but that doesn't mean people aren't dead." Frank, close to tears, tugged his mustache.

"I'm sure some kind of deal can be worked out with him," PD said comfortingly.

Frank sighed. "He has eyes like a crocodile. They never blink. He's a bad thing for all Italians." He sat a bit straighter. "PD, you mean what you just said? You could work out a deal?"

For the first time in his life PD experienced the visceral responsibility that occurs when a parent becomes the dependent.

"Piece of cake," he lied.

PD sat in his car several minutes before he turned the ignition key, revolving the problem in his mind. Raising the money seemed as impossible as raising the dead.

As he drove along Santa Monica Boulevard in the direction of his apartment, he saw the lit façade of Good Shepherd. He hadn't been inside the twin-towered, Mission-style building since he'd bought Beth's ring a year ago. He turned left. Parking on Bedford Drive, he told himself that this would be no disloyalty, that he merely needed a quiet place to get his head together.

He passed between the heavily carved doors and was assailed by the familiarly mingled smells of Lysol and incense. Without conscious volition, he dipped his hand in the cool water, crossing himself and genuflecting.

A modicum of peace descended on him as he slid into the pew. His mind no longer twitched with the impossible amount of four hundred and twenty-five thousand dollars. Folding his hands on his lap, he closed his eyes, letting himself float the way he had as a boy, and soon he was in a mental sanctuary where spacious calm prevailed. He found himself murmuring, "Hail Mary full of Grace, blessed art thou among women. . . ."

Alyssia, he thought suddenly. She was vacationing in Italy with Hap.

"Alyssia," he said aloud.

He accepted the name as the answered prayer for his family's salvation.

35

"Yes?" said the soft masculine voice at the other end of the line.

"Mr. Lang, this is PD Zaffarano, Frank Zaffarano's son. There's some business I need to discuss with you."

"You're talking for your father, then?"

"Yes, for Dad. When can I see you?"

"I'm free anytime tonight."

It was after eleven. "Tonight?" PD echoed.

"You'll have no problem getting a flight. Ask for me at the desk."

Though all other forms of high living attracted PD, his father's abiding and unfortunate passion had given him an aversion to the extravagances that surrounded gambling. He never used the Zaffarano box at Santa Anita, he avoided the Friars Club because of its high-stake card games and had availed himself of Bartolomeo Lanzoni's offers of a gratis run of the Fabulador just that one time ten years ago.

Since the broiling day of Barry and Alyssia's elopement, the hotel had tripled in size.

Though it was long after midnight, a half dozen red-jacketed clerks still busily manned the reception desk. When PD explained he had an appointment with Robert Lang, the clerk's bored smile changed to respect. With a snap of fingers, he summoned a bellhop. "Show this gentleman to Mr. Lang's entry." PD was led past crowded cocktail lounges and clattering slots, through a maze of crimson-carpeted halls, until they came to an elevator door marked PRIVATE. "Here you are, sir."

Tipping the boy a five, PD rode up to the elevator's sole destination.

When the door slid open he couldn't prevent his gasp. He had been anticipating more of the same garish red decor, but in front of him stretched a softly lit library with obviously old, honey-colored bookcases. The chintz upholstery was faded to soft pastels; the tabletops sagged a bit with age. No interior decorator could have designed such a room, it had been achieved only by several generations of soft living and hard money.

"Mr. Zaffarano?" said the same soft bass he'd heard on the phone. A man hidden by the back of the sofa rose to his feet. "I'm Robert Lang."

He was about thirty, approximately six foot tall, and slight—no, weedy was a better description—with thinning, rumpled brown hair. His v-necked sweater was so well worn that the sleeves were transparent at both elbows, while his equally antiquated, creaseless flannel pants appeared to have been bought decades earlier for attendance at some Eastern prep school.

There was no way PD could reconcile Robert Lang with Bartolomeo Lanzoni, a very short, ebullient Sicilian who wore loud ties and puffed at smelly cigars. Other mental cogs refused to slip into place. How could this obvious gentleman be threatening the lives of the entire Zaffarano family even unto the third generation?

"My father spoke of you often," Lang said.

"Uncle Bart was my idol. Mom and Dad always said there was no holding me down when Uncle Bart came to the house." Though PD's warmth for his father's dead buddy came naturally enough, the staking of a familial claim by reiterating Uncle Bart was quite deliberate.

"May I offer you a drink?" Lang gestured at three crystal decanters incarcerated in a silver tantalus.

PD never touched alcohol during any form of negotiation. "Thanks, but no," he replied. "This room is amazing, really amazing."

"It was moved intact from my mother's place."

All that PD knew of Uncle Bart's wife was she had died in her early twenties. Could she possibly have been English upper crust? *Gatsby*, he thought suddenly. At Beth's insistence he had read the property and fallen in love with Fitzgerald's blue lawns and the gangster whose every far-out claim turns out to be true.

Lang poured himself a Scotch. "You're representing your father, Mr. Zaffarano."

PD formed a smile. "That's my line. I'm an agent, Mr.

Lang." He paused, awaiting the usual suggestion to drop the formality and go onto a first-name basis. His host said nothing. After a couple of beats, PD continued. "I suppose you realize Dad's flat broke?"

Lang watched him silently.

"But if you'll hold off a few months, we could make five, six times the money he owes you."

"We? You mean you and your father?"

"No, this is strictly between you and me." PD paused. "I handle major talent, including Alyssia del Mar."

"Yes, I've heard that. I'm a great admirer of her work."

"Alyssia's the definition of the word star. On her next film I can get her to defer salary to you."

Lang continued to watch him.

All at once PD could hear his father's words: *eyes like a crocodile. They never blink.*

"I suppose you're wondering why she'd do all this for me," PD said. "The truth is I helped her out once and she owes me. Just like Dad owes you."

Lang sipped his Scotch. "As a matter of fact," he said finally, "I have been considering branching out in Southern California."

"Movies?"

"I'm not positive. Real estate interests me too."

"If you're thinking of Dad's house, I better warn you that it's mortgaged to the roof shakes."

"Land development is more what I have in mind. An industrial park surrounded by green belts, tracts of variously priced houses. Shopping malls."

"*Major* development," PD said, wishing he didn't sound so impressed.

Another of those long, staring silences.

PD longed to mop his forehead and upper lip, but all his well-developed instincts warned him to remain both quiet and still. He forced himself to concentrate on the peculiar absence of sound in the library. Fifteen stories below, gamblers reveled and traffic flowed and honked on the Strip, yet PD might have been profoundly deaf for all he heard of the night bustle.

"Mr. Zaffarano," Lang said slowly, "one thing you must understand about me. I deal in good faith with others. I expect that same treatment in return."

"Dad sincerely felt he could pay his debt."

"I don't wish Miss del Mar to consider I'm forcing her into a difficult position."

"It's me she'd be doing this for," PD said, while thinking, *What makes you so sure she'll do it?* He wasn't sure, but his gut instinct was that she would help him.

"*Wandering On,*" Lang said. "I've seen it five times and it's impressed me each time."

"Tremendous at the box office, too. If that's what you have in mind, no problem. Alyssia would be delighted to do a quality project."

"And what about your other cousins? The director, the producer, the writer. The deal would have to include all four of them."

PD was dead positive of Barry, who had indicated at their meeting this afternoon—no, yesterday afternoon—that he'd sell his sozzled soul to do a feature. The Wasps, as he and Beth privately called their Episcopalian cousins, were another story entirely. Maxim, who spent most of his time stuck away on his Mexican island, hadn't done another film after *Wandering On*, and might easily tell him to fuck off. And as for Hap—if Hap were ignorant of Lang's Vegas background, his father would set him straight. Hap assuredly would refuse.

He evaded the question. "Are we talking that you'll finance?"

"I'll put up the money, yes."

"Have you considered the sort of percentages you'll give?"

"Percentages?"

"Of the gross. The director gets anywhere up to five, and so does the producer. Even the writer expects something."

"I thought you understood, Mr. Zaffarano. The others would get scale."

"Scale?" PD cried. "Only beginners work for scale! These are top people!"

"Then it's up to you to negotiate with them."

"And what about Alyssia? It's usual for a superstar like her to get someplace close to ten percent of the action."

"As you yourself suggested, Miss del Mar will turn her earnings over to me."

"I only meant her salary! Am I hearing you right? She stands to make zero on the film."

Lang poured himself a Scotch. "You said she was indebted to you."

"Mr. Lang, be realistic. You could make millions on an arrangement like this."

"You're acting for your father, aren't you?" The tone remained soft, gentlemanly.

"Yes, sure, but—"

"Then I'll need to know whether you'll be paying his debt. Or whether I'll be financing this film."

"We don't have a property or even a story idea. It takes a long time to get together the crucial elements, and to put it mildly, this deal's complicated."

Lang was thumbing through a hand-tooled leather datebook. "Get back to me by the twenty-eighth," he said.

"Of September?"

"Certainly."

"But that only gives me a week. And Alyssia and Hap and Maxim are out of the country!"

"Possibly your father will have paid his debt by then," Lang said, and courteously escorted PD to the elevator.

Beth, tying the sash of her pink robe, came to the front door of her apartment. After their official engagement, she had moved out of her parents' house but still continued to pay the Salvadorian woman she had hired to help Clara.

"PD, dearest. You look like you haven't been to bed," she said in that soothing voice.

He felt a bit less annihilated. "I haven't, I've been in Vegas. It's a long story, and right now I could kill for a shower."

Showered, wearing his own robe, which was kept discreetly in the back of Beth's walk-in closet, he sat on the couch and drank cup after cup of fresh brewed black coffee as he told her the story of his father's debacle with Lang. "You wouldn't believe this guy. On the outside he's an English duke or something, but I swear if you took his temperature it'd be below freezing."

"He really has people killed?"

"Nothing crude—it's always accidents." PD set down his cup. "Jesus, Bethie, what am I going to do?"

"There's no choice, darling. You have to convince Barry, Maxim, Hap and Alyssia."

"Barry's no problem, he's hot to do a feature—I did say I'm representing him? And I'm pretty positive of Alyssia. But what about the Wasps? How in hell do I convince *them*? For God's sake, Hap's the only truly incorruptible man alive, and you know the spectacular offers Maxim's refused."

"Tell them exactly what you told me."

"Beth," he said hopelessly. "Lang gave me exactly one week. Hap and Alyssia are in Italy; Maxim on that island. I don't even know how you get to that godforsaken part of Mexico." PD's voice cracked, and he had to fight back the urge to weep.

"My poor sweetie," Beth said, tenderly stroking back his hair. "You're exhausted. Things'll fall into place after you've slept."

"Sleep? Who has time to sleep?"

"You can grab an hour while I call my travel agent."

In the bedroom he got between flowered sheets that smelled of her, and as she bent to kiss him, his lips clung to hers until she stretched out next to him. "You're the only person I can count on," he whispered.

"I love you even more for doing all this for your father."

He untied her robe, pulling up her nightgown, caressing her breasts and what lay beneath the brown triangle, the touch that cherished her above all others. While birds chirped outside the windows, they made love gently and caringly. Some of the girls of PD's youth had been exquisitely skilled, others adept with accoutrements and drugs, but only with his cousin did he feel unfettered by raging ambitions. With her he was the decent, honestly open man he yearned to be.

He drowsed to the sound of her serene voice discussing itineraries.

36

As the Alitalia plane slowed for its descent into the Milan airport, PD closed his eyes. He was perennially dubious about those laws of aerodynamics which enable a large metal object to dangle semistationary in midair.

The dangerous part of the trip is over, he assured himself. *Successfully over.*

Beth's travel agent had arranged his journey to Izumel first, a bouncily nerve-racking Aeromex flight to Vera Cruz, and an eternal taxi ride through humid jungle to Puerto Santiago. On the dock passengers, including PD, crossed themselves before boarding an archaic motor launch. The island, a four-mile-long crescent, was defaced at its northern tip by a cluster of shacks. Maxim's broad-verandaed adobe at the southern end was the only other habitation.

PD, not having seen Maxim in the three years since the premiere of *Wandering On,* was frankly shocked by his cousin's appearance. Maxim was yet thinner. And somehow his deep, reddish tan seemed a cosmetic to hide his pallor—had PD not known better, he would have believed Maxim recovering from a dear one's death or a mortal love affair.

They sat on the porch facing a tumbled Mayan pyramid which Maxim gazed at as PD unfolded the Zaffarano family's peril. When PD asked—no, begged—for help, Maxim got up to open a Dos Equis. Drinking it, he launched into the history of Izumel: in Mayan times the island had been sacred to Ix Shell, goddess of fertility and basket weaving, whose temple the ruin had been.

PD could bear no more yattering. "Jesus, Maxim! I can see you're not interested, so why not level with me? Are you permanently through with producing? Or does the Vegas backing turn you off?" He paused, adding in a choked tone, "Or don't you want to help me out?"

Maxim opened another beer. "Stop me if I'm wrong, but you don't have a script?"

PD shook his head. Barry's feature ideas, spilled hastily on the drive to LAX, had been unmitigated crapola, giving PD yet another problem: finding a vehicle.

Maxim, an artist at jerking people around, halted to chugalug his beer. "Then, old buddy, I'll produce on one condition."

"You're coming in?" PD's voice broke with excitement.

"*If* we make this novel I happen to own."

"You've optioned a property?"

"Bought it. Three thousand bucks."

PD's sudden hopes had plummeted. Slumping into his deck chair, he had said, "Nothing producible ever comes that cheap."

But, reading the thin book, *Transformations,* during the flight to Milan, PD had realized price wasn't an infallible indicator of quality. If ever there was material alive with cinematic possibilities, *Transformations* was it.

The plane wheels bounced onto the runway and PD gripped the seat arms. Dizzy with fatigue, he yearned to head for Milan's top hotel, the Principe e Savoia, where he could shower, dine on veal and fresh porcini mushrooms, then sink into a long sleep.

But he had exactly fifty hours left.

He rented a Fiat, following the signs to Lake Como. A warm, drab mist blotted out the view of the Alps and most of the lake. The season was over, so vacationers no longer swarmed in the tiny pastel towns that tumbled precipitously toward the waterfront. On the hairpin curve before the village of Bellagio, PD slowed at a stone gatepost on which was carved VILLA ADRIANA. Swerving across the narrow road, he braked down a steep, cobbled drive. The nineteenth-century house with its peaked roof appeared a smallish bungalow, but from a previous visit, PD knew that five commodious stories descended the hillside.

Hap and Alyssia had leased the Villa Adriana each September of the three years they had lived together. The month was inviolably set apart from the anxieties and pressures of their work. They fell into a drowsy, pleasurable routine—leisurely forays on Bellagio to buy the pungent local salamis and cheeses, or explorations of other villages that surrounded Lake Como. They sat on the terrace, watching the turbulent clouds above the mountain peaks or admiring the panorama—from here they could see all three fingers of Lake Como. They strolled hand in hand around the sculptures and follies in the gardens of Villa Serballone and Villa Melzi. The only shadow on the Septembral happiness was Hap's seldom mentioned but omnipresent desire to legalize their relationship.

Each time they arrived back at the leased house on Laurel Canyon, Alyssia would phone Barry to set up a date to discuss a divorce. Invariably he would reply that nothing could please him more. When they were together, though, his willingness always came with a disclaimer—they could start with attorneys as soon as he finished this urgent rewrite, as soon as he moved to his new apartment, the day his mother recovered from her latest illness. If Alyssia remained adamant, he would drink incredible amounts, then turn lachrimose, playing on her guilts, her sense of loyalty, her pity.

PD banged the rococo bronze mermaid door knocker. Though the furnished villa came with three servants, and though Alyssia traveled no place without her bespectacled personal maid, she answered the door herself. In a gauzy yellow kaftan that showed the outlines of her bikini, without makeup, her glossy black hair sleeked into a ponytail, she looked younger, more beautiful and far softer than her image on the screen.

"PD!" she cried. "PD! I don't believe this! What a mess I must look! Why didn't you tell us you were coming?"

"A spur-of-the-moment trip," he said smoothly.

"We'd have driven to Milan to meet you. God! Won't you shock Hap! Come on, we're outside."

In clear weather the garden had a view that could only be described as magnificent, and even on a hazy, obscured day like today, the pool deck, set into the bougainvillea-covered hillside and graced with ancient Roman pots from which sprang red geraniums, was romantically spectacular.

Hap, wearing faded khaki shorts and zinc oxide on his nose, his feet adangle in the water, sat reading a script. The ferry was hooting its way into the Bellagio dock, so he didn't hear them emerge. Alyssia paused to look at him, her eyes bedazzled as if he shone.

Then she called, "Look who's here!"

Hap jumped to his feet.

In spite of his exclamations and warm welcome, PD detected a lack of surprise, almost a hint of wariness. *Hap's always laid-back,* he told himself to calm his nerves.

"Hey PD," Hap was saying. "A long flight. You must be beat. So why not bathe and take a nap?"

PD drew a breath. "Later," he said. "First I have a property I need to discuss."

"So *that's* why you dropped in from the sky." Alyssia smiled. "Before you start agenting, I'll get you a drink."

PD gulped Pellegrino water, then used his considerable skills to pitch the story line of *Transformations.*

Alyssia's role, a bawdily outspoken young Detroit assembly line worker, sets off with her crude stud of a boyfriend to New Mexico, where her father is dying. The father turns out to be a billionaire along the lines of J. Paul Getty, and though the heroine is rebellious and disrespectful to the old bastard, she alone of the assembled, greedy family cares about him. The plot turns on past incest and the willing of the fortune.

When PD finished, Alyssia said enthusiastically, "What a story, and what a role—what a fantastic role."

"The concept's brilliant," Hap said. "Before we go any further, though—PD, does this project have any connection with a man called Robert Lang?"

PD felt as if somebody had punched the air out of both lungs. "Then Maxim spoke to you—"

"Maxim?" Alyssia interrupted. "Is he in on this? He's going to do a movie after all these years?"

"The property belongs to him," PD said. "It's a novel."

"You haven't answered me about Lang," Hap said.

"Uhh. . . ." PD shrugged. "He's only on the financial end."

"Dad called late yesterday. He said you'd probably be contacting us. Forget it, PD. The answer is no. We are not doing this film. We are not working with Robert Lang."

"I'm not even going to have a chance to explain the deep hole I'm in?"

"What are you two talking about? Who's Robert Lang?" Alyssia asked.

"Somebody to avoid," Hap said.

"PD," Alyssia asked, "what did you mean, a deep hole?"

"Let's sit down," PD said, mopping his forehead.

He and Alyssia took two of the wrought-iron chairs under the jacaranda tree. Hap remained standing. Brief and unadorned, PD laid out his family's plight.

"This Lang." Alyssia leaned forward. "All he wants is for us to do one film, then he'll cancel your father's debt?"

"You'd only get scale," PD said, deciding not to mention the deferral of her salary until they were away from Hap's narrowed gray eyes. "No percentages, either."

"But he's agreed to this story?"

"Not yet, but I can't see him turning thumbs down. He was quite explicit that he wanted an artistically meaningful project—and what else is this?"

Hap's fists were clenched against his shorts. "We are out! O,U,T!" Hap almost never lost his temper, but when he did, PD was remembering from boyhood, he was a far more implacable opponent than the terrifying but changeable Desmond Cordiner.

"Hap," Alyssia said, "sit down. PD's not asking that much. Why can't we do a film for only salary?"

"Money's the last thing I'm talking about."

"I wouldn't have hauled ass all over the world," PD said, "if I had anyplace left to turn."

"Why shouldn't you come to us?" Alyssia said. "You saved my life."

A muscle moved at Hap's jaw. "Can't you see he's playing on that? You never change, PD, do you? You're always that weasel Tony Curtis played in *Sweet Smell of Success*."

"Tell me what the fuck I *should* do. Let my family go down the tubes?"

"Maybe I'm obtuse, but I don't see any big deal, Hap." Alyssia's tone was no longer pleading, but gutsy. "So Lang owns a hotel and casino—"

"He also controls a big hunk of the US heroin trade," Hap said.

Stunned, PD took off his dark glasses, peering at his cousin. Hap stared back. Near naked, furious, he looked invincibly large.

PD said the first thing that came into his mind. "There's an unfounded rumor."

"Dad quoted considerable evidence to back it up."

"If Lang's rough," Alyssia said, "then all the more reason to help PD."

"Dad's fought for years to keep slime like this out of the studio."

"Oh?" Alyssia raised her chin. "It's news to me that your father has the same corner on virtue that you do."

Through the mist came the foghorns and deep throbbing hum of the ferry's departure.

Hap asked quietly, "Are you telling me I'm a sanctimonious prig?"

"You're behaving like one!" she snapped.

Hap picked up his script and went into the house. The quiet click as he closed the French doors had more finality than a thunderous slam.

"How could I have said that to him, PD?" Alyssia's lips were white.

"I'm sorry," he mumbled, ashamed of having destroyed the unmitigated happiness he had witnessed earlier.

"He's so much above me—smarter, more decent, top-notch family, everything."

PD was perpetually astonished at his top client's lack of confidence in her true worth. "Sure," he said. "You're only incredible-looking, talented and famous."

"I'm terrified one day he'll come to his senses and leave."

"He's mad about you."

"Not now, not anymore."

"Crazy talk. Hap's nothing if not steadfast." PD sighed and slumped forward in his chair. "Alyssia, I swear to you it came as a total shock, hearing that Lang dealt in big H."

She tilted her head at PD, as if finally noting his dejection. "It's the world's most fantastic part," she said brightly. "How could I turn it down? And my guess is Barry'll be delighted to do the screenplay. Maxim'll produce. So you have a trio of us."

"It's all four." PD's voice wavered. "Four or nothing."

She bit her lip thoughtfully: the marks showed in the tender flesh when she spoke. "How long do I have to change his mind?"

PD stared down at his hands. "The day after tomorrow."

37

Hap did not fight the same way the men of her youth had, shouting with hard blows to emphasize a point, nor did he turn petulant, like Barry. Reserved courtesy was his style. He kept to his own territory in their king-size bed, and beyond the bedroom walls treated her as if she were a fellow houseguest to whom he had just been introduced. Alyssia was generally the first to extend the olive branch, not because he was in the right, though she conceded that almost without exception he was, but because she was positive a prolonged quarrel might cause an irreparable tear in the fabric of their relationship.

Showing PD to the room he'd occupied before, she was already atremble with the need to surrender. But how could she, when she owed an incalculable debt to her guest? She went slowly down the flight of stairs to the master bedroom, finding Hap in the low-slung easy chair, reading the same script. He hadn't turned a page in twenty minutes, but she couldn't know that.

"I'd like to discuss *Transformations*," she said. Her voice was level though her hands trembled.

"Of course." Gravely, he marked his place. "But what's the point? We aren't doing it."

"We?"

"I'd prefer that you didn't, but of course I can't tell you what parts to take."

Alyssia heard in Hap's tone a modicum of the aloof precision that Rosalynd Cordiner used on her.

"Well *I* can't ignore PD!" she snapped. "And I don't see how you can either—he's your cousin. His family's your family! Don't you give a damn about family? Or do only the dirt-poor learn to help one another out?"

"I refuse to be involved with heroin."

"Lang's not sticking needles in you. He's financing a film."

"Taking his money means I condone the needles."

"Terrific!" She was shouting now. "PD or one of your other relations get their skulls bashed in while Mr. Morally Superior Cordiner soliloquizes about right and wrong!"

She ran into the dressing room. As she yanked on slacks and a loose sweater, she grew more and more frightened that Hap would decamp. Throwing open the door, she shouted, "I'm going into town!"

She drove the mile into Bellagio, parking in the square that abutted the little town's ancient, square-spired church. Striding down a cobbled alley in the direction of the lake, she ignored the tall, narrow houses with flowers that fell raffishly from every cranny—normally the little town's opera-buffa vistas delighted her.

Reaching the lake, she hurried past the ranked, outdoor tables where locals were leisurely taking their afternoon snacks, continuing to the end of the promenade, where she paid to enter the gardens of the Villa Melzi. The extensive grounds bordering the shore were empty in the twilit mist. As she passed the little Moorish temple where Liszt had composed, her footsteps crunched slower on the gravel and she hugged her arms around herself. *I'll have to use strategy*, she thought bleakly. She considered it wrong to bring psychology to bear against anyone, and to work Hap seemed the ultimate treachery to love.

"Signorina del Mar."

The desiccated little guard, Rizzio, was running after her to explain it was closing hour. She replied in her serviceable Italian, picked up while doing the Fellini film, that she was just about to leave.

PD peered at her through the ocher light coming from the outside lantern. It was a few minutes before dinner, and she had just brought a bottle of Marzemino d'Isera to the guest-room terrace.

"Take off?" he asked. "You've got me baffled. There's no way I can convince Hap if I take off."

She looked away. "Alone, I can, uhh, convince him."

He picked up the wine. "You're the boss," he said.

At her insistence, he hired a driver to return his car to Hertz.

No matter where she fell asleep in a bed, she invariably awoke curled around Hap. That night she retired to the adjacent room.

The triumvirate arose before dawn, driving to the Milan airport.

After they waved PD onto his plane, Alyssia turned to Hap. "I need a couple of things on Via Monte Napoleone."

Via Monte Napoleone, a short, narrow street in the old central part of Milan not far from the Duomo, was where wealthy, superhumanly well-groomed Milanese shopped at Gucci, Ferragamo, Valentino and other top designers.

Leading Hap into a perfumed boutique, Alyssia said, "I won't be long."

He sat on one of the uncomfortable gilt chairs, which were far too small for him, while she disappeared into an elegant fitting room. She chose several feloniously expensive silk outfits for herself, then asked to see clothes in Juanita's size, buying the two high-priced suits that would fit her sister. The beaming manageress offered to deliver her purchases to her car—or even to Bellagio—but Alyssia said no, she'd take everything with her. She piled her packages into Hap's arms, leading him to Gucci's, where she selected two dozen richly flowered silk scarves to take home as gifts, handing him these, too. If they hadn't been embroiled, he would have told her to knock it off, but instead, he carried his burdens like the perfect gentleman. At Ferragamo, her saleslady stayed past the inviolable lunch closing hour of one o'clock to sell this American movie star all the shoes that fitted her slim, high-arched feet.

Outside, Alyssia exclaimed, "I'm ravenous." Hap crammed her purchases in the trunk and drove the few deserted blocks to Don Lisander's charming eighteenth-century courtyard restaurant.

"What's the matter?" she demanded. "Isn't the *zuppa inglese* good? It's usually marvelous here."

"I'm not hungry."

"You barely took two bites of your *risotto* and your veal." She had eaten less of hers.

"Alyssia, they're waiting for us to finish," he said with patient courtesy.

The other tables were deserted and their waiters leaned disconsolately against the famed antipasto buffet. As Hap raised his finger, the short waiter with the mustache darted over.

"Signore?"

"I'd like a brandy," Alyssia said.

Again she slept in the adjacent room.

At first, unable to place the odd, rusty little sounds, she imagined some wounded animal had found refuge in their hilly garden. Then she realized it was crying.

Running into the next room, she dropped on the bed to clutch Hap's large, overwarm body. "Oh, darling, darling, don't."

His controlling breath shuddered against her. "This kind of situation," he muttered, "when something's right and wrong at the same time, is something I can't handle."

"I've been a total bitch."

"You don't have to tell *me*." He rubbed his wet cheeks against her breasts. "Alyssia, I'll do the film."

"Hap. . . ."

"I should be doing it for PD and Uncle Frank, but I'm not. I'm going ahead strictly because I just can't fight you."

38

Lang's demands included a swift release. Luck was with them and there were incredibly few foulups. *Transformations* was ready for release seven months later, at the end of April. Members of the Motion Picture Academy were treated to a preview showing of *Transformations*. The downstairs lobby of the Academy's big, comfortable new theater on Wilshire was jammed, and some casually clad people were still making their way down the broad, thickly carpeted staircase to the larger, brilliantly lit lobby where the temporary bars and buffets were besieged—in honor of the New Mexico locale, the caterers were serving *chile verde, carne asada* and gold puffs of *sopapillas*.

Well-wishers formed kaleidoscoping groups around those connected with *Transformations*. (An invitation had been sent to Robert Lang, but he had preferred to view his investment privately—thus far he'd had no contact whatsoever with any member of the cast or crew.)

Maxim received his adulation in front of a glass-encased exhibit of Billy Bitzer's cameras.

Barry held court on the steps.

Alyssia stuck close to Hap. She had no belief in her own talent, and lavish compliments always made her feel an imposter. The only way she could get through functions like this was to play a role she had long ago prepared for herself. Wearing blue velvet hip-huggers and a blue fitted tie-dyed chiffon top, she continually tossed her head, flashing her new ultralong gold earrings as, eyes asparkle, lips moist, she uttered breathless disclaimers.

Desmond Cordiner had come over. "Alyssia, it's a damn blessing you've got an obligation to do a picture for us," he said. "I wouldn't want Magnum to be at the tail end of the line."

"Those lines, Mr. Cordiner, are for the buffet," she bubbled.

Rosalynd Cordiner embraced Hap. Smiling at a point a few inches above Alyssia's head, she said, "You were excellent, dear, as always."

"Wonderful direction, Mrs. Cordiner," Alyssia said.

But Rosalynd was already making her stately way toward a pair of gray-haired matrons in designer pantsuits.

Alyssia flushed. She reflected that at least she didn't have to worry about a run-in with Clara and Tim. The demand for tickets had been so great that Maxim had decreed two Academy screenings: her in-laws had insulated themselves from her by requesting the second night's performance. So had Frank and Lily Zaffarano. Frank and Lily had yet to invite her to their home, and though she feigned indifference, she couldn't control her bitterness—or her desolation. Rejection hurts.

A minute later Beth was there. "You were fabulous," she said.

"With a role like that, who wouldn't be?"

Beth lowered her pleasant voice to a whisper. "I'm really grateful, Alyssia. PD told me the entire story."

"It's nothing compared to what he did for me."

Beth touched her arm. "Will you look at Barry!" Barry was laughing with an oval-shaped, long-haired older man whom Alyssia recognized as a Metro big gun. "He's finally out of his slump . . . thanks to you."

Beth had never showed her warmth before: Alyssia felt her throat tighten. Then William Holden came over, his weathered face creased into a smile.

The next time Alyssia glimpsed Barry, he was at the buffet with one arm around a blonde wearing a brief, metallic gold top.

Alyssia decided that when major executives hung on Barry's words and blondes pressed their spectacularly tanned bodies up to his, that was the time to bring up a divorce.

Leaving Hap, she went over to make a date with her husband.

When the phone rang at eleven thirty the following morning, she glared balefully at the instrument, positive that it was Barry canceling.

"Hello?" she snapped.

"May I speak to Miss del Mar?"

Puzzled, she tried to place the soft masculine voice. Their phones were unlisted, therefore she knew everyone who rang the Laurel Canyon house.

"This is she."

"Miss del Mar, Robert Lang here. I'm in Los Angeles today and I'd like to lunch with you."

Taken completely by surprise, she blurted, "Hap's at the office for a press conference."

"I'm aware of that. And considering how Mr. Cordiner feels about me, don't you agree it would be easier if we meet without him? Shall we say at the Bel Air? At one."

"I can't—" she started. But the phone had gone dead.

She slammed down the instrument. *I'll call and cancel,* she thought. But the incident had roused her uncertainties, and she examined herself in the mirror.

For her meeting with Barry she had put on a black turtleneck and jeans. Mightn't he think she was too casual and get his back up? She changed to a crimson midi with matching boots. But this outfit might also be a demerit—Barry had always felt that she overdressed.

She was wearing one of the silk Valentinos she'd bought in Milan when she finally went into the living room. Barry was well into a fifth of Chivas Regal.

"I'm sorry, Barry," she said. "But you know me, late for my own funeral."

"Juanita gave me a drink," he responded cheerfully. "But I do have an appointment at the Brown Derby." He took a sip. "Last night went well, think?"

"How not? Another fabulous script." As he beamed, she continued, "I wanted to get things rolling with the divorce. It's been dragging on too long."

He was still smiling. "You're the Catholic, remember."

In all the years they had lived together as man and wife she had never once entered a church or uttered a prayer, yet he continued to perceive her as Alicia Lopez, devout housemaid.

"It's better to get it settled," she said.

"Any time you want, hon. As I've told you *ad nauseam.*"

Had he been too drunk to remember those times when he had sobbed and begged her not to cut him out of her life, not to turn him adrift?

"I'm not up on the community property, but we'll make a date with the business manager."

"Why?" Barry blinked rapidly. "Your finances are of no concern to me."

Too late she remembered his touchiness about her success, financial and otherwise. "You're right," she soothed. "It's better to let the lawyers handle everything. But we can get rolling?"

"Alyssia, it so happens I'm more eager than you to dissolve this long-defunct marriage."

After he left, she stared at the door, trying to remember how Barry had appeared to her years ago—a godlike college man, erudite, sophisticated, impossibly successful.

Sighing, she dialed Information for the number of the Bel Air Hotel.

"I'd like to speak to Robert Lang."

"Robert Lang?" A long silence. "I'm sorry, but we have no Mr. Lang registered."

"Oh. I thought he was staying with you. Then please give me the dining room."

The captain informed her there was no luncheon reservation for anyone by the name of Lang.

Juanita had come to clear away the drink. "What's wrong? Barry cry in his beer again?"

"No, no. He said it's fine with him."

"Now *there's* a new tune." Juanita set the glass on the tray. "So why d'you look like the end of the world?"

"Robert Lang called awhile ago—"

"Lang?"

"Yes. He said he'd meet me at the Bel Air. And hung up before I could refuse. I just tried to give him a message that I won't be there, but he's not registered—he doesn't even have a table for lunch."

"Maybe they always give him one when he shows up. D'you think he's about to make a pass?"

"I won't be there to find out."

"You can handle his passes, Alice," Juanita said firmly. "And from everything I've heard, Robert Lang isn't the type anybody stands up."

The Hotel Bel Air shelters presidents, royalty and other celebrities desiring luxurious privacy. At casual glance, the rambling, vaguely Hispanic compound appears to be another of the surrounding Bel Air estates, and the hostelry's noncommercial aspects were further corroborated inside. At that time the lobby was without a reception desk or bellboys, appearing to be a large, gracious drawing room.

A man sat reading near the fireplace. His head was bent, so Alyssia couldn't see his features, but the way his thinning brown hair was a bit rumpled and the easy, somewhat out-of-date cut of his well-tailored suit made her think, *One of those Boston brahmins*.

He looked up and recognized her. Slipping his small book in his pocket, he came over, a tall, weedy man supremely confident of his surroundings. She formed a set little smile, anticipating a request for an autograph—it no longer surprised her that the rich and powerful were wowed by her film persona. At least he wasn't pricing her. Most tycoons eyed her with lascivious appraisal, as if figuring to the dollar what it might cost to spend a night with the object of universal desire.

"Miss del Mar," he said. "I'm Robert Lang."

She couldn't control the stiffening of her muscles. PD had described their Las Vegas connection as having class, but that Robert Lang looked like old money came as a shock.

"You seem surprised to see me," he said.

"I didn't think you'd be here." She extemporized with the truth, adding, "The moment I hung up I realized I already had a lunch date. I called back. They told me you weren't registered. The dining room had no reservation for you." She cut off her sentences as if with a scissors.

"My secretary never uses my name. My apologies about your other appointment, but I'm grateful you're here." There was an ambassadorial formality in Lang's tone, and he ushered her across the patio as if this were his official residence.

In the dining room, after their orders were taken, he said, "*Transformations* is everything I hoped."

"It's too upscale for a broad market," she retorted.

"The excellence means more to me. You were magnificent," he said, and launched into further praise, never looking away from her face.

Makeup artists, cinematographers, studio executives, directors, focused trained eyes on her. Out in the world, she was public property. Nobody was more accustomed to being stared at than she. Yet under Robert Lang's gaze, she found herself fidgeting with her silverware.

"I was just rereading this." Fishing a book from his pocket, he extended it across the table.

"*Medea,*" she read.

"I'd like to see it made into a film."

"Have you signed Euripides? And Dame Judith?"

"Judith Anderson isn't Medea."

"She *owns* the part."

"Medea's not an old, mannered actress. She's young, vital—and rough around the edges. She comes from a savage land, where survival is difficult." He tapped the well-worn leather binding. "If this were a modern play, she'd be from some urban ghetto or rural poverty pocket."

Alyssia wondered how much Robert Lang knew of her past. "There's a thousand interpretations."

"I see it as a big-budget epic."

"Oh, the bigger the better," she said. "And modern, too—isn't that what you said?"

He ignored her jibing tone. "Turn of this century. And shot overseas."

"Greece, I suppose."

"No, somewhere wilder. Africa maybe." He paused. "Miss del Mar, you could bring Medea to life."

"One picture is all I contracted for, and that's it. Period."

"The terms would be negotiated by your agent."

"Forget it!" She spoke so vehemently that the nearby trio of withered, natty old men who had been darting discreet glances in her direction now stared with diagnostic intensity at her face and breasts.

"You'd find me more than generous."

"I'll *never* do another film for you."

She excused herself before coffee. As she crossed the arched bridge over the hotel's pond, she was accepting that Robert Lang had done something worse than proposition her or threaten her, eventualities for which she had been primed. He had tempted her with the role of a lifetime.

In the late afternoon she taped a guest appearance on *The Merv Griffin Show,* then her PR people whisked her to CBS for a live interview on the news, afterward depositing her in the El Padrino Room of the Beverly Wilshire for a tête-à-tête dinner interview with a reporter from the *View* section of the *Los Angeles Times*—all were part of her promo obligations to launch a film.

She was reading in bed by the time Hap got home from the second screening, which, he reported, was equally as gratifying as the previous night.

Because he remained implacably hostile to their Las Vegas backer, she did not mention her lunch.

As Hap turned out the light, he asked, "What happened with Barry?"

"He came by in the morning—the divorce is fine with him. He even called to give me his lawyer's number."

"God, I can't believe it!" Hap's exultant chortle resounded in the darkness. "Barry actually said yes, with no delays?"

"You're about to be stuck with me."

She expected Hap, in high spirits, to retort in teasing kind. Instead, he reached for her hand, holding the palm against his chest. "I thought it'd never happen," he said huskily.

"But we've been together, darling."

"It's always seemed flimsy."

"Flimsy?"

"Remember that first time I drove you home from Magnum?"

"You were wearing a pale gray sweater."

"I can still remember thinking, *This is how it would be, married to somebody*. I've always wanted the solid things with you. A family, a lifetime commitment."

He pushed up on his elbow, kissing her tenderly, insistently. Outside, in the cool California night, crickets chittered and a coyote faraway in the canyon howled at the orange half-moon. She put both arms around him, spreading her hands above and below his waist to bring him closer. After a few moments she raised up and the bedclothes slithered onto the carpet. She straddled him, and they both gasped as she sank down on his penis. Her interior muscles caressed him, his hands traced patterns on her breasts, the scents of their moistures mingled, and all at once she was still, her eyes wide open, her pulses violent. As she began to gasp, he gripped her hips roughly, pulling her into his rhythm, and she rode swiftly.

Just before they fell asleep, he said drowsily, "We'll be together always."

39

The filing of the Cordiner/del Mar divorce on the grounds of her desertion caused a rush of publicity, but with the absence of titillating malice there was nothing to fan the gossip. The story quickly dropped into media limbo.

A few weeks before the divorce would become final, on a vigorously bright Tuesday in December, Alyssia, wearing outsize dark glasses, introduced herself at the West Los Angeles Police Station.

"I'm here for Barry Cordiner," she said.

"Please come with me, Miss del Mar."

The sergeant's voice was apologetic, his hazel eyes faded with awe, yet she heard a warning buzz in her ears. Dark-blue uniforms meant the enemy, the repressive, legally empowered hasslers of her girlhood.

Her delicate nostrils grew pinched. "Oh?" she said coldly.

"He has no ID on him." The sergeant hacked a few dry little coughs. "You'll need to identify him."

The cell, with its stained toilet and tiny corner washbowl, had two pairs of mattressless bunks, but Barry was alone, snoring gustily on steel springs. The bruise that swelled his left eye made his lashes appear embedded in the maroon-black flesh. The rest of his face was so pale that his freckles stood out like eczema. Lumpy, rust-colored stains ran down his shirt. His tweed sport jacket was ripped at the shoulder and one black loafer was missing.

Drunk and disorderly.

Assaulting an officer.

Until this moment she had been certain that the police had somehow concocted the second charge. Barry, even blotto, was the last man to put up his dukes with a cop.

"Miss del Mar, is this your husband?"

"Yes." What point dragging in their interlocutory decree? According to California statutes, for another three weeks he was indeed her husband.

Barry stirred, opening his eyes—the left was a slit. Groaning, he mumbled, "'Lyssia? Whatcha doin' here?"

"Bailing you out," she said tersely.

She signed papers, counted out twenties, and Barry was released.

As he pushed open the heavy glass exterior door for her, she caught a strong whiff of his sour odor. She stepped a bit apart, her memory flashing the image of Barry at the screening of *Transformations*. Clad in the latest hip leisure suit from Eric Ross, wooed by the powerful, embraced by the beautiful, a man at the top of his world. Since then she had seen him only twice, at the business manager's office and amid a cadre of lawyers when they filed for the divorce, but from PD she knew that he had turned down a television job to clear the decks for his re-entry into feature writing and that no film work had materialized.

As Barry opened the car door for her, he mumbled, "I don't know why they called you, but I'm grateful you came."

"No problem." She pulled out of the parking lot. "What happened, Barry?"

"Last night? I'm not sure. My memory's edited out certain crucial passages." He paused. "I was in a bar on Wilshire with Christmas decorations everywhere and some black guy was telling an antisemitic joke. Who knows? Maybe I retaliated with an antiblack remark—Alyssia, you know I'm no racist. The next thing I can recollect is us being hauled apart. Then, it seemed a moment later, the local gendarmerie arrived. I had a dream of socking one, so maybe I did. The next thing I knew I was waking up incarcerated, with you there."

"Were you alone at the bar?"

"I arrived with a Clairol blonde by the name of Wilma, her patronym will forever remain shrouded in mystery, and she was what the less generous might describe as an old pig. We'd connected a bit earlier at Fat Fred's, that's on Westwood Boulevard a block from me."

"Is this the first time?"

"For what? Picking up a decrepit sow when under the influence?"

"Getting booked."

Barry's hands clenched on his knees. "Two other 'drunks and disorderlies' mar my escutcheon."

"Barry. . . . Maybe you need help."

"The obligatory call to AA?"

"Yes, AA."

"Around a year ago Beth arranged a sponsor for me. He gave me a booklet with places and times of meetings, and we agreed on one at a Unitarian church. It was a Wednesday night. Alyssia, I swear to God I was going. But I was working on *Transformations*, and there was a flurry of rewrites."

Barry Cordiner, creator of screenplays and excuses.

The light changed and she concentrated on turning right. "There's other places for people with your problem."

"A private dry-out, you mean?"

"I heard about a first-rate one in Santa Barbara."

"It's a sound idea," he admitted. "But one has to be rich as Croesus."

"I'll give you whatever you need."

Barry jerked erect in his seat and she heard the rip as his jacket separated yet further from its sleeve.

"I am not a charity case!"

The strength of the sun burned through her dark glasses, striking against her pupils. How could she have forgotten that during their marriage Barry had always obliquely indicated the object of his material desire, letting her be the one to suggest he get it, then raising objections, forcing her to plead?

The remembrance of their old tugs-of-war roused not animosity but a perverse flood of tenderness. "Barry, it'll be a loan," she said. "You'll write me an IOU."

She persisted until they reached his beige stucco apartment building, where he surrendered.

"It's obvious," he said, "that you won't feel properly ennobled until I'm locked up in this pseudoclinic."

"Let me find out the details."

Villa Pacifica, Southern California's classiest spot for treating chemical dependencies, happened to have a vacant suite with an ocean view. Leaving it to Barry to set the time and date of his entrance, Alyssia transacted the hefty financial arrangements.

"Hap, they usually have a waiting list, they only take thirty patients—guests, they're called. And there was this one space. How's that for luck?"

"Amazing."

"Why that tone?"

"Have you ever considered that you're always helping Barry?"

"A few loans—" She broke off, jumping as something rustled swiftly in the dark manzanita. "A rabbit," she said.

They were taking their evening stroll along the unsidewalked curves of Laurel Canyon. This tall mountain formation that divided the city from the San Fernando Valley remained rustic, and was home to extended families of rabbits, mule deer, coyotes, foxes and quail.

"And you're lending him more," Hap said.

"If only you'd seen him this morning."

"But he didn't send for me. Or his parents, or Beth, or anybody else. He sent for you."

"He didn't *tell* them who to get in touch with."

"No?"

"He was asleep when I got there, and seeing me came as a total shock."

"Alyssia, the police couldn't have picked an unlisted number out of a hat."

"Oh, stop badgering me!" she snapped.

"I'm not. I'm trying to figure out your relationship."

"It's an ex-relationship."

"Are you sure?"

"What should I have done? Not pay his fine?"

"If you'd asked my opinion, I'd have told you to let somebody else go. Like Beth. She's his twin, she's closer to him. Or PD—he's the agent."

"Hap, Barry's drowning. I'm sorry, but I didn't stop to figure out the protocol of which Cordiner should throw in the life preserver."

A car swept around the curve, its headlights illuminating the various sized houses that clung to the steep, chaparral-covered walls of the canyon.

"These past few months," Hap said in a low voice, "have been the best of my whole life."

"Mine, too, Hap."

"God, how it hurt, all those years that you put off the divorce."

"But you knew exactly how I felt about you."

He walked slower. "Did I?"

"The only thing I missed was a skywriter spelling out 'Alyssia belongs to Hap.' Believe me, I'm only helping out of guilt. Why won't you understand?"

"Do you understand it completely?"

"Barry and I got married too young. I didn't realize that I didn't love him. I screwed up his life."

"That's open to interpretation."

"Anyway, you will admit that he didn't drink before he married me."

They had reached their driveway. Halting at the steep, cracking asphalt, he gripped her shoulders. "Alyssia, you have to understand where I'm coming from as well. I'm crazy about you. Everything about you turns me on. The way your eyes turn almost black when we make love. The way you smell, earthy and sweet. Your voice. Your walk when you're not being a movie star. Your courage when the whole deck is stacked against you. Your generosity, your loyalty."

"You're treading on my lines," she murmured shakily.

"Love, let me finish. However much you mean to me, I can't go back to the way we were. Too much self-loathing was involved."

"Has anyone ever told you you're too decent?"

"Decent? Barry was married to you, he hung on to you, he's my cousin."

"What's the point going into this now?" she asked. "In exactly three weeks and two days we'll be married."

40

Barry drank nothing the day of his release from jail, yet when he awoke the following morning his hangover, rather than lessening, had become monumental. His tongue felt like a length of thick hose, sourness packed his chest up to his gullet, and his eye throbbed meanly. His greatest misery, though, was his belly, which seemed packed with sharp hunks of steel. He'd had stomach pains before, but none had ever approached this intensity. Every movement was agony, and it took him several minutes to crawl out of bed.

I'm killing myself, he thought. He had never been so terrified. As he drank black Nescafé, the phone rang, and he answered before the second buzz, blazing with the hope that it was Alyssia.

It was. "The place is called Villa Pacifica," she said. "Here's the number and the name you're meant to contact."

Humiliated by his tears of relieved gratitude, he snarled, "Can't wait to get me there, can you?"

As soon as she hung up, he dialed 805, the Santa Barbara area code, arranging to enter Villa Pacifica the following morning, Thursday.

He went through the emptying of bottles. Wincing, he raised an open fifth of Wild Turkey theatrically high above the sink. How many times had he performed this rite? Best not to remember. When the last bottle of alcohol had gurgled down the drain, he dressed. Moving slowly because of the pain, he packed his bound scripts, the stained old typing paper boxes that held his two unpublished novels, his dishes, sheets and books, leaving the cartons on the floor for the manager to cart down to the storeroom.

He completed stowing away his worldly possessions around seven that evening. By then his gut-ache had receded to bearable proportions, and although the thought of eating brought a wave of nausea, he knew from experience that food would make him feel better, so he shoved a frozen Stouffer's macaroni and cheese in the oven. While waiting for it to heat, he suddenly asked himself how he would get to Santa Barbara.

His beat-up Peugeot wouldn't start, which was why he'd walked to Fat Fred's the other night, and Beth was in New York negotiating on Magnum's behalf for a best-seller. He had no real friends to call on. It was out of the question to ask his parents.

So he phoned Alyssia.

In a tone of subdued reluctance, she agreed to pick him up at nine.

A headache started behind his neck. *Villa Pacifica,* he thought. Did they confine "guests"? Did they use aversion therapy? He'd heard that it resembled medieval torture. Or did they prefer drug therapy? He cringed from injections as if from rattlesnakes. What about psychoanalysis? If a shrink were obligatory, he might as well stay home.

Pulling on his argyle sweater, he headed south along Westwood Boulevard in the direction of Vendome, whose gondolas displayed an impressive number of fine wines and liquors.

At half past nine the next morning, when Alyssia arrived at the apartment, she found Barry deep into the belligerent stage of inebriation. Shouting that she was dragging him to Bedlam, he refused to pick up his suitcase. She lugged it to the Jaguar: he sat in the car, staring straight ahead, ignoring her effort to hoist the heavy valise into the trunk.

As they passed through Calabasas, Thousand Oaks, Camarillo, the small towns that were joining the megalopolis, his pugnacity lessened.

"Remember in the château how we used to snuggle in bed when it snowed?" he asked. "In those days I drank a bit of wine, that's all. We'd still be happy if Hap hadn't gone after you. He always looked down on me because Dad's poor and Mom's Jewish."

"Oh, Barry," she sighed.

"You still care. If you didn't, would you be going to this kind of trouble?"

Hap had posed the same question in different words.

She looked out the window at the flat, fertile land of the Oxnard plain where, in another life, she had stooped at Juanita's side. Why hadn't she shucked her legal bonds to Barry years ago? Pity, yes. She was drenched with pity whenever he pleaded that she hold off on a divorce. Guilt, yes. She blamed herself for his failures, his drinking. But were pity and guilt the sole emotions that held her?

Why this stubborn refusal to give him up? She stared at the immense celery fields. *The very worst part wasn't the picking,* she thought. *It was having no family, the sense of not belonging anyplace.*

Villa Pacifica, hidden in the green folds of the Santa Barbara foothills that climbed from the ocean, had been named by the oil baron who had built the Italianate mansion decades earlier.

Entering the security gate, they passed a trio of middle-aged men strolling in and out of the blue shadows of tall old trees, then an oversized pool churned by a single swimmer, a gazebo where two young women sat. Mixed foursomes bounded on both of the red clay tennis courts. Alyssia was buoyed by the sense that she was bringing Barry to a weekend party. Then she saw the white-clad nurse slowly walking along the terrace with a frail-looking man and the two, large, watchful orderlies.

As she parked in the flagstoned courtyard, a French window opened and a short, bald man wearing an Izod shirt and slacks came onto the terrace. "Welcome," he said with a broad, Eisenhower grin. "I'm Al Ryker, the chief psychiatrist here."

"I'm Alyssia Cordiner."

"I'm not blind," he said, laughing. "And you must be Barry Cordiner. I can't tell you how I've admired your movies and your teleplays. They have a real feeling."

The compliments alleviated Barry's qualms about psychiatry. "The grounds are superb," he said.

"We think so. I'll show you around before lunch." Dr. Ryker paused. "Mrs. Cordiner, why not have a bite in Santa Barbara, maybe catch up on some of your Christmas shopping. We'll talk around three."

"Come back?"

Hap had raised no arguments when she explained she must drive Barry up here, but when he left this morning (he was looping the film they'd just completed for Orion) she promised to be home in the early afternoon. Santa Barbara was a long two hours' drive from Los Angeles, and in the late afternoon traffic, it took more like three.

"We believe family involvement is vital for the treatment's success," Ryker explained.

The doctor, apparently not a devotee of journalistic trivia, didn't know about their separation. She looked at Barry, hoping he would clarify matters. He gazed studiedly at the tennis players.

"It's not obligatory, of course," Dr. Ryker said, his brown eyes judgmental.

"Three," she acquiesced.

Stopping at the first gas station, she called home, telling Juanita to explain to Hap that she would be late. Picking up a taco at Taco Bell, she ate as she drove aimlessly through the University of California at Santa Barbara. The campus spread above the beach, and quite a few of the tall, tanned students were carrying surfboards.

At quarter to three she was waiting in Dr. Ryker's large, bright office. She kept getting up to peer edgily out the French windows. At twenty past three, she gathered up her purse, scarf and dark glasses.

Before she reached the door, it opened, and Dr. Ryker came in. He had changed to a brown suit.

"Sorry about the delay," he said in a flat voice. "I've been with Barry at the hospital."

"Hospital?" She returned to her chair, sinking down.

"He was late to lunch so I went up to his room. He was on his bathroom floor, vomiting blood."

"God. . . ." Shuddering, she remembered those lumpy, rusty stains on his shirt.

Ryker moved briskly around his desk to sit facing her. "Dr. Olesham, our staff internist, has ordered tests."

"Barry didn't look well, but I thought it was the fight and the hangover—" She paused. "I hadn't seen him for quite a few months."

"Yes, while I gave him the grand tour he told me that your marriage is on the skids."

"We're in the process of getting a divorce."

"That, he didn't mention. But he's extremely disturbed about your relationship with his cousin—"

"Hap and I've been together many years."

"Yet you've remained married to Barry?"

"The decree will be final in less than a month," she said. "How long will Barry be in hospital?"

"At this point we don't know. Probably three or four days. But the length of his stay isn't important. Mrs. Cordiner, I won't mince words. He'll be dead within the year if he continues this drinking pattern. So the major problem is to reclaim him from his dependency."

"That's why he's here."

Dr. Ryker tapped his pen on his desk. "About the divorce. I'm going to ask you to consider waiting."

"But why? I'll handle the expenses. I'll visit him."

"Barry's on extremely fragile ground right now. His marriage is all he has to hang on to."

"All he has?" Her voice was shaking. "Didn't he tell you about his family? He's very close to his parents; he has a twin sister he sees all the time. Uncles, aunts, cousins—"

"In his mind, when he married you he cut them off."

"That's about as far from the truth as you can get!"

"We're not discussing truth, we're discussing Barry's emotional responses."

"For years Barry's manipulated me," she said.

"And you," the doctor pointed out, "have let yourself be manipulated."

She bit her lip.

"Alyssia, look. I've talked less than an hour to Barry, but I can tell you this. He has a great many problems, and we must deal with them before he can give up his crutch. He's not manipulating you now. I am."

"You're saying it'll be *my* fault if he leaves here and starts drinking?"

"He's exceptionally proud of you. Being your husband is a major part of his self-esteem. Without your total support it will be nearly impossible for us to make any headway."

"We've put off the divorce far too long," she said.

"Of course I can't make your decision for you." Dr. Ryker got to his feet. "But right now Barry's a very ill, very frightened man."

She sighed and stood up, too. "Tell me how to get to the hospital."

41

The large room on the second floor of Maude FitzSimmons Memorial Hospital had windows overlooking the ocean, but the fine view was wasted on Barry. He lay flat in the bed, and the way he turned on the pillow as she came in told her he was too weak to lift his head. She couldn't reconcile this gray-faced invalid with the belligerent then plaintive man who had sat next to her in the car this morning.

"One good thing," he said in a thin voice as she set down the floral arrangement she had bought at the gift shop. "I'll have plenty of material for a medical series."

"Young Doctor Kildare Returns?"

"Good title," he said, reaching for her hand. His grip was lax. "God, Alyssia, I feel like I've stepped into somebody else's nightmare."

"Doctor Ryker said you'll be out of here in a couple of days."

"Ulcers," he said. "I have bleeding ulcers and other as yet unknown ailments."

"Want me to call your folks?"

"No!" His head jerked up an inch or so, then fell back. "Don't do that. Mom's been having chest pains, so I told them I'd borrowed a friend's cabin to work on a screenplay."

"Beth?"

"She's in New York until the day after tomorrow." He had not released her hand. "When I started to vomit I felt so rotten that I lay down on the bathroom tiles. If I'd been at home, I would've passed out and drowned in my own effluvium. Hon, you bringing me here to Santa Barbara saved my life."

"You're going to be fine."

He closed his eyes.

"Tired?"

"I keep drifting in and out."

"I can come back."

"Stay."

She sat by the bed until he slept. Then she went up the broad, airy hallway, the hospital staff goggling after her. Using the wall phone, she called the Laurel Canyon house. Hap answered and she outlined Barry's physical symptoms.

"The poor guy," Hap said.

"He looks so awful. I kept wanting to cry."

"I'll come right up."

Hap was in Santa Barbara before eight, PD driving him.

The childhood affection binding Hap and Barry reasserted itself, and Hap leaned down, hugging his cousin. "Barry," he said huskily.

"Hey, that's some shiner," PD said. Another embrace.

Barry blinked away tears, mumbling, "You should see the other guy."

To the sounds of masculine laughter, Alyssia slipped from the room.

In less than five minutes a wiry black male nurse banished the other two visitors.

Emerging into the corridor, PD shook his head. "Did you ever see anyone look crappier? Hap, he's our age, our exact age."

Hap nodded. His shoulders were slumped, his hands balled into his pockets.

They had reached the waiting area, where Alyssia sat staring down at an open but unread magazine.

"That was short," she said.

"The nurse shoved us out," PD said.

"Can we go back later?" she asked.

"The nurse said not tonight," Hap replied. Then, as if forcing himself from his despondency, he said, "Well, what about dinner?"

"Three's a crowd," PD said.

"Come off it, PD," Hap said.

"There's a big bash for a client." PD glanced at his watch. "If I go like hell, I can still make it. Ciao."

They watched the short, well-tailored man strut to the elevators, then Hap hugged Alyssia's shoulders.

"Any ideas where to eat?" he asked.

"I booked us into the Biltmore," she said. "How about room service?"

They ate guacamole dip and steaks in silence. They were often companionably quiet, but tonight the lack of communication had a strained quality. Alyssia's mind was filled with her conversation with Ryker, but she couldn't bring herself to broach the subject.

When they were in bed, lying side by side in the darkness, she was finally able to say, "Doctor Ryker thinks this is a rotten time for the divorce."

The surf beat loudly against her ears.

Then Hap's voice. "Did he explain why?" He sounded the way he did on the set, sincere and questioning, holding his own thoughts in abeyance until the other person had voiced an opinion.

"The drinking's killing Barry, and if he keeps it up he'll be dead in a year."

"That's laying it on the line."

"He also said there won't be any headway in the drying-out process without my total support."

"Alyssia, look. I'm not going to push you anymore." Hap's voice was drained and flat.

"But if I don't go ahead with the divorce. . . . What will happen?"

He sighed deeply. "I wish I could hang loose like Maxim." Currently on Izumel with the young actress wife of a complaisant engineering magnate.

"Barry won't be like this forever," she said. "For the time being, why can't we keep on the way we have been?"

"We could," he said quietly. "Except for two things."

"What are they?"

He took her hand, holding it to his chest. "First of all, Barry's never going to get better."

"Doctor Ryker said—"

"I don't mean he'll be lying in the hospital. But every time you're ready to get the divorce, something'll happen. He'll fall down and you'll prop him up."

"But—"

"No, let me finish. The second reason is that every day I'll be a bit more ashamed of what I'm doing, hate myself another iota."

"Oh, Hap."

"I'll get more and more dour. I'll brood about the kids I wanted. And you, being you, will hit out. We'll argue all the time."

"I want us to be married; I want us to have children—you know that, Hap."

"But you can't give up Barry."

"He's deathly ill, you saw him."

"Love, I'm not arguing. The thing I don't want is for us to end up hating one another."

"It doesn't have to be so grim."

"It does," he said.

For a long time there was only the rumbling of the sea. Then she rolled closer to him. Her throat ached, but she didn't cry. Her grief was too immense for tears. *Being your husband is a major part of his self-esteem,* Dr. Ryker had said, and she was accepting the truth of the statement. Barry, in his weakness, would always come up with an unarguable reason for not getting a divorce.

Arms around each other, naked bodies pressed together, she and Hap mourned for Alice Hollister, who could never let go; they mourned for the old-fashioned decency somehow inculcated into Hap Cordiner. They mourned for the entwined life they both wanted that was impossibly beyond reach.

42

The weather stayed good for Christmas and the New Year's day Rose Parade, but as if exacting payment, torrential rains hit in the middle of January.

PD was grateful that he and Beth didn't have to leave her snug apartment and brave the storm. Over the holidays he had been feeling somberly mortal, his mood caused by that visit to poor old Barry, who was now out of the hospital and locked up in Villa Pacifica. While PD caught up on *Variety,* Beth stacked their dinner plates in the dishwasher. The phone rang.

She answered it in the kitchen. "Hello?" There was a long pause. "Yes, he is. Wait a sec, Uncle Frank."

Never once had his parents called him here. PD jumped to his feet as if his father could see him on Beth's couch, naked beneath his robe. The boyhood guilts, harsh and untamable, still shackled him even though their roles had been reversed. Frank was now the dependent, pathetically thankful to PD for representing him gratis. (PD sweated harder to place Frank Zaffarano than to place any other client, and with lackluster results: Frank's string of flops barred him from features, and television demanded a younger director schooled in the medium's breakneck speed.)

Beth came to the dining ell, muffling the phone against her hip. "It's Uncle Frank—and he sounds spaced out," she whispered. "You better take it in the bedroom."

PD went into the other room, sitting on the chair rather than stretching on the rumpled bed. "Say hey, Dad. What's up?"

"Nothing . . . I just wanted to talk to you." Frank's voice was hollow and thin, as if he were calling from some remote archipelago.

"This is a rotten connection," PD said. "Let me call you back."

"I'm not home."

"Where are you?"

"I just wanted to talk. . . ."

After a long pause, PD spoke. "I'm sorry the job with Aaron Spelling fell through. I figured we had it nailed."

"You did your best, Paolo."

The old-country name. Imprinted on his birth certificate and draft card, used nowhere else.

"Everything okay, Dad?"

"Remember when I took you to school on your first day?"

"Dad, you didn't take me, it was Mom." Lily had deposited him in kindergarten, informing him in her most no-nonsense voice that it was a sin to disobey the teacher, a nun whose chin bobbled like Jell-O over her wimple.

"Oh. It must have been one of your sisters. Also I was thinking about the good times the family had at dinner, enjoying your mother's good food and all of us talking." Frank had dominated every mealtime conversation, generally regaling them with his latest method of outmaneuvering the enemy, Art Garrison.

"It's pissing bullets out there. Dad, tell me where you are and I'll come drive you home."

"We used to have fun together, didn't we? Those Sunday barbecues at your Uncle Desmond's I remember you tearing around, wild and free. All that energy! Your mother was always trying to get you to behave, but me, I was so proud of you that I thought my heart would bust. You, the leader, your cousins following."

The group had been ruled predominantly by Hap, with forays into mischief led by Maxim. The crackle on the line worsened. "Dad, where are you?" PD asked anxiously.

"God bless you, Paolo."

The valedictory remark increased PD's fears. "Dad, I don't want you driving. For God's sake, tell me where you are!"

PD heard the click and knew that the conversation had ended, either by some problem the storm was causing General Telephone or by his father's volition.

Beth, rubbing sweet-odored cream into her hands, came to the door. "What did Uncle Frank want?" she asked.

"He kept telling me I was a good boy and remembering stuff."

"That's not like him at all. You better call back."

"He wasn't home."

"Where was he?"

"I kept asking but he never told me."

"Aunt Lily'll know."

Predictably, Lily's line was busy. PD dialed the other number. (The Frank Zaffaranos had pared their standard of living to what they considered the bone, firing one of the maids, avoiding Chasen's, canceling the standing order at the florist and visits from the masseuse and facial lady, but it never occurred to either that it was possible to manage with only one phone line.)

His mother answered the first ring.

"Mom, it's me. Where's Dad?"

"Working," Lily said. "Dear, let me call you right back.

Mallie Ryan and I're in the middle of planning that Knights of Columbus fund-raiser."

"What do you mean, working?"

"You know, that series at MGM," she said with a touch of asperity. "He called around six to say they were doing some night shooting."

PD had difficulty catching his breath. "Dad doesn't have a job at MGM."

"But he said—"

"No job, Mom. He hasn't worked since he finished that *Bonanza* episode. He's in some poker game."

"Impossible," Lily said flatly. "PD, I didn't mean to tell you this, but last month I had to sell my emerald ring. Dad knows he simply cannot afford to play." On the last sentence her voice rose, a shrill wail reminiscent of her atypical hysteria when the IOU from Lang had arrived so mysteriously.

"Beth and I'll be right over."

"Beth?"

"I'm at her place," PD admitted. What use yet another Zaffarano denying the truth?

Lily wore a trim heliotrope knit suit, and her hair was immaculately coiffed, but her rounded face was the color of oatmeal.

"What a night," she said in her normal sensible tone. "You children go sit in the den while I make some good hot espresso."

"Let me fix it," said Beth, fully conversant with the magnificently equipped kitchen—her childhood treat had been to make cannoli with her aunt.

They compromised, Lily grinding the beans and mashing down the handle of the espresso machine—the large, elaborate type used in Italian cafés—while Beth set out the demitasse cups and spoons. PD, watching, wondered by what vicious quirk of fate he had fallen for his cousin, whom his mother loved and viewed as a daughter.

They were drinking the coffee when the door chimes sounded.

"That can't be Dad." Lily's full cheeks shook. "He never uses the front door."

The trio stared at one another.

PD couldn't move. Numbly he watched his mother go

into the front hall and admit the two policemen in dark slickers.

That was the last time he let anyone else take charge.

A few minutes later he was calling the family members, telling them that his father had been killed in an accident on the dangerous, rain-slippery curves of Sunset Boulevard. His Uncle Desmond and Uncle Tim wept, and he comforted them. The superpolite Beverly Hills police drove him to the station to claim a brown paper bag filled with his father's effects: the keys to the highly financed Rolls, which was totaled; a gold Dunhill lighter; a gold Mark Cross pen and pencil set; a worn Cartier wallet containing a new driver's license and two dollar bills. Also in the wallet was a note written in Frank's spiky, European hand, reminding himself of the exact amount of that night's IOU to his buddy, Joshua Fernauld: $5016.

Later that night, when the family and close friends like the Fernaulds showed up, PD made out a check for the amount. Joshua, who had written the screenplay for Frank's Oscar nomination, refused it. "I can't take your fucking money, PD. *Mea culpa, mea culpa.* Poor Frank—he put on a big act that he didn't give a damn about losing, but I saw the fear in his eyes."

"Dad frightened? Not on your life. And he'd have wanted this paid off!" With violent purpose, PD shoved the check into Joshua's large, liver-spotted hand, thus proving Frank Zaffarano could pay his debts—and proving, too, that the heap of expensive wreckage being towed from Sunset was indeed a rain-caused accident.

PD spoke to Monsignor about the funeral Mass. He arranged the financing on an ornate bronze coffin with white satin lining; he hired the public relations firm of Rogers and Cowan to ensure that adequate space and news time were given to Frank's obituary.

A considerable crowd came to honor Frank Zaffarano's passing.

PD stood at graveside with his arm around his quietly weeping mother. Ranged on either side of them were his sisters, his brothers-in-law and little Jeffrey, who was stamping a foot into the implausibly green grass, which was still soggy from the storm. The rest of the family was grouped on the other side of the deep gash. Aunt Clara with a thin arm consolingly around Uncle Tim, who wept hoarsely. Beth next to her parents. Uncle Desmond and Aunt Rosalynd, who looked like the impressive cow that she was in her black suit and pearls. Maxim stood with his live-in, the married actress. Hap was out of the country.

PD's mind wandered to the last time he'd seen Hap, who had come to the office to explain that as soon as he'd finished the job at Orion, he was going to Africa.

PD, who wasn't yet aware that Hap had moved out of the Laurel Canyon house, had innocently asked why.

"Is that any of your goddamn business?" Hap had flared.

"What's with you, *paisan*? Your business *is* my business—and Alyssia's starting a new film in ten days."

"She's not coming."

"Because of Barry?"

"All I came in to do was to tell you that I'm leaving for Africa and not to line me up for anything!" Hap had stridden from the office, his expression tormented.

PD glanced across the grave at Alyssia. She was standing apart from the family, halfway between them and the first row of nonrelated mourners. Her makeup didn't hide her pallor or the shadows under her eyes. There was something compelling about her grief, which, PD told himself bitterly, had nothing to do with his father. Her presence grated on him.

His mother was murmuring the responses, and PD joined in, finding comfort with every familiar word.

In this, the ultimate hour of his father's passage on this earth, he accepted how irrevocably his Catholicism was part of him.

A creaking mechanism lowered the coffin into its final resting place, and PD looked toward Beth. She appeared a will-o'-the-wisp creature forever shimmering beyond his reach. The salt tears blurred his eyes and a chaotic bitterness swept through him, carrying with it an ugly urge to blame someone.

He had arranged for a catering firm to be at the house, and there was the usual Hollywood wake complete with bartenders, hot hors d'oeuvres, sentimental reminiscences and Industry gossip.

Lily and the girls circulated, pale, red-eyed, but sociable.

PD attempted his usual conviviality, but he couldn't control his tears. He retreated to the small downstairs room that had been his father's office.

"PD?"

Alyssia had followed him. "I haven't had a chance to tell you how sorry I am."

Angry that she had caught him weeping, he blew his nose.

"It was so sudden," she said. "What a terrible loss for you."

Leave me alone, bitch. "I came in here to be alone."

She backed toward the door.

Realizing he had barked at his top client, he said with forced warmth, "Dad was very appreciative of you making *Transformations*. Did he ever tell you?"

She gave him a stricken look. For a moment he thought she would break down. Then she said, "Not exactly, but that's how the older part of the family is."

Was that a reproach? He decided it was. She was slamming his dead father, blaming his dead father.

When time had mythologized and blurred the moment, he would forget that Alyssia had done the film for zip to pay his father's debts—and coerced the intransigent Hap into the production, too. He would forget that she had helped raise the PD Zaffarano Agency from a joke to its present substantiality.

He would remember only that Alyssia, the eternal outsider, had slurred his father on the day of the funeral.

PD had his scapegoat.

"It's over, isn't it?" Beth said quietly.

"Jesus, Beth, give me time."

"Darling, I'm not pushing you about *that*."

They were in her living room, fully clothed. Dinner finished, he'd just told her he'd be heading home; tomorrow was a weekday. It was exactly four weeks to the day after the funeral, and he had yet to make love to her.

"Like hell you haven't been!" he snapped.

"PD, it's not bed, it's everything—either you're avoiding me or barking at me. You've done everything but tell me to get out of your life." Tears ran down Beth's smooth cheeks.

Hunched in his chair, he watched her weep. He longed to comfort her but he couldn't. After a minute he said haltingly. "It's the Church. Bethie, when Dad died, I saw I couldn't give it up. I'm pretty sure we could get a dispensation . . . that is, if you—"

"Converted?"

"Yes. Aunt Clara's stronger than you think."

"When we told them about the engagement, she was ill for months. . . ." Beth's melodious voice choked. Holding a Kleenex near her eyes, she whispered, "But it's not only Mother. It's me. I'm not Aunt Lily, I couldn't throw myself into Catholicism the way she has."

"I don't ask that of you."

"Judaism's more than a religion, it's an entire heritage."

"Your father isn't."

"I've told you, PD. In Jewish law, it's the mother who counts. And what about the children?"

"You know the Church's position," he muttered.

"Darling, if I do what you want, every single morning I'd wake up feeling a traitor to my ancestors. I can't do it, I just can't."

She struggled to get the engagement ring from her finger: the diamond clinked as she set it on the marble coffee table.

Though his sigh shook his entire body, he didn't argue with her to keep it. There was no point in argument. She was right. He loved her still, but it was over.

Picking up the ring, he mumbled, "I'll see you at Uncle Desmond's on Sunday."

After Beth was gone, he began to cry hopelessly. And by some mental quirk, he also bound this ineluctable loss to Alyssia.

BEVERLY HILLS, 1986

Remembering, PD sighed and took a long drink of his Campari and soda. "After Dad died," he said, "I got a bee up my ass that his death and also certain personal problems were somehow connected to Alyssia. Going through a rough time you dream up crazy things."

"Dream up?" Beth's mellifluous voice rose as she turned to her erstwhile fiancé. "She treated you disgustingly."

"She was my major client for years, Beth, and believe me, the major clients dish out far more crap than she ever did."

Beth sat up straighter. "Who took the brunt every time she didn't show up on the set—or walked off?"

"The unreliability," Barry put in, "didn't start until after she lost her confidence. From then on she had to fight attacks of unameliorated panic."

"Yet she always radiated when the camera hit her," PD said.

"If it weren't for her, Hap would still be alive." Beth's voice shook. "I can't understand why you're all defending her."

"Stop me if I'm wrong, Madame Gold," Maxim said. "But for a while there weren't the two of you closer than Cagney and Lacey?"

"She happened to be my sister-in-law. I did my utmost to get along." As Beth spoke, she felt oddly mean-spirited. But why? It was true. *We had nothing in common, but I was so grateful when she reconciled with Barry that I made an effort to be her friend.*

Yet, even as this went through her mind, Beth knew it was an ex-post-facto thought.

A decade earlier, her affection for her sister-in-law had been honest and pure. Only later did she come to hate and fear Alyssia for the destruction that she could wreak on Jonathon.

BETH

1979

43

In the white leather datebook embossed MRS. IRVING GOLD, 1979, the neat notation for September 1 showed: *Alyssia, lunch, 12:45.* Beth finished dabbing on her Norell perfume before twelve thirty.

There's time to visit Clarrie, she thought.

Clarrie, her only child, had been born June 12, 1974, a few weeks after Clara Friedman Cordiner was buried by a reform rabbi at Hillside, a cemetery not far from where she had lived. Abiding by Jewish custom, the Golds had named their daughter after her deceased grandmother.

As Beth crossed the airy, bright upstairs hall which was hung with Irving's da Vinci sketches, the now permanent twin lines between her hazel eyes grew deeper. With an air of resolve, she pushed open the heavy fire door.

Clarrie did not glance up.

The child sat at the small, brightly painted table, knotting the length of string stretched between her hands. A pretty, redheaded five-year-old wearing meticulously ironed yellow corduroy pants with a yellow shirt on which a smiling bear had been appliquéd. In the walk-in closet hung twenty identical sets, which when she outgrew them would be replaced with others in the next size. Clarrie refused to wear any other style.

Beth glanced at Mrs. Patrick, whose thick legs were propped on an ottoman. The nurse nodded. It was all right to come in. Beth glided past the deep shelves crammed with toys in pristine condition, moving toward her daughter with the same caution she would employ cozying up to a bird.

Clarrie continued knotting and looping the dark-brown twine. The macramé developing between her small hands would bring pride to an adult—if the adult were without artistic talent. She did not appear to notice her mother. But of course she did. When Clarrie was less than a year old they had learned by her piercing screams that she noticed the most minuscule alteration in her immediate environment. By the time Clarrie was two, she had developed an uncanny awareness of every minor discrepancy in the household. The Golds stopped inviting people to the house, entertaining either at Hillcrest Country Club or in the upstairs banquet room of the Bistro. If the slightest change—a forgetful servant whistling, a delivery truck turning in at the front door rather than the back—occurred during one of Clarrie's bad times, she would shriek, sometimes for so long that Dr. Severin would have to be called to okay a sedating injection.

Perching on a childsized chair, Beth turned to the nurse. "How is she today?"

Mrs. Patrick, like the others rotating in the nursery, was a pediatric RN. Picking up her chart, she read in her Alabama drawl: "'Woke at five past seven. Dressed self. Breakfast, the usual.'" If anything other than oatmeal was set in front of Clarrie for breakfast, lunch or supper, she would hurl her much-dented sterling porringer across the room. The cereal was fortified with a special mixture of liquid vitamins, protein powder and dried milk. "'Bowel movement in commode at twenty past eight. Walked in garden for thirty minutes, then heard helicopter and grew distraught.'"

"Yes, we heard her crying."

"'Came inside at nine oh five. Nine thirty-five, calmed. Watched cartoons.'"

Watched? Beth thought. Who knew what transpired in Clarrie's brain when she gazed at the television screen?

Clarrie raised her strings higher.

"It's beautiful, just beautiful," Beth said. "Daddy and I framed your last macramé." As she described the frame, its position in the house, her pretty voice assumed a false brightness.

With Clarrie, she was completely out of her element.

Beth's self-esteem was intricately connected with helping others. She wasn't sure whether this had developed from the psychology of being a twin, half of a person—the lesser, female half at that—and having to earn her share of attention and love, or whether she was born with an innate urge to make herself useful to others. In earliest childhood she had toddled off to perform errands for her parents and Barry. Later she had worked for good grades to please the teachers as well as her mother. At Magnum she had delighted in her long work hours and her efficiency. When PD started his first agency, she had volunteered to do his books. After marrying Irving, a widower, she threw herself into caring for him and his homes—a sprawling pink bungalow in Palm Springs, a house in Aspen, this Holmby Hills mansion.

The specialists whom Irving brought here, sometimes at vast expense, gave a name to the child's disorder. Acute chronic childhood psychosis. Beth didn't care what they called it. She knew only that she was unnecessary in her child's life, and no type of hideous physical or mental birth defect could have been more damaging to her.

At the sound of a car moving up the long driveway, Beth stiffened, waiting for Clarrie's shriek. She rested a light, comforting hand on her daughter's silken hair, which was the same coppery shade of red as Barry's had been at her age. Clarrie squirmed away, standing to continue her knotting.

"The car's not disturbing her," Beth said.

"She knows it's her Auntie Alyssia."

How does she know? Beth wondered.

Smiling and waving unacknowledged bye-byes, she left the nursery and felt five pounds lighter. She ran down the stairs to greet her sister-in-law.

Alyssia wore yet another of those tee shirts studded with a pattern of rhinestones. Beth unconsciously smoothed the pleated skirt of her classic beige silk, thinking with rueful affection, *Poor Alyssia, she has the tackiest taste.*

The two women hugged fondly, chatting as they went through the hall, which was designed specifically for Irving's huge Rubenses—yards of stoutly rosy female nudes. They wound through the Oriental garden to the blue-tile-roofed teahouse, where a table was set for two.

Pouring the iced coffee, Beth asked, "How's Barry?"

"He's been busy on the book." During the long hiatuses between Barry's infrequent TV assignments, he rewrote the novel that he had started in the early weeks of their marriage.

"And he hasn't . . ." In the September sunlight hovered Beth's unspoken words: *Fallen off the wagon?* Since Clarrie's birth, she saw impending disaster everywhere. Barry hit the bottle less than once a year, and never stayed on a toot long enough to further damage his internal organs, yet Beth agonized incessantly about his drinking problem.

"He's great. As a matter of fact, he's at L'Ermitage having lunch with a visiting editor from New York."

"Wonderful!" Beth cried wholeheartedly. Then, incapable of escaping her new and unwanted role of pessimist, she added, "Let's hope it's not another false alarm." Last year the oft-revised novel had roused interest from a local publishing house, but no contract had been forthcoming.

"Not to worry. He's braced for this to be only a friendly lunch." Alyssia sipped her iced coffee. "You said there was good news about Clarrie."

"Yes. Mrs. Patrick explained you were coming, and when your car turned into the drive, she didn't get worried." Even with Irving, Beth spoke in euphemisms, keeping up the fiction that Clarrie was a normal child going through a stage. But on the last word her lips turned downward.

"Bethie," Alyssia said sympathetically, "why don't you and Irving have another child?"

"He's sixty-two and I'm forty. It's out of the question."

"A lot of men his age have second families."

Beth looked at the pretty artificial pond, unable to banish the thought of her joinings with her husband. Irving, lacking any trace of PD's amatory skill, followed a single routine. He French-kissed her until his erection was established, then climbed on top missionary style to grip the custom-made headboard with both hands as he pounded away for a maximum of two minutes. Yet, despite the inadequacies of their sex life, she cared deeply for him. She hadn't married him for his money. In fact, she'd had no idea he was immensely wealthy when she met him at one of Uncle Desmond's barbecues. It was a few months after she and PD had broken up, and she had been drawn to him because of his kind expression and sympathetic voice. "You look blue," he had said. "I am, a bit," she admitted. They talked about her work, and he diffidently invited her to a movie—"If you don't mind being with an older man, that is." She took him to an Academy showing because she didn't want him to throw away more money than he could afford.

Those first years the act hadn't excited her, but neither had she found it repellent. When Clarrie's problems were discovered, though, she had become convinced that the failure stemmed from her—after all, Irving in his first marriage had fathered three sons, energetic men with healthy families of their own. From then on sex became a nightmare. Legs spread, molars gritted, she would pray that she wasn't conceiving. Already on the Pill, she went to a second gynecologist to be fitted for an IUD. She also used vaginal foam, in part for the now necessary lubrication, but mainly for contraception.

Alyssia was inquiring gently, ". . . What about adoption?"

"I won't adopt. I absolutely couldn't."

"A lot of people say that, then go bananas over the baby."

"The child wouldn't be part of me."

"But a newborn—"

Beth sighed deeply. "Alyssia, I wish I were different. But I've said it before and I'll say it again. I could never accept a child who didn't have my genetic makeup."

"But you can't know how you'd feel."

"I do know," Beth said, her melodious voice going flat. "I know exactly. A stranger's baby would be a placebo and nothing else. What could be more unfair?"

She fell silent as Roscoe labored up the path with the tray.

Eating thin-sliced papaya and freshly broiled shrimp (Beth was on a perpetual maintenance diet), they talked about the movie Alyssia was finishing at Universal.

"So the retakes are almost done," Beth said. "Then what?"

"A little vacation time. After that, PD's put together a package."

"Who's in on it?"

"Old times revisited." An Alyssia del Mar chuckle. "Me. Maxim. Hap."

"Hap?"

"It surprised me," Alyssia said. "I figured after he finished that movie in Yugoslavia, he'd be going back to Zaire."

Beth had assumed so, too. She donated lavishly to the relief center that Hap had founded in Zaire (she still inwardly thought of the new country as the Belgian Congo), feeling a deep shame that the checks she mailed were not for good deeds but to keep her cousin geographically separated from her brother's wife. Photographs of the center, which was in a remote section of tropical rain forest near the Ruwenzori Mountains, showed why it possessed no more ornate name. It was a twenty by twenty-five frame house on stilts with a thatch roof and broad veranda where those receiving medical care were nursed by their families. The supervisor was Dr. Arthur Kleefeld, a bearded young New Yorker, a graduate of Johns Hopkins. Those first five years Hap spent all of his time in Zaire. When he resumed directing, Beth was overjoyed that his films were made on location. He hadn't come back to Los Angeles on a permanent basis until three years ago, when he married Madeleine Van Vliet, of the Van Vliet supermarket chain. At the big June wedding in All Saints Episcopal, Beth had felt a great burden lifted from her.

Madeleine never accompanied Hap on his African jaunts, and seldom went on location with him, but in all other respects they were a golden couple. They looked magnificent together—Madeleine was as tall for a woman as Hap was for a man, as fair-haired as he. They never argued. She swam in a sea of Blue Book friends, a sociability that the Cordiner clan agreed was the perfect antidote to Hap's tendency to shy away from large-scale parties.

At the rare family gatherings when Alyssia showed up with Barry, Beth kept a sharp eye on the onetime lovers. They would exchange a few cousinly pleasantries, then move apart.

Beth watched the goldfish darting below the placid surface of the pond. "What's the story line?" she asked.

"It's called *The Baobab Tree* and it's set in Africa."

"Probably that's what attracted him."

Alyssia shrugged. "Who knows? All I can tell you is why *I* agreed to do it. Beth, after they see this, they won't dare offer me any more of those dumb sex comedies."

The faint assertiveness of her tone disturbed Beth yet more. Her fingers shook as she emptied the pink paper of Sweet'n'Low in her iced coffee, and traces of white powder spilled on the table. "It sounds fabulous," she said.

In truth Alyssia had no idea what her role was or what the film was about. She knew the locale, East Africa, and the title, nothing more. She had agreed to do *The Baobab Tree* for a single reason. PD had told her that Hap was already signed to direct.

44

Upon Barry's release from Villa Pacifica, Alyssia had bought a new, one-story home in the Santa Monica Mountains a mile or so north of the Beverly Hills Hotel. The builder had developed five of what he called luxury manors, getting the utmost view from his expensive crag by layering the pads. The Cordiners', the topmost of these, was reached by a long, steeply zigzagging private lane.

Alyssia wound up the hill, and as she pulled into the large parking area, Barry opened the front door, waving to her.

On the short drive from the Golds' Holmby Hills estate, she had been thinking about Hap. How his gray eyes had darkened before they made love, the brief hesitation before he answered a question that gave his reply weight. The total security she had felt with him both on and off the set.

Seeing Barry, she experienced a cockeyed sense of alienation. It was as if she were observing a woman in white slacks and a smashing tee shirt emerge from a car and walk to a tall, balding man.

A concerned, wifely voice inquired, "How did your lunch go?"

"Come on inside." Barry's eyes glinted with boyish excitement.

She followed him into a large, sun-splashed living area, which a decorator had strewn with sleek pale woods and large pieces of squashy red upholstery. Beyond plate glass glittered the heart-shaped pool that she'd recently put in.

"Mrs. Cordiner." Juanita emerged from the kitchen wing. "You got some calls."

"Tell Mrs. Cordiner about them later," Barry said.

Leading Alyssia to his study, he closed the door and then tamped tobacco in his pipe, an obvious attempt to prolong the mystery.

More to oblige him than out of curiosity, she asked, "What happened at lunch?"

"Gebhardt"—the visiting editor—"offered me a contract."

"He didn't!" Every trace of spectatorhood vanished and she hugged Barry. "Tell me what he said! Every word!"

"He called *The Drifting Tide*" (the much rewritten novel whose numerous versions she had never glimpsed) "overly literate for the marketplace."

Her exultation waned. "That other editor said it was a work of art!"

"Hon, Gebhardt's right. Commercial novels are what the readership buys. So I pitched him the espionage thriller, the script outline I've been laboring over for lo these many weeks." Barry's chest expanded. "That's what they'll publish."

Alyssia kissed his cheek. "Fabulous!"

"Since it's only a sketch, not a real outline, Gebhardt warned me the advance will be minuscule."

"That's PD's worry."

"PD's not a literary agent."

"The woman in his office who handles books—isn't she meant to be tops?"

"For out here, maybe. But to have the proper élan, the necessary prestige, one needs a New York agent. I'll fly back east and interview them."

"Can you wait a few days until I finish the retakes on *Counter Point*? I'll go with you."

"Great idea," Barry said, adding in the stilted tone that he used to voice compliments to her, "Hon, I told Gebhardt how supportive you are."

That night Barry edged over to her side of the outsize bed, curving his hands on her breasts, squeezing and kneading. Before turning to face him, she experienced a moment of disbelief. They had made love less than a month earlier.

Fans of the second-sexiest woman in Hollywood (according to an *Esquire* poll, she was close runner-up to Jacqueline Bisset) would be stunned to hear how seldom her husband availed himself of his conjugal rights—and possibly yet more astounded to learn that she had not attained orgasm in nearly a decade.

When Barry fell asleep, she cupped a hand to her pubis, then pulled her fingers away. She had never achieved anything but self-contempt in the solitary vice.

Rolling onto her stomach, she thought, *I really ought to start a little discreet adultery.* But what was the point? She had voluntarily separated herself from the man she still loved, and now he was married to Madeleine. Then she sighed deeply. When she'd heard Hap would direct *The Baobab Tree* she had been unable to turn the film down, but now she was asking herself how she would feel, facing the class couple during the lengthy shooting schedule. Mercifully, Barry would be with her.

The following afternoon she was sensually fondling a telephone while flashing a come-hither smile at Edgar Wiatt, the romantic lead of three decades' endurance who was her costar in *Counter Point.*

Edgar said, "What makes you so sure—"

She didn't hear the remainder of his line.

A sudden pain was shooting down her left arm, an agony that intensified so swiftly that it seemed to explode from within the marrow. Simultaneously, a heavy weight clamped against her chest.

Edgar was looking down at her questioningly; the short, black assistant propman was holding up a chalk board with her line.

Alyssia's pupils registered only the corruscating brilliance of the lights. The ghastly pressure increased against her rib cage. In her urgent need to draw air into her lungs, she opened her mouth.

"Alyssia, what is it?" Edgar asked.

I'm having an acute coronary, I'm dying.

"Cut," the director called peevishly. "Cut!"

Aware of eyes fixed on her, Alyssia gasped, "'Scuse me." And fled from the circle of brilliant suns.

She left a wake of disgruntled voices.

"What is it *this* time?"

"You know, stars. They feel like leaving, they leave."

She stumbled into her dressing room, locking the door behind her. Dizzy from lack of oxygen, afraid she couldn't make it to the couch, she lowered herself onto the floor, and, open mouthed, sucked in dust odors of white carpet fibers.

"Miss del Mar." A masculine voice.

It's only an attack, she informed herself. *It happened on the set, so it has to be an attack.*

A light tap on the door. "Miss del Mar?"

The attacks had begun immediately after she broke up with Hap, which meant she'd been having them for approximately ten years. Thus far she had discerned only one rule. They invariably occurred while she was working. Beyond that, nothing could be calculated, all was random. Sometimes, as today, she would be felled in the midst of some simpleminded dialogue. It could happen when hordes of union-scale extras surrounded her or when she was alone with her makeup woman. Sometimes two or three would blitz her in a single week, then several months would pass, raising her hopes of a cure, making the inevitable recurrence more devastating. She had told nobody but Juanita, safe repository of secrets. And to Juanita she had revealed only a tiny fraction of the physical dimension of her problem and none of the terror—this awesome, primal terror. Through the years she had consulted with cardiologists, internists, an oncologist or two. Each gave her a clean bill of health. She tried a psychiatrist. He stated unequivocally that the problem must be uncovered before the symptoms could be cured. Accordingly, she visited him five evenings a week after leaving the studio. Within six months the attacks were coming so fast and furious that she was forced to choose between analysis or her career. To the disgruntlement of her psychiatrist, she chose her work. The attacks again became sporadic.

A series of knocks sounded on the door. Prone on the rug, she felt the jarring vibrations.

"Miss del Mar, can you hear me?" The peevish voice of the director.

Go away, leave me alone.

"Miss del Mar, we need you on the set!"

From a book on phobics, she had gleaned a useful tip: count backward: . . . *ninety . . . eight . . . ninety . . . seven . . .*

A muttered but intentionally audible, "The last time I work with the fucking bitch."

She had a reputation for being difficult.

The attack, while demonic, was not long-lasting. The worst of her terror and excruciating agony ended within fifteen minutes. She crawled to the sofa, lying with her hand over her still struggling chest. Her face was slack, her makeup sweat-streaked.

An hour later she was back on the set, glowing and simpering at Edgar Wiatt.

In New York she and Barry took an apartment at the Sherry Netherland—Juanita was housed many flights below in the comfortable rooms reserved for servants of hotel guests.

While Barry made the rounds of literary agents, Alyssia foraged through Bergdorf's, Bendel's and the nearby shops and boutiques. She bought a floor-length white Arctic fox cape and a red-dyed "fun" mink, sweaters and slacks and low-cut dresses; she chose a bakers' dozen pairs of Maud Frizon shoes and three Hermès bags. She dropped in at Van Cleef's, selecting a gold minaudière and a pavé diamond pin shaped like a bee. She dragged Juanita to Saks, charging four outfits plus a Persian lamb coat and six strands of freshwater pearls. "Where will I wear all this, in the kitchen?" Juanita protested. She bought gifts for Edgar Wiatt and everyone connected with *Counter Point,* even the snippy director. She bought exorbitant presents for Beth, Irving and Clarrie, for PD. She bought luxuries for her husband—cuff links in gold, in platinum; Dunhill pipes, a score of Turnbull and Asser shirts, Sulka cravats—he never wore ties—and hand-knit sweaters. She was in the grips of what she called the shoppees, a recklessness that salespeople blessed and her business manager deplored but could not stem. Bourgeois caution in spending was not part of Alyssia del Mar's background.

Barry became a client of the Karl Balduff Agency.

During the two days that Balduff negotiated the contract for the four-page outline of *Spy,* the author and his wife explored the galleries of SoHo and wandered through Central Park, munching ethnic food from pushcarts. In horn-rimmed dark glasses, with a scarf covering her glossy black hair, Alyssia was seldom recognized.

After Barry signed the contract, he said, "What a magnificent few days!"

"I have until November. Let's bum around Europe."

"My book!" he cried in outrage. "What about my book?"

"You always liked working in the château," she said. The family who had leased it from them had moved out three months previously.

"The perfect environs for literary endeavors," he said, kissing her fondly. "We'll go to Belleville-sur-Loire."

They arrived late one September afternoon when a golden haze endowed the run-down nineteenth-century house with the same beglamoured mystery as the nearby historical châteaux. Getting out of the chauffeured Mercedes, Barry stared around.

"I'd almost forgotten what a jewel it is. We'll start the renovations. First the roof. And the shed's falling, so we might as well demolish it and incorporate a proper garage into the house."

"Barry, we're only going to be here a few weeks," Alyssia reminded him.

"I'll pay you back when my royalties start rolling in," he said stiffly.

"Oh, Barry, that's not what I meant at all. But you know me. I'm not much with decorating and that kind of thing. So everything'll be up to you. And you're here to work on *Spy*."

"There are firms who specialize in modernization."

"You really don't mind putting in the effort?"

"*I* didn't earn the wherewithal. And I can tell you're not interested."

It took her a week to convince him to go ahead.

Barry engaged Dupont et Cie, the pre-eminent Paris renovators, and work started immediately. Roofers swarmed above the expanse of broken slate. Masons matched stone, chiseling and fitting missing portions of the Norman fireplaces and main staircase. Two additional bathrooms were carved from the never-used upstairs sewing room; the kitchen was gutted.

Mornings Barry withdrew to the library—the one untouched room. Oblivious to the hammering, the ear-destroying power tools, the shouting, he scratched hastily across long sheets of yellow paper. Afternoons he spent with the workers, marking mistakes, offering suggestions, thoroughly enjoying himself.

Alyssia, on the other hand, found the tumult unbearable. She was growing more and more edgy. What in God's name had possessed her to make this film? Tormenting enough to work with Hap, but being on location with him and Madeleine would be pure, unadulterated hell. And how could she give a performance when she hadn't yet seen a script? She put in a call to PD.

"Alyssia, we're talking a period piece. Period-type scripts need more polishing—you should *capisce*, you're married to a writer."

"I don't mind if there's changes, PD. But I need an idea of what I'm about. How else can I get inside my character?"

"*Cara*, you deserve a vacation," he said.

Alyssia was due in Los Angeles for fittings and preproduction rehearsals the first week in November. The day before they were due to depart, Barry dropped his bombshell.

"I've given this great thought," he said. "I can't leave now."

"*What?*"

"I've canceled my flight."

"Barry, you promised." Her voice rose an octave. To face Hap and Madeleine without him? Impossible. "You can't back out on me."

"My opus, the restorations. . . ."

"It'll be quieter for you to write in Los Angeles," she said, managing a reasonable tone. "And Monsieur Dupont has everything in hand."

"The creative juices are flowing; the novel's taking shape. How can you ask me to risk everything?"

"But you'll only miss a day's travel time," she said, longing to ask, *What about Hap? Aren't you the least bit concerned?*

"Have I ever uttered one syllable about where you work?"

"No, but—"

"Well, *I* am remaining here!" He stamped around the sawhorses, slamming the new, unpainted door after himself.

A few hours later he was saying apologetically, "Hon, I have my thrust. I can't risk losing it. But I don't like thinking of you alone in the Beverly Hills house. It's so isolated."

He placed a call to Beth. She requested that Alyssia be put on the phone.

"You'll stay with Irving and me," Beth said firmly.

"I can't. It's a huge imposition."

"Don't be an idiot. Irving's your biggest fan. And Clarrie adores you."

"Thanks, Bethie. You really are a doll," Alyssia said to her sister-in-law, who was also her friend. "I'll see you in a couple of days."

45

Waiting for Alyssia outside the LAX customs area was Bernard Whitson, senior partner of Ares and Whitson, her public relations firm. Bernard beamed proudly because he was surrounded by at least fifty newspeople. Alyssia, who had not anticipated the press, took a figurative step backward. The eleven-hour flight had zonked her more than usual. Briefly gripping Juanita's hand to steady herself, she tilted her head back, smiling for the photographers, parrying with humor the storm of snoopy questions about Barry's absence, about her rumored hot romance with Edgar Wiatt, about her upcoming direction by her former lover, Hap Cordiner.

By the time she and Juanita arrived at the Golds' Holmby Hills estate, Beth had been called away. Alyssia showered and napped. When she awoke it was dark, and her hostess had returned.

The sisters-in-law embraced and went into the living room, which was dominated by Irving's prized Monet "Nymphéas"—the great drifts of water lilies set the room's color scheme of floaty mauves and celadons.

"There was an emergency about the big United Way luncheon," Beth apologized. "I feel terrible, not being at the airport."

"We wouldn't have had a word, Beth. The hungry horde was waiting. I could've killed Bernard—except he thought he was doing a fine job, alerting the press. And besides, didn't you promise not to fuss if I stayed here?"

"At least you got a nap."

"And did I ever need it!" Alyssia took one of the thin curls of carrot. "Did a script arrive from PD's office?" She paused, recollecting her gushy enthusiasm for *The Baobab Tree*. "I'm expecting the rewrite."

"No, but he phoned while you were asleep. There's quite a few calls." Beth held out a small sheaf of monogrammed scratchpaper. "You can answer the urgent ones while I go kiss Clarrie goodnight."

The top two messages were from Maxim and PD. Maxim's said welcome home and he'd see her tomorrow. PD had left a schedule with phone numbers where he could be reached.

At this hour, six thirty, he was at the Polo Lounge. Alyssia waited while a phone was jacked into his booth. She could hear cheery background noises before he spoke.

"Alyssia, *cara*. How was the flight?"

"Fine. PD, I thought you said you'd have a script here for me."

"You don't have it?"

"No."

"That damn girl! She must've screwed up. I'll give you one tomorrow morning personally. You and I are taking a meeting at eleven with Hap and Maxim."

"None of the money people?"

"Just the creative end."

"PD, who's putting up the cash?"

"Not to worry, they're staying clear."

"But who are they?"

"Meadstar."

"Should I know them?"

"They're very highly thought of. And besides, *cara,* aren't they giving you the moon?"

Did his voice contain yet more of that artificiality than usual? How could she gauge over the telephone, and with all the background chatter?

"We'll talk details later," he said. "Come by the office ten thirtyish and I'll zip you over to Magnum. I'd pick you up, but . . . you know how things are. Poor Beth." The sigh that came through the receiver was genuine and filled with regret.

She answered her calls until the discreet hum of an engine drawing up to the front steps told her that Irving was home. She went into the hall with the paintings of fat naked women to greet her brother-in-law.

In repose, Irving Gold's narrow face had a friendly warmth. He was short, thin and possessed of huge vigor. Born to oppressive poverty in the South Bronx, he had built his first low-priced, high-quality housing tract immediately after World War II, and since then his fortune had multiplied geometrically. He, though, had never taken on the arrogant smugness of many self-made men.

"Some host I am," he said, kissing Alyssia's cheek. She could smell his weariness.

"You're here, that's what counts," Alyssia said, kissing him back. Her affection for him was not a spill-off from her friendship with Beth, but an entity of itself.

Three places were set at one end of a table long enough to accommodate sixteen. Irving took the chair at the head, Alyssia and Beth faced each other over a low silver epergne filled with grapes, plums and pears.

While waiting for the sliced tomatoes and broiled sea bass, Alyssia asked, "Irving, ever hear of a company called Meadstar?"

"Meadstar?" He shook his head. "Doesn't ring any bells."

"They're putting a fortune into *The Baobab Tree*. Over twenty million."

"Their own cash?"

"Yes. They're financing."

"Then it's an extremely well capitalized outfit. My guess is it operates out of Nevada."

"Why?" Beth inquired.

"Lake Mead," he said.

Upstairs with Juanita, Alyssia said, "We had the low-cholesterol, low-calorie, I-never-eat-red-meat menu. What did you have?"

"Avocado salad, spareribs, cornbread. And hot caramel over coffee ice cream for dessert."

"Whipped cream?"

"Cool Whip. Roscoe opened a can of Planter's salted peanuts to sprinkle on top."

"Heaven."

"Want me to fix you one?"

"You're a doll. I'm still ravenous."

Alyssia was in bed when Juanita brought up the sundae. Alone, she luxuriated in the oversweet goo, her thoughts drifting to the conversation at dinner. Nevada, Irving had said.

Nevada?

The spoon fell from her hand onto the pale-blue silk blanket cover.

She was remembering that lunch at the Bel Air Hotel. Robert Lang, drug dealer and reader of Greek tragedy, had tempted her with the role of Medea. In his version the play had been set in the turn of the century, and—what had been his words? Not in Greece but "somewhere wilder. Africa maybe. . . ."

It fit.

And if PD had gulled her, if Meadstar were indeed a front for Lang, he assuredly would have kept the information from Hap. *If it's true, when Hap discovers it, he'll bow out,* she thought.

She set the melting dessert on the bedside table. Her appetite had vanished.

46

Roscoe drove her in the Golds' Daimler to the Zaffarano Building—a three-year-old, glinting-windowed structure for which PD was profoundly in hock. PD ceremoniously handed her a script. As he drove eastward along Sunset toward Magnum, where the resurrected Harvard Productions leased offices, he kept up a barrage of talk. His mother, he said, was emerging from her long grief. Lily Cordiner Zaffarano was seeing Ken O'Herlihy, a well-to-do widower, and PD, for one, heartily approved of his mother's sensible choice. His nephew Jeffrey. . . .

Alyssia wasn't listening. Her mind flashed like a prism, reflecting a hundred thoughts about the upcoming meeting with Hap.

"PD," she interrupted. "Is Meadstar a Nevada company?"

He stared at the beat-up Ford directly ahead of them. "For tax purposes it's based in the Bahamas."

From PD's hastily spoken response she accepted that it was not only possible but probable that illegal money, Lang's or somebody else's, was financing *The Baobab Tree*. In the last few years such backing had become commonplace. Those battles fought to keep out the underworld proved to have been rear-guard actions of aging tycoons like Desmond Cordiner. The studio system was dead. The splintered new Hollywood, in frantic search for venture capital, had a far more laissez-faire attitude.

PD changed the subject. "Did you hear that Uncle Desmond and Aunt Rosalynd bought a condo on Maui? In my opinion, Hawaii should be their permanent headquarters. Retirement's been hell on Uncle Desmond. He was one of the true power guys in this town and it's killing him to sit on the sidelines."

She felt a ripple of sympathy for her old enemy, and started to say something to this effect, but PD, evidently fearing she might return to questions about Meadstar, rushed on with his outpouring.

He told her about Tim Cordiner's roostering over the widows at Golden Crest Retirement Hotel. (She knew all about the geriatric romances: Barry, as the son of the family, insisted on being his father's sole support, so her business manager made out checks each month to cover not only the Golden Crest's substantial rates but also the limo service and restaurant tabs incurred by the father-in-law, who still turned his back whenever she entered a room.)

PD slowed under Magnum's wrought-iron archway, and the gatekeeper waved them on in.

During Alicia Lopez's career as an extra, the back lot had been eerily deserted, devoted as it was to Magnum's minimum production. Rio Garrison's astute second husband, who had taken the reins from Desmond Cordiner, had restored the studio to bustling life by renting out the facilities. Actors in cop uniforms and actresses sporting hooker hot pants were streaming into a sound stage. A TV miniseries was being shot on the Western street. PD swerved around a brightly painted open trolley: Magnum's guided studio tours now rivaled the popularity of those at Universal. A Japanese group stared after them, exultantly snapping away at the back of the Rolls that carried Alyssia del Mar.

PD parked in a reserved slot outside the row of flimsy stucco bungalows that once had housed Magnum's publicity department.

Maxim met them at the door of Bungalow One. "Sorry about missing you when I called yesterday," he said, bending to touch a kiss on Alyssia's cheek. "Mmm, you smell of Joy."

He led them through the dinky foyer and down the narrow hall to his stifling little office. Framed, yellowing posters for his movies decorated the walls: across from his desk hung the one of her and Diller in *Wandering On*.

"What's wrong with putting in an air conditioning unit?" PD inquired, mopping his forehead.

"UCLA has this new surgery to correct abnormal sweat glands," Maxim retorted. "Strictly in the experimental stage—but for a terminal case like you, PD, I'd suggest taking the risk." He opened a small refrigerator. "How about a soft drink?"

Alyssia refused; PD requested a Perrier.

Handing the green bottle to his cousin, Maxim said, "Hap'll be right in. So let's administer the oath of loyalty to Alyssia."

She smiled uncertainly.

"You're on the side of capital, right?" Maxim asked.

"Capital? You mean the money people? All I know for certain is the name Meadstar."

Maxim glowered at PD. "What about the explanations?"

"I figure we save time and energy talking to both of them at once."

"*You*, PD. *You* talk. *You're* their fucking agent. *You* put together the deal—"

He stopped as the door swung open.

The small office seemed to dwindle yet further as Hap stepped inside. As always when they had been apart a long time, his size and the easy way that he moved came as a shock to Alyssia.

"Welcome home," he said. He did not give her the

ritual Hollywood greeting kiss. "Did you have a good flight?"

Though he spoke in a friendly, pleasant tone, she sensed his code of manners lacked a proviso for how to treat a former mistress.

"Smooth and on time," she said, smiling. "It's good to be back in warm weather."

He took the free chair, which was next to hers. Conscious of the gravitational pull, she leaned slightly in the opposite direction.

"Before you people get down to creative talk," PD said, "we need to iron out a few details about the business end."

"The backers?" Hap said. "Meadstar. You already checked them out. What's up?"

"When I came to you with *The Baobab Tree,* did I have to sell you?"

"It's a brilliant script."

"A project of this scope requires fat financing."

"What are you trying to say?" Hap asked.

PD ran the bottle over his sweating forehead. "We needed to find a backer with major bucks."

"Quit the waffling, PD," Hap snapped.

"Meadstar is Robert Lang."

"Lang!"

"You think every shmegegge who wants to be in show biz can come up with twenty-five mil?"

Hap was on his feet. Leaning across Maxim's desk, he asked in the quiet tone that meant he was furious, "You knew about Lang?"

"It's like this, older brother," Maxim replied. "I'm not the latter-day Father Damien."

"Cut the sarcasm. Well?"

"Lacking your altruistic faith in humanity, I investigate before signing a contract."

"So you *did* know. And never said a word." Hap's eyes narrowed.

"Why should I? As you just pointed out, the script's brilliant."

"You and PD are both aware I don't work for guys like Lang."

"You already did," Maxim said, glancing at the poster

for *Transformations.* "Or have these many full moons re-virginated you?"

A muscle twitched at Hap's jaw, and he turned to Alyssia. "Did you know?"

"I never heard the name Meadstar until last night. When I asked Irving if he knew the company, he said no, but it sounded like Nevada—Lake Mead." She hesitated. "I took it from there."

"I see," he said, his face expressionless. "Maxim, any number of top directors'll be interested in a film of this caliber. You'll have no problem replacing me."

PD ran his fingers through his hair and the moist, black strands stood up. "You mean you're walking?"

"That's the general idea."

"You and your impossibly high moral standards!" PD cried.

"I'm hardly the only person in America who refuses to do business with drug pushers."

"It's too late for the ethics shit," PD said. "For Christ's sake, the contracts are signed!"

"You always put in escape clauses."

"Be serious!" PD was shouting. "Nobody steps into the ring with guys like Robert Lang."

"You do business with him often?" Hap inquired.

"*Transformations.*"

"And?" Hap prodded.

"You don't know how iffy financing has gotten nowadays," PD said defensively.

"How often?" Hap persisted.

"Okay, have me excommunicated. I've put together five—no six packages with Meadstar as an element."

"Then by now you've learned how to explain a situation like this to Lang," Hap said.

He walked out of the office, quietly closing the door.

Alyssia rose to her feet. The pressure against her chest was faintly reminiscent of an attack; her thighs felt spongy. PD and Maxim were staring at her. Following Hap would be tantamount to an open confession of everything she still felt for him, and her formidable pride rose up against such exposure. Yet her feet were moving.

"Are you crazy, too?" PD cried. "Alyssia—"

She shut the door, diminishing the sound of his voice to a gnat's buzz.

Hap stood by the water cooler, his head bent. As she emerged, he looked up.

"Big exits," she said breathily.

"Why're you leaving?"

"I'm on your side."

"Oh?" Again that polite wariness.

"I told you. I was shocked as you about Lang."

"That doesn't mean you have to bow out."

Her knees wobbled. "I feel a bit shaky is all," she murmured.

"I'm sorry." Opening a door, he said, "Come in and sit down."

His office was as dun-drab as Maxim's, lacking even the spartan decoration of old posters.

He pulled out the chair facing the desk (even in her wooziness, she noted it was unadorned by a photograph of Madeleine) and she sank gratefully down.

"Let me get you something to drink?"

"Water, please."

He went outside to the water cooler. She sipped the restorative liquid. They were silent until she set down the Dixie cup. "That's better," she said, her voice still a bit tremulous.

"Sure you're okay?"

She nodded. "I can't seem to remember my line, but it goes something like, 'Lang's dangerous to fool around with.'"

"I agree. You definitely ought to stay on the film. My decision, though, is made." He pulled back his chin, a slight but well-remembered gesture meaning he was adamant.

"Hap . . . you've done so few movies lately."

"I've been looking for projects." He spoke rapidly. "I don't need to explain the piles of garbage I waded through before I came to this. The role's tailored for you."

"Is it?"

He tapped his pen on a Filmex program. "You know it is."

"I've never read the script," she said.

"But . . . but PD said you flipped over it."

"He didn't give me a copy until this morning." She patted her Gucci carryall. "It's in here."

"Are you saying you signed without any idea of *The Baobab Tree*'s basic concept?"

"Yes," she murmured.

"You never used to let PD pick your scripts."

Her cheeks were hot. "He told me you'd agreed to direct."

At a burst of feminine voices and laughter, she looked at the window. A trio of happy, gesturing, middle-aged women, possibly secretaries, were passing. Composing her face, she turned back to Hap.

He was gazing down at his hands. She couldn't see his expression but his posture denoted acute embarrassment.

"Enough confessions for the day," she said lightly. "May I use your phone? Roscoe's going to pick me up here—I'm staying with Beth."

"Jesus, poor Beth," Hap said.

After Alyssia finished her call, Hap sent out for donuts and iced coffee. They ate at his desk and talked. Alyssia did not bring up *The Baobab Tree* or Robert Lang.

It was difficult not to stare at Hap, but she managed to chat with him in a reasonably normal tone. *The only thing worse than being with him*, she thought, *is not being with him.*

47

As Alyssia stepped into the Golds' front hall, she felt smothered by the silence. Clarrie was napping, Beth lunching for charity, and Juanita had gone to Disneyland with Salvador Cardenas, a widower with whom she had been friendly since North Hollywood days. Alyssia raced up the wide, circular staircase, swift as a child. Kicking off her shoes as she dropped the now unnecessary script on the bedside table, she sprawled on the custom-quilted spread.

She gave herself up to intolerable embarrassment. How could she have confessed her never dormant involvement to Hap? And let PD and Maxim in on it, too? What a poor, pathetic masochist she was!

In the midst of her self-flagellation, her mind took the peculiar lurch that she knew meant she was dozing off. *Been sleeping a lot the last couple of weeks. . . ,* she thought as she dropped into heavy slumber.

A discreet jangle woke her. She toppled the script to the floor as she groped for the phone.

"Miss del Mar?" said the soft masculine voice. "Robert Lang here."

Fully awake, she jerked to sit on the edge of the bed. "Alias Meadstar," she said tartly.

"It's one of my corporations, yes. PD told me you left the meeting when you found out."

"I don't like games," she said.

"First of all let me assure you that I have no intention of holding you to any contract that you consider onerous."

"Good," she said. "I'm flying back to France at the end of the week." As she spoke, she saw that the spur-of-the-moment decision was a perfect retreat from her humiliation.

"I'm releasing you from your obligation," he went on, "because I feel I owe you something for your work on *Transformations.*" There was only generosity and respect in his soft voice, yet a chill settled between her shoulders.

"I did the film for PD," she said.

"Nevertheless I earned far more from it than I had anticipated. Miss del Mar, I attempt to be absolutely fastidious in my business affairs. I expect others to behave in the same manner."

"Oh oh—that sounds ominous."

"Mr. Cordiner signed a contract to direct."

"He liked the script."

"Possibly. However, he had turned it down twice before he was informed that you'd agreed to star."

She gasped, incapable of believing what Lang had told her. If it were true, why hadn't Hap said something when she'd unbosomed herself?

Lang was saying, ". . . hoping that you can convince him to remain on the film."

"He doesn't direct often nowadays. If he says he doesn't want to do it, he means it."

"Miss del Mar, as I just told you, I'm scrupulous in my own dealings. And I use whatever means are available to me to insure that others behave in the same manner. Mr. Cordiner has a valid contract with Meadstar. I'm suggesting—suggesting strongly—that you convince him not to back away from his commitment."

Just as the phone went dead, Clarrie shrieked, a cry somehow the more disturbing for being muted by the nursery firedoor. Alyssia tensed for a second yell, but there was only the muffling silence.

That night the Golds took her to Ma Maison, where the booths were dark and the diners sophisticated enough not to gawk at celebrated faces. Her mind in a turmoil about the morning's contretemps and the afternoon's telephone call, she made a remarkably poor dinner companion.

Back at the house, she was surprised to find Juanita watching TV in her room—Juanita waited up only to help her out of some problematically fastened gown.

"How was Disneyland?" Alyssia asked.

"Great. . . ." Juanita's beautiful eyes sparkled, and she looked no more than five years older than her chronological age. "Alice, Sal wants me to move in with him."

Salvador Cardenas, a retired mailman, a short and prim widower, from his manner and appearance would be the last man to live the swinging new mores. Alyssia dropped her red mink and it slithered onto the carpet.

Juanita laughed excitedly. "Shocked you, didn't I?"

"Yes. Totally. I thought you guys were, like they say, just friends."

Juanita bent to pick up the fur. "Not anymore. He spent the day making plans for the two of us."

"He really *does* have it bad," Alyssia said. "I'll ask Barry to send the things you left in France."

"Sounds like somebody's trying to get rid of me."

"Oh, Nita, stop teasing. You know I'll miss you like cuh-razy," Alyssia said, hugging the sister who had given her childhood all that it had known of love. As they pulled apart, she couldn't hide her tears.

"Alice, look, if you need me, say the word. I'll tell Salvador the deal's off."

"I'm just happy for you." Alyssia blew her nose.

More than anything she longed to go over the day's events with Juanita—a good talk would act as a cathartic to free her both of humiliation and fear—but she knew that if she mentioned Robert Lang, Juanita would remain glued to her side. How could she kill this long-overdue romance?

After Juanita left, Alyssia stared into the cricket-haunted darkness, unable to sleep. What would Lang do if Hap continued to refuse to direct? *I use whatever means are available to me. . . .*

Switching on the bedside lamp, she opened her blue brocade address book, dialing the most recent number penciled under Hap's name.

After several rings the phone was answered by Madeleine's sleepy but irate voice. "Hello? Hello? Who is this?"

Without speaking, Alyssia hung up.

At ten after eight the next morning she was dialing again. This time the phone was answered on the first ring.

"Hap Cordiner."

"It's me, Alyssia. We have to talk. Lang called—"

"He phoned you? The bastard phoned *you*? Did you explain you were quitting?"

"That's what we need to go over."

"Was that you last night?"

"Last night?" she inquired, then that infuriating inability to lie to Hap jabbed at her. She mumbled, "Yes, me."

"How about breakfast?"

With a restaurantful of people watching her embarrassment as she attempted to convince him? "Eat first and I'll meet you. Tell me approximately how long you'll be, and I'll be walking up Delfern."

"Say ten minutes."

That meant he was leaving now. She brushed her teeth, hastily pulled a comb through her tumbled black hair and yanked on a white jogging suit. In the upstairs hall she heard a series of Clarrie's yells; downstairs she heard Beth and Irving's conversation. The last thing she needed now was Barry's sister and brother-in-law asking questions. She edged quietly out of the library's sliding glass door.

An opaline mist hugged the garden, fading the greens to tender grays. She hurried down the long, brick drive, pressing various buttons on the massive ironwork electric gate that guarded Clarrie's privacy and Irving's art collection.

She started along the rustic road, halting as a car slowed to park against a long hedge—there were no sidewalks here. In the fog she couldn't properly make out the emerging driver, but his height told her it was Hap.

He waved, trotting to her. Gripping her arm, he asked, "What did Lang say?"

"That you'd signed a contract and he expects people to keep their commitments."

"What about *your* commitment?"

"He's not holding me. He feels he owes me one. For doing *Transformations*."

"He wasn't threatening you, then?"

"Not me, no. But he's serious about *you*."

Hap released her arm, and without discussion they began walking away from Sunset in the direction of North Faring Road and the mist-shrouded hills.

"Alyssia . . ." Halting, he picked a camellia leaf, playing with it. "If I do direct *The Baobab Tree* it won't be because of threats. There's something I should have told you yesterday."

"You mean about refusing until you heard I'd already signed?"

"*PD* told you that?"

"Lang did. But why did you let me lay myself out and not say anything?"

Two men in shorts were jogging downhill toward them, and Hap was silent until they had passed.

"Things got in the way," he said in a low voice. "Loyalties that are an obligation. You understand?"

She nodded. He was telling her that all was not well between him and Madeleine, but nevertheless she was his wife.

"Another reason, and this isn't to excuse myself—yes it is," he said. "It hurt, you not getting a divorce those years we lived together. And when you finally decided to stay with Barry, I went sort of haywire."

"I was miserable too."

"The point is I swore I'd never let myself in for that kind of pain again. So now you know why I sat there, a voyeur hugging my privacy around me while I watched you strip."

She felt an erotic tingle, as if at this moment he were in actuality gazing at her nakedness.

"Last night," he said slowly, "after the call, I couldn't get back to sleep. It occurred to me that given the circumstances—that I was doing *The Baobab Tree* to work with you—backing out was not only idiotic but also hypocritical."

The oleanders trembled and a hummingbird darted out, hovering near them. She felt herself melting with desire; she yearned to press herself against him, longed for them to fall entangled on the damp grass. Yet something infinitely more complex than physical desire drew her to him. She was sick with longing for the lovely sensation of utter security, of complete freedom from danger, that she'd experienced only with him.

She whispered, "So we're doing the film?"

"Yes," he replied, his voice as low and shaken as hers.

They glanced away from each other, accepting that without so much as a fleeting touch or a word they had reinstated their love affair.

48

Irving had remained home that morning to choose a site to display his newest acquisition, a J. Seward Johnson, Jr., statue that would arrive the following week. As he and Beth went into the front garden, Alyssia and Hap were passing the gate. Irving's face pulled into lines of disapproval. Having maintained grim fidelity for over three decades to a wife who considered sex a messy martyrdom, he nursed a hidden distrust of the Cordiner family that was based solely on their relaxed attitude toward extramarital activity.

"I didn't even realize she was up yet," Beth said, quavering on the last word.

"Beth, maybe this makes me old-fashioned and out of it, but I can't for the life of me understand these open marriages."

"Me either," she sighed, then felt an obligation to set the record straight for her sister-in-law. "Before I got close to Alyssia, I blamed it all on her. When the chips were down, though, and Barry was at Villa Pacifica, I can't tell you how wonderful she was. But Irving, what if it's starting all over?"

"I shouldn't have said that about open marriages. Bethie, don't look so worried. In a few days she'll be safe with Barry at their Loire place." (At Ma Maison, Alyssia had glossed reality by saying there had been a misunderstanding at the financial end, so she and Hap were backing out of *The Baobab Tree,* an excuse Beth had swallowed with a vast sense of reprieve.) "I'm sure that they got together to discuss how to leave the production with the least embarrassment to Maxim and PD."

Irving was sure of no such thing—with a family that had every kind of meshugeneh arrangement, who could maintain such a certainty? Besides, the intense way the couple had been looking at each other bore no relationship to any kind of business except monkey business.

At a faraway shriek, the Golds turned in tandem.

"She's cranky this morning." Irving sighed. He had been overjoyed at the birth of the pretty pink and white child of his old age—finally a daughter!—and her disorder grieved him almost as much as it did Beth.

"Nurse said she has a temperature," Beth said distractedly.

"A temperature? How high?"

Beth continued gazing up at the nursery window. "A hundred!"

This time Irving, father of three healthy sons, could honestly allay the fears of his adored young second wife. "A hundred? At Clarrie's age that's nothing."

"But she's *never* sick."

"She's not exposed like other kids," Irving said. "She must've picked up a little cold from one of the nurses."

"She's never sick," Beth reiterated.

When Alyssia returned, her host and hostess were near the raised flower bed, Irving stooping over to press some sort of a post into the grass, Beth tilting her head appraisingly. At the whir of the gate mechanism they looked up. From Beth's hastily averted gaze and Irving's purposefully blank expression, she realized they had seen her with Hap.

Smiling, she went toward them. "I called Hap to discuss a few ideas I had about the script."

"But you said you were canceling." Beth nervously clenched and unclenched her fingers.

"There's no choice," Alyssia replied. "I didn't want to get you all upset, but what I told you last night wasn't total truth. Meadstar's the problem. Irving, you were right about Nevada. It's Robert Lang."

"Lang?" Beth breathed, flooded with memories of the dawn when she first heard the name. She felt herself flush. Though Irving knew everything about her and PD, she felt vaguely adulterous whenever she, now a married woman, recollected their intimacies.

"*He* owns Meadstar?" said Irving. "Then you're right, Alyssia. You have no choice but to go ahead. From what I've heard, smart people don't fool around with Lang."

"I better go phone Cyril about the costumes. I'll set up an appointment for this afternoon."

Beth had put aside the afternoon to clean up her Queen Anne desk, but Clarrie's crankiness continued, and at each shriek the numbers on the bills she was checking would jumble. For most people an ailing child would drown out all other problems. Not so for Beth. Though frantic about Clarrie, she kept seeing Hap and Alyssia—Barry's wife!—as they drifted past the gate. Beth, devoted to Irving, could never admit it even to herself, but her twin was the person she felt closest to on this earth.

A series of particularly piercing yells made her press both hands to her flat-set ears. When the cries ceased, she picked up her phone.

It was after midnight in France, but Barry answered on the first ring.

"Should I be superstitious and grumble?" he asked, his exuberant elation traveling six thousand miles. "Or should I dare the envious gods by telling you that the flow is incredible. Would you believe ten, sometimes twelve pages of original material in a day?"

"Wonderful." Beth hesitated, suddenly fearing that the problem might send him rushing to the bottle. But he seemed in high spirits, so she said cautiously, "Barry, have you ever considered this is the first movie Alyssia and Hap have made together since, uhh. . . ?"

"Bethie, Bethie." His chuckle was clear as if he were in the next room. "You're a compulsive worrier."

"They did, uhh, well, have a thing going for quite a few years."

"Don't give it a moment's thought. That's ancient history. Hap has a wife of his own now. And our marriage has settled into what I can unequivocally describe as felicitous harmony."

"Yes, but you will join her when they get to the Kenya location, won't you?"

"Of course."

"You'll be in Nairobi when they arrive?"

"I'll be there! Do I have to take an oath on both testaments!"

"I only meant—"

"Bethie, for God's sake, stop worrying. The affair is over. Moribund. Dead as a doornail."

When Beth hung up, she was shivering.

Three weeks passed. Three weeks during which Clarrie's temperature hovered around a hundred. Dr. Severin, the pediatrician, initially decided that chickenpox or measles or some other childhood disease was incubating, but when no symptoms developed, he consulted with other specialists, whose presence made Clarrie scream endlessly. Only the child psychiatrist ventured a diagnosis. The illness was Clarrie's method of weaning herself from her mother, and chances of recovery would be enhanced if Mrs. Gold would limit her visits.

Thus Beth was denied even her token role in the nursery.

Alyssia insisted that Clarrie's illness made her stay an imposition.

"The last thing you need right now is a houseguest," she said.

"Don't be ridiculous! Irving and I adore having you here," Beth remonstrated agitatedly.

"You're a doll, Beth, but I do have a home of my own."

Alyssia's maid had quit, so she hired a Guatemalan couple and returned to her isolated ledge in Beverly Hills.

On Thanksgiving the Golds shared turkey with Irving's side, afterward dropping by at Uncle Desmond and Aunt Rosalynd's mob scene. Hap was there with Madeleine. Beth asked the blonde and smiling Madeleine about her plans for Kenya.

Madeleine retorted, "I had enough of the dark continent for a lifetime that week I spent at the relief center. Hap's being a darling about my begging off."

Beth, who had called Barry with each development, phoned him the minute she got home, although it was only six thirty in the morning for him. To her surprise he, the perennial slugabed, was already working.

"To mangle Shakespeare," he said, "there comes a creative tide that must be taken at the flood."

She related her news, finishing, "So Madeleine won't be in Africa at all."

"I'm following suit," Barry said. "In a minor way."

"What do you mean?" She could hear her dismay in the echo on the long-distance cables.

"I already explained to Alyssia how magnificently *Spy* is coming, and she agreed that I ought to hold off joining her until the Nairobi sequences are finished."

"Oh, Barry."

"Will you stop dreaming up fictive drama, Beth? Madeleine isn't worried, I'm not worried. Why should you be? Anyway, I'll be there for the bulk of the shooting."

The rest of the Thanksgiving weekend Clarrie's temperature remained normal.

Sunday night Beth brushed her hair at her dressing table. Irving watched her from the bed.

"Why so pensive?" he asked.

"Just thinking. . . . Dear, if Clarrie stays well, I'll take a vacation. Since you're still tied up with Tahoe—" He was opening a major vacation complex on the north shore of Lake Tahoe. "—I'll have to go alone. So East Africa seems the obvious choice. I've never been, and the family'll be there."

Irving had been deeply involved in Clarrie's illness, but it was watching his adored Beth crumble that had hit him hardest.

Smiling, he raised up on his elbow. "A wonderful idea."

"You don't think Clarrie needs me?"

Clarrie, alas, had never needed her mother. "She's on the road, Beth," he reassured. "And besides, won't I be here, keeping an eye on her?"

She came to the bed, kissing the deeply grooved forehead. "You're so good to me, dear."

"While they're shooting, you can safari around with Barry."

"He's coming later. He won't be in Nairobi."

Shrewdly astute, Irving immediately accepted that Beth was traveling around the globe to protect her brother's interests. Though he considered his brother-in-law a weakling, and also a fool for abdicating his marital responsibilities to an opulently beautiful wife, at this moment he was blessing him.

Beth had turned out the light. He embraced her slim, sweetly scented body. Obediently she placed her arms around his neck. *What a woman!* Irving thought.

49

Alyssia left the doctor's office white and dazed, stumbling as she got into the elevator. Reaching the parking structure, she stared around the gasoline-odored dimness, tears clogging her throat because she couldn't spot her Jaguar.

After two full minutes she realized she'd left it on the next level. In the car, she closed her eyes, leaning back against the headrest and breathing shallowly.

"God," she muttered to herself. "God. . . ."

She had made this appointment with her internist because since before leaving France she had been having digestive problems—not nausea, which would have been a dead tipoff. Everything tasted as though it had been dipped in a coppery substance. Afterward, she suffered. In her entire life she'd never gotten indigestion from the stalest hamburger, hottest chili, the greasiest junk food. She had shrugged off her new problem as a trivial manifestation of the same psychological disorder that caused her anxiety attacks. And her schedule on *The Baobab Tree* was hectic. Pre-production rehearsals were in full, acrimonious swing. Her fittings generally escalated into high-pitched arguments—Cyril Lewin had designed each of her fifty costumes to be soft, delicate replicas of 1910 Worth gowns, refusing to listen when she insisted that a parsimonious Cockney miner's daughter living in Kenya would scarcely spend her toil-filled days in the latest Paris creation. Even missing a period hadn't seemed all that significant—occasionally when working hard she'd be late, or even skip a month. Today, however, the doctor, stripping the glove from his right hand after her internal, had inquired about her last menses. The implied diagnosis had sunk into her consciousness with the sureness of an arrow finding its target.

Several years earlier, when the airwaves were jammed with connections between cancer and the Pill, she had decided that with her near-nil sex life there was no need to court malignancy. Since then she'd used her Delft-blue diaphragm only about half of the times. The same old problem: if she left the bed, Barry might lose his erection and turn defensive or sad. The infrequency gave her a sense of security. Barry's contract for *Spy*, however, had acted like a shot of testosterone. There had been one time here, twice in New York, and several more encounters at the château.

On the stirrup table, she had immediately acknowledged that the baby couldn't be Hap's. They hadn't started again until three weeks ago. As if reading her mind, the doctor had said, "You're well into your second month."

She looked at her pale reflection in the rearview mirror. *An abortion?* she thought.

They weren't leaving on location for three days, so she still had time.

Of course—an abortion.

All at once she could hear her mother's stentorian groans, could see the blood-smeared, party-partying thighs.

Why think about that? Abortion was legal now. And she wasn't May Sue Hollister, tended by a warty crone and two terrified children. Alyssia del Mar, movie star, would have a safe, sterile procedure.

I'll go back to ask the doctor for the name of the top person, she thought. She left the car, plodding between slant-parked automobiles. She didn't hear the first honk, or the second. Not until a lengthy, irate blast did she shift onto the zebra-striped pedestrian path. The parking attendant eyed her questioningly, as did the elevator man. She didn't notice. When she got to her doctor's door, she gazed at his gilt-painted name and saw a meaningless jumble of letters.

The door swung open. A woman in a magenta velour warm-up suit swept out, giving an irritated sniff as she was forced to circle Alyssia. All at once the puffy, wrinkled face did a comic double-take. "Aren't you—"

"No!" Alyssia shouted. "I'm not!"

She raced up the hall to the emergency stairwell. Gasping, she leaned her full weight against the door until the danger of pursuit had passed, then she sank down, huddling on the snow-coldness of a metal-edged cement step.

I can't do it.

Her mind was stripped of all pretense by her burst of primal emotions, and she knew that no matter how inconvenient the small cluster of cells multiplying in her womb, abortion was an impossibility for her. *Why?*

What's the difference? I just can't.

Driving home, she decided that *The Baobab Tree* was entirely feasible. They had an eleven-week schedule, which would put her only in her fifth month at the conclusion of shooting. She would be wearing a period corset, so nothing would show. She was still in a state of shock, otherwise she would have realized that her sanguine planning had less to do with the realities of filmmaking and childbearing than with her intense desire to be with Hap.

* * *

"What happened this afternoon?" Hap asked.

Naked in bed, she had one arm behind her neck and was smiling somnolently as she watched him dress. He had dropped by on his way home from Magnum—he dropped by whenever possible, and they always ended up in bed. (What the Guatemalan couple thought, she didn't know, but chances were that they considered visits from a lover normal for Alyssia del Mar.)

At his question, she shifted her arm, pulling the sheet over her breasts. "I'm fine," she said.

Hap sat on the edge of the bed. "Then why have you been chugalugging Pepto-Bismol?" It was he who had insisted she make the doctor's appointment.

"As my director you'll have to get used to the new me. Sometimes when I'm working I get . . . edgy." The most understated truth of the year.

"What, exactly, did the doctor say?" he pressed.

This was the question she had been dreading. Even in her most catatonic state she had known that she couldn't share her news with Hap, who never made any secret about his hurt jealousy of Barry.

After a long pause, Hap took her hand, pressing it against his firm, naked thigh. "Love, look—if there's a problem, better to face it here at home than when we're in Africa. Is he running gastrointestinal tests?"

"He says it's not necessary. He thinks the problem's either the cholera and typhoid shots or the malaria pills."

"So he's positive you're only having a reaction?"

"That's his opinion. I already told you mine. Nervous stomach. So take your choice."

Hap released her hand, picking up his watch. "I better get a move on," he said.

"Only three more days," she said, feeling tendrils of anticipation.

Madeleine's complete absence during the eleven weeks of shooting and Barry's recently announced postponement had given her a fuzzy sense that she and Hap were setting out on a holiday. But of course they would not be vacationing, they would be in equatorial Africa, working with several hundred sensitive, gossipy people. During preproduction she'd had a foretaste of those speculative eyes glancing from her to Hap. The utmost discretion was called for.

She pulled on her robe and went outside to give Hap a goodbye kiss. After he drove away she stood on the doorstep gazing up at the near-full moon.

The phone rang. Positive it was Juanita, she darted inside. She couldn't tell her sister, either. Juanita would insist on leaving Salvador to accompany her on location.

"Alyssia?" It was Beth's voice.

"I was going to call. How's Clarrie?"

"Still normal."

"Thank God."

"This whole thing's really dragged me down," Beth said.

"You ought to get away."

"That's what Irving says. But he's totally tied up with the Tahoe project. I was thinking I'd zip on over to Kenya. I've never been to the game reserves."

"Oh. . . ."

"Do you think I'd be in the way?"

"It's a fabulous idea, Bethie. But wouldn't someplace closer be easier?"

Beth sighed. "I would be a nuisance."

"Oh, Beth, don't be silly—Maxim and Hap would love to have you. And Barry won't be there at the beginning, so when I'm not working we could chum around—I've never been to Kenya, either."

Alyssia hung up thinking, *If I had a brain in my head, I'd have scheduled an abortion for first thing tomorrow morning.*

50

To the west, the deep blackness of the sky showed a silvered edge that dimmed the enormous stars. The curve of horizon became visible, and suddenly one could make out a silhouetted march of elephants.

Watching the swift ascent of dawn, Alyssia stood at the mosquito webbing that substituted for windows in the tents. She had never expected to be enthralled by the panorama of Africa—having had her fill of the outdoors during her first fifteen years, she was no nature lover. Yet on the untouched land of Masai Mara Game Reserve, which is Kenya's side of the vast Serengeti, she would find herself imagining that she'd been thrust back through uncountable eons to the cruel, miraculous age before humankind reared up on two legs. Nights were mysterious and velvety, days vast, with clean, limitless distances. The sleek, tawny lions were a different breed from their brethren incarcerated in zoos, as were the elephants, the giraffes, the herds of trim zebra, the hundreds of species of antelope, the magnificent profusion of brilliant birds.

"Miss Alyssia, the shower is ready." Sara's lilting soprano was behind her. (Alyssia's contract specified that she have a personal maid on the company payroll and Sara, hired in Nairobi, was Juanita's replacement.)

In the rear of the tent were two beds: only one had been slept in. The eight weeks that Alyssia had been in Africa, Barry had remained at the château, finishing *Spy,* hassling with the clatterous workmen, and dispatching wordy explanations for his continued absence.

Alyssia's thongs flapped across the tent's raised wooden floor and down the two exterior steps to a canvas-fenced private yard lit by a kerosene lamp. Next to the open-topped, six-foot-high, corrugated iron shower enclosure stood two young black men wearing khaki shorts and sweatshirts imprinted THE BAOBAB TREE.

"Jambo," they chorused.

"Jambo," she replied, adding, *"Asante sana."* Unlike most of the company, Alyssia had picked up a serviceable Swahili vocabulary. *Jambo* meant hello, *asante sana,* thank you very much.

Inside, she shucked her terry robe, slinging it over the corrugated iron. Nights were cold on the highlands, and goosebumps rose on her flesh. The bathboys had heated the water at the kitchen cooking fires before pouring it into an overhead contraption. She pulled a cord to release the hot flow through the inaccurate showerhead, then began soaping herself vigorously. Her breasts were a fraction fuller and their blue tracery of veins more visible. Her stomach curved slightly between her pelvic bones. She reassured herself with the thought: *Even Hap hasn't noticed.*

An overladen tray had been delivered to her tent. The head cook, a long-time fan, personally fixed her breakfast, and nothing she said could persuade him not to include a half dozen of the strongly odored, brighter-yolked Kenyan eggs crisscrossed with bacon rashers. Leaving on the metal cover, she helped herself to fruit, scarcely making a dip in the terraced slices of mango, papaya and pineapple.

The tent flap was pushed aside. Beth came in carrying a coffee cup. She wore a crisply ironed safari suit and a broad-brimmed khaki hat adorned with a fish-eagle feather. Her delicate nose was red and peeling, her eyelids puffed from sunburn, her bare arms splashed with freckles. Though she never left her tent without a hat and slatherings of #15 sunscreen, the equatorial sun had marked its vengeance on her fair skin.

"Did the lions keep you up?" she asked.

"Lions? What lions?" replied Alyssia, who had sunk into a heavy sleep a minute after Hap had slipped from her tent.

"The lions that Masai Mara's famous for, the lions who roared until four this morning," said Beth.

"Oh, *those* lions. No, I didn't hear them. But then, Bethie, I'm a star—and stars get soundproofed tents."

Beth chuckled, then pressed a finger to her temple. Already the nerves behind her eyes were vibrating, not yet a headache, but moving toward one.

Africa was Beth's nemesis.

She couldn't take the intransigent brightness. She loathed the emptiness of the rolling grassland. The free-roaming animals terrified her. And as for the nights—she had never imagined anything so hostile as Masai Mara's predatory nights. She and Alyssia generally ate dinner at the trestle table outside Hap and Maxim's tent: long before nine thirty, when the generator went off and light bulbs all over *The Baobab Tree* encampment faded, Beth was rushing Alyssia to their neighboring tents. Striding a bit ahead, she would grip her large Eveready flashlight like a truncheon. Once zipped inside, she didn't emerge until morning, not even when her bladder begged her to use the chemical toilet two steps down from the rear tent-flap.

In the eight weeks she had been in Africa she had never ceased fretting about Clarrie's health: the cheerful letters from Irving that arrived in the Harvard Productions pouch did nothing to allay her worries.

Yet, for all Beth's acute discomfort and maternal brooding, she never considered going home.

On the surface she had no cause for alarm. While filming, Hap and Alyssia displayed only professionalism. At the supper table, they were friendly and never worked the seating to be next to each other. They hadn't renewed their affair, of that Beth was positive. She was equally positive that the instant she left Masai Mara Game Reserve, her sister-in-law would leap naked into Hap's narrow camp cot.

Beth's suspicions and Alyssia's semiamused resentfulness of her sister-in-law's chaperonage should have dulled the edge of their friendship. Instead, their existing warmth had grown and they were closer than ever. Beth would help Alyssia learn her lines; they shared paperbacks, magazines, worries about Clarrie, dreams of success for Barry's novel, light gossip and laughter.

The makeup artist arrived, also carrying coffee. She, Beth and Alyssia chattered, and continued to talk while the hairdresser ratted Alyssia's hair into a period pompadour.

The chain-smoking wardrobe mistress came to perform her task.

"Alyssia, you really oughta let me lace the corset," she said, cigarette dangling from her lips, nicotine-stained fingers moving deftly to adjust the white organza gown. "Sara doesn't get the damn thing tight enough."

"Why do you think I let her do it?" Alyssia replied, winking.

"I'll have to move these hooks. Again."

"Africa gives me an appetite."

"You're telling me!" said Beth. "I've gained ten pounds at least." In actuality she had lost three.

A minibus was waiting for Alyssia, and Beth climbed in with her. There were few roads on Masai Mara, and none in this remote section. The bus traveled across the open land in a cloud of red-yellow dust. A herd of Thomson's gazelles pronged away, their white butts bouncing. One of the giraffes around a clump of acacia trees glanced at them, then the entire group shifted in their slow grace to browse at more distant vegetation.

From the top of a slight rise they could look down on the set. As always, Alyssia caught her breath at the superbly cinematic image. The sweep of empty beige savannah, the baobab tree of the title with its barren branches resembling upside-down roots, the solitary, gardenless brick villa backed by the era's ubiquitous carriage house/stable that belonged in some middle-class London suburb.

This was the home of Mellie, the role that Alyssia played. Her miserly Cockney father, having struck it rich in the Transvaal, has come to Kenya with a mineral map showing rich veins of gold in the Rift Valley. (Mellie will steal the map for her lover, Jason Mattingly.)

As the minibus jounced down the slope amid a maze of tire ruts, the turmoil in the dip to the left of the house became visible. Land-Rovers, jeeps, minibuses were parked higgledy-piggledy near trailers. Wranglers and animal trainers bustled around the corrals, an assistant director raised his megaphone to a crowd of elegantly tall *moran*—Masai warriors—whose hair was reddened with ocher.

The minibus braked at a trailer above whose door was painted: PRODUCTION.

Maxim greeted Alyssia and his cousin, then cocked an eyebrow toward a drifting continent of gray-black clouds. "That's one mean mother," he said sourly.

"The short rains, don't you know," said the ruddy-faced Kenyan who was their so-called local expert.

"'I say, there might be a spot of rain in November and December.'" Maxim mimicked the Kenyan's rather high-pitched voice. "You call twenty-one days of rain in eight weeks a spot?"

Hap had emerged. Fatigue lined his face, but his calm manner invited confidence. "So let's shoot while we can," he said.

The very young second assistant director, whose shirt and shorts already showed dark sweatstains, jogged to one of the trailers. In two minutes he emerged.

"Mr. Camron's having a massage," he reported. Cliff

Camron had been signed for the role of Jason Mattingly after Jack Nicholson and Robert Redford had turned it down.

"I'll bet he is." Maxim gave an acid laugh. "Get your butt back in there and tell him we're ready for him."

The young assistant director trudged to the trailer. Returning, he said, "Mr. Camron said his back's been acting up and he can't stand straight. The masseur is trying to work out the knots."

"In case you've forgotten," Maxim said, "we're shooting a film here. You, as part of the crew, are paid handsomely to do your job, which is getting Mr. Camron out from under the nimble fingers."

The young assistant director was as crimson as if he were suffering from heatstroke. "Mr. Cordiner, I can't drag—"

"The fuck you can't!"

"Maxim." Hap pushed back his hair, which the sun had streaked yet lighter. "It's nobody's fault. If you keep sending for Cliff—you know what happened yesterday."

The previous day, Cliff had departed during lunch with Cameo Hannaway, a pretty, frizzy-permanented blonde bit player. All afternoon the two-hundred-plus Hollywood crew and the forty-seven Masai extras were paid to wait while Cliff Camron had a boff and blow job. He had returned to the location just as the sun began its swift descent.

Alyssia went to her trailer with Beth.

The clouds increased and darkened as they shared the new *Vogue*.

An hour and a half later, Cliff trotted jauntily from his trailer. Fair-haired, barely taller than Alyssia, he bore a resemblance to Alan Ladd, the movie idol of the forties, but projected his own good-natured, highly sensual charm.

"Hi, guys," he said. "Sorry about that, but the old lower lumbar's been acting up. Ready for me?"

"Ready, Cliff," Hap said calmly.

As Cliff started toward the setup, where his brother, who was his stand-in, sat reading a week-old *Variety*, rain began falling in large drops, denting the carefully smoothed soil. "Jeez, rain. What a tough break," Cliff said. "Well, maybe it'll let up after lunch."

"Mr. Cordiner." The script girl held up her big hat to protect herself from the sudden deluge. "This scene comes right after fifty-three, so we can't have mud. Even if the rain stops, we won't be able to shoot."

"Jeez, what a fucking lousy break," said Camron, and jogged through the downpour to the waiting Mercedes that was one of his production perks.

It rained intermittently through the afternoon and evening. Beth and Alyssia dined alone in Beth's tent to the reverberation of huge drops on waterproof canvas roof.

"This puts us exactly thirty days behind schedule," Alyssia said.

Beth, sawing on a rubbery chicken wing, looked glumly at her. "This afternoon I was talking to Maxim. He figures they're more than six million dollars over budget already."

"At least Lang's keeping hands off."

Beth abandoned her battle with the chicken. "Will he when he hears he has to put up another six million?"

"Everybody knows filming on a remote location like this can skyrocket costs. He must've known we'd go over."

"Yes," Beth said. "And he knew Uncle Frank had no money to pay his gambling debts."

Since this was the supposed onset of her period, they did not make love. Hap took off his safari boots and lay dressed next to her on top of the blanket.

"Hap," she asked. "Aren't you at all worried about Lang?"

"No."

"With anyone else, you'd feel responsible for the delays."

"So let him pull the plug," Hap said. "Why're we wasting time on him? Let's talk about us. What're we going to do about us?"

"It's too complicated," she sighed.

"About me and Madeleine." Hap's voice was a low rumble. "I once heard somebody call us the gold-dust couple. I guess that's how we look from the outside. We're constantly on the move. Tennis, sailing, the big charity things, parties, weekends with people she knows or I know. Alone with her, I often can't find a word to say. Literally, we spend entire evenings without exchanging a sentence. If she wants to talk, she does it on the phone. And, uhh, we haven't, uhh, had sex for nearly a year."

"You don't have to tell me this, Hap," she said, kissing his cheek.

"I'm not blaming Madeleine. We just don't belong together." He paused. "One thing I've always wanted is to be the same on the outside as on the inside."

"You're the least phony person I know."

"Not anymore I'm not. I started the relief center to forget you and now I'm positive that's the main reason I married Madeleine. On the set I'm faking it, pretending to be the Rock of Ages, total self-assurance, and all the time gnawing and worrying."

She traced his jaw—the fair stubble never showed, which made the toughness of the bristles surprising. "At least you know you're Hap Cordiner. What about me? Am I Alice Hollister, Alicia Lopez or Alyssia del Mar? Or any of the above?"

"I know who you are. I know every inch of you."

No, you don't, she thought.

51

During the night the rain ceased. Before dawn electricians were adjusting huge lamps to dry the earth, which turned the color of oxblood when wet.

It was eleven before the art director, the cinematographer and Hap were all satisfied that the ground was the right shade.

Before this they had never shot through the noon hours, when the rays of the equatorial sun are most intense, but today Maxim insisted. They were filming Mellie and Jason tossing horseshoes in front of a group of fascinated Masai, an intensely physical scene with technical problems.

On the fourth take, Alyssia could feel her head getting lighter and lighter, as if her large, gauze-swathed period hat were filling with helium. And then the sun turned black.

"I should've told Maxim to forget it when he insisted we shoot through lunch."

"Hap, why won't you believe me? The rest fixed me just fine," she said. But she clung to his solid strength.

He had come into her tent two or three minutes earlier, shucking his clothes, as he had not done the previous night.

"The truth is," he said, his voice level, "you shouldn't be working at all—especially not here."

Her skin prickled with apprehension. "The rushes are that bad?" she asked with a little chuckle.

"Alyssia." His hand curved over her naked stomach, a large, authoritative presence.

Gripping his wrist, she attempted to shift the hand. It refused to budge.

"Hap, why're you making such a big deal? I'm not the first person to pass out. The midday sun here is murder."

The mattress shifted as he raised up and the flashlight he'd set on the bedside table flared. The beam shone starkly on his face, flattening and whitening the features as if he were a player in an early silent film.

"How pregnant are you?" he asked.

The hunting lions, the bane of Beth's nights, roared. The pride was close, and the intensity of the sound was like a drumroll reverberating inside Alyssia's chest.

"In my fourth month," she whispered unhappily.

A low, sibilant breath escaped Hap. "So it's Barry's?"

"Yes—Barry's."

Clicking off the light, he shifted on the cot so he no longer touched her.

"Why did you do the film?" His voice in the darkness was courteous and measured.

"I told you in your office that first day. I wanted to be with you."

"What were your plans for the future?"

"I wasn't thinking, Hap, I was feeling."

"Not one thought about completion?"

"I wear the corset; we were meant to be finished a

couple of weeks from now. You and Maxim both have the reputation of getting in on schedule."

"Did you," he asked, "consider abortion?"

"Please stop."

"Stop what?"

"Talking like that."

"Rationally, you mean?"

"I know you're hurting, Hap."

"Shouldn't I ask a few questions that've occurred to me through the weeks?"

"I *did* think about it," she said. "It took me less than ten minutes to realize I couldn't."

"Because the baby's Barry's?"

"Because I'm *me.* Oh, what's the point of logic? I just couldn't do it."

"How does Barry feel?"

"He doesn't know."

"What?"

"I haven't told him."

"Why the secrecy?"

By now she was so frightened by Hap's politely questioning tone that she burst out, "Would you rather hear that I've told him and he's dancing jigs?"

"Even you aren't a good enough actress to carry it off."

"What does *that* mean?"

"Barry's not much in evidence."

"All right—you've made your point. I've been tried and convicted of the crime of the century. I hid something from you—"

"Something?" For the first time Hap's voice shook.

"If you want to know, I thought of telling you after I saw the doctor, but I put it off because I wanted to be with you and I knew that this would happen. You're predictable—entirely predictable."

He made an odd little sound in his throat before he said, "Yes, I imagine I am."

"Well, now you can quit slumming!" she hissed, holding back her tears.

She felt the mattress shift beneath her. *Don't go, don't leave me,* she thought. *Please, I'm sorry—I didn't mean any of that. Don't leave like this.* But she could not speak.

She heard him fumble for his clothes, heard fabric slither on flesh, heard and felt the reverberations of bare feet padding on boards. For a moment she saw a dim outline against the moonless night, a large masculine body with slumped shoulders. The canvas fell into place and she was alone.

Alyssia—no, it was Alice—began to weep in loud sobs that drowned out the hunting lions.

The following morning on the set they exchanged amicable greetings and discussed the nuances of Mellie's first kiss.

It was a close-up. Cliff and Alyssia swung gently on a hammock that hung by chains from the roof of the veranda. The sound people had booms over them, the camera crew was less than three feet away, grips stood by the flat, shimmering reflectors, and Hap leaned over the veranda rail.

"I think we ought to go inside. . . ." Alyssia murmured her line, her lips parting.

The instant before she would meet Cliff's kiss, a sudden pain infiltrated her left arm. She gasped.

The sound men exchanged glances. The gasp would be picked up and amplified with Dolbyized fidelity.

The pain curved swiftly across her chest. Rocking the hammock askew, she lurched to her feet, pushing through the encirclement of technicians. She didn't hear the concerned, questioning voices. She was racing across carefully tended, pale-brown wild grasses—she never considered taking the hard-packed path because the grass was the shortest distance to her trailer. Hauling herself up the steps, she gasped into Sara's frightened dark face, "Get out! Get out!"

The maid, galvanized, darted away, leaving the door open. Alyssia locked it. *How can I breathe with this damn corset?* Dizzily, she fumbled through the things on her dressing table, overturning bottles and jars before finding her nail scissors. With the short, curved blades, she severed her way down both her exquisitely fragile Edwardian bodice and the constrictive corset. She could hear her own whimpering gasps.

"Alyssia! It's me—Beth. What is it, dear? What's wrong?"

"Be all right. . . ."

She collapsed on the daybed. Knocks were accompanied by worried queries. Her breathing had eased a bit when Maxim's voice came through the window louvers.

"Let me in."

"Be fine."

"Just open the damn door before I get a hacksaw."

Later, she would ponder what there had been in his low, furious voice that made her obey. But now she wasn't thinking coherently. Yanking off the ruined costume and corset, she tied a yellow robe over her nakedness.

She unlocked the door.

Maxim came in, blanching as he surveyed her.

"Jesus!"

She hadn't realized that spotlets of crimson were oozing through the buttery silk. "I . . . I cut myself."

"Suicide?"

"The corset was too tight. . . ." She glanced at the strew of pale, jaggedly cut costumery on the floor. "I had to use scissors."

He took a step, standing over her. Sweat gleamed on his long, angular face. "No more of this shit, Alyssia. If you and Hap have a blow-up, that's between the two of you."

Hap told him? Unbelievable. Impossible. "What're you . . . talking about?"

"You and Hap."

She turned away. "That was years ago."

"Put the crap in the can where it belongs, Alyssia. I know what's been going on in tent city. Who gives a shit? All I care about is that you earn your two mil when you're in front of the camera."

"Get out of my trailer!"

"Not until I'm finished."

"One more word and you'll be talking to my lawyers." Though her breathing had somewhat regulated itself, she still needed abnormal effort to control her voice.

"Robert Lang isn't into talking," Maxim said.

"Lang?"

"He knows far better than Dad ever did how to keep his people in line."

"I gather that's a threat?"

"Alyssia, are you trying to destroy my brother?"

"Hap?"

"He's the only brother I have. I love him. I prefer to

keep him around. Or hasn't it occurred to you that Lang might conclude that Hap's sabotaging the production?"

She sank into the makeup chair. "But Maxim, why would he blame Hap?"

"It's too obvious to need explanation. Hap tried to back out of the film. Under Hap's direction, we've shot exactly half the number of scenes we should have."

"The rain, Cliff, the first-time extras—"

"Sure, *we* know that. But Lang's got it in for Hap. So you tell me. Is Lang more likely to lay it on the weather, Cliff, the local darkies? Or lay it on Hap?"

52

The rain started again three evenings later, just after dinner. Beth draped a bush jacket over her shoulders before she sat under the dangling light bulb to write her letter:

> Irving, dear,
>
> Even though this is going in the pouch, you will probably see me first. . . .

Since Alyssia had passed out in front of the camera, Beth felt as if a skillful ophthalmologist had removed cataracts from both her eyes. She no longer viewed Hap and Alyssia through the obscuring lens of the years that they had lived together: instead, she saw them as they were now, two professionals related by marriage who were making a film together.

"Beth, are you decent?" The familiar masculine voice rose over the aggressive counterpoint of rain. "It's me, Hap."

Speak of the devil, she thought. "Don't stand on ceremony, Hap," she called. "You could drown out there."

He took off his yellow slicker, and as he hung it on the hook, streaming water darkened the floor planks. Using the towel that she handed him, he wiped his face, then rubbed his hair. He did not speak. Instead, he gazed at her with bloodshot eyes.

All at once she was positive that her cousin was the bearer of evil news. Who was it? Clarrie? Irving? Her father? Barry—had something awful happened to Barry?

"Hap . . ." she faltered. "What is it?"

"At dinner you said something about leaving tomorrow morning."

She relaxed and her voice returned to its normal serenity. "Tomorrow morning at nine. Derek"—the White Hunter whom she had hired to keep up her pretense of being on a camera safari—"has chartered a plane to get us to Nairobi. From there I'm booked on a Lufthansa flight. Hap, you sweet idiot you, did you come out in all this rain just to say goodbye?"

Hap didn't seem to hear her. Gazing down at his ankle-high boots, which were slathered with brown mud, he asked, "Have you noticed anything different about Alyssia the last couple of days?"

Beth's warning antennae immediately shot up. "Isn't she incredible? If it had been me passing out, I'd have taken off a few days—but not my sister-in-law. She's a real trouper."

"Bethie, I've directed her too many times. I know her work. Since she fainted, the spark's gone."

Beth had a habit of remaining silent while she puzzled through new information. What hidden reason had propelled Hap through the downpour? It couldn't be to discuss Alyssia's performance with her. Had her suspicions indeed been well grounded? Had there been a lovers' quarrel? Did Hap expect her—of all people—to patch it up? But on the other hand, Hap had never been devious.

His red-streaked eyes were fixed on her.

"She seems in top form to me," Beth said guardedly.

"She's running on technique. I can't put my finger on anything specific, except to know something's missing."

"Have you talked to her?"

"Bethie, how can I go to an actress with this line of questioning? It'd be the kiss of death for any working relationship." He paused. "If Barry were here, I'd talk it over with him."

"She did rush off the set," Beth said thoughtfully.

"I've spent hours trying to figure it. Maybe I've somehow offended her. Maybe the film's too rugged physically. Maybe the sun's too much for her. Or maybe it's just her period."

Beth looked down at her large emerald engagement ring, wishing he hadn't brought up anything so intimate. "Hap, you haven't worked with her for years. Maybe you've just forgotten that she's like all actors—she has her good days and her bad."

"I thought of that, too," he said. "Beth, does this seem completely off the wall? I even figured the fainting might mean she's pregnant."

"She'd certainly have told me." But as she spoke, Beth's eyes narrowed reflectively. Hadn't the chain-smoking wardrobe woman been talking about loosely laced corsets and altering hooks on costumes?

"I can't work like this. Will you do me a big favor? Find out what's bothering her."

"Of course."

"I'll wait here."

"You mean I should talk to her *now*?"

"You're leaving tomorrow morning."

"Hap, the rain—"

"It's almost stopped."

The thrumming on the roof had indeed lessened. "But the lights're ready to go out—"

"Isn't she in the next tent?"

"Yes, but—"

He was gazing at her with those bloodshot eyes. One of Our Own Gang pleading for help. . . .

Sighing, she reached for her umbrella and flashlight.

"Hi, Beth. What a surprise." Alyssia splayed her book face down on the khaki blanket.

Minus makeup, her beautiful face shadowed by thick, glossy black hair, she looked haggard. No—more than haggard. Alyssia looked ill. Then she sat up straighter, smiling. The picture of health.

But Beth knew an actress's bag of tricks. And she didn't

have time to spar around with words. Setting down her wet, still open umbrella, she asked, "Alyssia, maybe this is way off base, but are you pregnant?"

Alyssia's thick, dark eyelashes fluttered, her pale lips quivered briefly. Then she recovered. "A little," she said with a tiny chuckle. *"Un peu."*

Beth's fingertips curved involuntarily, as if to scratch or gouge.

Alyssia, having a child!

Alyssia doing what she, Beth, desired to do above all things—and feared most. Not having an envious nature, Beth didn't recognize her sudden surge of hotly violent emotion as jealousy.

"Wonderful!" she said in a strangled tone. "After all these years! I'm so happy for you and Barry. But whatever possessed you, doing *The Baobab Tree*?"

"I signed long before the baby was started, and by the time I found out, we were leaving in a couple of days. Beth, look—will you keep this under wraps?"

"Why? I don't understand the whole thing."

"It's just easier if people don't know. You're the only one who does know."

"You mean you haven't told *Barry*?"

"Especially not Barry. I'll tell him when he finishes *Spy*."

"This is *his* baby, too." Beth couldn't repress her punitive note.

"Bethie, this book's so important to him." Alyssia's voice broke with sincerity. "You know he's never respected his television work or even his screenplays for *Wandering On* and *Transformations*. Ever since I met him, his goal has been to be a novelist."

"You can't hide this."

"His last letter said he's almost done."

After a brief pause, Beth said in that same vaguely punitive tone, "It's hard to believe your OB okayed doing this particular role."

"I'm in tiptop shape, Beth. How did you guess?"

Beth stirred uneasily. "Oh, observation, and something the wardrobe woman said."

The low-watt bulb flickered, dimming until only the filament showed. Beth's fears crowded into the darkness. She clicked on the flashlight, holding it straight-armed in front of her the way actors hold crosses to ward off vampires.

"You promise not to spread the word?" Alyssia asked from beyond the shadows. "Or tell Barry?"

"I won't." Forgetting her umbrella, Beth charged into the dripping, terrifying African night.

Hap, sitting in the clammy, pitch-black tent, squinted into her flashlight. "Well?" he asked in a low voice.

Beth told him that Alyssia was indeed having a baby and had sworn her to secrecy. "You mustn't let on that you know," she finished.

"I'll do my best to make it easy on her, that's all." Hap's hands were clenched tightly. "If only Barry were around—"

Beth interrupted, whispering. "He's nearly done with the book and she wants him to finish. She hasn't told him yet, and she'll be furious if anyone else does."

"Even that maid of hers isn't here. Your leaving is going to be very rough on her."

"Hap, I've been away *two* months!"

"Couldn't you stretch it out just a bit longer until Barry gets here?"

A pair of white moths circled around the flashlight. Something about the way the shadows moved across Hap's face made Beth sense that this was what had brought her cousin to her tent in the first place. He wanted her to stay so Alyssia would have somebody to lean on. His eyes were pleading with her.

"Clarrie and Irving have managed this long." She sighed, then added reluctantly, "A few more days won't be the end of the world."

"I knew I could count on you, Bethie," he said with that warm smile of his.

After he left, Beth tore up the letter to Irving and set the flashlight on the table to compose another. Writing about Alyssia's secret in some manner eased her jealousy, and by the time she pulled the blankets up over her ears, she considered herself delighted with the news of her impending niece or nephew.

* * *

The following dawn, over coffee, Beth told Alyssia she was staying—"Just a bit longer."

"I knew I never should have told you," Alyssia retorted.

"Don't be so conceited. The African mystique has finally gotten through. Irving and Clarrie are having a wonderful time together. Aren't I entitled to a holiday?"

Alyssia and Beth were nibbling iodine-washed lunch salads in the trailer when a faraway buzz intruded, growing louder and angrier.

"Sounds like a helicopter," Beth said.

"Doesn't it, though? But I thought Maxim paid off enough Nairobi officials to ward off every chopper, plane and minibus for miles around." She set down her fork, pulling aside the curtain.

The two women watched the machine land amid great, swirling clouds of yellow-brown dust. A man emerged, ducking under blades that whipped his thinning brown hair.

Alyssia sat back abruptly.

"Oh, my God," she whispered. "It's Lang."

Beth, deafened by the roar, shook her head to show she hadn't heard.

"It's Robert Lang!" Alyssia shouted.

Ten minutes later, when the din had subsided, Beth was still asking, "What's he doing here?"

"Checking up, Beth, that's all it can be."

"Nobody drops down out of the blue like that."

"It's his style."

"Close again, please, Miss del Mar," said the makeup artist, applying another of the six pinks that enhanced the soft fullness of Alyssia's lips.

Beth stared out the trailer window. Hap and Lang stood talking. They were too far away to make out expressions, but Hap's feet were braced apart, as if he were a soldier standing guard.

"Perfect," said the makeup woman. "There you go, Miss del Mar."

Alyssia left the trailer, hurrying along the path. In the shadow of the stable/carriage house, Cliff Camron sat on a stool while his hairdresser stuck bits of straw in his tinted yellow hair.

"So the moneybags has arrived," Cliff said.

"It's probably come to his attention that we're a mite over budget," Alyssia replied.

"Stop worrying, chick. Isn't old Cliff here to protect you?" He ogled the open neckline of her shirtwaist with his boyish grin. "Don't you look eminently seducible."

"Thank you," she said, smiling. Cliff might be an irresponsible egotist, but he was a likable one.

Entering the stable, she saw Hap peering through the camera.

As she approached, he looked up.

"Alyssia," he said. "Have a minute?"

"Any number of minutes."

He led her to a dim corner where their privacy would be respected.

"Lang's here," he said.

"Descended from the heavens," she said.

"He wants to watch the afternoon's shooting."

"Funny. I never thought of him as a masochist."

"Is it okay with you?"

A wintry shiver ran through her. Under Lang's unblinking gaze, how could she respond with a young girl's timidly awakening passion to Cliff's baring of her breasts? But it was Maxim's warning that Lang would blame Hap for everything and anything that dictated her response. "Delighted to have him aboard," she said.

"You're positive?"

"Isn't he putting up his illegally gotten gains to make this Euripidean tale of love and revenge?"

"You're upset enough as it is."

"Upset? Flattered's more like it. After all, he's flown to Africa to view my anatomy."

"You're reaching. You always reach when you're shook."

"I must remember it's a no-no to be directed by former lovers."

Hap was standing with his back to the lights of the setup. Shadows pooled in his eye sockets.

"Alyssia, what happened the other night—I'd been building myself up in a major way that the baby was mine.

When you told me it was Barry's, I couldn't deal with it." He sighed. "I still can't deal with it."

Numbness prickled on her face and she wondered if she had gone white under her makeup. "Not to fret," she said. "We each have our own little adjustment problems."

"I'm trying to apologize."

"For what?"

"I behaved badly. Look, I want to be able to deal with it, God how I want to! Alyssia, give me time."

"How about another few months? Let me see, what will you two be? First cousin once removed, does that sound right?"

"Stop putting up barriers. At least let's talk about it."

"But we are talking," she said. "Very heavy stuff."

"You can't punish me any more than I'm punishing myself."

"What's the problem, Hap? We had a little location fling for old time's sake."

He swallowed sharply, as if he were going to respond. Instead, he walked away.

She called after him, "Please tell Mr. Lang if he wants to watch, as far as I'm concerned he's welcome."

Hap nodded but didn't turn. As she watched him go toward the brightly lit setup, she leaned against the plank wall, weakened by inconsolable misery.

Lang sat just out of camera range, his chin in his hand, and though she couldn't see him, she could never forget he was staring at her. She found it impossible to keep her mind away from the conversation with Hap. No wonder she couldn't rouse up the appropriately enamored rapture as Cliff's hands began their maneuvering. She fluffed her lines.

On the twelfth take, Hap called, "People, be back in fifteen minutes."

"Upsydaisy," Cliff said, extending his hand.

"Sorry," she murmured.

"Happens to all of us," he replied good-naturedly.

The chain-smoking wardrobe mistress handed her a duster to pull over her now gaping shirtwaist.

Lang was approaching. "Miss del Mar," he said. Though he didn't incline his head, he gave the impression of making a courtly bow. "What a pleasure this is. I've always wanted to see you work."

"Not my finest hour." *Laugh,* she told herself.

Lang was looking over her shoulder. Turning, she saw that Hap had come up behind her.

"Lang," he said, "you'll have to leave."

"Jesus Christ, Hap!" Maxim had followed his brother.

Hap ignored the interruption. "You're disturbing my actors."

"Mr. Cordiner," Lang said, "I don't need to point out that I have every right to be here."

"Not while I'm the director."

"Hap, cool it," Maxim interjected.

Hap continued to ignore him. "My contract gives me complete control of visitors to the set."

"That is correct," Lang replied in a manner that implied he knew every clause of the sixty-odd pages of single-spaced print.

"Hap's trying to protect me," Alyssia said. "It's been a rotten afternoon for me and I'll handle it better without an audience."

"My last wish is to delay production," Lang said. "But I would like a meeting with Mr. Camron and the three of you."

"Whenever you want," Maxim said.

"This evening at seven in the production tent," Lang said.

53

Alyssia pulled forward a wisp of bang. For the evening's meeting she had swept up her hair in a sexy tumble, piled on eye makeup and worn one of her glitzy tee shirts to cover the bulge in her white slacks, which were now so tight that she had to lie on her back to zip them.

Beth was saying, ". . . even when we were little kids Hap was the same way. Calm and reasonable until somebody messed with his ethical ideals or acted unfairly—then watch out!" Having heard the true events in the stable, as well as the embellished versions, she couldn't control her anxious fretting. "How could he have barred Lang from the set? He's gone totally berserk."

Alyssia's fingers trembled as she reached into her satin jewel folder for another narrow gold chain to add to the dozen or so already dangling on her sequined bosom.

"If I were you," Beth advised, "I'd look more businesslike."

"For me, Beth, this *is* businesslike." Alyssia glanced at her clock. "God! I said I'd be there at six thirty, and it's nearly seven. See you later!"

Hurrying past the tents, she ignored the aroma of barbecuing beef, the sounds of convivial pre-dinner conversation, the soft, restless thrumming of a guitar, the tape of a Haydn symphony. Beth's compulsive worrying had stretched her already taut nerves. *Don't say one word,* she commanded herself. Any remark could ignite Hap into an overt display of his loathing. *No wiseass cracks to cover up how terrified you are.*

At the production tent she pressed a hand over her racing heart, then lifted the flap.

The rear, where Hap worked on uncut footage at the Kem editing machine, was hidden by a wall of canvas. The front area served both brothers as an office.

They were sitting on the swivel chairs of their facing desks, while Lang had taken the narrow, slip-covered sofa that sometimes served as a bed.

Seeing her, the three men rose.

"Ahh, Miss del Mar," Lang said. "We've been waiting to start."

She smiled. "Am I late?"

"Late?" Maxim said. "I didn't realize the word was in your vocabulary."

"Bitchy, bitchy," she said, then realized that she had unwittingly trod too close to the castle keep wherein Maxim guarded his secret life. Hastily she inquired, "Where's Cliff?"

"Treetops," Hap replied. "Before this came up he'd chartered a plane to go to Treetops."

Treetops was a hotel built high in the Cape chestnut trees of the Aberdares National Park: here visitors passed the night looking down on the wild animals attracted to a floodlit watering hole. Cliff repeatedly swept his entire entourage (masseur, barber, chauffeur, makeup artist, aerobicist, hairdresser, secretary, the brother who was his stand-in and Cameo Hannaway) into such exotic excursions.

"I'm distressed that Mr. Camron isn't with us," Lang said. "But my message is simple and can be passed on to him: these constant delays must stop."

Maxim leaned forward. "The short rains," he said, "have broken Kenya's fifty-year record."

"The weather's unfortunate." Lang's unwavering eyes were fixed on Hap. "And the footage you just showed me is exceptional. But Meadstar went into this venture in good faith that the budget you presented—"

"*I* worked up the budget," Maxim interrupted protectively. "Not Hap."

"At any rate, it was a budget that Harvard Productions could live with. Meadstar did not balk at the considerable costs. Or rather, I as Meadstar's sole shareholder did not balk. I had anticipated that my good faith would be reciprocated."

"You've been here since noon," Hap said. "That's hardly enough time to understand the problems of shooting in a difficult location like this."

Lang nodded judiciously. "I agree. And as I just said, I also accept the difficulties with the weather, even though such contingencies should certainly have been included in the original budget and schedule. What I cannot condone is the manner with which you, as director, indulge your cast."

Alyssia stared down at her fingernails, unpolished and short for her role as Mellie. *Me,* she thought. *He means me.*

"After you left," Hap said, "we got the scene in one take."

"This afternoon you pointed out that you have the right to regulate visitors to the set. There is another clause in your contract that states if you fall behind schedule, Meadstar producers may come in to assist."

"Take over for us, you mean?" Hap asked.

"No. Precisely as I said. You continue to work while our personnel remains on hand to insure there's no further falling behind."

Hap looked at Maxim. "Did you see that clause?"

"It's there," Maxim replied tersely.

Lang tugged at a blue-striped shirt cuff, adjusting the plain gold link. "My people have worked out a revised schedule for you. It's more than reasonable. You have twenty-nine days to complete principal shooting."

"Twenty-nine days!" Alyssia forgot her vow of silence. "No way! It's impossible! We can't do it. The schedule calls for almost that much time in Africa alone. And what if there's more rain?"

"Miss del Mar, I have the highest regard for your acting talent, but I refuse to permit directorial excesses to destroy this film."

"Destroy it? You're the one talking artistic impossibilities."

"No, Miss del Mar, I'm talking about simple arithmetic. I have already poured an additional six million into *The Baobab Tree*. The original budget to complete was twenty-five million. The sum of six and twenty-five is thirty-one. Thirty-one million dollars is scarcely a niggardly budget for even the most 'artistic' film."

"Don't use that tone with Alyssia," Hap said.

"It's a math lesson," Alyssia said lightly. "Mr. Lang, you have my solemn promise I won't muff another line." Her trill of laughter was drowned out by the high-pitched whistle that announced the dinner buffet had opened.

When the penetrating squeal ended, Lang said, "You see, Mr. Cordiner? Miss del Mar understands that *she* has responsibilities."

Hap, already on his feet, rounded the desk. "That's enough, Lang. The meeting's over."

Lang's composed expression didn't falter, though a gloss that might have been excitement showed on his high forehead. "I'm sure that you can bring *The Baobab Tree* in on the revised schedule—if you learn how to manage your stars."

Hap's tan mottled red, but he repeated levelly, "The meeting's over."

Lang nodded. "I've said everything that needs to be said."

"Good. I can get back to work."

Not rising from the narrow couch, Lang said, "Your zeal is gratifying. It means that my purpose in coming to Kenya has been accomplished." He turned to Alyssia. "Miss del Mar, wasn't that the dinner signal?"

"Yes, it was." Alyssia formed a smile.

"I'd be delighted if you'd accompany me."

"Let's understand one another, Lang," Hap said. "She and I work for you—"

"Cool it, Hap." Maxim hovered between his brother and the couch.

"I contracted to work for Meadstar, not to entertain Lang. And that goes for my cast."

Lang said in a musing tone, "Possibly *I* could be the Meadstar producer."

"In that case," Hap said, "you'll need another director to replace me."

"That might be an excellent idea. From what I witnessed today, you aren't drawing a performance from Miss del Mar commensurate with her salary."

Hap's fists clenched. "Just fuck off, Lang."

Lang rose to his feet, and as part of the same swift, smooth motion, closed his right fist, aiming it at Hap's mouth, the hard uppercut of a professional boxer. Caught by surprise, Hap reeled backward, toppling a swivel chair, which fell to the floorboards with a hollow clatter.

Blood spurted from the left corner of his mouth, and his eyes were momentarily glazed, but he remained on his feet. Lang swarmed after him, snaking a left hook at his chin and a savage right to his chest. Again Hap fell back, putting out a hand to brace himself against Maxim's desk. A neat pile of papers scattered.

"Leave him alone, Lang!" Alyssia cried.

"Mr. Cordiner needs a lesson in simple courtesy," Lang retorted. His breathing was normal, his voice level.

"You were baiting him!"

Hap had recovered. Lunging, he grappled Lang around the waist, a bearlike hug. Three inches taller, considerably the heavier, Hap never would have physically attacked Lang whatever the taunts and provocation. But Lang had thrown the first punches, and Hap's compunctions were gone. He squeezed tighter. Lang jackhammered a series of ferocious, clubbing blows to Hap's kidneys.

Maxim tugged at his brother's right arm. "Jesus Christ, Hap! Cut the Muhammad Ali crap!"

While Hap was shrugging off Maxim, Lang raised his knee between Hap's legs. At this same instant Hap pulled back to deliver a punch, his first. Lang therefore was off balance as Hap's fist landed just above his belt buckle. The blow was delivered with all of Hap's outrage and all of his baffled misery at losing Alyssia.

Lang's breath exploded from his lungs with a harsh, dry sound. While Maxim and Alyssia watched horror-struck, he sank onto one knee. In this position of supplication, he clasped both hands to his stomach.

The whole fight couldn't have taken a half minute.

Hap stood with his chest heaving, hands dangling, blood dripping down his chin onto his shirt. When Lang didn't rise, he dunked his handkerchief in the water pitcher, handing it to his fallen opponent.

Lang took the sodden wad, touching the moisture to his wrists. He said nothing. With the stooped posture and slow shuffle of an octogenarian, he left the tent.

Maxim started to follow, then halted, shrugging as if to say, *Let the bastard go.*

Alyssia took a step toward Hap. He was picking up the wet handkerchief, wiping his mouth. He stared at the redness in surprise.

"It's not ketchup, buddy," Maxim said.

Hap jabbed a finger toward his brother. "Just keep him away from me."

54

Beth, anxious to hear about the meeting, stayed in Alyssia's tent: Sara had brought two dinner trays, and the roar from the departing helicopter set off vibrations in the pot-metal dish covers.

As Alyssia came in, Beth jumped to her feet. "What's all that? Lang can't be leaving already?"

"He and Hap got into a fight."

"Didn't I say Hap could go berserk?" Beth cried. "What sort of fight?"

"The physical kind. With fists."

"Oh, God. . . ."

"The worst part is, Lang kept goading Hap because he was positive he'd win—he handled himself like a professional boxer—but Hap knocked him down."

"He really *is* demented, my cousin." Beth groaned. "You just don't go around humiliating men like Lang."

Alyssia closed her eyes. "It's my fault, Beth," she said. In a low voice she capsulized the conversation that led up to the fisticuffs.

Beth shook her head mournfully. "What a mess."

Alyssia clasped her arms around herself. "I'm freezing." She bent to pull a sweater from the gaudy pile on her bottom shelf.

"What's that on the seat of your pants?" Beth asked.

Standing, Alyssia craned her neck, twisting.

"Alyssia." Beth's voice shook. "It looks like blood."

Alyssia lay on her back with a pillow elevating her hips. The bleeding was like a heavy period, dark and steadily copious. She had changed the maxipads that Beth had lent her twice in two hours.

I could be losing my baby.

A hyena howled its ugly bray, and others joined in. Hyenas, the foremost and strongest in the chain of scavengers that gather around Africa's dead, wounded and newborn.

At the realization she was maybe miscarrying, Alyssia's pretense of invulnerability had shattered. She had been shaking so hard that her sister-in-law had to help her undress. In her dulcetly soothing voice, Beth had quoted statistics to prove that this type of spotting was commonplace. Indeed, it had happened to her, Beth, in her fourth month.

Which isn't much of a reassurance, Alyssia thought, shivering.

A strange, watery movement within her, a flutter she

had never felt before. A good omen? A warning of impending disaster? She pressed both hands protectively to her stomach.

At first, her pregnancy had been an unwelcome burden that she—for whatever rationale of her subconscious—could not rid herself of, then it had become a growth to be hidden, disguised, lied about. A few days ago she had seen it as a barrier forever separating her from Hap. Now, for the first time, she was accepting that the child was part of her, yet a separate being, a vulnerable being who was utterly dependent on her.

If the baby's dead, I have only myself to blame, she thought and began to cry.

After a couple of minutes the hot, sparse tears stopped and she stared into the darkness.

Please let it be all right.

I'll be careful, so careful.

She began compiling a list.

First thing tomorrow morning announce your condition.

Refuse to wear any form of corset. Let them figure out camera angles or close-ups that do not show your body.

No more impersonations of Superwoman. No more twelve-hour days—and the hell with Lang's schedule.

Every day drink a quart of milk. Forget that it's chalky, unpalatable, canned Carnation. No, better yet have Harvard Productions fly in long-life milk from England.

Don't lunch on a Hershey bar and Fritos. Go on a health kick, eat those iodine-flavored salads that Beth's been pestering you to.

Insist on a Mercedes like Cliff's to drive you to the location. No more bumpy minibus.

Do not pretend you have nerves of steel. Take it slow and easy. Do everything in your power to avoid an attack.

A prospective baby needs its prospective father, so tell Barry right away.

The hyenas started howling again.

"They're right near the kitchen area," Beth said as she barged into the office tent.

"Hi, Beth." Hap was sitting at his desk. There was blood on his collar, and a small Band-Aid taped to the left corner of his swollen mouth.

For once he didn't rise for her, so she came to hover uncertainly near him. "The hyenas, I mean," she said.

"Sit down," he said, his injured lips forming the words slowly. As she picked up a fallen swivel chair, he asked, "Want a drink?"

She hadn't noticed the open Scotch in front of him. *He's drunk*, she thought. *He's not even bothering with a glass. Barry's the family boozehound. Never Hap.*

"Nothing for me, thank you," she said.

"Are you here to give some good advice?" he asked, a hint of rancor surfacing.

She frowned. Despite her cousin's puffed mouth and bloody shirt, his fight with Lang had skipped her mind. She kept seeing Alyssia, trembling and sobbing. The collapse had terrified Beth to the point that she wasn't sure whom she was more concerned about, her sister-in-law or Barry's unborn baby. "You'll have to shoot around Alyssia tomorrow," she said.

"That heroin pusher got through to her so much?"

"It's not Lang." Beth's face grew hot. She found sex difficult to discuss even with Irving—only with PD had "it," and the nimbus of accompanying vagaries and symptoms, seemed a natural part of life. "When she got back to the tent I noticed she was, uhh . . . staining."

"Jesus!" Hap's apathy and inebriation vanished and he jumped to his feet. "I'll radio for a plane! We'll get her straight to Nairobi Hospital!"

"Hap, there's no cramping, she's resting—"

"She needs proper care!"

"They'd only put her to bed."

"Damn it, she can't stay here!"

"It happened to me and I just stayed home."

"Medication—"

"Doctors used to prescribe stilbestrol to prevent threatened miscarriages. But the women turned out to have cancer-prone daughters. So now the OBs are afraid to use it."

"She could die!"

"Hap, the baby's in danger, not her."

"How can you be so positive? You're not a doctor."

"For tonight, believe me, a doctor would only order bedrest."

"We're getting her to the damn hospital!"

"You know as well as I do that no plane can land or take off from here at night." Nocturnal animals foraged on the level area they used as a landing strip.

"We'll find a pilot who can handle it." Hap's pacing safari boots crumpled and dirtied the strew of production papers.

"I have a charter arranged for tomorrow morning—I'm going into Nairobi to put through a call to Irving."

"What time?"

"Nine."

"Nine!" Lines cut deep into Hap's tanned skin. "That's twelve hours!"

He still cares, Beth thought. *Does Alyssia still care?*

Hap was saying, ". . . and line up the cars and buses so the headlights make a runway."

"Hap, be reasonable," she said gently. "Frightened animals maybe would barge in, hit the propellers and then you'd have a plane wreck on your hands."

Hap hit his fist into his palm, then sighed. "What can we do?"

"Radio the hospital and ask their advice. Then radio Wilson—" Wilson, the smaller of the two Nairobi airports, catered to charter companies. "Tell them to have my plane here by first light, at six. I'll have Derek arrange for a doctor in Nairobi."

Alyssia was in the white-tiled bathroom of the suite at the Norfolk that she and Beth were sharing. Dr. Jozef Kazimir, whom Derek, the White Hunter, had alerted, had just ended his hotel call. Kazimir, an emigré Pole with dyed black hair and courtly manners, had felt her torso with his soft hands, then passed his cold stethoscope up and down and across her abdomen. "My dear Miss del Mar," he had finally pronounced, "I am most delighted to inform you that the little one is safe in his snug nest."

With Alyssia's distrust of the medical community in general, it was not Dr. Kazimir with his overblack hair and ornate English who reassured her, but the fact that the bleeding had stopped entirely.

She turned her profile to the long mirror, pulling her silk robe close to show the bulge.

The outer door opened and closed. "It's me, I'm back,"

Beth called. In the hopes of garnering more obstetrical information, she had walked Dr. Kazimir across the tropically planted courtyard to the hotel's broad veranda.

Alyssia went into the living room. "What else did he tell you?"

"Nothing. He just repeated that you're both fine but you must be very cautious."

"That's for sure. No more corset. Hap and I'll have to work it out." Catching a flicker in her sister-in-law's eye, Alyssia added, "Before I say anything to him or anyone, though, I'll get the dope on Barry's progress."

"You'll tell him," Beth said with firm fondness. "The baby's more important than any novel."

"Shhh." Alyssia held a finger to her lips. "Never say that to a writer—or a writer's wife."

"Why don't you lie back down? I'll tell the desk to put in the call." Beth had already booked her call to Irving.

The call from Belleville-sur-Loire came through first. The sisters-in-law were having tea, and Alyssia, who was stretched on the couch, set down her plate of thin-sliced watercress and cucumber sandwiches, going into her bedroom for privacy.

"Hon, what a coincidence!" Barry's voice emerged tinny and exultant. "I was about to cable *you.* Exactly eleven minutes ago I typed The End."

"Barry! How fabulous!"

"Of course there's still the copy editing and the galleys."

"I have some news for you," she said.

"How *is* the movie progressing?"

"This is about us." She swallowed. "I should have told you before."

"What is it?"

"It's dumb, but I can't say the words."

"You've faded away."

"I'm going to have a baby."

"What?"

"I'm having a baby."

The line crackled loudly, then there was a hum.

"Barry, are you still there?"

"Should I present my congratulations to anyone in particular?" Barry sounded as if he were in his cups, sullen, petulant.

"Don't be angry."

"Tell me what other response I could have?" he shouted. "You and I, we haven't been in proximity for over three months."

She held the phone tighter. The previous night she had determined that her child would have all that she had been denied, and a father was the main advantage.

"I'm sure that's an eminently negligible fact, of course," he barked.

"I'm in my fifth month, Barry."

"Oh? Well I accept that the male plays a minimal role in the drama of parturition, and therefore you haven't said a word to me. But what about the press? I get the papers and the trades here. I read the rumors about disasters on the *Baobab Tree* location. Thus far, though, I haven't seen one infinitesimal hint about the star's pregnancy."

"I've felt life," she persisted.

"And everybody there is too astigmatic to notice your advanced condition?"

"I'm sorry, really sorry. I didn't say anything because I wanted you to finish *Spy*."

"My ever self-sacrificing spouse."

"Yesterday I had a little problem, so I can't work so hard. I'm going to have to tell them."

"It's the least you can do."

"Barry," she said, forcing the pleading note from her voice. "The book's finished. Why don't you come down and we'll make the announcement together."

"They're laying the parquet."

The baby needs a father, so don't scream at him. She drew a shaky breath. "It would look better if we both tell the press."

"Oh, indubitably it would look better!" he shouted.

She heard the click and knew he'd hung up.

The hotel courtyard was centered with an aviary of brilliantly plumaged Kenyan birds, and she lay on the bed listening to the harsh caws and trills of alien fowl.

When the phone rang, positive it was Irving, she let Beth answer in the living room.

"It's Barry," Beth called. "He said you were cut off."

Alyssia picked up the extension. "Barry?" she whispered.

"You took me by surprise," he said apologetically. "I'll be there as soon as I can."

The sisters-in-law had retired to their bedrooms when Irving's call finally came through.

Beth said, "I was getting worried if I'd reach you, dear."

"My Beth . . . how good to hear your lovely voice." The connection roiled Irving's words, as if passing them through mountainous waves. "I've missed you so."

"I've missed you, too. And Clarrie. How is she?"

"She's not well."

Beth leaped up, standing by the bed. "I knew something was wrong! I knew it! The fever?"

"Yes—a fever. For a couple of days she's had a fever."

"The same as the last time?"

"Higher."

"How high?"

"A hundred and three."

"Oh my God! Is it connected to her last illness?"

"They aren't sure. Maybe."

"Do they know what it is this time?"

"Her arms and legs are weak. The neurologist says it's a form of encephalitis—"

"Encephalitis?" Her voice rose in terror. "Brain fever? Sleeping sickness?"

"Beth, it's not that bad—"

"I should have been with her! Oh, Irving, how could you not tell me?"

"Bethie, I sent the cable today. She only got sick the day before yesterday."

"You should have radioed me immediately!"

"Listen to me, Beth. Clarrie's Clarrie. There's nothing we can do. And they have the encephalitis diagnosed, so everything's in hand—"

"I'll be on the first flight I can get."

"You're already ticketed on the PanAm flight to New York. It leaves Nairobi at six A.M. I'll have the jet at Kennedy to meet you. Beth, I don't want you all frantic.

The doctors say there's no reason on earth to think the worst."

"Oh, God. Why wasn't I there?"

As Beth hung up, she saw the reason.

Alyssia stood in the doorway, the lights behind her shining through her sheer nightgown to display the fecund curves below. Beth's entire body shook with surges of mortal fury. This sister-in-law—this cheesy creature, this brassy bitch who had risen to world fame by flaunting her nakedness—had needed a curb against her whoring. That was why she, Beth, wasn't with her desperately ill child.

"What is it?" Alyssia asked. "You're all white. Beth, you're shaking. What's wrong?"

"Clarrie's got encephalitis. She's burning up with fever," Beth said tautly. "I'm leaving first thing, so I have arrangements and packing. If you'll go back to bed, I can get started."

55

ALYSSIA DEL MAR'S HUSBAND JOINS HER ON LOCATION IN MASAI MARA

—Kenya's *The Nation,* February 6, 1980

Alyssia del Mar and her husband, writer Barry Cordiner, are expecting their first child sometime in May. Good news for the long-married couple, but just one more problem for already problem-beset *The Baobab Tree,* which is being shot in the wilds of Kenya. The film is already reportedly in excess of $30 million over budget.

—*CBS Evening News,* February 8, 1980

Budget fizzles and tempers sizzle as Harvard Productions' *The Baobab Tree* approaches its third month on location in Africa. More delays expected because of Alyssia del Mar's anticipations.

—*The Hollywood Reporter,* February 8, 1980

Meadstar, financing Harvard Productions' *The Baobab Tree,* has sent in two veteran producers.

—*Daily Variety,* February 11, 1980

A Land-Rover bounced to a halt near the small kraal erected for Alyssia's scenes with the Masai, and a mismatched twosome climbed from the back seat. The small man with narrow shoulders and thin gray hair wore the first dark suit seen on location, while his outsize companion's superfluity of flesh was stuffed into a creased but new-looking bush jacket.

Alyssia pulled away from her hairdresser's ministrations to go to the open door of the trailer.

Barry came up behind her. "Who are *they*?" he asked.

"I never saw them before."

"Definitely not tourists. What tourist comes to a game reserve in a business suit?" Barry snaked an arm around her waist, resting his hand fondly on her stomach.

"I wonder if. . . . Maybe Lang sent them."

Barry released her. "What about Lang?"

"When he was here he threatened Maxim and Hap that if we didn't speed up, he'd send in his people."

"Watchdogs, you mean?"

"Exactly."

Barry picked up a shiny, red plastic loose-leaf notebook. With a long, penetrating glance at the two dissimilar men, he began to write rapidly.

He was keeping a journal. Alyssia, warmly grateful that his acceptance of their child had escalated to proud pleasure, was delighted that he'd discovered something to occupy himself. (There is nothing more stultifyingly boring than being trapped on somebody else's location.) He wandered around chatting with grips, electricians, wranglers, the assistant directors, the cameramen, the script supervisor, the bit players, and over dinner at the long trestle table he initiated earnest discussions about the delays and production problems with his cousins.

The newcomers' first meeting with Hap and Maxim took place that night in the production tent. Paul Trapani of the wild hair and overstuffed bush jacket lounged back in his chair: a diamond-surrounded gold Piaget adorned the thick wrist of the hand that held a quart bottle of Tusker's beer. He had volunteered nothing about himself beyond his name, so his connection with Meadstar remained hazy. However, the man in the suit, Herrold Jones—he had spelled his Christian name twice—had informed them that he was the company's vice president and treasurer.

Jones tapped his index finger on a shooting schedule that he'd just unrolled on Maxim's desk. "Mr. Lang has worked out how you can leave this location by the nineteenth of February." He articulated each syllable.

"You realize, of course," Hap said, "that gives us only a week. We need a minimum of twelve more days here." Moving to the schedule glued to the canvas tent-divider, he pointed. "This sequence will take four days at least, probably longer. Difficulties are bound to crop up when you deal with so many animals and unskilled extras."

"Mr. Lang specifically mentioned that sequence. He believes it's extraneous."

"It'll run behind the opening credits," Hap said in the same unruffled tone. "It's our way of letting the audience know that they're watching an epic-scale film."

"We estimate a million dollars to shoot it," Jones said.

"I want this straight," Hap replied. "The sequence stays. It's non-negotiable."

Herrold Jones adjusted his bifocals. "Mr. Lang asked me to convey his respect and understanding for your artistic dedication. However, *The Baobab Tree* had a shooting schedule of sixty-six days, which is eleven weeks, and you have already been here for longer than that with the English scenes still to shoot."

"I told Lang that he can replace me anytime," Hap said icily.

Jones glanced at his associate.

The chair creaked as Trapani sat forward. "Mr. Lang's poured a bundle into this movie, Cordiner. You're finishing it. *And* you're splitting from Africa in one week."

"You can tell your boss that we're already shooting as many setups per day as we possibly can and still maintain quality."

"Better figure out a way to get what-all you need in seven days," Trapani said. "Because that's how long we're staying here with the jungle bunnies."

"We?" Hap asked.

"You, me, Jones and the rest of the two hundred people."

Jones, who was fastidiously polishing his glasses with a felt cloth, looked up. "Two hundred and thirty-four," he said.

Trapani took a gulp of beer, wiping his mouth. "The way I see it, Cordiner, you better get every one of them overpaid slobs working. No more sitting around on your fat asses."

Hap moved a step closer to Trapani.

Maxim said hastily, "I'll see to it we're on our way to England in a week."

Cliff Camron had finished his scenes ten days earlier, and—with his retinue—was already in Los Angeles doing a film for Paramount. Jones and Trapani took over the tent he had vacated. Each evening the two of them strolled to the radio tent, where Jones sent a report to Nairobi that would be forwarded by cable to Las Vegas. So many pages of script had been shot, so many feet of film exposed.

Maxim was everywhere, ensuring that the newest schedule was being adhered to.

He did not have to cajole Alyssia to be on time. Since the arrival of Jones and Trapani, she had forsworn her program of short workdays. Despite her bone-weariness, she rose before five for makeup, and on two nights shot until after ten. She had no control over her attacks, and suffered three fairly substantial ones during the week, but prodded herself back to the set in less than a half hour. On a certain level the hectic pace suited her. She had no energy left to brood about her disastrous relationship with Hap.

* * *

They filmed the final Kenyan sequence amid special-effects rifle shots, swirls of fuller's earth, a melee of big game, Masai warriors and actors dressed as white hunters.

On the eighth day after their arrival, Jones and Trapani, along with *The Baobab Tree* principals, boarded a flight to London. (The crew, who would not be able to get work permits in England, were returning to California in a chartered plane.)

Alyssia sat sipping the warmish milk that the stewardess had brought her. She couldn't shake her doom and gloom.

56

The English interiors would be shot in the Pinewood Studios. For the exteriors, which were scheduled first, Hap and Maxim had rented the grounds of a small, romantically turreted manor house in Sussex. The English crew were bused in from an inexpensive modern hotel in the seaside resort of Worthing, while the upper echelon stayed at a charmingly restored old inn near the location.

While they filmed, drizzle fell unabated and a plague of colds descended.

Alyssia, awakened by a coughing spell, was reaching for the tin of blackcurrant pastilles when the phone jangled. "Hello," she said, stifling a cough.

"Alyssia—is that you?" her brother-in-law inquired.

Any call at this hour was bad news. She sat up. "Irving, Irving—what's wrong?"

"Clarrie. . . ." His voice disappeared, and for several long seconds there was only the sibilance of the interminable rain. "She died a few hours ago. . . ."

"Oh, Irving. I'm so sorry. Poor Beth, poor, poor Beth. How's she taking it?"

"Not too well. Dear, let me talk to Barry."

Barry, who had trained himself to sleep through his wife's wake-up calls, was snoring gently.

She pressed his arm.

"Mmmf?"

"It's Irving," she whispered. "Clarrie's dead."

Barry jerked up on his elbow, grabbing for the phone. "Irving, I had no idea the encephalitis wasn't under control." Silence. "Yes, but if we could distance ourselves, we would see that in the long run Clarrie—and you and Beth—are being saved from incalculable heartbreak."

A long silence.

"Yes, that's precisely the way she would take it," Barry sighed. "She's always been a totally responsible person."

Another lengthy silence.

"Of course it's no problem."

Handing Alyssia the phone to replace, he jammed on his glasses and hopped out of bed, hastily stripping off his flannel pajamas.

"What is it, Barry?"

"Beth's refusing to talk to anyone, even Irving. We agreed if anyone could help her, I could." Barry was pulling on his underwear. "Call the airport and get me a seat on the early TWA flight, will you? And ask the desk to have a production car brought around. Oh, and pack my toothpaste and shaving gear."

Rotund in a swaddle of wool clothing under his fleece-lined raincoat, he grabbed the flight bag she had hastily packed and the red plastic loose-leaf journal in which he was keeping his notes about the production. For Barry the ailments and problems of his blood kin superseded any that might beset Alyssia. Filled with concern for his twin, he blew his pregnant, sneezing wife a kiss and dashed out.

Alyssia returned to bed, but couldn't fall back to sleep. Her mind formed an image: a pretty, redheaded little girl in crimson corduroy overalls skipping along the sun-dappled paths of elaborately landscaped grounds, a child seemingly all things bright and beautiful, yet followed by a uniformed registered nurse. All at once a pink-faced infant was superimposed over Clarrie. Alyssia blew her nose violently. The double image refused to separate.

She turned the pillow. *Sleep, sleep,* she told herself. *Your call's at five fifteen. Go back to sleep.* Finally she turned on the light, asking the drowsy-voiced desk clerk to ring room 37, which was located in the annex across the gravel courtyard.

"Ho?" Hap said. Though she knew she must have awakened him, his monosyllabic query was alert.

"Hap, I thought you'd want to know. Clarrie died a few hours ago." Alyssia took a woebegone pride in her performance: family member imparting sad tidings. Her voice held no trace of either her incipient hysteria or her urgent need to touch base with him. "Irving called to tell us."

"Clarrie? When did it happen?"

"A few hours ago."

"I didn't know she was so ill."

"Nobody did," Alyssia said. "Beth's in a bad way. Barry just left to be with her. Will you tell Maxim?"

The call had done nothing to allay her anxieties. Coughing, she went to get some vitamin C and an antihistamine. She was at the medicine cabinet when a tap sounded.

"It's me," Hap called softly.

She spilled half the phial of chewable vitamin C into the sink. After weeks of polite estrangement, what was Hap doing at her door in the middle of the night? More aware than ever of her ungainliness, she drew the blue velvet lapels of her peignoir to her throat as she went to undo the chain.

He wore Nikes and a rain-dotted Burberry. She looked swiftly away from the long intervening stretch of tanned, blond-haired legs.

"You sounded rotten," he said. It was the first personal remark he had addressed to her since that disastrous day when Lang had watched her flub every line and nuance of the seduction scene in the stable.

"My cold," she said. "It's very nice of you to come over, but also nuts. It's a mean night out there."

"Alyssia, look—I know things are rotten between us, but what's the point in kidding one another? You called because you were touching bottom."

She shook her head in denial, then moved from the doorway. "I am feeling pretty bleak," she admitted.

He followed her into the suite's sitting room. "Want to talk about it?"

"I was thinking about"—she colored—"the baby."

"Is something wrong?"

"What if it's like Clarrie?"

"Clarrie was unique."

"They'd be first cousins—closer, because Barry and Beth are twins."

"Fraternal twins are no different than any other brother and sister," he said. "Irving told me that the doctors called what she had an acute chronic childhood psychosis, and that there was never a hint the problem was genetic."

"Yes, I know. . . . But Beth's terrified of having another child." She put a lozenge in her mouth, asking, "Think I'm overreacting?"

"A bit," he said. "At three o'clock in the morning it's permissible."

She smiled faintly.

After a couple of moments he said, "I'll go back for the funeral."

"Hap, that's crazy! Jones and Trapani—"

"Screw them. Beth's my cousin. I'm going."

"The new schedule—"

Hap interrupted with low vehemence, "You don't understand how sick I am of being Lang's creature. I can't look myself in the eye when I shave."

"I'll be there, too," Alyssia said, and broke off in a sneeze.

"You're what?" Maxim was saying to Hap ten minutes later.

"Going to the funeral. And save your breath. Nothing you say'll change my mind."

"Hap, I feel enough of a turd for dragging you into this mess. But here's the cold fact. You go to Los Angeles and we lose three more days."

"My flight's already booked. And so's Alyssia's."

The star and director of *The Baobab Tree* stood with their respective spouses amid the family-only mourners at Hillside Memorial Park as a small white coffin was lowered into the California adobe next to the basalt plaque marking the burial site of Clara Friedman Cordiner.

Hap and Alyssia had not requested adjoining seats on either flight. On their return to London, after the fasten-seatbelts sign went off, he moved through the first-class cabin to take the empty chair next to her.

"I thought you ought to know before it's all over everywhere," he said. "In the car coming back from the funeral, Madeleine suggested we make our separation permanent."

Alyssia felt a weakness tremble through her, and for an irrational moment waited for him—the director—to tell her how to react. "Madeleine has great timing," she said, and knew instantly the remark was wrong, cheap.

"Actually, she was very decent. No recriminations." The plane was banking, and the sudden blaze of sun made his eyes seem a flat, dead gray.

"Hap, I'm sorry," she said.

"Are you?" The sympathetic closeness he had shown in her suite the other night had been a transitory thing.

"I wanted things to work out for you."

"It's been coming for a long time," he said.

As she watched him return to his seat, the pressure in her ears increased unbearably because of her cold. She bent over, pressing her hands tight against her head.

They moved to London for the interiors of *The Baobab Tree*. Shooting concluded at the end of February with a boisterous wrap party at Pinewood. Alyssia, who had played her final scene in near numbness from heavy lacings of antihistamines and cough suppressants, returned directly to The Connaught. She did not join in the festivities.

The following morning's *Daily Mirror*, in line with the rash of negative publicity on *The Baobab Tree*, inquired: "Is Alyssia High-Hatting the Brits?"

57

At home, she stayed in bed for a week, sneezing or sleeping. Even after her cold was entirely gone, she continued to sleep a minimum of ten or eleven hours. Barry left long before she awoke—he had subleased an office in an old Beverly Hills building favored by writers. She was surprised, therefore, when he brought her coffee in bed one morning. Depositing the cup on her nightstand, he sat on the mattress next to her.

"Hon," he said, then paused portentously.

Stretching, she said, "Yes?"

"I sold a piece to *The New Yorker.*"

Realizing today was April first, she wondered if he were fooling her, but his exhilarated face told her otherwise.

"The New Yorker!" she cried, sitting up to hug him. She was as thrilled as he. "Oh, Barry . . . how fabulous! That's always been your ambition, to sell them a story."

"This is nonfiction. They're devoting almost the entire issue to me."

"The whole magazine! Barry, I'm dying! Is this what you've been working on in your office?"

"Yes."

"What's it about?"

He got up from the bed. "The Industry," he mumbled.

Since he had never shared any portion of his career with her, she had no reason to suspect anything more than his usual caginess lay behind this grudged response.

April Fools' Day brought another surprise.

Alyssia had invited Juanita for brunch. She was delivered by Yellow Cab. Leading the way around the heart-shaped pool to the cluster of outdoor furniture, Alyssia asked, "How come Salvador didn't drive you?"

At this, Juanita slumped into a wrought-iron chair and began to cry, between sobs explaining that Salvador had somebody else, a peroxide blonde who was sixty-five if she was a day.

Alyssia comforted her sister, then asked her to return to live at the house: "After all, the baby needs an aunt on my side to even things up," she said.

Juanita, still crying, refused. "Just give me my old job back." When Alyssia persisted that she wanted a relative, not a maid, Juanita blew her nose. "Listen to me, Alice. I know Barry. Once he hears about where you really come from, Momma and the picking and all, take my word, he won't be so excited about this baby."

Alyssia, thinking of Barry's initial reaction to paternity,

gave a long, wavery sigh. "I guess you're right," she said reluctantly.

That same afternoon Juanita was reinstated in the pleasant servants' quarters behind the kitchen.

A few days later a limousine arrived to take Alyssia to the studio for a couple of retakes of close-ups. As she drove east toward Magnum, she alternated between hopeful pleasure that she would be with Hap and dread for the distance he would inevitably place between them.

She had not seen him since London. He had flown home a couple of days after her, and since then had been immured in a Magnum editing room with a hundred hours of film to prune into a commercially viable movie that ran under three.

She had heard his name often enough, though.

Since the news broke about his and Madeleine's separation, there had been a fair amount of media coverage—and a storm of family gossip. Because neither Hap nor Madeleine gave any reason for their split, and because they had never even bickered and were so admirably mated in all respects, there was a paucity of hard facts to go on. The baffled Cordiners were reduced to endless speculation about the divorce.

Hap was waiting with a minimal crew on Stage 8. Alyssia wore her new white maternity slacks topped by her costume, an ecru lace shirtwaist that due to her girth was unhooked below the back of its high-stayed collar.

They were finished with both shots in less than an hour and Alyssia pulled on a loose cardigan to hide her naked back.

Hap came from behind the blaze of lights. "May I talk to you, Alyssia?"

Not having anticipated any interest on his part in prolonging the session, she blurted the first thing that popped into her mind. "Aren't you going back to the editing?"

"If you're in a hurry—"

"No, not at all. Come along to the dressing room."

There, she poured him coffee, taking a carton of low-fat milk from the mini-refrigerator, pouring it into a tumbler, adding a dash of coffee. She understood, as no doubt he did, too, that these bits of business were to cover her awkwardness. He waited until she was sitting.

"I'm going to Zaire," he said. "To the medical center."

She nodded. "When?"

"The day after tomorrow."

She had been taking a sip. Coffee-spiked milk went up her nostrils and she began to cough helplessly. He took the glass from her hand.

She controlled herself, wiping the milk that dribbled down her chin. "Hap, you're in the middle of editing."

"Jones and Trapani share our offices," he said.

"I heard." She had also heard about—and cringed at—his steadfast refusal to show any of the rough cut to the Meadstar duo. "But you can't leave the cutting and the scoring to other people."

"Why not?"

"You never did before."

"This time I am."

"Hap, you've put your whole self into *Baobab*. You're the only one who really knows the footage."

"I just wanted to say goodbye."

"What about Maxim? He's counting on you. You've never left anybody in the lurch."

"I've considered all that." Hap spoke evenly, but his expression was tired and sad.

"This isn't you."

"Maybe it is," he said.

She reflected that he'd told her he almost cracked after she went back to Barry. "I realize you're going through a rough time, Hap, with the divorce and everything. But at least stick around until you've finished the rough cut." She hated the begging tone in her voice.

"Hy Kelley"—the head editor—"can do the same job I can."

"Don't you understand? Why are you making me spell it out?" Fear made her loud. "First you refuse to show the film, then you quit—"

"I'm not indispensable."

"You're daring Lang!"

"I've already told Kleefeld I'm coming to the center."

"I won't let you do this!"

The gray eyes fixed on hers.

Confusion overcame her, and she was suddenly aware how she must appear to him: a shouting, very pregnant ex-mistress in grease makeup with a milk-stained sweater pulled over an undone blouse.

He went to the door. "Take care, Alyssia," he said.

The image her memory held was of his weary dejection as he raised a hand in a valedictory salute.

58

Beth sat in the day nursery. Her eyes were open but her face was relaxed and expressionless, almost as if she were asleep. Paradoxically, only in this room, where nothing had been changed, surrounded by shelves of pristine toys and a never-to-be-finished web of macramé—surrounded by tangible proofs of Clarrie's existence—could she abstain from her lacerating self-accusations. At the sound of a car turning in at the gate she tensed, then recalled that such intrusions no longer heralded high-pitched wails that could become interminable shrieking sessions.

"Beth?" Barry was calling from downstairs.

Tilting her head, she listened for another voice. If Alyssia were with her brother, she would have to tell him that she had a vicious migraine and couldn't see a soul. However much Beth avoided tearing the social fabric—to refuse to see a friend or relative had hitherto been beyond her scope—she could no longer bear being with her sister-in-law.

Barry's heavy tread sounded on the staircase. He was alone.

"Beth, where are you?"

"In here," she called. A trace of color and the worry lines had returned to her face. Glancing into the nursery mirror, she saw a woman in early middle age who showed evidence of mangled grief and guilt for a dead defective daughter.

Barry kissed her cheek. "You spend too much time in there, Bethie."

"It's the only room in the house without a phone. Why didn't you tell me you were coming? I'd've waited and had lunch with you. What's that?"

A plump blue folder was tucked under his arm. "My piece for *The New Yorker*," he said proudly.

"Oh, Barry!" She hugged him. "It's unbelievable! In less than a year you've done a complete novel, and this too."

"Editorial's been through it with me, but you're the first outside reader."

"I appreciate that," she said softly.

"I'll go in the garden while you digest it," he said. And bolted down the stairs. He always felt queasy watching anyone read his work, and one of his main complaints against TV was being forced to be present while some idiot producer or sharp-nosed network story editor went over his rewrites.

Sitting on the top stair rung, Beth opened the folder.

THE MAKING OF A DISASTER MOVIE

Even in the land of major deals and enormous egos, creativity thrives on innovation rather than cash. The grossly overbudget *The Baobab Tree* is a case in point. The brothers Cordiner have been producing (Maxim) and directing (Harvard) penetrating, deliciously watchable films since they burst on the screen nearly a decade and a half ago with the bargain-basement-budgeted *Wandering On*. On their latest, as yet unreleased film, with an apparently endless supply of the green stuff available, they have finally come a cropper. The media were barred from the location in Africa, but intrepid Hollywood correspondents interviewed members of cast and crew in the watering holes of Nairobi emerging with tales of the roaring of lions and executives. Rona Barrett has chirpily given America thirdhand information of the doings of the stars, Alyssia del Mar and Cliff Camron, on the inhospitable but sex-inviting veldt.

Because of my relationship to three of the four major participants, my reportage has more of an immediate, fly-on-the-wall quality. . . .

Beth, who had become a crack speed-reader during her

years in Magnum's story department, let her eyes travel swiftly down the center of the seventy-three double-spaced pages.

When she turned the last sheet, the permanent grooves above the bridge of her delicate nose were deep.

"Well?" Barry, at the foot of the staircase, was looking up at her with an expression that mingled truculence and nearly insupportable anxiety.

"Who else has seen this?"

"I told you! Outside of the literati, you're the only one!" He stamped up the curving staircase, halting a step before the top. "If you don't like it, just say so!"

"Why must you always be so touchy about your work?"

"The consensus from the East Coast is that it's lively, witty, candid, well-informed—"

"Barry, it's not a matter of quality. The writing's magnificent. But don't you see what you've done? The people in it aren't fictional characters. They're our family."

"I plead guilty to a writer's objectivity."

"You show Hap as an egomaniac intent on squandering millions of feet of film to prove what an artistic hotshot director he is. You show him wasting a fortune to get an effect you say won't be noticed by the audience, jettisoning his relationship with Meadstar. Maxim comes across as a high-strung wisecracker who would be selling used Chevys if his father hadn't been head of Magnum. You hint strongly that they both signed away their souls in blood to the Mafia so they could do the project."

"'*The Baobab Tree* was financed by Meadstar,'" he recited from memory, "'a Las Vegas–based production company whose major stockholder is Robert Lang. Lang, the son of Bartolomeo Lanzoni, founder of the Las Vegas Fabulador, is a longtime backer of the Cordiner brothers. The film was packaged by PD Zaffarano, the savvy, expensively tailored, iron-pumping Hollywood agent. Not too coincidentally, Zaffarano is cousin to the Cordiner brothers as well as related to Miss del Mar through her marriage to this writer. So it's all in the family.'"

"Barry, listen to the tone."

"What did you expect, fan magazine gush? It's for *The New Yorker!*"

"You've damned them all. Not only Maxim and Hap, but PD—he reads like you lifted him from *The Godfather*. And what about. . . ." Her voice trailed away. She could not bring herself to even say Alyssia's name anymore. But Barry had word-painted his wife as the ultimate bitch movie star who feels no compunction about letting cast and crew wither on location while she gets her beauty sleep.

Barry was saying, ". . . an entire issue of *The New Yorker,* in case you aren't aware of the fact, is considered the ultimate in status publicity."

"Oh, Barry, you more than hint that *The Baobab Tree* is the disaster of the decade—who wants that kind of promo?"

Snatching the manuscript from her hand, Barry stalked down the stairs.

Beth ran after him. "Barry, don't leave. Please, let's try to see how it can be changed."

"What you just read is the final draft! The exact wordage and punctuation that will appear in print!" He pulled open the heavy front door, slamming it after himself.

Beth stood amid the abundantly fleshed Rubens nudes for a full minute, and her mournful eyes fixed on the door might have belonged to a maternal forebear surveying the aftermath of a pogrom. Then she went slowly to the den and picked up the phone.

PD piled cream cheese on half of his bagel while the elderly, plump waitress poured expertly from the Pyrexes she held in both hands—coffee for him, decaf for Beth. Beth had invited him to breakfast at Nate 'n' Al's, the deli on Beverly Drive favored by film folk of every denomination.

When the waitress had departed, Beth looked down at her cup, suddenly prim. "I would have asked you to the house for dinner with Irving and me, but it seemed better to discuss this in private."

"I hear you, Beth. Now lay the problem on me."

"I saw Barry's *New Yorker* piece."

"What's the subject?"

"You don't know?"

"Barry's been as secretive as hell. The same way Hap's been about the editing—you do know he's refused to show a single frame?"

"Yes, I heard."

"Then this you won't believe. Before the crack of dawn

this morning, he calls to tell me he's off to Africa, to his medical center."

"The editing's finished? Already?"

"No way. After cracking the whip over every damn detail, he calls me before *six* to tell me he's taking off. Just like that."

"He's all shook up about the divorce," Beth said. "And Barry's fuming at *me*."

PD sighed. "How did two guys who were perfectly normal kids develop such temperaments?"

"*The Baobab Tree*—"

"Don't say another word!" PD interrupted. "Beth, give me a break. The effing movie's all I hear about. From Meadstar, from Maxim, from all my so-called friends. I've had it up to my gullet with *The Baobab Tree*."

"That's what Barry's written about. The making of it."

PD's hand jerked, and cream cheese smeared the barber-shaven skin around his mouth. *"Jesus!"*

"While he was in Kenya and England, he evidently took a lot of notes."

Beads of sweat stood out on PD's forehead. "Did he trash us?"

She looked away again. "It's investigative reporting done breezily."

"A real hatchet job, then. Who does he mention?"

"Everybody."

"Me? Lang?"

"Everybody," she repeated.

"What does he say about Lang?"

"He goes into his background. Uncle Bart's real name, that sort of thing. Nothing libelous—I'm sure lawyers have gone through it with a fine-tooth comb. But he—Lang—does appear starstruck, in love with show biz. And, well, naive for letting Hap go so far over the production budget."

"He comes off a total idiot, you mean?"

"There's a phrase: 'Las Vegas groupie.'"

"Holy Mother of God!"

PD was in Las Vegas early that evening. While he explained the little he knew about Barry's magazine sale, he maintained eye contact with Lang, no easy feat against that unfaltering gaze.

"Did Mrs. Gold infer that the material defamed me?"

"Only that you lived in Vegas and owned the Fabulador." PD forced his white smile. "Which isn't against any laws."

"Does it make me appear ridiculous? Mr. Zaffarano, I warn you, I have no sense of humor whatsoever when it comes to being the butt of humor."

"I haven't read the property. I only found out about the subject this morning. Immediately I called Barry's New York agent to special-deliver a copy to Vegas for you and another to my office. After we've read it through, we can strategize."

"When will it arrive?"

"Any time now. I had them take the packages to Kennedy."

Lang went to his desk, using a hidden intercom. "Has anything arrived for me from New York?"

A young female voice replied, "About ten minutes ago, Mr. Lang."

"Send it up, please."

Almost immediately a short, swarthy man wearing a Fabulador red jacket emerged from the elevator, respectfully handing over an outsize manila envelope.

Lang carried it to his desk, slitting it with an ivory paper knife, putting on half glasses. Paper rustled as he set the pages he had read on the worn, tooled leather of his Jacobean desk. His demeanor gave not the least clue whether or not the material enraged him.

PD attempted not to squirm or stare.

When Lang had finished reading, he sat back in his chair, gazing thoughtfully at his laced fingers. PD would have given a fortune to glance through the stacked sheets, but he knew Lang. He'd have to wait until he saw his own copy. In the meantime he'd be forced to wing it.

The old and valuable-looking pendulum clock loudly ticked away several minutes.

At last Lang looked up. "Is there any way to squelch this?" he asked in a dry rasp.

"That was the first question I asked Karl Balduff—he's Barry's East Coast representative. He said that since there was no libel or slander involved, his advice was to let it stand. If it doesn't run, a lot of talking heads would be asking questions. About . . . well, about the hotel and

Uncle Bart's connections. But if you find anything objectionable I'll try to get *The New Yorker* to cut it."

Lang came to stand in front of the unlit fireplace. His expression was normal, but his eyes were strange. The pupils had shrunk to pinpoints as if his outraged brain had secreted some form of drug.

Frightened, PD muttered, "On the upside, the publicity might help *Baobab.*"

"I hear that Harvard Cordiner's on his way to Africa."

"He's gone? Already?" PD blurted. "It was just this morning that he mentioned that he would be leaving."

"I don't need to tell you how disturbing his excesses on *The Baobab Tree* have been to me."

Beth had mentioned that Barry had skewered Lang as an incompetent dilettante for not controlling Hap. "They went way over budget, sure," PD soothed. "Once the box office grosses start rolling in, though, it won't matter."

"Then you've seen the footage?"

"Hap hasn't shown it to anyone. That's how he operates. He's a star director, with heat, so he has things his way until completion."

"Exactly. He's overseen the post-production work on his other films. And now with Meadstar, he's simply left."

"This Hy Kelley is a top film editor," PD said, openly using his handkerchief on his cheeks and forehead. "Maxim's still here."

"Mr. Zaffarano, Harvard Cordiner is your client. I suggest you tell him to return and finish the job he signed to do for me."

"I already begged him to stay." PD shrugged, a helpless gesture. "He explained he'd gone stale. He's got problems—he's splitting up with his wife."

"His personal life is no concern to Meadstar."

"Believe me, Mr. Lang, I've known the guy forever, and he's gone haywire. In my opinion we're lucky he's off our backs."

Lang continued to stare at him. Under that strange, pinpoint gaze, PD mopped his face again.

Then Lang looked away. "I appreciate your alerting me about these matters," he said in an almost warm tone. "And I agree with you. It's best if we leave *The New Yorker* alone." He escorted PD to the elevator.

By the time PD was on the plane, he had forgotten how

terrified he had been in the Fabulador penthouse while Lang was denouncing Hap. He was congratulating himself on having smoothed over what obviously was a rough situation for his cousin.

Even though it was late when he arrived in Los Angeles, and he was hungry, he went directly to the office.

The large envelope from New York lay neatly on his blotter.

As he scanned Barry's material, he understood Lang's fury against Hap.

PD's own rage was directed at Barry. Never before had PD been in the power of the Cordiner rage. His body was poised for battle, his mind was consumed by a great heat, as if he were in the middle of a forest fire. How dare that writer turd say such things about him, about his family! If Barry were in the office, he would have killed him, and this was no figure of speech. He called Barry, getting his answering machine. PD could never remember what he screamed into the phone. Then, to prevent himself from some form of violence, he stormed to the small inner office he had fixed up as a gym, pumping iron until he was drenched with sweat and too exhausted to move.

He told nobody that he'd read the article—he couldn't even think about it without that hot conflagration of murderous urges. He avoided Barry.

59

Barry, haunted by what he considered Beth's negative response to his magazine article and horrified by PD's long, recorded shriek of obscene insults, which he immediately erased from his Ansafone, was in a panic lest *Spy* also provoke disgust or outrage. The galley proofs were due to arrive from the publisher in the middle of April. In order to go through them carefully and prune away every word that might be objectionable, he needed solitude. Lake Arrowhead being out of season, the mountain area was pretty much deserted and he was able to make a loose reservation for a remote cabin that lacked television and telephone.

The fat, quilted brown envelope containing the proofs arrived on April 14, a few days after Hap had left for Africa. Barry raced between the house and his car, filling the trunk with his manuscript, the galley proofs, a full pack of ball-points, his portable electric Olympia, his bulky Webster's Unabridged, Roget's Thesaurus, two cartons of groceries and a huge chicken casserole prepared by Juanita.

A late storm had dumped several inches of snow on Arrowhead, and at the last minute Alyssia remembered blankets and the heavy hunting jacket that he wore at the château. While she went to get them, Barry gunned the engine impatiently.

Watching the car disappear down the steep, winding drive, Alyssia heard a high, thin voice that she didn't recognize as her own call out, "Barry, don't go, don't leave me."

That evening, Z Channel was showing *Scarlet Empress*. Alyssia's legs ached, she felt alone and spiritless, so she decided to indulge herself by eating a dinner of buttery mashed potatoes in bed while taking in the Marlene Dietrich classic. Waiting for the movie, she watched network news. Later, it would seem impossible that she heard in this, the most cliché manner imaginable.

The anchorwoman was a pretty Oriental.

"We have just received a dispatch from Associated Press in Africa. The body of Hollywood director Harvard Cordiner, three-time Oscar nominee, reportedly has been found amid the wreckage of an automobile in a remote area of equatorial Zaire."

This isn't real, Alyssia thought wildly. She didn't realize it, but she was breathing in loud, ragged gasps that resembled an attack, yet came from purely mental torment. *I didn't hear her say that!*

". . . Cordiner endowed a medical relief center in Zaire, a third-world country, and often worked there. He recently completed *The Baobab Tree,* an as yet unreleased film starring Alyssia del Mar and Cliff Camron. Inhabitants of a nearby village reportedly found the charred automobile upended with Cordiner's remains inside."

Charred.

Alyssia shuddered convulsively.

Charred.

Once, she couldn't have been more than five, May Sue had punished her for interrupting a party-party by holding her hand over the butane stove flame. *This'll learn you to stay out when I tell you to stay out.* Now, decades later, Alyssia could feel the incendiary heat searing her palm, smell the charred meat odor. She was again experiencing the awesome pain, her helpless terror.

"We'll keep you up to date as more reports come in. Now we return to Humphrey Shaw for today's news of the stock market—"

The voice halted abruptly. Alyssia had jammed down on the remote. Rushing to the set, she gave the heavy piece of furniture a vindictive shove that wrenched at her shoulder and abdominal muscles, then she stumbled into the corridor, her legs weakening so that she would have fallen if she hadn't leaned against the wall.

"Alice?" Juanita's frightened voice reverberated as if in a distant echo chamber. "Is it the baby?"

"Hap. . . ."

Juanita set down the tray on the carpet. "You're panting. You're having one of them bad spells. Here, come back to bed."

Alyssia let herself be guided into her room. Falling across the bed, she started to weep in soft, animal-like howls.

Juanita sat beside her, draping an arm about the shuddering shoulders. "Tell Nita what's wrong," she soothed.

"Hap. . . ."

"Hap?"

". . . television . . . news . . . he's burned in a car."

"No," Juanita denied. "I was watching in the kitchen. I didn't see—"

"Near the relief . . . center. . . ."

The phone rang. Juanita answered. "Cordiner residence. No, she can't talk now. No. She don't have any information on any accident!" Hanging up, she left the instrument off, letting it buzz. "I don't know how they get this number," she said, tears streaming from beneath her glasses.

Alyssia asked in a choked tone, "So you believe me?"

"He was asking if it was true, so maybe it ain't."

Juanita's remark, intended as mollification, struck hope into Alyssia's precarious mental workings.

Maybe he's alive. Yes. He's alive.

Energy pulsed through her. She jumped to her feet, pacing to the dressing room door, then to the curtained window and back again. The baby, who was active, kicked. She didn't feel the neural jabs.

"Alice," Juanita said uneasily, "come lie down again."

Alyssia paced faster. "'Reportedly' means it doesn't have to be true, right? Besides, she said it was a car crash. And you know what a terrific driver Hap is. He never had a single accident, not even on those hairpin turns around Lake Como with all those crazy Italians going a hundred miles an hour. He told me there's no traffic in Zaire once you leave Kinshasa—that's the capital. How could he've had an accident? You're absolutely right."

"I . . . I only said it didn't have to be true," Juanita sighed.

"But you're right!"

"Alice, you look awful, I never seen you look this awful."

"We have to find out."

"Think of the baby."

"Maxim'll know."

Alyssia's hands shook, and she could not open the gilt-edged paper of her address book to the C pages. Juanita, blowing her nose and replacing her glasses, did it for her.

Maxim's line was busy. Alyssia's urgent, quaking index finger pressed the numbers continuously.

"He probably took it off like we done."

"Of course!" A febrile intensity glinted behind the blue of Alyssia's eyes. "I'll have to go over."

Maxim, whiling away his current bachelorhood in the heavily publicized company of a jet-setting oil heiress, had bought a condominium on Spalding Drive opposite Beverly Hills High School. He discouraged all visitors, including family. His address was penciled in her book only because she'd needed to have a signed revision in her *Baobab Tree* contract messengered over to him.

"We'll have to wait until morning when Gisele's here," Juanita said. Gisele, who came in daily, did the driving: Alyssia hadn't taken the wheel since her return from location.

She was already in the dressing room, yanking out purses of every shade and shape, opening each in her search for the car keys. Suddenly she recalled she'd dumped a set in one of her jewelry boxes. Grasping the keys tightly, coatless, in her loose, white-silk shorty robe which the pregnancy pulled up in front, she dashed into the chill evening. Juanita, still protesting, climbed in the Jaguar next to her. At the bottom of the long driveway there were stomach-lurching jolts. The car went off the blacktop, bumping from the ivy to the curb and onto the street.

"Alice, be careful!"

Alyssia continued to ignore her. Juanita gripped the dashboard, begging her to slow down as they sped through red lights and stop signs on the three-mile drive southward. They jerked to a halt at Maxim's chocolate-brown condominium complex. Double parking, leaving Juanita in the car with the engine running, Alyssia ran between mounded modern landscaping to Maxim's apartment, pressing the bell, then banging with both fists.

The door was opened by a barefoot, shirtless young man holding a drink. The muscles of his smoothly tanned, hairless chest were well delineated, his teeth capped and even.

She stared at him bewildered. He was completely at home. Could she be at the wrong address? He stared back, and she realized he was seeing a very pregnant woman in a short robe, her feet encased in sheepskin slippers, her glossy black hair falling uncombed over her shoulders.

Recognition dawned on the small, neat, masculine features, and he called, "Hey, Max. You've got a famous visitor."

Maxim came to the door, tying a hapi coat about his long, bony nakedness. Seeing her, he flinched and reddened. Then, an implacably sardonic smile curved his narrow lips. He did not invite her in.

"Well," he said. "If it isn't Alyssia del Mar, mother of future Cordiners."

"Maxim, I need to talk to you."

"Not exactly the garb for a social call, but then maybe you've elected me to drive you to the hospital for the blessed event as stand-in for the fathers—there are two possibilities, aren't there?"

Maxim's cruelty, which he couldn't help or control, came from being caught out in his meticulously guarded secret. Alyssia was too distraught to notice what he said.

The young man, looking at neither of them, mumbled, "I'll leave you guys."

Alyssia reached for Maxim's arm. "What have you heard about Hap?"

Maxim stepped backward. "I don't keep tabs on him, star lady. Or Barry-boy, either."

"But why did you take your phone off?"

Redness showed on Maxim's cheeks. "Doubtless I've missed some vital point," he said. "I'm not following this conversation."

"His car's been found near the relief center."

Maxim's smile disappeared. "Car?"

"She said it was burned and he was in it—but she only said reportedly."

"Who the fuck is 'she'?"

"The newswoman. It was on the news."

He glared at her with the same expression of loathing she had vented on her television set, then strode to his phone. Holding her breath, she watched him press numbers.

"Jessica?" he said. "Maxim here. Let me talk to Dad."

A short pause.

The long body convulsed. Standing in the doorway she could not see his expression, but she heard his hoarse, shaking whisper. "Oh my God. . . ." A long pause. "He is? Which hospital? The number?" He fumbled with a telephone pad, then shoved it onto the floor. "Call and tell Mom I'll be right there."

As he hung up, she asked, "What's happened?"

"Oh, nothing much." Maxim spoke with a labored parody of his caustic tone. "My father's had a stroke because my brother's been fried in his car, that's all."

"Oh, my poor love. . . . No!"

"And the one thing I don't need now is you!"

"He really has been identified?"

"His body. My brother's dead. Dead." Tears trickled down Maxim's hollowed cheeks. "He should have been cutting the fucking picture. And you know why he was in Zaire—fucking Zaire? Because of you! I don't know what the hell you did to him, but he was sick to his soul because of you!"

Maxim shoved her backward and slammed the door.

Because of you. I don't know what the hell you did to him, but he was sick to his soul because of you.

She dropped to her knees on an exposed aggregate paving block and vomited over a spiky cactus.

60

Barry, reddish stubble covering his cheeks and chin, unlocked the front door.

"Alyssia," he called. "The task is done. The galleys are en route to New York."

There was no reply from his wife or either of the servants.

He made his way through the house to the bedroom, where maternity clothes strewed the carpet and a small, partially packed suitcase stood open on the bed. He peered around in bewilderment. Was she at the hospital? Her due date wasn't until May 17, was it?

He was dialing the OB's number when he saw the note on the bedside table.

Barry, I'm going to Zaire to see what I can find out about Hap. Juanita's with me.

Why would she go to Africa when the baby—*his* baby—was due in a few weeks? And what was that about Hap?

Him, Barry thought.

Always the damn Wasp!

"It's time to go on home," Juanita said.

"I can't," Alyssia replied apathetically.

They were in Kenya, in the Norfolk Hotel's largest cottage. Though it was midafternoon, the bedroom curtains remained drawn, for Alyssia was in bed.

"You ain't been eating. You get them awful spells. You're due in less than three weeks."

"Hap's here in Africa."

Juanita said uneasily, "Alice, he's dead."

"I know. But he's buried here in Africa."

Hap had often expressed a desire to be buried in the garden of the relief center, or so Art Kleefeld—Dr. Arthur Kleefeld—had radioed the bereaved family. The wish, Art told everyone, was a blessing, given the rapid decomposition of mortal flesh in a hot and humid climate. Art had told

Alyssia all the details of the simple burial service, which was presided over by a black Episcopal priest.

When she had radioed the center that she was in Nairobi and planned to visit, a journey that involved a small plane, a four-wheel-drive vehicle skittering along unpaved roads, plus two unscheduled ferries, Kleefeld had insisted on coming to the Norfolk. The youngish, dark-bearded doctor had remained with her from before lunchtime to well after midnight.

"He was on his way home," Kleefeld had said. "He'd been to Lunda, a village thirty miles from the center, to deliver soy flour—protein deficiency is rampant in the area, and I do my level best to get women to add soy to their cornmeal when they make *posho,* that's their diet staple, a kind of porridge—"

"How long did he stay in Lunda?"

"He arrived that day. I figured he'd spend the night."

"Why, if it's so close?"

"You have to take into account that we're in the middle of tropical rain forest. There's so many swampy areas that the roads, such as they are, wind all over the place. People just don't travel at night."

"Why did he?"

"He probably never gave it a thought. You know Hap, he was totally fearless." Kleefeld scratched his beard as if to give himself time to consider his next remark. "There was one thing that did bother me. At first, that is. I stumbled on the burned jeep myself. News travels fast in Zaire. There's no phone lines in our area, so I've never really figured how word spreads, but it does. The cook should have known and told me."

"Didn't you find that significant?"

"In the beginning, yes, like I said. Then I heard there'd been a group of Kenyan bigwigs traveling around."

"What difference does that make?"

"With ranking strangers around, the local higher-ups wouldn't want any bad publicity, so everyone kept quiet."

"Everyone?"

"Closing ranks, it's called."

"I don't mean to cross-examine you," Alyssia sighed. "But I just can't believe he's dead."

"It is difficult to realize. He was such a vital, beautiful

man. But, Alyssia, I prepared the body for burial myself. He's dead."

"I know what you're going through," Juanita was saying. "After my little Petey went, I wanted to die, too. But you'll have the baby. If you can't stand going back to LA, what's wrong with France? We could—"

Alyssia gave a deep sigh and then gasped. Lines of pain appeared above the suddenly glittery blue eyes.

Juanita poised over the bed, accepting that this was the onset of what she termed a spell. Since the report of Hap's death, there hadn't been a day when her sister was free of the merciless symptoms.

This made the third of the day—a new record. Juanita, sponging the contorted, sweat-drenched face, knew she could no longer handle it herself. Later, when Alyssia napped, she went to the desk. Never in her life having dispatched a cable, unable to read or write worth a damn, she stuffed her glasses in her uniform pocket, explaining to the dark blur of the clerk's face that she had misplaced her specs and therefore needed assistance in composing and sending a telegram to Miss del Mar's husband, Mr. Barry Cordiner, in Beverly Hills.

At his request, the nasal female voice reread: "'Miss del Mar ill at Norfolk Hotel Nairobi Kenya stop says she needs you stop Juanita.'"

When Beth had told him about the accident in Zaire, Barry's sorrow had been so genuine and profound that he had believed himself purged and cleansed of the lesser emotions he'd nourished toward his dead cousin. Yet, hearing the message repeated, he felt his ears and neck burn with resentful anger.

"Would you like a copy mailed to you?" asked the nasal voice.

"That won't be necessary," he barked. *Like hell I'll go to her!*

"You're sure you have everything you need?" Beth asked, eyeing Barry's Vuitton overnighter, which was his total baggage.

"I'll have her back in three or four days." He stepped aside to allow an obese young couple laden with plastic

Disneyland shopping bags to waddle past him onto the plane.

"When I was having Clarrie, I was careful, so careful. To travel around like this in her last month!"

"Stop worrying, Beth. There's one consistent fact about Alyssia. She's strong. She's sturdy as a Percheron horse."

The skin around his eyes was red with weariness. This past week he'd been up until all hours with the galley proofs of *Spy,* and last night he had slept not at all. His mourning for Hap had been intensified by guilt—those malicious chopping remarks would soon be seen by all who read *The New Yorker.*

"Oh God," Beth said in a low, fervent tone. "What wouldn't I give to be having this baby!"

The final boarding call came over the intercom, and Barry's kiss was more consolation for her losses than farewell.

The handsome young desk clerk at the Norfolk bore a marked resemblance to Leontyne Price. She said apologetically, "I'm sorry, Mr. Cordiner, but Miss del Mar is no longer with us."

"That's impossible! She just cabled me."

The ledger was turned to face him. "Third line down, sir. See? She checked out two days ago."

"Doubtless to the hospital," he said. "I'll phone around."

"I wasn't here, you understand, but, well, naturally we discuss the arrivals and departures of our famous guests. She went to the Embakasi Airport."

A Lufthansa flight was about to depart, and Embakasi bubbled with redly tanned German tourists as well as the usual mass of Kenyans in dashikis and Asians whose women in their bright, gilt-embroidered saris resembled fantastic, flightless birds. Barry shoved his way from ticket counter to ticket counter. Everyone he spoke to knew who Alyssia was, of course, but nobody had seen her. Finally a baggage handler sidled over. He had been working the Air France counter yesterday and there had been a very expecting lady with a big hat who looked like Alyssia. She and a much older woman wearing glasses had left on the flight to Paris.

61

Barry landed at Charles de Gaulle Airport after nearly two full days of travel, his ankles swollen, his nerves frayed from sleeplessness and uncertainty. Alyssia! The inconsiderate bitch! Couldn't she have at least left an address for him? In Nairobi he had ascertained that France was their final destination. But where were they? At the château? Somewhere in Paris? His lips were set in a line as he went through passport control, and he decided to begin his search at the Plaza-Athénée, the Paris hostelry favored by Alyssia. But when his Avis car reached the Périphérique, the freeway that belts the capital, he found traffic at a curdled standstill. It took him fifteen agonizing minutes to reach the first ramp. Getting off, he headed for Belleville-sur-Loire.

As he drove between the stone-ball entry posts into the small park, the sun emerged from behind a cloud. A good augury, he decided, and was not surprised to see that the new garage stood open to show a dark-green Peugeot whose license plates indicated it a rental.

Flinging open the front door, he called, "Alyssia?" His voice echoed through the bare, stone-floored hall. There was no answer. He shouted again, with no response, and was on the verge of going outside to reassure himself there was indeed a car in the garage when footsteps sounded upstairs.

Juanita came down to the first landing. "What are you doing here?" she demanded.

He was so taken aback by her tone—not an iota of her normal servility—that he felt his jaw drop. Then his indignant wrath, reinforced on the two-hour drive from Paris, exploded. "That's a bottomlessly stupid question! If you cudgel your brain, you might possibly recollect sending a cable informing me that my wife was ill and needed me. Where is she?"

"She don't want to see anyone right now."

"Well, I intend to see *her*." Barry was climbing the stairs with ponderous purpose.

"She's feeling awful low at the minute," Juanita said, not shifting from her position in the center of the landing. Arms bent at the elbows, thick legs flexed, she reminded him of a Masai Mara lioness guarding her cub.

He reached the step below her. "Having circumnavigated the globe, I am not about to be turned away by you!"

"It's never been any secret that you don't think much of me—but don't take it out on her."

"Is she in the bedroom?"

"Please, Mr. Cordiner." Now the maid was all humility. "Won't you hold off a few minutes?"

Brushing past her, he stamped up the remainder of the staircase, noting that one of the replaced balustrades was too white. He silently denounced Alyssia for the mismatch. If she hadn't dragged him to Africa to announce the baby—was it really his?—he would have been here to oversee the stonemasons.

"At least let me warn her you're here," Juanita was pleading behind him.

Barry flung open the bedroom door.

Alyssia lay on the high, old-fashioned bed, a mount of pillows propping her. Eyes closed, she labored for breath, her swollen torso arching with each stentorian gasp.

Fear doused Barry's ichor with such force that he leaned against the doorjamb. He had taken no prenatal classes; his limited knowledge of childbirth was gleaned from reading Tolstoy, and his sleep-deprived brain leaped to the assumption that he'd found his wife in the final convulsions of labor.

"Where's the doctor?" he whispered urgently.

"She don't need him," Juanita replied.

"But she's having the baby!"

"Not yet."

Discounting this as a servant's ignorance, he snapped, "I'll call him. Where's the number?"

Juanita didn't answer. She had gone to the bed to wring

out a washcloth and sponge Alyssia's pale, sweating face. "Barry's here," she said quietly.

Alyssia, in the midst of a battle to inhale, opened her eyes, staring at him with an expression that mingled agony and humiliation.

"Get out!" she cried through clenched teeth.

He retreated to the hall. By now he was no longer positive she was in labor. She could equally well be in the acute stage of some pulmonary disorder like pneumonia. In either case, medical aid should be summoned. But whom would he call? And how could he explain the problem when he didn't have a clue to it himself?

Juanita has matters in hand, he told himself. But he felt an inept craven as he trudged downstairs. Using the espresso machine to squeeze an elixir so strong that his heart palpitated, he waited in the library—his writing room—until, finally, the maid came down.

"I'm sorry about yelling at you, Mr. Cordiner," she said, contrite. "But when Mrs. Cordiner gets like that she don't want anyone to see her."

"What's wrong?"

"Uhh . . . she'll explain. She'd like for you to go on up."

Alyssia lay on top of the smoothed bed. A fresh negligee trailing about her, her face a delicate white porcelain, she resembled one of those full-skirted dolls that women once had used to adorn their pillows.

Why, she's fragile, he thought. *Small and frail.*

For Barry, Alyssia's strength had been the cornerstone of their relationship. From that first meeting at Ship's Coffee Shop in Westwood, he had perceived her as ebulliently healthy, a plucky fighter with street smarts. Never once had he considered that she could be prey to the physical and psychological megrims prevalent among delicately reared females. This view of his wife as an invincibly tough broad had permitted him to depend on her, and to neglect her.

Now, staring at the bed, his mouth went dry. He was experiencing an actual physical wrench, as if some inner organ had burst within him. The image he'd always held of Alyssia was crashing down, shattering into a thousand irreparable pieces.

"I can't bear anyone around when I'm like that." Her murmur was flat, apathetic.

"Juanita says it's not connected with the pregnancy."

"I can't catch my breath, that's all."

"Hon, what I saw was distinctly worse than mild hyperventilation."

"It's called an anxiety attack. It happens to me at work."

"Is that why you sometimes go dashing from the set?"

"How can I let people see me?"

"Right now you're not working," he pointed out.

"The thing's been getting worse and worse since I heard about Hap."

"Why didn't you ever mention these attacks to me?" he asked, unable to repress the thought of how little of his own emotional landscape he had shared with her.

"Everything connected to them seems weak, shameful."

"What about a shrink?"

"I tried one, years ago. It didn't help. Later I tried a psychologist. For a while she did me some good."

"You need some type of therapy now."

"What good would it do? Hap's dead. He's dead. . . ." Her head sank back in the heaped pillows and she appeared yet more friable.

Sitting on the edge of the bed, Barry took her lax hand. "Hon, he was a unique person. Honorable, clean, decent. All my life I tried to emulate him."

She withdrew her hand. "Did you?"

Barry's lips creased downward as the tears he'd not yet been able to shed for Hap pooled in his sinuses. "I did love and admire him . . . but always I envied him, sometimes unbearably. Long before I ever met you, I saw him with the monster's green eyes. Not because he was rich, a Wasp, but because he was immeasurably decent and generous and brave. After you and he. . . . I felt so unworthy. How dare I compete with somebody like him? I . . . I thought the baby was his."

"So did he."

Barry heard the confession, yet his tears for his dead cousin continued flowing.

The remainder of that afternoon he felt as if his brain were floating several inches above his skull, a peculiar sensation he attributed to lack of sleep. Whatever the reason, he was able for the first time to accept the truth about his relationship to Alyssia.

His crusade to stay married to her had been a ridiculous mistake. They didn't belong together.

Yet paradoxically, his tenderness toward her had never been greater.

He sat next to the bed, lighting pipe after pipe as he told her how it had bolstered his poor, weak ego to be her husband, and how grateful he was that she had earned their living at the beginning—he even admitted his shame that she had done housework. He told her he had admired her courage ever since the first day of their marriage, when she had faced down the motel manager. He said if it weren't for her, he would have drunk himself into the grave. He told her that she was the most beautiful woman he had ever seen and he cherished her flesh insofar as he was able—"I must be lacking in androgen."

When a reply was called for she would nod torpidly, as if speech were beyond her strength. Her unresponsiveness did not slow his confessions.

Nothing could have silenced him.

He was unwinding the spool of their marriage.

He asked Juanita to bring his dinner up to the bedroom. Alyssia dipped her spoon in the cream soup, a dutiful gesture that she soon ceased. He ate hungrily. He was finishing the wedge of brie when Alyssia gasped. The awful racked breathing started again.

"Go away!" she panted shrilly.

"Hon, you need a doctor—"

"No! Get out!"

Hurrying to the kitchen, he summoned Juanita, then waited on the top step, a vicious draft whirling away his pipe smoke.

His usual mode when faced with unpleasant decisions was avoidance, but as a carryover from his recent beatific state he accepted that it was up to him to take charge. *Alyssia can't stay here, isolated in the country with only me and an illiterate servant to take care of her,* he thought. *She ought to be under medical supervision.*

He went to dial the Tours number on the card that he'd glimpsed on the telephone ledge.

In less than an hour Dr. Fauchery arrived. After he examined his famous new patient, he drew Barry downstairs. He spoke no English. Enunciating slowly and loudly for the American, he voiced Barry's own belief that it was imperative that Madame Cordiner spend the remainder of her term at his private lying-in facilities.

"I am not going, and that's that!" Alyssia walked agitatedly up and back the length of the bedroom.

Barry was already in bed. Weariness had hit him like a blow. Yawning, he said, "Hon, be reasonable."

"*You* had to call the quack! Now the two of you have decided I need locking up."

"It's nothing like that," Barry said in the calmest tone he could muster. "He explained to me that many of his patients who live outside of Tours come to stay at the clinic before their due date. He's thinking of the baby."

She began to cry. Woozily he got up and went to her—had her shoulders always been this slight?—leading her to her side of the bed.

When the lights were out, she whispered in a tear-clogged voice, "You're right. I can't risk the baby. But I don't want any nurses, Barry."

"Who'll look after you?"

"Juanita."

He rolled onto his side. It seemed reasonable enough that she wouldn't want strangers seeing Alyssia del Mar in her weakness, possibly selling the story to a gossip sheet.

"Let me see what I can arrange," he said, and fell asleep.

After breakfast the following day the three of them drove to Tours. The lying-in clinic was a commodious private house near the *cathédrale*. The rooms were booked months in advance, but a *comtesse* had delivered her fourth son before she could leave her country estate, so the second-floor suite was vacant. The airy bedroom came with a small, adjacent sitting room where a cradle could be installed with a private nurse.

That same morning, Dr. Fauchery ushered up Dr. Plon, a goateed psychiatrist. Plon stayed, talking to Alyssia in formal English for about an hour, witnessing an attack. He then retired to consult with the obstetrician. An ardent convert to drug therapy, Plon wanted to use pharmaceuticals to alleviate her hyperventilation, but Fauchery flatly refused this course until after the delivery. The two physicians compromised on a minimal dosage of Librium.

Barry, who had taken a room at the Trois-Rivières Méridien, could see no benefit whatsoever from the tranquilizer. Alyssia's attacks came as frequently and were equally severe.

The third day after Alyssia's arrival, April 30, a balmy sun shone on Tours. Dr. Fauchery, making his morning rounds, coaxed Alyssia to sit by the open window of her small sitting room. She was in the armchair when Barry visited. Juanita took his hyacinths and daffodils to arrange, tactfully leaving them alone.

A strand of black hair blew over Alyssia's forehead. She didn't push it away. "I've been thinking," she said in a dulled tone.

"About what, hon?"

She sighed. "Us. It's over, Barry."

"Yes," he agreed. "We've been tenacious for twenty-odd years. Nobody can say we didn't try."

After a long pause, she said, "The baby? What are we going to do about the baby?"

"That's the prime consideration, of course."

"I won't be much of a mother."

"You're going through a traumatic phase," he said.

She gave him a bleak look.

"Hon, eventually you'll get over Hap."

"I won't, Barry. Not ever. And the attacks—what about the attacks? I'm bad news for a baby."

A sparrow came to perch in the tender new greenery of the Virginia creeper outside the window. Barry gazed at the drab little bird and for the first time thought about fatherhood.

Oh, he had daydreamed often about the child, invariably visualizing it as male, seeing him a gleeful toddler being hoisted onto the merry-go-round at Santa Monica Pier; a small boy sharing peanuts at Dodger Stadium. (Barry disliked every type of sporting event, and found baseball an indescribable snore, but his mental imagery discounted this.) His most cherished projection, however, was of a tall adolescent rising to his feet in boisterous applause as he, Barry Cordiner, picked up his National Book Award.

Now, though, in the soft French sunlight, for the first

time he faced the realities. Unless *Spy* hit, and he could afford servants, he would be in for dirty diapers, two A.M. feedings, vomiting, car-pooling, as well as backtalk, drug involvement and teenage sex.

"Don't downgrade yourself," he said earnestly. "You'll be a marvelous mother. Erda personified."

"Oh, Barry. . . ."

"You're saying *I* should have custody?"

Abruptly she slipped into her agitated mode. Jumping to her feet, she exclaimed, "Of course not! What makes you say that?"

"This entire conversation."

"It never crossed my mind for one instant that I wouldn't have the baby. How could I not? It's mine." She tugged at her fingers. "But it's awful to be raised by somebody who can't function as a mother."

In spite of her persistent denials, it appeared to him that she was offering justifiable excuses to avoid custody of the baby.

All at once he recalled his twin's despairing tone as they'd said goodbye at the Los Angeles Airport. What were her words? *What wouldn't I give to be having this baby!*

62

That evening he ate at Barrier, Tours' two star restaurant, which had previously been known as *Le Nègre*. After the rich terrine, the *saumon en papillottes*, the delicate white veal, the cheeses and an ethereal raspberry soufflé, he felt in need of a walk, so he strolled along the embankment of the Loire.

He had been thinking about his unborn child ever since he'd left Alyssia this afternoon. However much he attempted to evade the unpalatable fact, he was accepting that she was in no shape to look after a baby. He, temporarily at least, would be the parent in charge.

And who was Barry Cordiner to take on the responsibility of a helpless infant?

He stared disconsolately at the Pont-Napoléon, seeing neither the bridge nor the reflection of its looped lights in the blackness of the river. In a rare moment of total self-honesty, he was seeing exactly who Barry Cordiner was.

An alcoholic. A hack writer who without his Cordiner connections would never have earned a living. A son who had abdicated his filial responsibilities to Beth. An unfaithful husband whose infidelities seldom reached honest consummation—he pawed women's breasts and pubic triangles as an act of vengeance toward Alyssia, punishment for making him feel third rate, which he probably was. He had played on her weaknesses to keep her apart from his immensely more worthy cousin. (In his morbid honesty, however, he conceded that here fault lay partially with Alyssia, whose dogged loyalty had always made her his patsy.)

I can't look after a baby. It's impossible.

His twin, not he, had inherited the genes that constitute a sense of responsibility.

"Beth, it's Barry."

"Where are you? I've been beside myself. I called the Norfolk. They said you'd never registered. And that *she* had checked out."

"We're in Tours. Alyssia's at a maternity clinic. She's in rotten shape, Beth."

"I knew it! At her age doing that difficult role in Africa, then chasing around—"

"This has nothing to do with the pregnancy."

"Is the baby a breech?"

"There's no problem whatsoever with the child."

"Then what's wrong?"

"Uhh, she appears to be, uhh, having what we laymen call a breakdown."

"A *nervous* breakdown?"

"Yes. Hap's death has hit her very hard. That's why she's at the clinic early."

"Was she violent?"

"The reverse. Most of the time she's numbed and lethargic, the way people get in deep depression. Also, she has attacks of hyperventilation."

"You're *positive* the baby hasn't been brain damaged?"

"Will you stop harping on the baby? Not being a prenatal expert, I am taking the highest regarded local obstetrician's opinion that all is well!" After a moment he said, "Sorry I lashed out there, Beth, but I've been under an annihilating strain. Alyssia and I have decided to split."

"*Now?*"

"Our marriage should have been dissolved many years ago."

"Yes, I know. But now? When she's ill? And having a baby?"

"Yes, the baby." Drawing a deep breath, he spoke rapidly. "Beth, even the youngest infant has an awareness of its surroundings. It's unfair to burden the baby with our problems. Could you take over for a while?"

"What do you mean, take over?"

"Uhh, could you, uhh, look after the baby until Alyssia's well?"

"No."

"What?"

"I said no."

His entire life Beth had been a soft touch—had she ever refused him? Their mother had often repeated the tale that in their shared playpen when he demanded a toy Beth would docilely hand it over.

"Beth, you don't understand. Alyssia's in no condition to manage a new infant. I'm only asking you to become custodian until she's past the worst of her depression."

"No. And it's not fair to ask me." From the honking sound of a nose being blown, he realized his sister was crying.

"I'm sorry, Bethie. I should've realized. You have your own problems."

"Don't you see? I'd become attached all over again, and then *she* would take the baby away. It'd break my heart. Again. I can't do it."

Barry replaced the receiver with a shaking hand.

That night Alyssia went into labor. She was run-down physically, and after twenty-five hours, at a point when Dr. Fauchery was readying himself to do a cesarean, she dilated so rapidly that she felt as if she were being torn apart from the rectum. Her agonized cries skittered through the clinic's corridors as she was wheeled into the well-equipped delivery room. Fauchery was forced to administer gas, then inject a potent mixture of sedatives.

Within short minutes after Alyssia's placement on the delivery table, her newborn son was complaining vigorously.

To Alyssia, however, the drugged labor seemed eternal. She was condemned to a murky, Götterdämmerung world where the only brightness was her mother's crimson blood and the flames consuming Hap's jeep, a world where the single inhabitant was death.

63

When she awoke, Barry was sitting at her bedside.

"We have a little boy," he said proudly.

She was still enmeshed in that nightmare existence, and her glazed eyes fixed on him.

"A boy?" she whispered, sighing. "He's dead."

"He's absolutely fine. Healthy as they come. And a real screamer."

Her head turned slowly from side to side in denial.

"Hon, he's with his nurse in the next room."

"He's dead. . . ."

Barry went to the little adjoining parlor. To ensure Alyssia's privacy, Fauchery had brought in an ugly, placid nursing nun from Alsace. At Barry's request, the white-coiffed sister carried in her cocooned charge, holding him close to his mother's pillow. The baby moved his mouth, letting out a mewling sound. His nose was temporarily squashed to one side, but otherwise he was pretty and pink—even his fuzz of hair was rosy.

"It can't be my baby—my baby's dead," Alyssia whimpered. She began to cry. She cried so long that Fauchery summoned Plon, his goateed psychiatric colleague. Although the anesthesia had not yet worn off, Plon started his treatment.

Barry visited again that evening. The bed was cranked up to a sitting position, and Alyssia sat bolt upright, but her face was lax, as if she were asleep.

"Hon?" he whispered.

She peered at him as if he were out of focus.

He asked, "Did I wake you?"

"No," she said in a faded murmur.

"Seen our boy again?"

"Did I?"

"But you know he's fine?" Barry asked.

"I think so. Barry, they've got me so doped up I can't tell what's happening."

"Your other doctor"—he couldn't bring himself to mention the consultant's specialty—"explained that the birth was extremely traumatic. He prescribed medication for that, and also for your, uhh, breathing difficulty."

"I can't feel or think. It's like my brain is wrapped in long strands of horrible gray pasta. . . ." Her voice faded entirely.

"Why don't you get some sleep," he said, retreating.

When he visited the following morning, she stared blankly at him, without recognition.

"Hi, hon," he said.

She closed her eyes.

Juanita hovered outside the door, her worry showing on her broad, pitted face. "Did she know you, Mr. Cordiner?"

"She didn't, uhh, pay much attention."

"She's been out of it all morning. Never saying a word. These pills they're pushing into her—they're no good."

"Since when are you a medical expert?" He spoke vehemently because of his own fears.

After handing her the flowers—more daffodils—he walked in a dignified pace along the corridor. Downstairs, though, he galloped, racing next door to the house where Fauchery lived and practiced. The dining room served as his waiting room. Every needlepoint chair was occupied, and Barry, under the gaze of a dozen pregnant Tours matrons, banged urgently on the office door.

The doctor, after a glance at the new father's face, excused himself from his patient.

The minute they were alone, Barry said, "My wife's overmedicated." He used his awkwardly accented French in the authoritative tone he put on during story conferences.

To his surprise, the obstetrician agreed. "My colleague, he has prescribed an antidepressant, a tranquilizer and a new medication that he says has been successful in your country for the relief from the panic." Fauchery clasped his hands on the desk. "He would have started the treatment earlier, but there was the infant to consider. Last night Madame Cordiner became extremely agitated about somebody who recently passed away."

"Yes, my cousin."

"So he also prescribed Thorazine."

"Thorazine? Isn't that for schizophrenia? I've heard it's dangerous. Especially since he's using all those other drugs."

"He believes the medications are necessary for Madame Cordiner." Fauchery's expression indicated that such heroic measures were not his own preference, but the matter being beyond his expertise, he was going along with the specialist whom he had brought in.

"How long should it be before she's completely well?"

Dr. Fauchery raised his clean, plump hands. "Dr. Plon, he believes that the deeprootedness of Madame's symptoms prove her recovery will be slow."

"Beth? It's a boy, exactly three kilos—six and a half pounds. He hasn't got much hair, but what there is looks red."

"Irving, wake up! Barry has a boy."

Irving said, "*Mazeltov*! Barry, give Alyssia and your new son a big kiss from me."

Beth was back on the line. "When was he born?"

"A while ago . . . actually yesterday."

"And you didn't call?" she reproached.

"We must talk."

"Let me go in the other room." After a minute she was on the line again. "Poor Irving didn't get in until a couple of hours ago, and he needs his sleep. Have you phoned Dad? What took you so long to call?"

"Alyssia's been . . . distraught. Beth, it's worse than before. We're in dire straits here."

After a long pause Beth said, "I'm sorry, Barry, but the answer's still no." Her voice sounded faraway and regretful.

"You told me you wanted a child; you told me you could never accept a child who didn't have your genes. This baby fills your specifications."

"Why are you being so cruel?"

"I'm talking about . . . adoption."

"Adoption?"

"Yes, adoption."

There was a silence. "What about Alyssia? Does she agree?"

"She's thinking it over," Barry lied.

"What . . . about the baby. . . ?"

"Alyssia, you can't manage him right now."

"It's all the stuff they've got me on."

"Hon, you've been having problems for years, you told me so yourself. That's what they're treating." He paused. "I'm not capable of taking charge of an infant."

"Juanita."

"The physical care isn't what I'm talking about. It's the responsibility."

"Juanita's reliable. . . ."

"She quit a few months ago, hon. If another man comes on the scene, she'll depart again. Besides, she's a personal maid, not a nurse. Do you want our son raised by a series of hired nannies?"

Alyssia began panting.

Though this attack had none of the stridency of her previous struggles for air, her expression of dazed terror made it far more unnerving.

After summoning Juanita, who was waiting in the hall, he went into the tiny parlor-nursery.

The white-coiffed Alsatian nun placidly continued her embroidery. He stood over the antique brass cradle with its elaborate festoons of Valenciennes lace. The cradle accused him. Alyssia, before the birth and despite her precarious mental and physical state, had insisted on leaving the clinic to lovingly select baby furniture and an extensive hand-stitched yellow and white layette.

The baby was awake. The frown lines in his forehead reached to the pale, reddish fuzz. With jerky lack of coordination he rubbed the back of his curled fingers at his unfocused blue eyes.

Barry felt love aching painfully inside his throat and chest. His previous fantasies were nothing compared to the overwhelming emotional attachment he felt for this tiny scrap of humanity. *He's all that matters,* Barry thought. *Alyssia and I must be the worst set of parents since the Borgias, and I mustn't let my squeamishness about pressing her interfere with what's best for him.*

When he returned to Alyssia's room, she was pale and limp, but breathing normally.

"Hon, there's no other choice. In this type of thing, the sooner the better. We have to let Beth take over."

She stared dully at him. "Beth?"

"He needs her."

"I'm not following you," she murmured. "It's all this junk in me."

"Beth is instinctively responsible. She's kind and loving, a true *mensch* of a person. She has every qualification to be an outstanding parent."

"Clarrie," Alyssia whispered, a spark in her glazed eyes telling him that someplace behind the pharmaceutical fog dwelt the old, spirited Alyssia.

"Beth did the best she could with Clarrie, under the circumstances."

"How long . . . will Beth look after him?"

"Uhh, permanently."

"You mean, adopt him?"

"It's the only way."

Alyssia half rose up. "Never!" she cried, then fell back in the pillow, turning her head away from him.

"Listen to me. What sort of life can we give him, you and I? To put it brutally, I'm an alcoholic and you're in a highly questionable mental state. It's not how *we* feel that counts, it's what's right for him."

"I can't lose everything. . . ." Alyssia whispered. "First Hap, then my baby. . . ."

"Hon, I never thought I'd love him so much." Barry's voice shook with emotion.

Then, steeling himself, he went to the escritoire for a sheet of the clinic notepaper.

He knew nothing of the legalities involved in giving up a child for adoption, and doubtless the Napoleonic Code differed vastly from the laws of the state of California. He did, however, know his wife.

She kept her contracts.

He wrote with careful legibility:

> We, Barry Cordiner and Alyssia del Mar Cordiner, do hereby agree to surrender our male infant to Elizabeth Cordiner Gold and Irving Gold in order that they might adopt him. We will not make ourselves known to said male child, or make any claims on him.
>
> May 5, 1980.

He returned to the bed. "Hon, write your name here," he said gently.

"Never. . . ."

Tears were rolling from Alyssia's eyes, but she showed no other sign that she was weeping. Her face didn't crinkle, she made no sound. Just those tears runneling down her cheeks.

He set his informal adoption paper on the nightstand. "When you think it through, hon," he said quietly, "you'll see there's no other choice."

"Where's the paper?" Barry asked when he returned at dusk.

Alyssia, who hadn't greeted him, didn't reply. He wondered if she were playing a silent game with him or if she were heavily drugged. It wasn't important. All that mattered, he told himself, was their son.

He fished the quasilegal document from the nightstand drawer, holding it in front of her face. "Have you decided about this?"

She closed her eyes.

"The maternity clinic's responsible for him now. But what about when you leave?"

She turned her head.

"Alice, I ain't letting you do it."

Barry had left a few minutes earlier, and they were in the baby's room, Alyssia sitting next to the cradle in the chair vacated by the Alsatian nun, who was downstairs eating dinner with the staff.

"I'm just trying to think it through," she said in a low, flat voice that sounded computerized. "Beth's good, decent. She knows all the right things to do . . . she'll teach him the college kind of things."

"You're worth more'n all of them Cordiners put together."

Alyssia rocked the cradle gently.

"You'll be better soon," Juanita argued. "I know you're all stoned now, but you mustn't let Barry wheedle you around the way he always done."

"Maybe he's right, Nita . . . I'm a mess."

"They've turned you into a zombie. You can't make a decision now."

The baby waved his fists.

"Look at how sweet he is," Juanita said. "Here."

She lifted the child, setting him in Alyssia's arms. Alyssia snuggled him closer, resting her cheek against his head.

Juanita said, "You mustn't even think about giving him up."

Suddenly Alyssia tensed, giving a soft gasp, and the baby slipped onto her lap. He inhaled for a scream, turning crimson. Juanita took him, soothing him.

Alyssia, gasping for air, returned unsteadily to the bedroom.

When Barry had left the clinic, he walked along the quiet, tree-lined streets without a goal in mind. The sky grew completely dark, and he found himself again in front of the vine-covered house. He halted, staring up at the dim yellow glow coming through the curtains of the second-floor suite. Torn between his desire to give his son the best possible life and his self-loathing at pressing his sorely beset wife, he had reached the limit of his self-control.

Pounding his fist into his palm, he hurried away from the clinic. Previously he had noted a bistro, Le Chat Noir, opposite the cathedral.

The following morning he awoke fully clothed on his bed at the Trois-Rivières Méridien. He attempted to recall the events of the previous night, but a wave of nausea sent him staggering to the bathroom. After he finished vomiting, he remembered. He ordered a bottle of cognac sent to his room.

Two days later, when he visited Alyssia, he was shaven, wearing a clean shirt, but the sour odor emanating from his skin and his red-streaked eyes told her, drugged as she was, what he had been up to.

"Sorry—I haven't been by, hon," he said with a sheepish little grin. "Been celebrating fatherhood."

For several minutes they were silent, then the baby began crying in the next room.

She sighed, closing her eyes. "You're right," she murmured. "I can't take care of him."

A shudder passed down Barry's spine, as if a window had blown open. He hastily searched the nightstand drawer, finding his de facto adoption paper, signing his name, then resting the paper on a magazine, giving Alyssia his pen.

Her hand shook and her signature—the autograph that she had scribbled so many thousands of times—wobbled unrecognizably.

Barry folded the paper, carefully putting it in his inside pocket.

Then he rested his head on his wife's milk-swollen breasts and began to sob. She, dry-eyed, stared dully at the flowering horse chestnut tree outside the window.

The news was broken by Dan Rather. Yet another tragedy had overtaken the Cordiner family. Alyssia del Mar had given birth to a stillborn girl.

Irving was tired after the long haul of the Tahoe condominium project, Beth told her family and friends, so she was taking him away. They leased a large, handsome chalet isolated in the foothills of the Alps.

When they returned a month later, they had a six-day-old adopted son, Jonathon. He was a large, healthy infant, able to hold his blue eyes in a fixed position, exceptional in a baby so young. By some stroke of fortune or precise Swiss adoption proceedings, he had a trace of the red hair common in Beth's branch of the Cordiner family.

BEVERLY HILLS, 1986

Beth gripped her wineglass so tightly that the tendons of her hand stood out. She was recalling her measured walk down the chalet's front steps to Barry's rental car. She had been warning herself to remain aloof for a year or so, until she could be positive that this baby had none of Clarrie's abnormalities. Yet, as she unfastened the straps of the car crib and lifted the small weight, an exultant stir twisted within her abdomen, a blood knot tying itself. And so it had began, her bedazzled maternity. Sometimes she even forgot the nightmare of Clarrie, connecting her own pregnancy to Jonathon. God knows, the family traits showed up in abundance—her son had Tim's impetuousness, a strong hint of the Cordiner temper; he had Barry's intelligence without the laziness.

Beth sighed. "What I can't understand is why Alyssia wanted Jonathon here," she said.

"Stop worrying, Beth," Barry said.

"Yes," Maxim said. "Can't you see that this is just a friendly Cordiner family get-together?"

Giving her cousin a reproachful look, Beth got to her feet. "I can't take another minute of this waiting. Besides, I have a PTA board meeting and—" She broke off as a car in low gear came up the steep drive.

Though the house blocked the foursome's view, the sound captured their attention, and none of them spoke.

A car door slammed.

A faraway child piped, "Mommy!"

"She had a baby?" Beth whispered. "But how could she? It would have been in the news."

They heard the front door open, then Alyssia's intonations but not her words.

At the lower rumble of a masculine response, Maxim's head jerked. Slowly all color drained from his lips.

"Maxim, what is it?" Beth asked, her charming voice solicitous.

He didn't reply. He, who normally moved with total assurance, stumbled to his feet, barging to the house, attempting to slide open one of the mirror-treated windows. It was locked.

Slapping his palms on the glass, his voice almost unrecognizable, Maxim shouted, "Open up! Open up!"

HAP

1980

64

Within three months of Hap's death, Desmond Cordiner had recovered as much as he ever would from his stroke. The limbs of his right side were alien appendages devoid of all sensation, and his speech was nearly incomprehensible. Yet the brain trapped within this wreckage retained its agile wiliness. He spent his long, invalid days planning means to keep his beloved older son's memory alive. With lavish donations from himself and the rest of the family, he endowed the Harvard Cordiner chair at the USC film department, the Harvard Cordiner Gallery of Cinematic Art at UCLA, he founded Harvard Cordiner film scholarships at Columbia and the University of Chicago. (Desmond's life had circled like a compass around the fixed point of the Industry, so it never occurred to him to build up the relief center in Zaire that had meant so much to Hap.)

Hap's lack of a proper funeral preyed continuously on him.

The left side of his face working, Desmond sputtered out an idea to Maxim. Art Garrison and Harry Cohn had each had a funeral on a sound stage of the studio he founded—Cohn at Columbia, Garrison at Magnum. Why not give Hap a memorial on this grand scale?

Maxim, who was finishing the great slag heap of post-production work with the urgency of his grief, fully agreed with the concept and promised to implement it. By chance that was the week *The New Yorker* with Barry's article hit the stands. Maxim read the piece in a cold fury. That jealous shit—no wonder he was skulking in France!—had painted Hap as an egomaniacal spendthrift, a hack director with delusions of grandeur. What better refutation for this poison could there be than to premiere *The Baobab Tree,* which would be completed in August, at the memorial? Assuredly the film was Hap's crowning achievement. He and the studio would see to it that all the important people were there, as well as the world press.

The August hot spell continued and that Saturday afternoon the thermometer rose to a hundred and three.

Outside Magnum's iron-arched main gate, sweat-drenched onlookers strained against the cordon of equally sweaty off-duty LAPD cops hired for this occasion. The crowd ignored those mourners who lacked a VIP gold-embossed card and therefore were not permitted to drive onto the lot: for the most part these people who trudged inside mopping their saddened faces were the craftsmen from studio shops, the seamstresses, the extras, the hairdressers, the stuntmen, the makeup people. Many had worked with Hap, and others, the elderly retirees, had known him as a boy, the straw-haired son of Desmond Cordiner. He had been popular with them all.

The limousines carrying upper-echelon executives were greeted with near sullen disappointment, but the uncomfortable crowd came to exultant life, pushing and elbowing one another for a better view of Burt Lancaster and Richard Burton and Cliff Camron and Dustin Hoffman and Rain Fairburn and Shirley MacLaine. A small cheer went up for latecomer and star of the film Alyssia del Mar, arriving alone in a hired white stretch limousine. She glanced out the open window with an almost baffled expression, as if not sure why anyone should cry her name. Her Van Nuys fan club had heard on *Good Morning America* that for the first time she was emerging from her seclusion following the loss of her child to pay homage to her ofttimes director, with whom, as everyone in the club knew, she once had lived. A cognoscente announced that her soon-to-be ex-husband, Barry Cordiner, was staying in France because the family was pissed at something he had written about them.

On Stage 8, Magnum's largest sound stage, the outsize screen seemed an insignificant blank postage stamp. Facing it were thousands of folding chairs in neat rows, and a dais banked with red roses that was reserved for the family.

Desmond Cordiner, slumping awkwardly in a wheelchair, was shielded from public view by an enormous arrangement of American Beauties. On each of the white leather seats on the dais had rested a place card. In expansive Hollywood style the family included its divorced members. Two of Maxim's spectacular exes sat with their current spouses, and Madeleine Van Vliet Cordiner, as putative widow, had the place of honor behind the lectern. Every place was filled.

The ceremony had started with the full studio orchestra's rendition of Quincy Jones's haunting love theme for *The Baobab Tree,* and all eyes were fixed on Alyssia del Mar as she hurried toward the dais. She had lost considerable weight, but her new black silk Galanos was bloused to disguise this, and her pallor was hidden by several hours of effort on the part of her makeup artist.

"Can you believe it? The cunt even shows up late for this," snarled a Hearst columnist, not bothering to lower her voice.

The "stillbirth" might have attracted sympathy for Alyssia among her die-hard fans, but Barry's much-quoted article had fanned a general animosity toward her. To the media, and therefore to all of America, she had become the tardy star whose shenanigans had turned Hap Cordiner's final film into a nightmare.

Alyssia climbed three of the plank steps, then halted, faced by a solid phalanx of staring Cordiners. A wave of vertigo passed through her as she realized there was no chair for her.

Maxim gazed coldly down. It was no accident she didn't have a place, this woman who had somehow ensnared his brother. (Later Maxim would be ashamed of his vindictiveness, but at this moment he was relishing Alyssia's public humiliation.)

Beth cleared her throat delicately, wondering if she ought to relieve the hideous awkwardness by smiling, but Irving took her hand, and she decided this was a reminder of the power that Alyssia had over them. *Jonathon,* she thought, and stared fixedly at an overblown rose.

PD was grateful he was no longer forced to fake cordiality. Two months ago Alyssia had called to inform him that she had given up her career, maybe permanently. She was therefore no longer represented by the PD Zaffarano Agency.

To combat the dizziness, Alyssia dug her recently manicured nails into her palms. *Just find another seat—don't think about it—you might have an attack. . . .* She turned toward the central aisle. She didn't recognize Richard Burton as he stepped by her to the podium. A stuntman in the second row stood to give her his place, but she didn't see him, or the gaffer farther back who offered her the same courtesy. Somehow managing to impersonate the del Mar strut, she got to the last row, where a few seats remained.

"How short is the time of man," the amplified Burton voice was intoning. "We've come here to honor one of our best and brightest, felled long before his time by his own unquenchable generosity. . . ."

Alyssia, forcing an actress's semblance of control, saw and heard nothing of the eulogies.

In a way she was grateful not to be on the dais. Everyone would be staring at her. She had not been out in public since she had left Dr. Fauchery's place.

Plon had argued with Barry that she ought to be transferred to a nearby psychiatric hospital where he was on the staff, but Barry, apologetic and filled with empathy after they had signed the baby over to Beth and Irving, had understood how she felt. She would rather submit to physical torture or a lifetime of illness than those drugs. Juanita at her side, she had flown immediately home to Beverly Hills, where her body supplied its own opiate, depression. She moved like a somnambulist through her days.

Her mind stumbled to attention as the mourners on the dais noisily turned their chairs around to face the screen. The sound stage darkened and the opening credits showed over a big-game hunt.

Every scene prompted memories. This had been shot when they were happy; this when they were shattered apart.

Watching the seduction episode in the stable, she felt a peculiar prickling sensation travel down her spine, as if somebody behind were peering intently at her. She continued to watch the screen, but her concentration was gone. The pins and needles sense of uneasiness grew stronger.

After several minutes she could no longer prevent herself from turning. In the darkness she made out the figure of a man standing about twenty feet behind her. She couldn't tell much about him except that he was tall, and unlike the formally clad audience, wore jeans and a pale windbreaker. She decided it must be embarrassment at not having the proper clothes that had kept him from taking one of the folding chairs. Then she tried to turn back to the film. She was powerless to look away from him.

As her eyes adjusted to the darkness, she saw he was bearded. The scene with the electric storm was playing now, and in the special effects department's most hectic burst of lightning, she could see him quite clearly.

His beard was considerably darker than his streaked blond hair, and the eyes staring at her were deep-set. Her heart beat rapidly, and with clear recognition she understood she was looking at Hap. An older, bearded Hap.

She knew this was a hallucination.

But the queer part was that the hallucination didn't seem beyond the range of normalcy.

She started to rise from her chair.

Then he was gone.

Replacing him was a dark outline that she identified as one of the large tubbed ficus trees that propmen had set around to decorate the barren reaches of Stage 8.

She knew it was impossible to will a phantasm into being, yet a thought jittered through her.

Maybe if I wait, then look back, I'll see him again.

She fidgeted with her black silk skirt, then, after an unbearably long half minute, turned her head. The tree remained a tree. She pushed aside her chair and ran unevenly to the red lights that spelled EXIT.

65

"Of course it sounds crazy!" Alyssia said for the dozenth time. "But I'm telling you I saw Hap."

"The movie," Juanita said uneasily. "You told me how every part of it reminded you of him."

Alyssia dropped the earrings she had worn to the memorial in the jewelry box, then jerked them out again, her fingers agitatedly flattening the long onyx and diamond strands on the marble dressing table ledge. Juanita, hanging up the black outfit, watched covertly. The past couple of months she'd been worried silly by her sister's long silences and torpor, but this burst of frenzied activity and spate of words was far worse, almost as bad as when the medicines at the maternity clinic had turned the poor kid into a zombie. Once again Juanita was fearing for Alyssia's sanity.

Alyssia went into the bathroom, poking a cotton ball into a jar of eye-makeup remover, then dropping the saturated wad. "He'd lost his tan and grown a beard."

"Alice," Juanita said gently, "he's dead."

"I'm aware he wasn't at the studio! I'm aware I didn't actually see him. But, Nita, don't you understand—it was a sign."

"A sign of what?"

"That he's alive."

"You spent hours with that doctor in Africa. He told you everything about the accident and the funeral."

Alyssia yanked out a Kleenex. "Remember how Momma sometimes had premonitions and they turned out to be true?"

Juanita mumbled, "I never believed her when she got like that."

"And you don't believe me, either, do you?" Alyssia said belligerently. "Well, *I* once had a dream that happened. It was in Mendocino—just before Diller died. I dreamed Mr. Cordiner showed up. And he arrived there the next day!"

"A coincidence."

"Oh, must you be so damn sensible! Maybe she *did* have the gift. Maybe *I* inherited it! Loads of highly intelligent people believe in extrasensory perception."

"Alice, calm down."

"All right," Alyssia said. "You're above that kind of cuckoo stuff. But I'm going to look into it!"

"Look into what?"

"Whether he's alive, of course!"

"How?"

Alyssia slumped down at the dressing table, abruptly

devoid of her benzedrine energy. "I don't know," she sighed. "I'll have to figure it out."

Alyssia found John Ivanovich's number in the Beverly Hills Yellow Pages. There was a surprisingly long list of names under *Private Investigators*, but her selection was made easy by the third line of his ad: *Agents Stationed Worldwide.*

The following morning at ten promptly, as they had agreed, Ivanovich came to the house. Alyssia, who had been dressed and waiting since before nine, answered the front doorbell herself. Ivanovich, a leathery, hollow-cheeked middle-aged man, gave her the old up and down, then hastily averted his eyes as the area around his protuberant adam's apple turned brick color. His embarrassment was typical of men who had ravished her in their fantasies. She offered him coffee, and over the first cup he confessed in his wheezing, asthmatic voice that he was a fan.

"From way back when. I saw all of your French movies," he said. "How may I be of service to you, Miss del Mar?"

Assuming a businesslike tone, she inquired, "Are your investigations confidential?"

"More so than dealing with a doctor or lawyer," he reassured her.

She nodded. "I want Harvard Cordiner's death investigated." Having rehearsed in front of her bathroom mirror, the sentence came out with a low-key matter of factness.

His brown eyes narrowed. "Then you suspect foul play?"

She rose, walking away from him toward the window. Turning, she said, "I'd like you to find out all you can about the accident."

"Nobody else has opened this up, not his family nor the studio—yesterday they put on a big memorial for him. Miss del Mar, is it clear in your own mind why you're doing this?"

"Yes, of course." *I saw a vision . . .*

"Some years back you and he lived together."

"What's that got to do with your job?"

"I haven't taken it yet," he said. "You have to understand, Miss del Mar, that all of our clients have a reason. And usually the reason is spelled C-A-S-H. At least ninety percent of our work is tracking down ex-husbands who aren't paying property settlements or who've skipped out on the child support."

"And that's all?"

"Occasionally we're called in on other things, of course. We find missing assets, missing wives, missing kids and teenagers, missing witnesses. Sometimes we debug houses and offices. One thing I can tell you, though. Since I started this agency in 1954, we've never been asked to investigate somebody who's dead and buried."

"I think he might be alive."

Ivanovich's expression was keenly alert. "Do you have any evidence?"

She shook her head. "No."

"Then why?"

"It doesn't make any rational sense. And I certainly can understand why you wouldn't want this case," she said in a drained voice. "But, John—I do appreciate your coming up to the house." She used his first name to ameliorate the waste of his working morning.

He stared at her, his sunken face taking on softness. "You understand the investigation'll be expensive?" he asked. "And that the chances of success are what you might call nil?"

"But you'll try?"

"I'm a fan," he said, shrugging.

She gave him a dazzling smile of relief. "Thank you."

Taking out his pad, he said crisply, "It'll save my time and your money if you give me all the information you have about Cordiner's life, his family, his business associates."

"How does any of that affect what happened in Africa?"

"If it wasn't an accident," he said, "everything's important."

That same afternoon the scent of Arpège joined with the motes of dusting powder in heady sweetness as Alyssia readied herself to meet with the droning-voiced business manager who for years had handled all of her financial transactions from paying the monthly bills to investing in tax shelters. Barry was flying in from France in a couple of days and she was to lay the groundwork for their property settlement, a task that he, by inclination and educational background, should have taken on.

"Alice?" Juanita pushed open the door. "That Maxim's here."

Alyssia snatched up the bath sheet, saronging it around herself as if Maxim, arbiter of yesterday's public humiliation on Stage 8, were witness to her glowing nudity. "What does he want?"

"He didn't say. Shall I tell him you're sick?"

Alyssia, although tempted by Juanita's suggestion, feared that a no-show might be construed as a sign that she had been weakened by the ugly contretemps. "No, tell him I'll be right out."

She piled on a palette of cosmetics. With a final dry brush over her mascara, she scrutinized herself. *You're even more spectacular without all the gunk,* Hap had often said. Maybe. But she couldn't face Maxim without her Alyssia del Mar mask.

It was nearly an hour before she made her entrance into the living room.

When Maxim had looked down on her from the dais yesterday she had been too emotionally unstrung to note his appearance. Now she realized how terrible he looked. He was pale, new lines were cut deeply into his face and he was far too thin.

After their muted greeting, he said, "I suppose you're wondering why I dropped by?"

"It crossed my mind, yes."

"To offer various apologies," he said.

"Apologies?"

"For one thing I was hardly a gentleman when you came to the condo to tell me about Hap."

She anticipated a twisted smile. But his expression remained somberly sincere. She had never comprehended which way Maxim's pendulum would swing. *Take it at face value,* she told herself.

"It's okay, Maxim," she said.

"And I should've gotten in touch after the baby."

Her mind filled with her last sight of her son, his mouth open in a yawn, his thin newborn arms and legs protruding from the hand-stitched yellow crepe de chine sacque that was part of his layette. "A lot of people didn't," she said in a level voice.

"Alyssia, I was not only sorry when I heard, but also *un peu* guilty. On location I worked you like a sled dog."

"The umbilical cord was wrapped around the baby's neck, strangling her." The cause for stillbirth in the press release given out by Dr. Fauchery, who was bound by kindness to keep her secret. (Plon, with his silly little goatee, was bound by his Hippocratic oath, and the Alsatian nun by her religious vows.)

"I'm sorry," Maxim repeated. "And as for the memorial yesterday, the cold truth is that Hap's death has hit me hard." His eyes squeezed shut and he bent his head into his hands. "Jesus, Alyssia—this even beats when Diller died."

Her pity welled, and she wanted to offer consolation, but it seemed to her that she would dishonor their mutual grief by making the conventional sympathy remarks. Then her mind ran a film of that tall, bearded figure in the windbreaker. She certainly couldn't offer Maxim the thin hope that had penetrated her own darkness. If she told him about the apparition—and her investigation—he would conclude that she was a certifiable loony.

Two days later, after Barry cleared customs at LAX, he took a taxi to Beth's house.

She immediately led him upstairs. "To meet Jonathon," she said.

No nurses this time round. She cared for her adopted son herself, redecorating her pretty office, which led off the master bedroom, into an equally charming nursery. The crib was custom made to resemble a sporty red racing car. Jonathon, in a blue tee shirt and matching diaper cover, lay fingering his toes.

"It's remarkable," Barry said. "The resemblance to you."

She said briskly, "Yes, a good match."

He glanced at her and nodded. "Those Swiss agencies."

Beth extended the child. "Go to Uncle Barry."

Jonathon snuggled briefly in his arms, then grabbed for Barry's nose, chortling. Barry gave a happy, embarrassed little smile. How wise he had been, ensuring this child had a good, stable home. "Hey, Jonathon Jonathon Telethon."

"It's time for his juice," Beth said, taking back the baby.

The phone rang in her bedroom.

"Darn," she said.

Barry followed her through the connecting door.

Settling Jonathon, who could not yet wiggle across his crib, in the exact center of her oversized mattress, she picked up the phone. After a moment she said, "Yes, this is she."

At the response, Beth's arms pressed stiffly against her sides. "Yes, I know who you are."

After a long half minute, she said, "Wait a moment, I'll find out."

Holding the phone against her Liberty-flowered cotton skirt, she whispered, "It's Lang. He knows you're here. He wants to see us."

"Now?" Barry whispered back.

"Tomorrow morning. At PD's offices. Can you make it?"

Barry shivered at the thought of being with Lang. But he knew absolutely that he could not face PD. He would never forget playing his Ansafone to hear his cousin's recorded fury upon reading a bootlegged manuscript of *The New Yorker* piece: *You motherfucking writer, how could you sell that garbage? About me, I don't care. But to condemn poor Dad, who was only good and generous to you, as Mafioso by linking his name with Bart Lanzoni's! And to write all that crap about Hap—what a shitty way to get back at him for balling Alyssia! Now Lang's really got it in for him—are you happy, rat-ass? You're a talentless pigfart, Barry, and you always were. I'd never have represented you if you weren't Beth's brother! You're no longer my client, you're my enemy, do you hear me, motherfucker? My enemy!* By the time the article was duly published Hap was dead, and the rest of the clan, including Maxim, had responded with a cold wall of silence.

Beth was watching him, worry in her eyes. "Barry, we *must* go," she whispered. "With Lang there's no choice."

As she took the phone from her hip to accept, they both could hear the buzzing. Lang had hung up.

Beth reached for the baby, clutching him close.

"How did he know I'm here?" Barry asked. "Why does he want to see us?"

"He didn't say." Beth's voice shook.

Jonathon let out a restive wail, either announcing his hunger or protesting the tightness of his mother's arms.

66

Lang had specified they meet at eleven.

It was not yet a quarter to when the porcelain-perfect Nisei receptionist ushered Beth and Barry into PD's office. A silver coffee service on the credenza was flanked by Imari cups and a mound of miniature coffee cakes whose fresh-baked aroma filled the overcooled air.

PD removed the horn-rims he now wore to read and came around his desk.

"Beth," he greeted. He pecked a kiss in the vicinity of her cheek. Since their breakup, they seldom touched. "That dress is great on you. How's your boy?"

"Wonderful," she said, knocking the rosewood of his desk.

PD said coldly to Barry, "I didn't know you were back."

"PD." The tendons of Beth's neck stood out. "What does Lang want?"

"Explanations aren't his style," PD replied. "But I can tell you from experience that unless he believes he's being handed a raw deal, he's a perfect gentleman. Maxim's taking this meeting, too. Also Alyssia."

Barry gave a shiver and stared out at the view. Maxim would be even more difficult to face than PD, for the article had contained more about him—and poor Hap. And how had Alyssia taken what he'd written about her? *Why did I have to be so damn honest?*

PD picked up the ornately chased coffeepot. "Beth?" he asked.

"Yes. Black, please," she said.

Glancing in Barry's direction, he said, "Help yourself."

Barry craved a good stiff drink. Instead, with shaky fingers he selected four of the largest sweet rolls. As he gulped down the rich morsels of pastry, PD continued to ignore him, pointedly addressing his conversation at Beth.

Just before eleven Maxim arrived.

With a quick, surprised glance at Barry, Maxim looked away. "You have yourself an odor problem in here, PD," he said. "You ought to get a good fumigator."

"Hello, Maxim," Barry said, rising to help himself to another coffee cake, which wouldn't, he knew, assuage his overpowering need for booze.

Maxim kissed Beth. "I didn't realize this was to be a family reunion. And where's our master of ceremonies, the king of drug dealers?"

PD darted an anxious glance at the closed door as if Lang might somehow have passed through the polished teak and be listening. "It's only five to."

At one minute after eleven, Lang was admitted.

He greeted each of them with formal propriety, thanking them for their promptness.

"Where's Miss del Mar?" he asked.

Though Alyssia was no longer his client, PD still felt responsible for her, and beads of moisture appeared on his forehead. What with his unanswered questions about this meeting and being in the same room with that fuckface Barry, he was already under a strain that even his considerable social savoir faire could not accommodate, and Alyssia's tardiness was more than he could take. "Stars and their entrances! But if you're in a hurry, Mr. Lang, why not go ahead without her?"

"I prefer to wait until everyone is here," Lang said courteously.

He refused coffee. PD kept up a mainly one-sided conversation about *The Baobab Tree,* which since its broad release two weeks earlier had drawn the top grosses countrywide.

At twenty-five past, when PD was surreptitiously mopping below his chin, Alyssia arrived.

Poised in the doorway with a tremulous smile, her thick tangle of black hair gleaming in the lights of the hallway, her dazzling white cleavage showing to advantage in her low-cut magenta dress, she transcended her own myth and gave no clue to the anxiety that quickened her pulse.

"Barry, you doll," she said. "*Spy* just arrived. I can't tell you how touched I was, getting an autographed copy. I can't wait to start it." She turned her sparkling blue gaze on Beth. "It's *fabulous* about the baby—I'm so happy for you and Irving. Jeremy, isn't that what you called him?"

"Jonathon," Beth whispered. She shrank back, her cream dress fading into the slubbed white silk of her chair.

Alyssia smiled at Maxim. "Aren't you *sportif*?" His bone-thin legs were displayed by Fila tennis shorts. "And, PD, you darling. You must have read my mind with those sweet rolls. I didn't have time for breakfast."

Only when PD went to serve her did she acknowledge Robert Lang's presence. "Good morning," she said, unsmiling.

"Miss del Mar—it's always a pleasure. Allow me to extend my condolences to you and Mr. Cordiner for the loss of your child."

Alyssia stifled a shiver. Even though she and Beth had just exchanged words about the baby, he was indeed lost—irrevocably lost—to her. She took a sip of the coffee that PD had just handed her. It had cooled unpleasantly in the pot.

"When you've finished your breakfast, Miss del Mar," Lang said, "I'd like to ask a question of you and the others."

"Don't wait for me. Fire away."

He bent his head, a small bow that indicated gratitude. "Who hired John Ivanovich?" he asked.

Tepid coffee sloshed, and she set down the Imariware cup with careful hands next to the plate that PD had heaped with small pastries.

"Ivanovich," PD said musingly. "I don't know the name. Maybe my office manager took him on. But then he'd be strictly clerical."

"We don't have anybody new at the house," Beth said. "Of course my husband has a great many employees on his business payroll."

"John Ivanovich." Maxim quirked an eyebrow. "Is he the newest Russian defector?"

Lang turned to Alyssia. She managed an actressy little smile. "Guilty," she said, her voice wavering.

"Then, Miss del Mar, I suggest you tell him you no longer need his services."

"Mr. Lang, what possible reason can you have to ask me to do that?" Because she was afraid, she boldly mimicked his excessive politeness.

"There's no point to hiring him."

"It's my money," Alyssia retorted.

"Who *is* Ivanovich, hon?" Barry asked.

"Yes," Beth said, wetting her lips. "I don't understand."

"He's a private detective," Alyssia said.

"Mysteries and more mysteries," Maxim said. "Why have you hired a detective, star-lady?"

"Miss del Mar desires to discover more about the accident in Zaire," Lang said.

"More?" Barry said. "Hon, when you went to Africa didn't that doctor tell you everything?"

"I'm not positive Hap's dead," Alyssia said levelly.

They all stared at her, and Beth asked, "You have some sort of clue he's alive?"

"I'm not sure. Call it feminine intuition."

"Miss del Mar," Lang said in an icy tone. "Do you understand me?"

"About Ivanovich?" she replied. "Frankly, no. Why should I fire him?"

"I'm telling you to."

"That's an order, not a reason. I don't respond well to orders."

"Harvard Cordiner is dead," Lang said.

"Yes, Mr. Lang—but it's not easy for the people who cared about him to accept." PD, the agent, found himself attempting to placate both sides.

"Miss del Mar." Lang spoke softly. "On stage and on the screen, the actor springs up after his death. In actuality, alas, such is not the case. Mr. Cordiner died on a road near a small town called Lunda, formerly King Baudoinville. He was driving at night, a dangerous thing to do in that part of the world. His jeep skidded into a fallen mahogany tree and burned."

"So many details," she whispered. "Way more than Art told me. How can you possibly know so many details?"

Lang didn't reply or move. He was so still that a freeze-frame might have captured him on film.

PD found himself staring into Lang's eyes, yet wanting to look away. The eyes had the same peculiar, shrunken pupils as on the night in Vegas when he'd read Barry's article. Then it had seemed odd to PD that Lang's fury was directed not at that miserable loser of a writer, Barry, but at Hap. Lang had blamed Hap because the piece made him look ridiculous and at the same time had thrown in accusations that Hap had welched out on his obligations to Meadstar.

Suddenly PD's head felt light, as if he might pass out. He was remembering his dead father tugging at his mustache and using the heavy Italian accent that he lapsed into when emotional: . . . *accidents happen to whoever Lang thinks owes him. Never anything provable, but that doesn't mean the people aren't dead.* . . .

Lang was rising to his feet. "Mrs. Gold, Mr. Cordiner, Mr. Cordiner, Mr. Zaffarano." He inclined his head to each of them. "I'm grateful to you for coming here this morning. And I feel secure that the four of you can convince Miss del Mar that she has reached the heart of the matter about the unfortunate accident, and that for her to continue her investigation is not only unnecessary but also most foolish."

67

Lang didn't quite close the door, and after he left, the cooled air seemed to pulsate as all of them stared at the crack.

Maxim's fingers were tensed on his bare thighs, his eyes shut tight. Barry clutched the bowl of his unlit pipe—it was one of the Dunhills Alyssia had bought him a year earlier in New York to celebrate his signing the contract for *Spy*. Beth breathed shallowly and tugged the gold chain of her beige alligator purse with sharp, unconscious movements.

PD's hands, too, were busy. He had unlocked the top drawer of his desk and was surreptitiously fingering his boyhood rosary as he prayed for the departed soul of his slain cousin. Then he pushed back his chair, going to close the door. Turning, he stared at Barry.

"I was there when he read your manuscript," he accused hoarsely. "He already had it in for Hap. He went into a cold rage. A few days later, Hap's dead in a car crash."

Alyssia gave a little whimper, but the others ignored her.

"That's Lang's method," PD went on. "He arranges accidents for people he thinks have cheated him—or made him look an asshole. The point of your story was that Hap had jerked him around."

"That wasn't the point. And *I* didn't arrange that Hap do the film," Barry said defensively. "*You* knew all about Lang and his ilk. Why did *you* put a clean guy like Hap in a package with him?"

Maxim turned to Barry. "Lang had the right idea," he said. "Except he picked the wrong Cordiner to do it to."

"*You* knew something was rotten, Maxim," Barry snapped. "I saw you. All your time on that film was spent soothing those two gunsels of Lang's. And it's hardly my fault you went millions over budget, is it?"

Alyssia didn't hear the sparring voices. *He's dead,* she thought. *So much for hallucinations. So much for hereditary second sight. All I was doing was playing mental leapfrog over the fixed and unalterable truth. Hap's dead. Lang had him killed.*

The tightness in her chest was swelling against her lungs and she could breathe only with severe pain. By far the most anguished of the five, her imperative from earliest childhood to hide all weakness made her appear the least affected. Her hands were loosely folded on her magenta silk lap, her expression serene.

Beth yanked at her chain. "It's too awful to believe."

"Possibly we're leaping to heinous conclusions, Beth," Barry soothed.

"Weren't the details specific enough for your great, poetic brain?" Maxim inquired. "If we'd asked, my guess is he could have told the brand of gasoline they used to ignite the blaze—God, how I hope Hap was dead before they lit it."

A peculiar gasp came from Alyssia, but her voice

retained its normal pitch, a well-trained, cool instrument. "Art Kleefeld mentioned there were strangers around."

The other four turned to her. The flesh of their faces hardened subtly. Though PD and Maxim now openly loathed Barry, and disliked each other for the parts each had played in inveigling Hap into doing *The Baobab Tree,* they were all locking her out. No non-Cordiners permitted in this private domain of grief, enmity and horror.

After a couple of beats Barry asked, "Strangers? Were they visiting the center?"

"Art never saw them. He said he assumed that they were big brass visiting the locals."

"But you're saying they were Lang's hit squad?" PD asked.

"It's obvious." How could her body still continue functioning when inside she was as cold and dead as Hap?

"But what's incomprehensible to me," Barry said, "is why Lang would make a covert admission to us, of all people, that he'd had Hap killed."

A link between Beth's nervous hands snapped loudly. She stared down at the broken chain. "Eighteen carat," she whispered.

"Good for it," Maxim said. "Now, Beth, will you explain to your genius brother, who has always been remarkable for his capacity to avoid unpalatable facts, why you have broken an eighteen-carat-gold purse chain."

Beth said, "Lang's threatening us, Barry, don't you see? He's reminding us he can have people killed. He's telling us he doesn't want any investigations that might become public property."

Once again the foursome stared at Alyssia.

She couldn't catch her breath. *I'm fine. The pain in my chest—ahh, the pain—is merely a psychosomatic symptom. I am fine.*

"PD's right," Beth said in a low, frightened voice. "Accidents are Lang's way. And they don't have to happen to the person—they can happen to somebody he cares about." She paused, looking at Alyssia. "You are going to get rid of the detective, aren't you, Alyssia?"

Alyssia didn't hear. She was accusing herself of causing some of the production delays by her attacks and by the limits she'd imposed because of her pregnancy. *Maybe I was seeing a ghost unable to rest.*

Beth cleared her throat. "Alyssia, whatever else, now you know for certain Hap's dead. So there's no point keeping on."

"Yes, hon," Barry said. "It's perilous."

"Exactly why I'm not firing Ivanovich," Alyssia said. But that wasn't the entire reason. Guilt was one part of it. And mistaking the shadow of a ficus tree for a man was another. She couldn't let the Cordiners see she was a crumbled cookie. Besides, how could she let Hap's murder slip by the boards?

"But what about the rest of us and our families?" Beth's voice rose alarmingly. "What about my baby?"

"Doesn't it matter to any of you that we just heard Lang confess he had Hap killed?"

"Is that what you're attempting to accomplish?" Barry asked. "To bring Lang to justice?"

"If that's it," PD interjected, "take it from me. Grand juries never touch guys like Lang. The small fry are put behind bars, but people of his caliber never even get indicted."

"In case PD's being too cryptic, Alyssia," Maxim said, "let me spell it out. The Langs of the world control the courts; they own the judges."

"You're all afraid, aren't you?" Alyssia said. "Hap wasn't a coward, but the rest of you are."

Maxim snapped his fingers. "Listen, bitch, Hap's my blood and sinew. If I thought I could get Lang, nothing would hold me back."

Alyssia stared at him until he looked away.

Then she got to her feet, sauntering across the large Kirman rug.

She paused at the door. "Great seeing you all," she said with light malice. "Let's do it again real soon."

She ran down the wide, print-hung corridor, slowing to cross the waiting room, where she ignored a trio of agency clients watching her from the deep chairs.

As the elevator door closed on her, she collapsed against a mirrored wall, her hoarse gasps filling the enclosed space. The elevator halted. She pulled erect, waiting with a faint smile for the blue-jacketed attendant to bring her car. Driving a block west on Sunset, she turned onto a side street and parked. There, hunched over the steering wheel, she shuddered, gasping for air.

After Alyssia had left, PD was first to speak. "All these years dealing with her and it never got through to me how unstable she is."

"Was Lang serious?" Beth gazed pleadingly around at the three men.

"Believe me, Lang's always serious," PD replied.

"So you really think he will blame us if we can't control her?" Beth asked.

"Yes," PD said, turning to Barry. "It's up to you to talk her out of it."

"Me?"

"You're married to the lady," Maxim retorted.

"Almost divorced. And I'm sick of being the goat here."

Beth turned anxiously to PD. "She's more likely to listen to you, PD. She always relied on you as her agent."

"I used to be her agent." PD bared his white teeth in a way that suggested a smile. "Beth, you and she are close."

"That was a long time ago," Beth said.

"Still, you *do* have a lot in common with her, Beth," Barry said, his voice lower and meaningful.

Beth held the broken links of the chain together as if the pressure of her nervous fingers could solder gold. "You saw how she behaved when I pleaded. I hate her!"

"We all do." Maxim spoke for the first time since Alyssia had left. "Didn't she just prove she's the only one of us with guts?"

"Where will arguing get us?" Beth asked shrilly. "What are we going to *do*? I'm so terrified for Jonathon I could die."

"Ahh yes," Maxim said. "Those adoptive ties are strong."

"What would you know about it?" Beth cried. "You've never managed to stay married long enough to have children."

Into the hermetically sealed atmosphere of the office came the muted howl of a siren on Sunset, and the angry voices were silent.

PD crossed his arms on the desk. "Okay—agreed that

none of us can handle Alyssia. Now what's the course of action?"

"Lang," Maxim said, scratching his thin, bare thigh.

"Lang?" PD exploded.

"Yes, Lang. You, PD, will go to your friend in Vegas and explain that we can do nothing with the lady, but explain also that we're devout cowards, so we're staunchly on his side, and none of us will ever raise a public accusatory finger. And furthermore, should Alyssia's friendly shamus dig up anything that might incriminate him, we're ready to do all in our power to consign her to the cuckoos' nest."

"Why should he buy it?" PD asked.

"Because you're a persuasive guy. And also you're laying the naked truth on him. Tell him that Beth's fearful for her infant, that you're fearful for the ten percent empire you've built up, that I'm fearful for my life, and that Barry's fearful period. And not one of us is in love with Alyssia."

"And that's your plan?" PD asked. "Dump her?"

"Exactly," Maxim said hoarsely. "Of course at the same time we'll also be dumping Hap. We'll let that Las Vegas prick get away with killing him."

They avoided one another's eyes.

The four living members of Our Own Gang had just forged an unspoken pact to ignore the murder of their fifth. With a rustling noise, they rose to their feet, exchanging overhearty farewells. Barry concocted an excuse to avoid returning to Beth's house. Nobody made any plans to get together in the future.

68

It was late afternoon before she felt calm enough to call Ivanovich.

A raspy-voiced woman answered the phone. "I'm sorry, but he's temporarily out of town."

Alyssia, having made up her apparently irrational mind,

was primed to tell the detective to go full speed ahead. Stymied, she said on a breathless, questioning note, "Oh?"

"We work very closely," the woman said. "Can I help you?"

"No, it's confidential. This is Alyssia del Mar."

"I thought it sounded like you. When he checks in, I'll tell him you called, Miss del Mar."

He didn't call back. After five days Alyssia was worn out by impatience, despair and lack of sleep. Her recent pattern of getting fifteen hours was altered drastically, and now she seldom slept as much as three. She lost more weight. Ivanovich was stalling her, avoiding her, and she had no conception how to deal with it. *Murder,* she would think, swimming urgent laps in the dumb, heart-shaped pool. *Murder, and the four of them are willing to let it go. But I won't—I can't. Why doesn't the asthmatic bastard call?*

"What about trying him again?" Juanita asked. They were eating a light dinner on the patio.

"I have." Six times. "The woman, she's his partner or something, keeps telling me he's still out of town."

"Alice, I don't like the way you been looking. Maybe we're the ones who ought to get away."

That same evening, the door chimes sounded just as Prime Time programming was making the ten o'clock change. Alyssia and Juanita, who were watching the outsized built-in screen in the living room, glanced at each other.

"Nobody comes by this late," Juanita said.

"Maybe it's Barry with some papers to sign."

"Or another one of them kooks," Juanita muttered. Alyssia del Mar's address and phone numbers were tightly guarded secrets, yet nonetheless in the spate of bad publicity about her following Hap's death there had been ugly incidents. Twice during the small hours of the night garbage had been carted up the long, steep drive and dumped by the front door. An androgynous voice phoned at random intervals to shriek, "Repent, repent!" until they let the answering service pick up every call. And yesterday, when Juanita had gone down to the mailbox, she found a creased sheet of paper. She couldn't read the string of words, but she knew from the appearance and smell that they had been scrawled in excrement. Hastily thrusting her feet into her slippers, she said, "I'll go."

It was Ivanovich.

Hearing his voice, Alyssia ran to the hall. "John, where've you been? I've called and called all week!"

"Yes, and I apologize for not getting back to you," he said, glancing at Juanita.

"I'll be in my room, Mrs. Cordiner, if you need anything," Juanita said.

Alyssia led Ivanovich to the low-slung red armchairs grouped around the fireplace.

After a long, wheezy exhalation, he said, "I've been told to lay off the case."

Naturally she had suspected something along these lines. "By Lang?" On Ivanovich's initial visit she had told him of the bad blood between Hap and Lang.

"No names were mentioned. A woman we sometimes work with, she's a very expensive call girl, passed on the message that in this particular case I was out of my depth."

"He, Lang, admitted to our faces that he'd had Hap killed."

"He did?"

"Not in words, but by implication."

Ivanovich wheezed again. "Well, it figures. Miss del Mar—"

"Alyssia."

He looked down at his veined hands. "Alyssia, I told you the kind of cases we take. I'm no Mike Hammer or Lew Archer, I'm a housebroken, sedentary, middle-aged man with two kids at UCLA and a wife who works with him. We've never taken a homicide of any kind. And Lang's big-time crime."

"Is that why you're here so late? You're afraid the agency's being watched?"

"It is."

She felt a spurt of anger. "You could've at least called!"

"My guess is your phones're bugged."

"Nobody's been here."

"Except the pest-control man, the United Parcel man,

Jurgensen's delivery truck, the two maids, the gardener, the pool man—"

"All right, maybe it *is* bugged!" she snapped. Then her temper evaporated. "John, don't you understand? We're talking about somebody who meant everything to me. He was murdered. Cold-bloodedly *murdered.*"

"I don't take homicides, Alyssia, but I know about them. Coverups happen. And with prominent people, you'd be surprised at how often the victim's family helps with the coverup."

"Not if they give a damn they don't."

"Oh, at first there's hot thoughts of crime and punishment. Then reality sets in and the family starts considering what a public investigation means. The prying and probing into everyone's life, including the victim's. His sexual patterns, his frailties, his toilet habits—but I don't have to tell you that nothing is sacred at a media circus."

"Could you recommend another agency?"

He shook his head regretfully. "Sorry."

"You won't help me at all?" For a brief moment her spine of pride melted, and she sank waiflike into the deep chair.

Ivanovich said softly, "It hurts to let go, Alyssia, but believe me, it's best all round."

Leading him to the door, she recovered. "I'll have the business manager mail your check. That should be safe, shouldn't it? How much do I owe you?"

"I'm a fan. This one's on the house."

Reaching inside his jacket, he handed her two clipped-together sheets of bond folded lengthwise. They were warm and slightly moist from his body.

Her expression bleak, she slowly returned to her chair and unfolded the papers. The first page was compiled in California by Ivanovich. Scanning the single-spaced typing, she learned that though Hap Cordiner had been a private sort of guy, he had been well liked by his friends and acquaintances. They praised him in every smarmy Hollywood term. Alyssia turned to the second page.

> Our African correspondent received mixed reports. The population of Lunda as well as those in surrounding villages appear to have been primed to obscure the facts. For one example, the matter of the

subject's work. Three different informants used the exact same phrasing: he had come "to make plans for a Hollywood movie." Arthur W. Kleefeld, MD, director of a nearby free health-care facility that he and the subject had founded together, told our investigator emphatically that the subject had no further interest in filmmaking and had intended to make the facility his career.

The Kleefeld report is also muddied. Kleefeld states that the subject left the facility on the morning of April 17, 1980, with the clear understanding that he would spend the night at Lunda, therefore he was not alarmed when subject did not return that evening. Only when subject remained away after lunch the following day did Kleefeld become concerned enough to search. He found the accident site and brought back the subject's body. As per request of the subject, Kleefeld arranged for Episcopal burial at the center.

This conflicts with the statements from the two facility employees and the Episcopalian minister, Reverend James Iboe. It should be noted that these statements were taken separately. All three concur that the coffin was already interred when Reverend Iboe arrived to conduct the services. Furthermore, the cook, Mr. Peter Mzelie, states that Kleefeld was highly secretive about the subject's corpse, not permitting anyone to see it, placing it in the coffin himself.

As to your information re Kenyan visitors in the area. The police emphatically state there were no foreigners. This is substantiated by both local inhabitants and government officials in Kinshasa.

The accident itself is the single issue on which there is no dissension. All those interviewed agreed that a fallen tree blocked the road, and that the subject's jeep had hit it with damaging force, causing the engine to ignite and—

Alyssia was aware of a well-defined nausea. If she read another typed word, she would vomit. Crumpling the papers in her hand, she knelt on the marble hearth. Her hand shook and she wasted three of the foot-long fireside matches before one caught.

Briefly, as the papers fluttered and stirred, glowing poisonously, she saw a burning jeep. *What's the point of endangering Maxim, Barry, Beth, PD?*

He's dead.

The following day, she and Juanita left the country.

69

Beverly Hills, Bel Air and Malibu reverberated with Industry condemnations of Alyssia del Mar, who had not given a single interview, had not appeared on early-morning news or late-night talk shows—who had totally abdicated her promotional duties to Hap Cordiner's last film. It wasn't even as if she were in depression after the stillbirth. People returning from holiday or location reported that she was seen water-skiing at Puerto Vallarta, buying out Mary Quant's in London, gambling for high stakes at the casino in Monte Carlo, dining on lobster bisque and prune soufflé at Baumanière in Provence, selecting sapphires at the Paris Van Cleef's, bidding on antique jewels at Sotheby's, sipping Dom Pérignon with Princess Grace and Prince Rainier, perching on the edge of her gilt chair at the Ungaro collection.

In actuality she was at Lake Como.

She had taken another lease on the nineteenth-century villa with the peaked roof where she and Hap had shared three sun-drenched Italian autumns. The place was now her jail and her refuge. She had not left the grounds once.

Alyssia sat facing the view of the lake, which today was the ugly grayish-brown of an elephant's hide. She held *War and Remembrance* open on her lap, but she was reading about the wartime escapades of the Henry family.

Alone, she inhabited a dim, underwater world. When she was with Juanita or the married couple who came with the villa, she revved herself up, conversing, smiling when it seemed appropriate, eating at least part of the meals set before her, strolling down the villa's raked dirt path to the lake.

Her eyes moved to the desk. She saw with a dulled surprise that there was a heap of the fat, outsize quilted envelopes in which Magnum, the business manager and PD's office forwarded her letters. She hadn't opened any of those big folders in—how long was it? Accumulations of unopened mail were a sign of poor mental health.

Putting aside the Wouk novel, she moved to the desk.

She had been dispatched the usual assortment. Fan letters with the sender's return address, and hate mail, which was always anonymous. The polite or peremptory requests for her appearance at benefits, the solicitations from those charities to which she previously had been generous. The queries from the business manager about credit card charges as well as a note inquiring whether he should send her annual check to Zaire, adding a punctilious reminder—as he did every year—that since the medical center was not an accredited nonprofit organization, her donation would not be tax deductible.

Taking out a sheet of stationery, she wrote: *Quadruple what I sent to the Zaire center last year.*

Staring at her heavily underlined writing, she thought of Art Kleefeld. Ivanovich's report that Kleefeld hadn't been totally candid about Hap's funeral was a constant hangnail irritation. For some incomprehensible reason nothing fretted her as much as those mismatched stories about the burial time. And now, for the first time, it occurred to her that Kleefeld, like the Cordiner cousins, had been frightened off by Lang.

Taking out another folded notecard, she wrote, *Lake Como is very lovely, Art, and it would be super if you would visit—the ticket is on me.*

She determined not to invest overmuch emotional capital in his response. Despite her resolution, the next week she threw herself sobbing on the mattress she once had shared with Hap an inordinate number of times.

* * *

Rain threatened that morning. At the villa, she always breakfasted in bed: she had finished her first cup of coffee and was nibbling the buttered crust of a roll that had emerged from the baker's oven less than an hour earlier.

The door opened and Juanita said, "Telegram."

Shoving aside the tray, Alyssia jumped from the bed to snatch the yellow envelope. One glance at its window and her animation faded. "It's for you."

"I know my own name," Juanita said. "It's just I don't have my specs with me."

Alyssia, long accustomed to this sadly transparent deception, slit the envelope to read the contents to her sister.

"Alice, you're white as a sheet. What does it say?"

"It's from Zaire," Alyssia said, reading in a hollow whisper. "'Château Neuchâtel stop Proximity of Davos.'"

"That's all? No name, no nothing?"

"It's signed Peter Mzelie, but it's *got* to be from Art. He's being super-cautious." Alyssia snatched up the phone. Dialing, she asked a question in rapid Italian, nodding at the reply. Hanging up, she cried, "I'll have to rush! I must be in Como by noon—the Milan–Zurich Express stops there at twelve eleven. If I can make the train, I'll be in Davos by six thirty-eight."

"Alice, say Art *did* send the telegram, he sent it from Africa. There's no way in the world he can be in Switzerland already."

"You're right!" Alyssia flung open the elaborately carved doors of the armoire. "I better pack a few things."

"I'll get my stuff."

"No!" Alyssia tugged at a sweater with such vehemence that two others toppled from the shelf. "I have to go alone."

"That's silly, Alice."

"If Art sees you he might never open up."

It made no sense to Juanita, but her sister, after all this time, again had that lively stubborn look, so instead of arguing, she picked up the sweaters, asking, "Which ones do you want?"

Ten minutes later they were pulling out of the garage—Juanita insisted on seeing Alyssia off at the Como station. The cook's husband, delighted to at last have an opportunity to display his driving expertise, swerved them maniacally around hairpin turns. They reached the depot on time. The Express, though, had as usual departed late from Milan. The sisters sat in the barnlike ristorante drinking *caffelatte* for a half hour before the engine chugged into the open terminal.

As they hurried through the rain to the platform, Juanita said, "Don't go getting your hopes up, baby. Art's not going to say one more word than he done before in Nairobi."

70

The steepness of the path forced him to traverse, so he was making slow progress up the hill.

Concentrating on his maneuvers back and forth over the configuration of ruts and puddles, he had no opportunity to notice the majestic conifers, the quaint Alpine village nestled into the opposing mountain, the jagged peaks covered with snow—yesterday's autumnal rain had melted the snow at this lower altitude. His world was filled with his own harsh breathing, the slithering sound his white and silver nylon ski jacket made against his crutches, the clink of the tips hitting small stones.

Halting, resting the crutch handles under his armpits, he took out a handkerchief, wiping the sweat from his forehead, dabbing his neck below the beard. As his breathing slowed, he could hear the cowbells, each cow with her own individual musical note.

About a quarter of a mile above him loomed Château Neuchâtel. The smaller buildings appeared to be paying fealty to the massive ugliness of the sanitorium proper. The verandas that encircled each of its four stories were railed with battleship-gray wood, and at precisely every twelve feet the mustard-colored walls extruded outward. Each room, as the colored brochure promised, came with its own private sun porch. On this gloomy afternoon, less than a dozen of these were occupied. Like the porches, the solitary figures bundled in their heavy gray blankets were indistinguishable.

The block of penitentiary architecture pointed up the postcard charms of the surrounding chalets, which had whitewashed walls, steep gables and red shutters with cut-out patterns. The sanitorium's venerable chief of staff lived in the chalet with garlands of onions looped below the peaked rooftop.

As he watched, its red-painted door opened and a scarfed woman in a green loden cape emerged, stepping with slow care down the steps. Her head was bent and her shoulders were pulled inward. *Correct posture for any new inmate who isn't wheeled into Magic Mountain,* he thought.

In the early part of the century, when it was built, the sanitorium had served only tuberculars, and for this reason he called it Magic Mountain, although he was well aware that the current patient roster included no TB cases. Sufferers from cancer and degenerative diseases came for cures that sometimes resulted in remission, and the remainder of the rooms were kept continuously occupied by those desirous of either the so-called sleep treatment for obesity or the rejuvenation process that involved both cosmetic surgery and injections made from the ovaries of newborn lambs.

The faraway woman, however, was not fat, and though she moved slowly, she did not appear old. He therefore placed her in the same category as himself. The walking dead.

He shook his head as if warding off conjectures. Thinking about people carried him dangerously close to memories of his parents, of his brother, of her. Shoving the handkerchief back in his parka, he started his laborious climbing. After several teeth-jarring hops, his view of Château Neuchâtel was hidden by a clump of firs.

The following morning more rain fell in sparse, cold drops from the thick clouds that shrouded the peaks. Jamming on a knit cap and shrugging on his ski jacket, he swung past the floor desk. The beet-faced German orderly shook his head. "*Nein, nein,* Herr Stevens. Not in this rain. It is difficult enough, the crutches. Last week is your first time on them. If you slip, who will find you?"

He shrugged, continuing to the elevator, which was deep enough to accommodate a stretcher and wide enough for two wheelchairs.

Emerging on the desolate terrace, where a few weeks ago others—not he—had sipped coffee or tea and eaten whipped-cream pastries, he shivered. In weather like this even the cows had enough sense to huddle near the barn.

A large black Mercedes was winding cautiously down the road from Davos. If he hung around, he risked having to greet whoever was in it. He could not face strangers. Any conversational exchange, even one as minor as with the red-faced German, cost him unbelievable psychic energy.

He made as rapidly as possible for the path. On the steep incline, he welcomed the slippery navigations downward.

Within five minutes his knit hat, beard and Levi's were drenched, and the freezing rain had penetrated beneath the collar of his waterproof parka.

One of his crutches hit a pebble, which skittered. He lost control.

He fell forward heavily, sprawling on his stomach.

The light aluminum crutch bounced down the incline, coming to a halt five yards away in the tall, drenched grass. For a minute he lay unmoving, staring at the half-hidden metal. *It's only fifteen lousy feet,* he told himself. *Crawl there, buddy.* Stripping off his muddy leather gloves, he folded them into his pockets, then reached for the nearby crutch, pressing it between his right bicep and rib cage. He began crawling. His hands were anesthetized by cold, yet jabs of discomfort told him the skin of the palms was torn. His dragging left leg shot with pain from his toes to his hip socket. *Christ, two episodes of pricey surgical work shot to hell!*

Completely absorbed in the pain, his crawl, his grip on his remaining crutch, he didn't realize anyone was on the path behind him until he had nearly attained his goal.

Then he saw the flash of high-heeled boots and a flurry of loden cloth. A woman retrieved his crutch.

His breath exploded in a gasp as he looked up at her.

A strand of soaking black hair poked out of the loden hood to rest like a pen mark against her cheek; a trickle of rain was running between her nostrils, like snot. His soppy daydreams, his erotic night dreams, could not have invented those details.

She was real. She was here.

As they stared at each other, the color drained from her wet face and she swayed. Fearing she was about to collapse, he unthinkingly tried to catch her. Pressing both hands flat against the muddy path, he rose up on his knees. The bad one, the left, gave way. He felt and heard the tendons snap like too tightly pulled rubber bands. The agony he experienced was disassociated from the joy jumping around inside him.

"You aren't dead," she whispered. "It *is* you."

Then he was flooded with the realization that he was steeped in mud, crawling like a crippled beggar, an object for either scorn or the profoundest pity. Hot embarrassment swept him. What right did she have to come here like this? For a moment he considered denying his old identity, telling her she had the wrong guy.

"I'm called Adam Stevens now," he said with the coolest politeness he could muster. Immediately he saw that he'd taken the only possible tack. During his escape from the so-called accident he had heard the name Lang repeated several times in urgent fear, so he accepted that Robert Lang had carried a vendetta to its ultimate conclusion. If the assassins hadn't been more afraid of the night-shrouded forest than of their remote American employer, he wouldn't be alive and sprawled in the mud this morning. He emphatically must not involve her in the danger.

"Adam Stevens," she murmured. They were so close he could see the tiny freckle to the left of her soft, full mouth, feel the warmth of her breath on his wet skin.

"Yes. Now will you please give me my crutch?"

"Here, let me help you."

He took the crutch. "Thank you, but that's not necessary."

"But your leg—didn't something just happen to your leg? You can't stand by yourself, Hap."

"Adam," he corrected. "And though you've been very kind, I manage best on my own."

"Use me to brace yourself—"

"I'd appreciate it if you'd leave." This time his voice was deliberately damaging.

A gust of wind shook the branches above them, and enormous drops pelted down. One fell on her hood, creeping onto her ashen face.

But she was, of course, an actress. With a faint smile, she said, "Sorry to have intruded on you."

She stepped around him. He didn't turn to watch her, but he knew from the slushy crunch of her boots that she was returning up the path. When the sound faded he began to cry in big, rasping sobs and the hot tears mingled with icy rain. After a couple of minutes he attempted to stand, but his left leg, which was at a peculiar angle, refused to cooperate, and he sank backward whimpering.

Two orderlies came running down the path.

Old Hans was waving his arms and moving his red face agitatedly. "Herr Stevens! Herr Stevens! It is not good to move!" he shouted.

The tall Italian boy, who was new, darted back to the sanitorium for a stretcher.

71

After the surgery he slept until nearly midnight. When he awoke, a linen hand towel was safety-pinned around his bedside lamp. The impenetrable black shadows at the end of the narrow room reminded him of the rain forest on the night of his official death. He looked away. A strong smell of antiseptic ointment came from his hands, which were swathed in gauze bandaging. His leg, in a plaster cast that reached his hip and bared only his toes, hung suspended by a traction device.

The delicate surgery on his hamstrung left knee, performed by the same Davos surgical team that had operated on him twice before, had lasted four and three quarter hours, and long before the final suturing his spine had ached intolerably in spite of the mixture of anesthetics dripping into the veins of his arm.

Though he didn't realize it, he was still stoned.

A mind in its normal state recollects myriad impressions. His brain lagged over one detail at a time. Alyssia's sudden appearance on the path. Her beauty. Her pallor—why that ashen pallor? He did not consider that she, believing him dead, might be shocked to find him alive. Instead, he decided it was his mud-soaked crawl that had shocked her.

He was too drugged for his leg to hurt, but the suspension bothered him, and he decided a change of position might help. Raising his bandaged hands to the metal bar above his chest, he shifted his torso.

The shadows surrounding the window came alive.

"You're awake," Alyssia said, coming to lean over the railed bed. The dimmed light sparked gold in her eyes.

Her presence soothed him and he smiled up at her.

"Uncomfortable?" she asked.

His mind lurched. *It's dangerous for her to be here,* he informed himself. *Get rid of her.* "I need the orderly."

"Tell me where to find whatever you need."

"Thank you, but it's the bedpan," he lied, taking a melancholy pride that his words, though weak and faraway, were clipped in a manner that sounded vaguely British.

She left to get the night orderly. Long before help came, he was sleeping. He stirred restlessly, trapped in nightmares. They were amputating his leg—no, he was at Mount Sinai Hospital and it was Alyssia's leg they were sawing off.

He opened his eyes to the drab strips of morning light coming through the shutters. Looking around for her, he saw only the familiar buff-colored walls with the three garish prints of the Engadine, the small, fumed-oak breakfast table where he took his solitary meals. (He had been encouraged to use the large, bright dining salon where local adolescents with red, bony wrists showing between their white cotton jackets and white cotton gloves served lunch and dinner. His invariable refusal, or so he believed, was accepted as a desire for solitude, a common enough wish at Château Neuchâtel.)

His mouth felt packed with dry wool.

He pressed the buzzer. The wizened nurse with the girlish smile came. Opening the shutters before pouring him water, she held the tumbler while he sucked at the glass straw.

"So, Mr. Stevens, you are a friend of a famous Hollywood movie star."

No longer under the influence, he got a quick mental purchase on the situation. "She does look a bit like Alyssia del Mar, doesn't she?" he said. "But she's called Hollister."

"Yes, this is the name she says. Hollister." At the corroboration, the wrinkled mouth formed a disappointed grimace. "She's very beautiful. You know, oftimes we have here theater folk and politicians who make pretend with other names."

"Come on, you know sailors like me don't meet movie stars."

In Kinshasa, Art had found a woman who specialized in fake IDs—she was the Rembrandt of forged papers. And for months now he had been Adam Stevens, American, second officer on the *Argo Pride,* an oil tanker that sailed under the Liberian flag. During a Mediterranean storm, the vessel had caught fire. Battling the blaze, Stevens had been badly injured.

"Would you like more water?" asked the nurse.

"No thanks. Did she leave?"

"She is in the lounge, resting."

"I'm not up to visitors yet."

A thermometer was thrust into his mouth, and thin, wrinkled fingers grasped his wrist. "The patients who have the family, the friends, the letters, yah? They recover quickest," the nurse said in her softly guttural English. "The ones who make no outside contact, ya? They make slow progression. It is a good thing to have visitors." The thermometer was removed.

"A long operation yesterday," he said. "What I need is rest." While his face was washed, his beard and hair combed, he reiterated that he would recuperate more rapidly if left in solitude.

The nurse's sole comment was, "For today the doctors have ordered the liquids."

After he drank the juice of blood oranges—the bright crimson color had never seemed natural to him—and finished his lukewarm chocolate, he drowsed.

He awoke at the creak of the door.

As Alyssia entered, he felt an involuntary surge of relief that she was still on the premises. In less than a second he was planning ways to get rid of her.

"You're looking more human." She smiled and touched her jawline. "I like it, the beard, but it's a lot darker than I imagined it'd be. The stubble was so fair—I never saw it, just got scratched."

At this revival of intimacy, he covered his mouth, pretending to yawn. "I was sleeping. Didn't the nurse tell you I'm not up to visitors?"

"No, she told me the staff have been worried that you stick to yourself. They're sending up flares that finally you have somebody."

"Complete privacy is meant to be one of the features of Château Neuchâtel, or so I was given to believe."

"Given to believe," she repeated with the mischievous, gamine grin that invariably melted him. "You're fuming."

"No, simply tired."

"That ultracourteous tone means you're ready to explode."

"Perhaps I didn't make myself clear?"

"Oh, you're very clear." The smile was gone, and he felt a sense of deprivation. "You don't want me around. But how's about if you'd be better off shouting at me than taking a nap?"

"That might be a possibility," he said.

"The name's different, but you haven't changed. You still fight by being politer and politer."

With an effort that stabbed through his upraised leg, he lifted up on his elbow. "Why can't you stay the hell out of my life?"

In the past she would have snapped back at him. Now, though, her mouth trembled and she sank into the chair sidewise. Her hair shadowed her face as she bent forward, weeping. The muffled sobs cut into him, and he called on reserves of control in order not to cry, too. His leg pulsed and throbbed beneath the cast.

She dried her eyes and blew her nose. "I'm sorry," she said. Her voice had lost its musical undertone: she sounded older—and defeated.

"I didn't mean to shout at you," he said quietly. "But I really would prefer to be alone."

She nodded. "I can understand that. I've screwed things up for you all the way round. Your life, your career. And since I got here, I've made you reinjure your leg so you needed another operation."

"I take credit for screwing up my life and my so-called career. And as for the leg, hamstrung men shouldn't go hiking in the rain." He paused, gathering his strength of will. "But this is my chance to start over again. A new life."

"Are you worried about Lang?"

He had been pulling on the metal bar in an effort to shift his leg. At her question, his grip slackened and he fell back into the tough Swiss bolster.

She said, "He honestly believes you're buried at the relief center."

"He does?"

"Yes, he's positive you're dead."

"*I* knew he tried to have me blown away, but how can *you* know it?"

"He told us."

"Us?"

"Barry, Beth, PD, Maxim. And me."

"You're saying that Robert Lang sat down with the five of you and conversationally mentioned he'd set hit men on me?"

"It wasn't exactly like that." She looked down at the wadded tissue she held. "I'd had a—well, a sort of sight of you at the memorial—did you know they had a memorial for you on Stage Eight, then showed *Baobab*?"

"I read something. What do you mean, a sight of me?"

"Don't laugh, but I saw you there. Looking the way you do now. The beard. Wearing that white ski parka. I mean, it was so real that I hired a detective. That's when Lang called us together. He knew there was an investigation, but he wasn't positive who was paying for it. He'd narrowed the choices down to us. He wanted it stopped."

"None of this makes sense."

"Lang was already furious at going over budget—he put the entire blame on you, especially after you knocked him down. But PD says it was the article that Barry did for *The New Yorker* that really set him off. You never saw it, did you? Well, it read as if you were throwing Lang's money away with both hands. Lang felt you'd made him into a public jackass."

"I have no problem buying that Lang would try to dispose of me. What I don't understand is why he'd let all of you in on it."

"It was a warning. Telling us exactly how you'd died was his way of saying that if any of us made waves, one or all would get the same treatment."

"So that's how you found me? A detective?"

"I was at the villa in Bellagio," she said, as if this answered his question.

"Maxim. And the others. What did they do after they'd heard?"

She shrugged.

"Nothing?" he asked.

"They thought you were dead."

"Christ!" He grimaced bitterly. "I get swatted like a fly and that's the end of it?"

"They had no reason *not* to believe you were dead. And Lang *is* very dangerous."

"How about giving justice a try?"

"Hap, they *were* broken up. Especially Maxim. He's been a mess since it happened."

Desolation swept him. He pressed deeper into the mattress, breathing shallowly until he could pull himself together. "I read about your little girl," he said awkwardly. "It was a rotten break."

The small muscles below her cheeks worked, and for a moment he feared she would start to cry again. "The baby's not dead, either," she said in a controlled voice. "It was a little boy and he's with Beth and Irving."

"*Your* baby?"

"They've adopted him."

"You gave up your baby?" he asked incredulously.

"This way he has a better life."

"Because of the divorce?"

"I can't talk about it."

"But you wanted her—him—so much. It doesn't make sense—"

She cut him off by going to the door. "It was wrong of me to come here," she said. "I'm truly sorry for making things worse for you. But that's me all over. I never did know when to give up on people. But I'm learning, I'm learning." She smiled.

Long after the door closed, he was haunted by that despairing little smile.

He went over the entire conversation, accepting that she had been fully honest with him. She had confessed that she had cared for him enough to search for him even when it had appeared impossible that she find a living man—even when his own brother and the cousins once as close as siblings to him had been frightened off by the danger—she had persevered.

Why can't you stay the hell out of my life?

How could he have shouted that at her? He deserved those unrewarding stints with bitches like Whitney; he deserved his marriage to Madeleine—blonde, smiling, ultrasociable Madeleine.

He thought about Lang and wondered what the odds were that top purveyors of the hard stuff—busy men—continued their vendettas beyond the grave. *Probably negligible. That is, if the deceased keeps a low profile.*

Moving his butt an inch, it occurred to him that he hadn't told Alyssia how he had escaped from the "accident." This lapse in her knowledge seemed to hold a promise of return.

She'll be back, he thought.

When the wizened nurse carried in his lunch tray—broth and tea—an envelope lay on the napkin.

His pulse jumped, and it was all he could do to wait until the old woman left to open it.

As usual, the joined block letters touched him profoundly. Years ago, in a cruddy Hollywood motel, Alicia had traced the central hairs of his chest, admitting that in her peripatetic education she had never learned cursive script.

Whatever its emotional connotations, the writing was highly legible. He read the few lines in one glance.

It was a mistake barging in on you. If I'd given up on the relationship years ago we'd both be happier, and none of the recent rotten events would have taken place.

On the other hand, it makes me so glad to have seen that you are (more or less) FINE. You are the most decent, most generous human being I have ever known.

Have a wonderful life, and do all the good things you are capable of.

Goodbye and God bless.

Holding the paper in his bandaged hand, he turned his face toward the ugly buff wall. He knew a farewell letter when he saw one.

72

Three months later he was limping off the ferry in Bellagio.

He had never been here in the middle of winter. Iron shutters hid the tourist shops, the narrow alleys swooping down to the lake were empty and the outdoor cafés along the shore were deserted except for a pair of bundled-up women.

Reaching the curve of benches, he halted to look out at the dancing line of wavelets that reflected the large, pale sun. His expression was brooding.

At the beginning of his slow recuperation from the repair surgery, each time the door was pushed open he would turn, hopeful that it was she.

Convinced of the reality that she wasn't coming back, though, he retreated into himself. *I've lost her,* he would think in a continuous refrain. *I've lost her.* Whole days would go by when he spoke less than a dozen sentences.

In his silence he brooded about his brother's betrayal of

him, and his cousins' betrayal. He was indeed dead, but without any of the advantages of forgetfulness.

He had a fourth surgery, an unsuccessful and exceedingly painful attempt to lengthen the tendons behind his knee.

During this convalescence he began to think of going to her. He used the thought sparingly, in much the same way that he doled out codeine pills to himself. At night, when the worst pain smothered him, he permitted himself to conjure up fantasies about their reunion.

Although he had retained his faintly forbidding air of command and confidence with the staff, the loneliness and the pain had done damage to his spirit: those inner uncertainties always present within him had multiplied. For the first time in his life he felt unworthy.

Then one sunny afternoon Hans, the red-faced German orderly, wheeled him onto the porch. Possibly it was the magnificent view, or the jovial tinkling of a horse-drawn sled coming up the hill, or the cold clear mountain air.

It no longer seemed a pipe dream to see her again.

Now that he had a goal for recovery, his natural excellent health asserted itself. Within the week he was back on crutches, riding the big elevator downstairs to scrutinize the most recent *London Times* and *Paris Match*—his French was excellent from working in Zaire, where, despite independence, French had remained the official language because there were at least eighty different Bantu dialects. From the week-old papers he learned that Alyssia del Mar was an Oscar nominee for Best Actress (he also learned Harvard Cordiner was receiving a posthumous Oscar for lifetime achievement) but not one clue of her whereabouts.

In the past he could have embarrassed himself by phoning his father to discover where she was. (In his reading, he hadn't come across any mention of Desmond Cordiner's paralyzing stroke.) Or he could have called Maxim or PD. He could have crawled to Barry.

But Adam Stevens must search for himself.

She had told him she was at the Bellagio villa, but that was three months ago and wasn't it highly improbable she would remain there? On the other hand, he didn't know where else to begin his search.

The ferry, with a series of mournful hoots, was pulling

away from the dock. He rose from the bench. At the taxi stand, two drivers in heavy black coats were gesticulating to each other. Briefly he considered asking one to take him to the villa. But Adam Stevens' account in Zurich's Swiss Credit Bank had been opened with money from the relief center: though he had been the center's main contributor, he never thought of the money as his, so whenever he considered extras like wine to pep up Château Neuchâtel's blandly soggy meals or this taxi ride, pangs of conscience would assail him.

He started to walk.

The gait he had developed, leaning on his cane while swinging his left leg from the hip, presented difficulties going uphill. When he reached the two-lane highway, the cars and trucks that occasionally careened around the hairpin bends forced him onto the shoulder. On slick pine needles, the going was yet tougher.

At the VILLA ADRIANA sign, he rested to catch his breath in the brisk, westerly wind. What was he doing here? He was no longer Hap Cordiner, child of Hollywood's royalty, award-winning director. He was a cripple, broke and without so much as an honest passport, seeking out a reclusive, world-famed movie star—who might or might not be in residence.

If a certain doggedness hadn't been a component of his character, he would have returned to the ferry. Instead, he toiled steadily down toward the nineteenth-century villa whose exterior mistakenly suggested a small bungalow.

He banged the familiar bronze mermaid knocker. After a brief wait, the door opened a few inches. Juanita stood framed there. His chest tightened and he wasn't sure whether the sensation were relief or terror.

"Hello, Juanita," he said quietly.

The dark, broad face remained impassive. She evinced no surprise at seeing him alive on the recently washed doorstep. "Miss del Mar's not here," she said.

He shifted his weight. "Is she down in Bellagio, shopping?"

"No."

"Will she be back soon?"

"Go away! Leave her alone! Ain't you Cordiners caused her enough grief?" In Juanita's sudden furious outburst concentric circles formed around her mouth, and she resembled one of those eternally outraged Mayan deities carved in pre-Columbian times.

Her anger, so completely atypical, threw him off balance mentally and physically. Leaning more weight on his stick, he coughed to give himself a moment. "I'd like to see her," he said.

"What for?"

"To talk."

"Talk, hahh! All of you Cordiners want something from her. The family's like crows gathering round to peck the life from her—"

Angry himself by now, he interrupted brusquely, "Will you please tell her I'm here."

Her tirade spilled on. "That Barry, he lived off her for years! She did everything for him. She was always there when he needed her. But the minute she's in trouble, where is he? He's getting the doctors to dope her up so he can take her baby to hand over to his high and mighty sister. And her, that Beth! She's always snubbed Alice and treated her like she was a Hollywood Boulevard hooker. And now *she's* got that darling little boy. Alice saved your father's studio for him, but did he or your mom ever give her the time of day? She paid off PD's dad's gambling debts, she made PD a billion, and when the chips were down, PD threw her to the wolves. And what about your brother, Maxim? He shoved her around so she almost lost her leg, then he wheedled her into making more movies with that crook, Lang!"

"You're being totally irrational," he snapped. Yet as he said this, it hit him that she had spoken the pure, undiluted essence of rationality. It was absolutely true. The Cordiner family had all fed off Alyssia.

"And you! You're the one who hurt her the worst. First of all she falls apart because she thinks you're dead. Then she risks all sorts of danger to find you. And you kick her in the teeth!"

Maxim would have come up with some clever witticism about scarcely being in condition to kick anyone anywhere, much less in the teeth. "I know I hurt her," he said. His voice lacked resonance, and he sounded as he had during the worst of his post-op weakness. "That's why I want to talk to her."

"That's you all over! You think a polite 'Sorry' cures every rotten thing. She never told me what you did to her, but when she crawled back here, she was ill, so ill again. Now she's finally snapping out of it and I ain't letting you or any of the rest near her. Sometimes I think she can survive anything including the plague—but not the Cordiners!"

So Alyssia had been ill. Lying in his hospital bed and hoping—no, praying—that she would open the door, he had never once considered illness as a reason for her absence. Remembering the defeated smile as she'd left his room, he swallowed.

"You're right, Juanita." He sighed. "I shouldn't have come."

He started up the driveway. At a sickening screech, he halted abruptly. Tires were skidding on the road above. His mind jumping with memories of a primitive, winding African road, his own tires screeching, he held his breath for the accident. But no glass shattered, no metal crumpled.

As the engine sounds faded in the direction of Bellagio, he turned. Juanita remained on sentry duty at the ornately carved front door. Aware of her unsympathetic gaze, he returned.

"I promise not to upset her, but I'm not moving until I see her."

"Nita, who's there?" It was Alyssia's voice.

She came running up the staircase. On the top step, she halted. Peering across the hall, she lifted her hand to her throat.

The long window behind her served as backlighting. In the nimbus of bright winter sunlight, her face was not clearly visible. Hair falling over her shoulders, white robe sashed taut at her slim waist to show the curves of her body, she seemed to shimmer, and as she once had caused Barry to think of the immortal goddesses of love—Astarte, Aphrodite—so now Hap saw her as the truth of his being.

He forgot his game leg, his exile from his parents and family and home; he accepted that his one-time goal of making a so-called perfect film and his omnipresent goal of bringing a marginal comfort to the earth's poor were all externals.

This gleaming woman was his truth.

In the sanitorium he had been nearly devoid of desire. Now, staring at her, he experienced a lust stronger than any sensation he had ever experienced—stronger than his fear and agony on the night he had been certain of his own death, stronger than any desire he had previously felt for her. He shifted his cane to hold it in front to hide his physical manifestations.

She moved a few steps toward the door, halting.

Now he could see her face more clearly. Her fine-pored skin glowed with a faint, translucent pinkness across the cheekbones; her eyes were clear and unshadowed. Obviously she had recovered from the illness.

"Hi," she said in a normal tone.

"Hello."

"Just passing by?"

"I have something for you." He reached in his pants pocket for the Lindt bar he'd bought when he changed trains for the second time at the Zurich station. Inside its wrapper, the white chocolate had taken on a curved shape.

Smiling, she came to the door. "For a top director, you're doing a rotten job on this scene," she said, glancing out at the courtyard. "Where's your car?"

"I walked up from the ferry."

Her eyes went down to his knee.

His desire wilted a fraction. "Exercise is good for me," he said tersely.

Turning to Juanita, she said, "We'd like to talk."

"I'm not having you get all shook up again," Juanita said.

"Why're you growling like a Doberman guard dog?"

"Because you need one."

"Not right now I don't. Hap's come a long way."

Juanita rolled her eyes up at the high, molded ceiling, as if inviting providence to note the feckless, improvident generosity of her younger sister, then she stamped across the parquet, disappearing down the staircase, opening and slamming a door.

He and Alyssia faced each other across the threshold. He was incapable of looking away from her eyes. There had always been a mystery in her eyes, a hint of a shadowed past, and this nuance, caught by the camera, contributed to her allure. Now the melting blue depth held yet more mysteries.

She looked away first. Taking the misshapen candy bar from him, she said, "Let's go in the study."

They had used the study often, and without thinking he headed for the big leather chair, then, recollecting it was no longer his, he went to stand at the window. A speedboat carved around the inlet, the vroom of the engine barely audible within the study. She came to stand next to him. Her proximity impinged on all his senses.

"You're pretty good with that," she said, glancing at the cane.

"Better than my mud crawl?"

"It's a really big deal I saw you, isn't it?"

He shrugged noncommittally, then shook his head. "I didn't come here to lie," he said. "Yeah, thinking about it still makes me go hot in the face."

"How about the way I humiliated myself?"

"There's another thing. I can't believe I sent you away."

"Why did you?"

"At the time I was worried for you—the Lang business. But maybe it was because you'd seen me like that. Who knows?"

"Maybe because you'd just had surgery." She was speaking more softly.

"I willed you to come back. God, how I wanted you back, Alyssia."

"I'm Alice now."

"Alice," he repeated. "Juanita said you'd been ill."

"Not exactly."

"What did she mean, then?"

"It's all part of the same thing as Alyssia and Alice." She gazed pensively at the small, uninhabited, pine-covered island across the lake. "Remember years ago when I told you it was like a wonderful dream, being on the other side of the screen—like being Alice through the looking glass? And you said dreams weren't enough?"

"We were at Don the Beachcomber's." The memory of that long-ago, uneaten meal, and what they had done afterward at the Cahuenga Inn Motel, revived his stallionoid condition.

"Yes, there. Well, after that Villa Pacifica business, when Barry and I got back together, sometimes Alice had a problem being on the other side of the screen. I couldn't breathe properly."

"Anxiety?"

"Yes—anxiety attacks. Later, when I thought you were dead, they got worse, and not only on the set. They'd come over me all the time. They tried to treat me for it when I went into the maternity clinic. I'm not sure what drugs they gave me, but they made me feel so awful, far worse than the attacks, which didn't go away," she sighed. "That's really why I gave him up, my baby."

"Juanita said Barry pushed you to."

"Only because he thought it was best for the baby. And that's why I agreed. Hap, it was the right thing." She sighed again.

His throat clogged and he couldn't speak. He, too, stared toward the uninhabited island.

"Don't look so sad," she said. "I'm a lot better; the baby's well off. Besides, think of the positive side for you. It's impossible to feel ashamed in front of *me*."

"I've missed you," he said in a low, shaken voice.

She took his hand, pressing it between her breasts. He could feel the savage pounding of her heart.

With an incoherent sound, he put his arms around her, covering her throat with kisses. She was clutching him as tightly as she could, as if to reassure herself of his living body. Backing her to the leather couch, he pulled her on top of himself. She threw aside the robe. He wanted to caress her, feel the warm cream softness of the astonishing breasts, feel the unique smoothness of her thighs, but he was unzipping his jeans. She rose up, straddling him. As she sank onto him, engulfing the world, he cried her name. "Alice . . . ahh, Alice. . . ."

73

She was lying on top of him, and he shifted a bit so that there was space for her on the couch. Still entwined, he pulled back, gazing at her, finding it nearly impossible to believe the reality of the flushed and beautiful face. For the past months she had been a continuous denizen of his dreams and reveries, yet no more accessible to him than to the audiences who idolized her in movie theaters.

"Hap, stop brooding. It was wonderful."

He gave a snort that was half laughter. "We'll do better next time. No, I was thinking you couldn't be real."

She tugged his beard. "Will a bit of pain convince you?"

Smiling, he moved her hand. "Know something? If I had to pick one minute in my life—lives—this would be it."

"Not while we were—"

"No. This minute."

"Was I heavy? Did I hurt your leg?"

"Who noticed? It was like a storm, an earthquake, something outside of me. I don't know if it could ever be like that again. Right now I'm just normal-human-being happy."

"Me too." She ran her hand down his stickily wet thigh, a gentle, wandering touch on the hard, raised scar tissue. "When are you going to tell me about how this happened?"

"Later," he said, resting his bearded cheek between her breasts. "Now let's just be happy."

They began to make slow, tender explorations of each other, and after he went into her they continued to move voluptuously until the end. When they got up from the couch, he realized he'd eaten nothing today and was ravenous. The squat, heavily muscled cook (and her husband who tended the garden and the car) were off, so Hap whipped up a huge omelet topped with provolone while Alice fixed coffee and set the scrubbed pine kitchen table. The pale gold melted cheese and eggs smelled and tasted more savory than any food he could remember, the bread immeasurably fresher, the butter sweeter, the coffee richer and stronger. They divvied the white chocolate for dessert.

As they were returning upstairs, Juanita came out of her room. "I guess you won't be wanting supper," she muttered, not looking at him.

To his surprise, his old fondness for her had been revitalized and even deviously enhanced by her refusal to let him in the villa: the barring, so hurtful at the time, he now accepted for what it was: a last-ditch effort to protect Alice.

"We'll be hungry later," he said. "Let's the three of us go to La Pergola." In the old days, when the cook was off they had sometimes dined à trois beneath the dim Japanese lanterns and grapevines on the trattoria's terrace. "It's open in the winter."

"You don't need me."

"Hey, Juanita," he said. "Cut that out."

Behind the glasses, her heavy eyelids drooped, then she looked directly at him, blurting, "I meant a lot of that stuff, but not about you, Hap."

"What exactly were you saying before I arrived?" Alice asked.

"That's between the two of us," he said, reaching out to clasp Juanita's thick body in a hug.

At La Pergola, fragrant pine logs blazed in the fireplace and they ate gnocchi and veal, finishing two bottles of Trebbiano. He hummed as he drove the black, winding road to the villa.

"Hap, Hap . . ." She was shaking his shoulder.

He awoke with sweat pouring from his naked body. "Nightmare," he muttered.

The luminous green numbers on the clock showed it was eleven thirty-seven. He couldn't have been asleep more than twenty minutes, yet he had been transported through an endless montage of malign, Grand Guignol dreams.

"You were crying," she said, stroking his shoulder.

After a few seconds he said, "That was the first time I've driven since . . . the jeep burned."

"I'm sorry. I should've realized."

"How could you?"

"Isn't it time you shared?"

Rolling onto his back, he stared into the darkness.

"Hap?" she prompted.

"Lunda's a few mud huts with thatched roofs. It's like thirty miles from the center." Hearing his slight tremor, he took the light tone with which in the old days he might have told her the plot of some idiotic script. "Nobody from Lunda, not even the terminal cases or the badly injured, had ever come to us for help."

"Why not?"

"A lot of people don't. Mostly it's pride. They don't like accepting things from strangers. But a few still believe that whites want to take them slave. Often there's a language barrier. Whenever I was at the center, I'd visit different areas and explain what we were up to. As you can recall, when I left Los Angeles I was in a bad way. To pull myself out of it, I immediately began traveling around, proselytizing. The people in Lunda all spoke French, so communication wasn't a problem. When I told them about a miracle food that makes children stronger, soy flour—it's a terrific protein source to prevent kwashiorkor—they agreed to give it a try. I felt I'd scored a major victory. A couple of days later I loaded the jeep with sacks of it and went back. The roads are miserable, and nobody drives after dark, so both Art and I figured I'd be spending the night in Lunda."

"Art told me there were strangers in the area."

"I knew that, too, but it didn't have any significance. 'Stranger' is the generic term for anyone not born in your village. Looking back, I can see that when I returned to Lunda with the flour, the locals were more effusive than the occasion warranted. At the time, though, the warmth made me feel we were finally being accepted." He said this last bitterly.

"You were only there to help."

"Reverse it, love. You're living in Lunda and some white fat cat comes along to dole out food."

Memories drenched her. May Sue and her daughters would have preferred starvation—or kwashiorkor—to the pallid turkey dinners served by benevolently smiling church ladies at Thanksgiving and Christmas.

"You're right, Hap. Go on."

"As I said, I expected to sleep there. But despite the overblown gratitude, no invitation was forthcoming. At that point I certainly should have guessed something was up. People never let you leave after nightfall."

"What about sleeping there in the jeep?"

"I didn't consider it. The forest never bothered me. Actually, I found it sort of like being in a cathedral. The trees are huge, and the foliage at the top spreads out so densely that it makes a roof. Sunlight is muted and dim. Once in a while you pass somebody walking on the road, or tooling along on an ancient bicycle, but mostly you see masses of red colobus monkeys leaping after one another along the branches, troops of baboons, and once in a while, the chimps. At night, though, it was something else. There was no moon, and the foliage hid the starlight. I'd never felt so utterly cut off. It was as if my headlights were boring through the black hole of the universe. Then, suddenly, a man was waving his thumb in violent hitching gestures. You don't see that in Zaire—there are so few cars that a ride is arranged in advance. And, as I said, nobody moves around at night. I knew something was wrong, but it could literally be a week before another car or truck came by to give him a lift. Besides, I was delighted to see another human being. I stopped. . . ." His voice faded as a phantom pain traveled down his leg.

"What was he like?"

"Tall, with crooked teeth and a strange, high-pitched laugh. He spoke English fairly well. He was carrying something heavy wrapped in a maroon-patterned *kanga*. I asked what he was doing out here at this time of night, and his answer seemed reasonable enough. He'd thought he could make it to Uele—that's a village between Lunda and the center. He asked questions about the jeep, what had it cost and where had I gotten it. Then he asked how fast it would go. Like an idiot, I stepped on the gas to demonstrate. The tree trunk sprawling across the road hadn't been there before. I jammed on the brakes, yelling at him to look out. But he stood up, balancing himself to lift whatever was in the *kanga* over my head. In that instant when he was about to crown me, everything came together in a gestalt. I understood that I'd been set up. That the people in Lunda had been frightened off. I should've been scared shitless. Instead I saw red—actually saw a reddish glaze in front of my eyes. Letting go of the wheel, I tackled him. A rock fell from the *kanga*, which fluttered away behind us. He toppled. The jeep slammed into the fallen tree. I blacked out. When I came to, it couldn't have been more than a half minute later, he was sprawled over the dash, unconscious—or maybe dead. Smoke was pouring from the hood. Something sharp was cutting into the back of my knee. Thin points of flashlights were beaming up the road, and I heard men shouting."

"In English or what?"

"English and Swahili. They probably were from Kenya. The engine was on fire. My thigh and knee were a mess, bones broken, tendons cut, but it's true that in dire moments you can perform impossible acts. Somehow I scrambled out of the jeep and began limping into the forest."

"And they believed the other man was you?"

"No. They could see he was black. I wasn't exactly running, as you can imagine, so they reached the jeep before I got very far. I heard one of them shout Lang's name several times. He sounded frightened. I was positive they'd come after me to finish the job they were obviously being paid to do. . . ."

Without embellishment he told her how he'd barged deeper into the blackness, every couple of steps colliding with a tree trunk or stumbling over roots. A faraway explosion and a faint, incandescent glow told him the gas tank had gone up. His lungs near bursting, he attempted to run. Then his leg gave way. He pitched forward on his stomach. Too exhausted to move, he lay waiting for the searching beam of flashlights. But nobody was following him. When his breathing quieted, he heard the faraway barking of a tribe of baboons. His scalp prickled. Baboons. They were known to kill humans. Adrenaline raced through him, willing him to flight. Unable to stand, he crawled through leaf mulch and foul-odored softnesses. All at once rain pelleted through the dense foliage high above his head, and almost immediately he was soaked. Snaking through puddles, he reached an outcropping of rock. He clawed to find a way around, but the jagged stone appeared to be a solid wall—in the morning, he saw that if he'd gone a few yards farther to the right, he would have reached the end of the barrier. He grappled around for a weapon, found a heavy piece of shale and tucked himself against the dripping roughness. No amount of mental exercise could cancel the enveloping blackness, the agony in his left leg, the distant chorus of baboons, the nearby slithering noises. All night he remained positive the killers were tracking him.

"Why didn't they?" she asked.

"They must have been even more terrified of the forest than I was. The way I figure it, they reached a decision to pass the other guy off as me to Lang. After all, nobody besides them knew I had a passenger."

"It's gruesome. . . ."

"Art found the charred body in the driver's seat. He knew right away, of course, that it wasn't me. Thank God he's bright. He threw a blanket over the body and acted out grief."

"Then went looking for the real you?"

"Yes. And kept people out of my room with a lie about a suspected plague case—there've been outbreaks in Zaire."

"What about the conflicting versions of the funeral?"

"Art needed to bury the corpse before anybody else got a good look at it. And, under the circumstances, didn't feel obligated to tell the press or my family that the services came late. By then I was out of the country. He had bribed the pilot of a Cessna; he'd made the arrangements for fake papers and a flight to Switzerland. By the time I arrived, Château Neuchâtel had itself a real challenge."

Her body trembled, and he realized she was crying.

Stroking between her quivering shoulder blades, he said, "It's in the past, love. The bad times are past for both of us."

74

His next physiotherapy session was in two days, on Friday at eight A.M. Much as he longed to remain at the villa, it was an incontrovertible fact that missing an appointment would attract the type of questions he must avoid. On Thursday he returned to Switzerland. As he rode in the wooden-seated, second-class car to Davos, snow began falling. The other passengers talked exuberantly about fresh powder on the Strela Pass. He watched the fat white splotches hit the window, cling to the glass, and slowly melt. His well-delineated eyebrows were raised, making indentations in his forehead, and his eyes appeared a darker gray, an expression he assumed when considering an apparently insoluble problem.

At the villa he had not thought of the future. But these past hours on three different trains he had been continuously turning over the divergence between Adam Stevens' need for anonymity and Alyssia del Mar's fame.

Dining at La Pergola, she had faced the fire, yet even so an elderly man with a walrus mustache had come over to say in awkwardly phrased English that he had the honor of seeing her in *Il Baobab*—he was, however, utterly convinced by Alice's flattered demurrals that she was no movie star but dull, ordinary Ms. Hollister, a teacher from Chicago, Illinois. Would other fans give up so easily? And if Adam Stevens were accompanied by Alyssia del Mar, how long before he was recognized?

People reached for skis and bags as the train pulled into the Davos Platz station. Though he still took the bus down to Château Neuchâtel for his therapy, he had moved to cheaper quarters, a spartan pension opposite the *Skischule*.

He limped homeward through the falling snow. In the twilight sleighbells jangled. Skiers crowded the sidewalk and the Hotel Central blazed with lights. A cluster of women in fluffy sport furs emerged from the hotel, talking loudly in American accents. One of the men following was turned away. With his black hair and strong, compact body he looked exactly like PD. Positive his cousin was in Davos, Hap stepped hastily into the doorway of a tearoom. The man looked in his direction.

The sleek black hair must be a dye job or a toupee, for the pouches beneath the man's eyes sagged onto his cheeks, and the flesh hung underneath his jaw. And now it was obvious that the body, too, was thicker than PD's. Hap moved back onto the snowy sidewalk with a clammy feeling of self-disgust.

"You're what?" she screamed over the phone.

"I'm tired of skulking. I want to see Dad." He had finally learned about the stroke that had stilled half of Desmond Cordiner's body. "I'm going home. It's the only solution."

"What flight are you taking? I'll phone Nevada. Lang'll be very busy. Or have you forgotten he's not only got it in for you, but me, Maxim, Barry, PD and Beth as well!" Her voice rose in shrill fear.

He soothed her, vowing not to do anything until they had a chance to talk it over in person.

At the end of the month Château Neuchâtel's conscientious medical staff reviewed the case of Adam Stevens. While surgery and physical therapy had not restored the patient's left knee to full weight-bearing serviceability, he was an athletic man and had achieved a high degree of mobility with his cane. There was no more the sanitorium could do for him.

He returned to Bellagio.

He found Alice with a cold and sore throat. On the second afternoon, deciding to cheer her up with some small gift, he told her he was going for a walk.

"Hold on a sec. I'll get my jacket."

"What about your cold? It's a mean wind today."

"You're going to the travel agent! You're arranging a flight to Los Angeles!" she cried.

Angered by her accusation that he was lying, he said, "Will I need a guard every time I leave the house? Or someday can I be a trustee?"

She drew a sharp breath and ran to the bedroom.

Pulling on his parka, he slammed out the front door. Evergreens soughed in the wind, and he stood on the front step, gazing up at the agitated branches. He was accepting that her fear made sense. After all, hadn't he told her he planned to return to Los Angeles?

He went back inside.

She didn't hear him open and close the bedroom door. She was sitting hunched on a chair, her chest rising and falling as she drew a stridently loud breath. He had never seen one of her panic episodes, and he ran to kneel in front of her.

She shot him a look of shamed horror. "Go away."

"Is this one of your attacks?" he asked gently.

"Yes."

"Don't shut me out, Alice."

She closed her eyes and let him stroke her back. When the hyperventilation finally released her, he explained that he'd wanted to get her a little surprise, that was all.

"I'm not going back, Alice, I swear. But we better figure out what, exactly, we are going to do."

She nodded.

"First off, how about your work? Eventually a good script'll come along."

"You just saw Alyssia del Mar in action," she said with a feeble shiver. "All I want, Hap, is for us to be together."

They spent two days working out what they both considered a reasonable course of action. While she went home to pick up her final decree and to arrange her finances with the business manager, he would head for Scandinavia, a part of the world where a large, fair-haired man would not attract undue attention. Reunited, they and Juanita would rent a house or flat. Every few months they would move on. As for her appearance, well, people take pride in being a look-alike to a celebrity, and so would she. To stifle the "Whatever-happened-to" school of journalism, she would show up publicly as Alyssia del Mar from time to time.

The lease on the villa was up on March first. They both wept, clung together, and went their separate ways.

He traveled on a series of trains and buses to Bergen. He had always felt at home in Norway: Norwegians were civilized, fluent in English, the country strove to banish social inequity, and besides, his grandmother, Hjordis Harvard, who had left Maxim and him the trust funds they'd put into *Wandering On,* was of Norwegian descent. He found a temporary job in the Hanseatic Museum, a draft-haunted, fifteenth-century merchant's house. Other than colleagues, his venerable, bent-over landlady and the waitresses who served him at the inexpensive fish place on Bryggen, he spoke to nobody. He and Alice had agreed phone calls or letters exchanged between Beverly Hills and Bergen might arouse curiosity, so he read the American newspapers for word of her.

75

Alyssia del Mar returns home. Shown here on her arrival at LAX.

—Caption under a photograph in the *Los Angeles Herald-Examiner,* March 2, 1981

Maxim Cordiner, his open tuxedo jacket flapping behind him to show its crimson lining, jogged up to the stage. "Thank you, everyone out there in Academyland," he said, then halted, clearly unable to continue his speech. Raising the statuette above his head, he muttered shakenly into the microphone, "This would have meant a lot to my brother."

—*Washington Post,* March 27, 1981

Though Alyssia del Mar was in Los Angeles, she was a no-show at the Oscars. Hollywood watchers say she was worried she might lose, which as everyone knows, proved correct.

—*Women's Wear Daily,* March 27, 1981

That the Oscars are an emotional issue has been proven over and over, but nowhere is it more evident than in the case of Alyssia del Mar not winning this year's award for Best Actress. Though she is magnificent as Mellie in *The Baobab Tree,* reports of her absences and habitual tardiness during filming of Harvard Cordiner's final masterpiece lost her the Academy's sympathy.

—Charles Champlin in the *Los Angeles Times,* April 8, 1981

When the no-fault Cordiner/del Mar divorce was granted, *Time* called her "Alyssia del Mar, superannuated sex kitten." In the same Milestone, Barry was identified as "bestselling author" although the sales of *Spy* had proved a disappointment and the book had appeared on no lists whatsoever.

In May, when Oslo's many fruit trees blossomed and sailboats scudded across the blue fjord, Adam Stevens and the recently divorced Alice Hollister arrived in the spring-happy Norwegian capital from different directions. Their presence went unnoticed.

Three days later, while Juanita clasped Alice's fragrant bridal bouquet of hyacinth, the couple were married in the home of a retired Anglican priest. There was a spectacular view of the fjord from the open window, which admitted a crisp, salty breeze. The pink-cheeked, forgetful old minister called the bride Edith and the groom Alan, but his flat-voweled English accent was loud and vigorous as he intoned the vows, which they repeated shakenly: "With this ring I thee wed, with my body I thee worship, and with my worldly goods I thee endow."

The rings in question didn't match, but both were several centuries old, with the workings of the heavy gold worn equally smooth—the couple had discovered them at Kaare Bentsen, Oslo's best-known antiques shop.

After they were pronounced husband and wife, they turned, gazing at one another until the breeze whipped a strand of her hair against his lips as a sort of reminder, then he pulled it aside to kiss her lightly, tenderly.

"Alyssia, Alyssia, Alyssia!" cried her loyal French fans when she emerged from the Carlton Hotel to attend the out-of-competition screening of *The Baobab Tree* at the Cannes Film Festival.

After returning from Cannes, she and Juanita packed an enormous quantity of clothes and furs while Hap crated the pieces of painted antique Scandinavian furniture they had bought in Oslo. After shipping their possessions by rail, the trio, in a new Volvo, drove leisurely across Norway and Sweden to Stockholm. They rented a spacious nineteenth-century apartment overlooking Lake Malar. Following their plan, in January they moved again, this time to Copenhagen. They found a narrow, four-story house near the Tivoli Gardens—this being winter, the famous amusement park was closed.

Hap's second marriage had made him more content than he'd ever been, yet paradoxically he felt claustrophobic at being trapped in the identity of Adam Stevens, the invention of a passport forger. Nevertheless, he was seldom out of sorts, his equability serving as a buffer between the sisters, who despite their abiding affection, had a tendency to bicker. His restlessness he worked off by limping for hours through the snow-covered brick city.

In February, Alice Stevens, the name printed in her newly issued, dark-blue United States passport, flew to New York, where Alyssia del Mar was to take part in a PBS fund-raiser called *The Night of Stars*.

The day after Hap saw her off at Kastrup Airport, a Saturday, was bitterly cold, but Juanita ignored the weather. A swap-meet buff, she seldom missed the weekly flea market held at Israel Plads. As she buttoned her heavy brown coat, Hap came into the hall, knotting his muffler—he was on his way to the class in English he gave gratis for the neighborhood children.

"There's something I been meaning to ask," Juanita said in a low, diffident voice. "You're teaching them kids to read English. Is it hopeless with somebody as old as me?"

"You're really interested, Nita?" he asked, surprised.

"If I don't catch on," she muttered, concentrating on the top button, "I'll just drop it."

"We'll start this afternoon," he promised.

A superlative teacher—patient, tolerantly firm, enthusiastic—he succeeded in dissolving Juanita's lifelong humiliation about her illiteracy. Freed of tensions, she caught on rapidly, and was devouring English and American paperback romances long before Alice left for the Yugoslavian Film Festival in Dubrovnik.

Alyssia del Mar surfaced not only for show-biz events, but also for occasional society functions, and wherever she appeared her progress was diligently recorded by the press. English newspapers showed Princess Anne saying something in her ear at the Royal Enclosure at Ascot, *Vogue* printed a photograph of her in a blue Egyptian wig as Cleopatra at the Gambaras' annual costume ball in

Puerto Vallarta. Cameras kept zooming in on the low-cut décolletage of her ice-blue satin Valentino as she sat in the audience of a televised recital at the White House—she was there by personal invitation of President and Mrs. Reagan.

As Vincent Canby wrote in the *New York Times,* "The public's fascination with Alyssia del Mar is rooted in the same ground as its enduring interest in Marilyn Monroe. Both stars made exits clouded in enigma. Why did Monroe take those pills? Why has del Mar abdicated her career at its peak?"

"You haven't had an attack since we got married," Hap said. The two of them were reading in bed.

"And you're letting up on the nightmares. What a good sex life will do for people." She gave a chuckle, then her expression changed and she bit her lip thoughtfully. "I'm not positive, but I'm pretty sure we're going to have a baby."

"I've been counting, too, love, but I didn't want to get my hopes up. You sometimes used to skip a month."

"There's other symptoms," she said.

"Yes?"

"I always have a spot of indigestion; I can't ever seem to get enough sleep. That's how it was before." Her voice clogged.

He took her novel, putting his arms around her. "If it's true, I'm glad," he said against her ear. "So very glad."

The pregnancy proved a watershed in the way they viewed their nomadic life.

Alice, having spent her own childhood without roots, became obsessed about a permanent home. Hap saw his idleness with a new intolerant eye, and privately longed for his child to be American-born, a hope he was afraid to voice lest it bring about a recurrence of Alice's attacks.

One night at dinner as they discussed whether or not their next move should be to Helsinki, Juanita, who seldom intruded, said, "You could work, Hap, if we were back in America."

"Go home?" Alice glared at her sister over the Royal Copenhagen soup tureen. "There's a brilliant idea."

"Nobody's hot on our trail, Alice," Juanita said calmly.

"If they were, they'd have tracked you and Hap down ages ago."

After a brief hesitation, Alice shrugged assent. "Okay, Lang's not actively looking for Hap—but if we jump out at him, he'll sure find us."

"Juanita knows that, love." Hap set down his large, European-style soup spoon and looked questioningly at his sister-in-law.

"I been thinking a lot how quick you taught me to read," she said. "Hap, there's a lot of kids who grow up believing they're dumb because nobody took that kind of trouble with them."

"You mean a school for farm workers?" he asked.

"Are the two of you insane?" Alice cried. "We know a million people in California—and they know us!"

"There's plenty of other states," Juanita said.

Hap's expression of eagerness was not lost on his wife.

By the following day it was no longer whether they would go back, but where.

They finally decided on the tobacco-growing eastern Piedmont part of North Carolina, a state where none of the three had set foot. Hap flew back to the States alone, scouting the area around Durham. That first weekend he found exactly what they wanted a few miles out of town. The fifty-year-old house had no particular style, but the rooms were large and there were three big screened porches. The upstairs they kept for themselves, using their Norwegian antiques and comfortable, inexpensive upholstery. The downstairs rooms, except for the big, square kitchen, which was dominated by their major extravagance, a restaurant-size Wolf stove, they gave over to floor pillows and bookshelves and reasonably indestructible toys and a pair of Radio Shack computers with reading-aid programs.

At first the quasi school remained empty; then Alice came up with the idea of offering a child-care program at a price so low it barely covered the cost of the hot meals.

Within a month they were attracting not only preschoolers—transient and local—but older children and adults, too.

Alice Stevens had a tendency to brag about her resemblance to Alyssia del Mar, keeping a boxful of clippings about the star, confessing that maybe this was dumb of her, but she had changed her first name to one more like her idol's. Astonishingly, her identity was never questioned—but then again, Hap would think, maybe it wasn't so strange. After all, who expected a world-class legend to be wearing a maternity smock from Sears as she stood in line next to you at the A&P, or ate a Big Mac, or held up the reading cards to a group of pre-schoolers, or huffed and puffed with the other pregnant mothers in her Lamaze class?

After a brief, completely unsedated labor, Ross was born. Strong, agile and quick, by the time he was three he knew the alphabet and insisted on playing with the older children, who more or less kept him in line.

On November 17, 1986, Hap sat at the breakfast table with the Durham paper propped on the milk carton in front of him. A paragraph on the obituary page caught his eyes.

"Robert Lang, Las Vegas businessman and owner of the Fabulador Hotel in that city, died yesterday after a lengthy bout with cancer. His father was the underworld figure Bartolomeo 'Bart' Lanzoni. Though Lang shunned the limelight, he had a keen interest in the film industry. His corporation, Meadstar, produced several films including the classic *The Baobab Tree,* Harvard Cordiner's last directorial stint."

Ross was mashing his grits around the plate, and rather than risk a spate of unanswerable questions, Hap handed the paper to Alice, holding his thumb at the obituary. She read, then looked up.

"Think it's okay to go back?" he asked.

He understood, of course, that without Lang they would be in no physical danger. What he wanted to know was her reaction. Clammy sweat broke out on her torso as she re-experienced the grief and terror-struck bravado of that awful morning in PD's office. How could she face Our Own Gang, who had cast her as scapegoat and eternal outsider?

The gray eyes remained fixed questioningly on her. She knew how intensely he yearned to make contact with what remained of his family. (When Desmond Cordiner had died in the summer of 1983, and Rosalynd had suffered a fatal heart attack on Thanksgiving night in 1984, Hap's long mourning periods had been exacerbated by his inability to attend the funerals.)

If I go back, maybe I'll lose him again. Maybe I'll lose Ross, like I lost my other baby. That her fears were absurdly irrational did not make them any the less real, and pains twinged through her chest.

Yet, after only the briefest hesitation, she proved that Alyssia del Mar still lived. "Sure it's okay," she bubbled excitedly.

BEVERLY HILLS, 1986

Maxim continued to bang urgently against the glass door. "Let me in!" he shouted.

The glass slab to his left moved. Alyssia stood there with a very young, jeans-clad boy whose tow-white hair flopped across his eyebrows. Maxim ignored both the woman and the child. His attention was riveted on the large man whose gray eyes were fixed on his.

Maxim took off his dark glasses. In his life he had never before experienced so profound a disbelief in his own witness. This bearded man with long legs in beige cords, the sleeves of his cotton shirt rolled up to show strong forearms, his blond hair darker underneath, this man could not be the incorruptibly just older brother who had ruled over his childhood. His brother was bleached bones under a marble cross in the garden of the wide-verandaed little house that was the relief center. He himself had selected the marble, had arranged for the simple engraving:

HARVARD CORDINER
BORN LOS ANGELES, CALIFORNIA, 1938
DIED ZAIRE, 1980

As an act of love—and contrition—he had made the long, difficult journey with the tombstone to personally see it set in the mulch-rich African earth.

"Hey . . ." he whispered.

"Hey, hey."

A greeting they had invariably exchanged when they passed in grammar school hallways, and had never used thereafter.

Hap limped forward.

Maxim took a step. As Hap's arms went around him, he hugged his brother, experiencing a tribal completion, a profound sense of being part of a larger whole. He felt the moisture on Hap's bearded cheek and his own eyes were wet, too.

"Daddy," the boy was shrilling. "*Daddy*! Is this my uncle?"

The threesome on the patio had stood poised like waxwork figures, peering into the living room at the masculine embrace. At the child's question, they came to life.

Beth, lifting a hand to her pulsing throat, sank back into her chair. The ladylike blusher stood out in slashes on her bloodless cheeks. Barry released his grip on his pipe, and it clattered on the stones as he pressed a hand to his stomach. His shock was visceral, striking him with an ulcerlike pain. How could the admired and envied cousin who had put the horns on him have returned to the land of the living? PD crossed himself, and a croak that was meant to be "Hap?" came from within his well-muscled chest. Then he crossed himself again.

The brothers pulled apart, Hap rubbing his knuckles over his eyes, Maxim blowing his nose.

"Hap, we thought you were dead. . . ." Beth whispered, still grasping at her throat. "Everybody thought—"

"I didn't mean to blow your minds like this," Hap said. "But we couldn't figure out any easier way—"

"Daddy!" The child stamped a sneakered foot.

"Yes, Ross, this *is* your Uncle Maxim. Maxim, this impatient guy is our son, Ross." He ruffled the boy's hair affectionately. The child squirmed away, scowling. In this irate moment, in spite of his near-white hair and blue eyes, he bore a striking resemblance to his dead grandfather, Desmond Cordiner.

"I'm very happy to meet you, Ross." Maxim, still pale, squatted and gravely extended his hand. "But you're going to have to help me out. I never had a nephew before, so tell me what I should do."

"You take him to Disneyland, silly!"

The adults burst out laughing, not so much in amusement but as a release.

Hap reached an arm around Alice's waist, drawing her closer. "And this is my wife," he said.

"That at least I did figure." Maxim embraced her. "Welcome to the good branch of the family."

Hap's cousins had surrounded him; Beth's kisses leaving pink lipstick on his jawline; PD pounding his shoulders, then kissing him, too; Barry continuously shaking his hand.

Voices throbbed.

"I can't believe it, I just can't believe it. If only poor Aunt Rosalynd and Uncle Desmond—and Irving—could be here."

"We're talking miracles, Hap. Major miracles!"

"Words fail me—a phantasmagora come to life."

A thick white cloud had passed over the sun, graying the unpruned garden and casting a film over the heart-shaped pool.

"Come on, Ross, let's go inside," Alice said, giving her son a poke between the shoulder blades.

"He hasn't had his snack yet, Alice," Hap called.

As the door slid shut after them, Barry asked, "Do you have to use pseudonyms?"

"We did," Hap said. "But Alice is her real name."

"Alicia," Barry muttered.

"Barry, it's always been Alice," he said. "And Juanita's her half sister."

"Juanita has the same surname, but there the relationship ends—she came to work for us in France," Barry protested. Then, under Hap's sympathetic gaze, he flushed and mumbled, "Alyssia—Alice never told me."

Maxim drew a breath as if forcing himself to speak. "Hap, stop me if I'm wrong, but is the timing of your return connected to a recent ball score: cancer one, Lang zip?"

Beth, Barry and PD swallowed sharply, averting their eyes from Hap and one another. Like Maxim, each was once again reliving that quintessential betrayal scene when Lang had terrified them into ignoring Hap's murder.

Hap sat on one of the rusty garden chairs, his bad leg thrust out straight in front of him. "Exactly," he said, ignoring the change in mood. "Lang's death is why we were able to come back here." Briefly he outlined his knowledge of Lang's complicity in the so-called accident, how the other man was killed in the jeep and been buried as Hap Cordiner while he had become Adam Stevens. He touched his leg. "While this was being patched up in Switzerland, Alice found me."

"And the two of you have been hiding out in Europe?"

Beth asked, her voice caring and serene, her hands tensed on her purse.

"No, we came back before Ross was born. We live in North Carolina. Part of the house is a kind of school we run for farm workers. With all the moving from crop to crop, they don't get much of a crack at an education."

"Perfecto." Maxim's smile had a plastic quality. "You, in your long robe, arms outstretched, suffering the little children to come unto you."

PD jumped to his feet. "Screw off, Maxim!"

"That was brotherly awe," Maxim said. "I never speak ill of the dead."

"It's a remarkable concept," Barry said overpolitely as he stooped to get his pipe. "How did you arrive at it?"

"Actually Juanita had the idea—she's running the place while we're gone. She and Alice didn't get much schooling—as kids they picked up and down California."

Barry, about to refute this with the Lopezes' rich family life in El Paso, changed his mind. "When you came back to this country, weren't you concerned Lang might find you? I know only too well you can't hide an identity like Alyss—like Alice's."

"She admits to being a look-alike," Hap said.

The glass slid open and Alice stood there. She had washed off the Alyssia del Mar makeup, tied back her hair, changed to a white jumpsuit with running shoes, and it was possible to see that, away from the precincts of the rich and famous, she might easily pass as a look-alike.

She glanced at Hap and he nodded.

"If you can," she said, smiling, "we'd like all of you to stay for lunch."

Beth said, "This is one meal I wouldn't miss for worlds." But her face was yet more drawn with apprehension.

The phones in the house hadn't been connected, so she went with PD and Barry to take her turn at the one in PD's Rolls as they canceled appointments and lunch dates.

Maxim stayed on the patio, one bony leg over the other, the foot jiggling nervously. "Why did you really come back?" he asked.

"Two reasons. Alice wants to sell the house. I wanted to see you—and the others."

"You're obviously aware that we knew your, uhh, death

was no accident, but Lang threatened us out of an investigation."

"Yes, Alice told me. So you and the others can stop walking on eggs as if I'm about to detonate."

"And you haven't voiced a single recrimination? You really are cut out to wear the long robes."

"Believe me, Maxim, I was plenty bitter at first. As a matter of fact, it took me nearly a year before I could think about you or the others without hot, murderous urges." He shrugged. "Today it's just good being here with you guys."

"I'd have liked to see Lang get his, Hap. Believe me, I'd have loved to see him rot in jail for several concurrent lifetimes. But I was chicken . . . chicken." The cloud had passed, and the remorseless December light carved hollows into Maxim's angular face.

"Don't you think I have my own guilts, Maxim? God, how I wanted to come back for Dad's funeral—and Mother's, too."

"She at least went in her sleep."

Hap held his fingers on his forehead, using his hand to shield his expression of misery.

After a minute's silence, Maxim said, "So you finally snagged Alyssia—Alice." Then he sighed deeply. "Another black mark against me. I wasn't invariably the soul of kindness to her. She knew too much for me to be kind. Did she tell you about . . . me?"

"Yes," Hap said, leaning forward to grip his brother's thin arm at the elbow. "Maxim, it doesn't mean a damn to me and never would have—except I'm sorry you went to such lengths to hide."

The plump black cook, who had been hired from an agency for the day, was busy preparing the meal, so Alice asked Beth to help her set the table. As they took pottery from the butler's pantry shelves, Alice asked, "How's Jonathon?"

Beth's hands trembled, and fearing the brightly glazed cups would fall, she clasped them against her gray silk blouse. This was the moment that she had dreaded and steeled herself against. "He's in school," she said coldly. "And if you've come back here to take him away from me, you might as well know that I'll spend every penny Irving left me to keep him."

"Beth, when I signed that paper giving him to you, I wanted to die. But I felt it was the right decision. I still feel that way."

Beth darted a suspicious glance at her former sister-in-law.

Alice pushed open the swinging door to the dining room. "Do you really think I want to destroy his life?" she asked quietly. "I'm interested in what he's doing, Bethie, that's all."

Beth set the cups on the built-in sideboard. "I didn't mean to snap at you. But ever since I got your letter this morning, I've been afraid, so afraid."

"There was no need. You're his mother." Alice was smiling, but small lines of sadness were visible below the blue eyes.

As they ate the creamy chicken salad and raspberry tarts, Our Own Gang found themselves reminiscing about their childhood in the so-called golden age of Hollywood: parties with Judy Garland, Bogey and Baby, Edward G. Robinson, Harry James playing his horn; they recollected the eternal studio intrigues that had seemed life and death at the time but now were quaintly humorous; they mythologized their own group mischief. Ross, thoroughly bored, disappeared to watch television in Barry's old study. The adults lingered over their coffee, prefacing each remark, "Do you remember. . . ?" The laughter was no longer forced, the courtesy toward Hap had given way to good-natured digs.

By four thirty, when the guests rose to leave, the long family rift was well on its way to being healed.

"I haven't had a better time in forever," Beth said emotionally. "Let's all have dinner at my house tomorrow."

There was a chorus of acceptances.

"Alice, you and Hap must bring Ross," Beth said, smiling euphorically. "I do so want him to meet his cousin Jonathon."

Hap saw his family to their cars. The group stood talking and laughing for another fifteen minutes before they were able to break apart until the following evening, hugging one another goodbye with a warmth utterly different from the constraint of a few hours earlier. Hap stood waving on the front step as one by one the cars disappeared down the steep, curving driveway.

Alice hadn't come out. The falsetto voices assigned to cartoon characters came from the study, but she didn't go in with Ross. Instead, she sat on the couch, watching the dusk fall over the canyon walls.

Hap returned, sitting in the gloom near her. "It is okay with you, Beth's dinner tomorrow? You won't be too upset, seeing Jonathon?"

"I'll be plenty shook. But on the other hand, it'd be worse not seeing him."

"At lunch you kept looking around at us."

"I was thinking about the wedding lunch at the Fabulador. You people glittered like gods."

He smiled. "Aren't you overromanticizing?"

"Not a shred. There's no other way to describe how glamorous you were to me. Maxim, and your father was head of Magnum, PD's a famous director, Barry and Beth were hotshot college students. I felt like dirt in my good red dress."

He smiled. "That dress. God, love, that dress!"

"I'd never owned anything so beautiful. But somehow I knew it was all wrong to wear with divinities. Hap, all the years I was married to Barry I never once got over the feeling I was in the family on probation."

"Even after you'd made it big?"

"Not until today did I feel like a genuine Cordiner."

"You glittered more than any of us." He reached out for her hand and their fingers twined. "Now that Lang's gone, if you want you can be Alyssia del Mar again."

"The wench is dead." Alice paused, adding pensively, "But I'm not saying I never miss her."

"At odd moments I regret the passing of the old Harvard Cordiner, hotshot director, too." He fumbled toward the lightswitch behind him.

As the lights came on they blinked, then smiled contentedly at each other. They were both thinking about the day after tomorrow, when they would return to their shared life, leaving behind everything of the past except the intangibles—family affection, memories, old dreams.

AFTER YOU'VE READ
DREAMS ARE NOT ENOUGH
WE'D APPRECIATE YOUR ANSWERS TO THESE QUESTIONS.

1. Did you enjoy Dreams Are Not Enough? ______________

2. Have you recommended it to anyone else? ______________

3. Which of Jacqueline Briskin's other Berkley books have you read? (Check all that apply) A. Everything and More B. Too Much Too Soon C. California Generation

4. What attracted you to buying Dreams Are Not Enough? (Circle those that apply.) A. Advertising B. Author C. Cover D. Recommendation E. Display

5. On average, how many books do you read a month? ______

6. What kinds of books do you read most often? (Check all that apply) A. Historical Romance B. Contemporary Romance C. Mystery/Suspense D. Action/Adventure E. Fantasy/Science Fiction

7. Where do you buy most of your books? (Check one) A. Supermarket B. Bookstore C. Newsstand D. Department Store E. Mail Order

8. How often do you borrow books from the library? A. Once a week B. Once a month C. Other: ______________

9. Who are some of your favorite authors? ______________

____

10. Would you be interested in reading books by other Berkley authors and letting us know what you think of them? _____

Name ____

Address ____

Store where you bought this book ______________________

Age ______________ M/F ______________

Highest level of education completed ______________